Everyone loves

Leslie Kelly!

"Sexy, funny and a little outrageous,
Leslie Kelly is a must read!"
—*New York Times* bestselling author Carly Phillips

"Leslie Kelly is a rising star of romance."
—*New York Times* bestselling author Debbie Macomber

"Ms. Kelly never fails to deliver a captivating story."
—*Romance Reviews Today*

"Leslie Kelly writes with a matchless combination of
sexiness and sassiness that makes every story a keeper."
—*Romance Junkies*

"Leslie Kelly writes hot, steamy stories with lots
of humor and tons of romance thrown in."
—*Romance and Friends*

"Leslie Kelly is a master of amusing
contemporary romance!"
—*WordWeaving*

Leslie Kelly

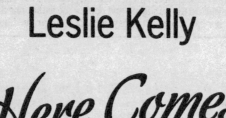

Here Comes Trouble

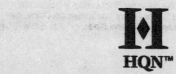

HQN™

ISBN-13: 978-0-373-77133-2
ISBN-10:   0-373-77133-9

HERE COMES TROUBLE

www.HQNBooks.com

Printed in U.S.A.

Dear Reader,

Hold on to your hats, because here comes trouble!

Trouble, Pennsylvania, that is.

If you've read my books in the past, you know I just love those funny, quirky small towns. From Pleasantville to Derryville to Joyful, I've had a fabulous time creating entire fictional communities populated by crazy, eccentric people.

Trouble, I must say, has quickly become my favorite. From the inn owner who likes to get naked when he prunes his roses to the two little old ladies who like to brew a little arsenic in with their chamomile tea, this town is one seething micrometropolis.

Max Taylor and Sabrina Cavanaugh are about to get their own crash-course introduction to Trouble. Since the two of them have been hiding who they *really* are from each other since day one, things are liable to get a little...wild.

After creating the wonderfully eccentric Mortimer Potts (the grandfather anyone would love to have!) and his three fabulously sexy grandsons, I knew all the boys would have to have stories of their own. (And they will!) But I didn't know that the town of Trouble was going to keep having to have its story told, too. A story too big to fit in just my HQN single-title romances.

So be sure to watch for more Trouble in my Harlequin series novels...starting with my October, 2006 title *Asking for Trouble*, for Harlequin Blaze.

In the meantime, hope you have lots of fun getting into Trouble!

Happy reading!

Leslie Kelly

Additional titles by Leslie Kelly

She's Got the Look
That's Amore!
"There Goes the Groom"
She Drives Me Crazy
Killing Time

This book is dedicated with utmost appreciation to my readers. Thank you from the bottom of my heart for your encouragement, support and enthusiasm. I hope you'll stick with me as we all get into Trouble.

Here Comes Trouble

PROLOGUE

MORTIMER POTTS was not insane.

He did, on occasion, like to slip into the past—at least in his mind—and relive his favorite days. Days that were certainly more exhilarating than those he lived now. But contrary to the belief of some of his detractors, he was able to separate fiction from reality. Usually.

The problem with reality was that it was boring. The idea of settling down into his role as elderly millionaire—sipping cognac and smoking cigars on the patio of his Manhattan penthouse as he watched the world go by—simply held no appeal.

He needed adventure. Excitement. Needed to ride through the desert on a fine black stallion, or sail into a secluded jetty on the coast of Malta to escape pirates. Or whisk three young boys away to an African safari.

That was one consolation—his grandsons, at least, did not think him mad. Eccentric? Yes. But not insane.

Or perhaps that wasn't a consolation. Having a bit of madness in the family would certainly invigorate the lives of those three young men, who'd become just a bit too pedestrian in their adult years. A little insanity could be good for the soul.

He *would* go insane if he was forced to ring in his eightieth year at a boring club filled with artificial people who wouldn't dream of walking unaccompanied in Central Park, much less fighting their way out of a smoky tavern in Singapore. *Ah, the good old days.*

At least, he *thought* they were his good old days. Sometimes his memory played tricks on him.

"Your morning papers, sir," said a familiar, well-modulated English voice.

Mortimer looked up to greet his manservant—and best friend. Roderick had been with him since 1945—a dispirited Brit tooling across Africa with a rich American once the Desert Fox had been defeated. He'd saved Mortimer's life on one occasion and, as incongruous as it seemed, had helped him raise his grandsons.

Roderick had taught the boys how to live responsibly. Mortimer had taught them how to *live.*

"Anything of interest?" Mortimer asked.

"Not particularly." Unruffled as always, Roderick, his dark, slicked-back hair now as gray as Mortimer's was white, spread the papers on the small café-style table on the penthouse patio. Then the butler-cum-mechanic-cum-partner-in-crime-on-occasion stepped back and cleared his throat.

"What is it?"

"I believe the boy might be headed for a storm, sir."

"Goodness, Roderick, how many times have I told you to call me Mortimer?" he asked. Then he focused on the man's words. "*The* boy?"

Roderick merely sighed. "With a woman."

Ah, Maxwell. A smile tugged at his mouth, even as Mortimer began to shake his head in feigned disapproval.

Mortimer did not play favorites with his grandchildren. But the rascally middle Taylor son, Max, was so much like *him* that he'd never been able to help being amused by his antics. Max was a rogue. A rapscallion, though a good-hearted one. At least, he *had* been. Before life had slapped him with a faithless wife.

Mortimer had had a few of those…wives, that is. Only one he'd wanted to keep. None, however, had sent him into the tailspin his grandson's had. She had apparently destroyed Max's faith in love. He seemed completely uninterested in trying marriage again…as were his two brothers, who'd never tried at all.

"What type of storm?" It probably didn't speak well of him that he had a quick hope that his grandson had gotten a young lady in trouble. He would rather enjoy a great-grandchild.

"I fear he may be flying toward some rough publicity."

Bad headlines. *Bah*. "Maxwell can handle rough publicity."

Too bad. The idea of having to help his grandson with something scandalous was more appealing than sitting here in the city waiting to die. And a wrong-side-of-the-blanket infant sounded much more exciting than a media scandal.

Lifting the London paper, he idly began to flip the pages, finding nothing of interest. Until… "Did you see this?" he asked. "Property For Sale—A Pennsylvania Township."

"A *township*, sir?"

Mortimer read on, barely hearing the other man. With each word, a surge of excitement built in his veins. Soon he was sitting straight in his chair, rereading, thinking, planning.

"I recognize that expression. You're going to do something outrageous," Roderick said, a note of resignation in his voice. "And I'm going to be dragged along, forced to

break you out of some prison or find a bottle of your
favorite Courvoisier XO Imperial cognac in a remote store
that carries little more than six-packs of—" he shuddered
"—Schlitz Malt Liquor."

Ignoring him, Mortimer said, "This town is looking for
a sheikh, a prince or a duke to save them from bankrupt-
cy."

"Is that possible? A town being *sold?*"

"It happens. Some actor bought a town last year, I
think." Mortimer read on. "Being offered in a once-in-a-
lifetime opportunity is the town of Trouble, Pennsylvania,
established 1821."

A dry chuckle told him what Roderick thought of the
name of the place. Most people would probably be put off
by it. Mortimer, however, had never been one to retreat,
had never liked to ride out of the way to avoid trouble.
"This might be just what I need," he murmured. "They did
say they wanted a sheikh."

He peered out of the corner of his eye, watching for
any sign of skepticism from his butler, as he occasionally
saw on the faces of others when the subject of some of
Mortimer's *adventures* arose. There was none, of course.
Roderick knew full well that Mortimer had been granted
an honorary sheikhdom from the head of a Bedouin tribe
after the winter of forty-eight.

"I wonder about the condition of the place, if it's bank-
rupt," Roderick said, reading over his shoulder. "A few
buildings, roads and parks for *that* amount? I should think
you'd be able to purchase an entire colony for such a sum."

"They're *states,*" Mortimer said. "Remember that tea
party and several years of revolution?"

Roderick lifted a disdainful brow.

Still, the man was correct. The amount named in the

ad was not a paltry one. "Well, see here, there *is* more for the price." He pointed. "Beyond the courthouse, town hall and fire station, some formerly private buildings are also included."

"Oh, goody," Roderick said, his voice as dry as the sawdust-flavored English biscuits he so enjoyed.

Mortimer's enthusiasm was not dampened as he finished reading the advertisement. "These include a movie theater, photo hut, school, barber shop, a big, furnished house, a gas station, two restaurants—one with working ice-cube maker—and a factory formerly occupied by Stuttgardt Cuckoo Clock Company."

Roderick sniffed. "How very appropriate."

"All government buildings are currently in use, all others are closed after bank foreclosure. Also included is the bank."

Well, that cinched it, didn't it? His family had been in banking for a hundred years. It was how the Potts family had made their fortune. Which had provided Mortimer with a comfortable inheritance that he'd parlayed into millions through prudent investing and a bit of international intrigue.

Destiny. He was a sheikh. He had the money. He loved trouble. And he would, most assuredly, love Trouble.

"About the boy…"

Mortimer set the paper down. "Is it serious?"

"It may be. He will likely need to do some reevaluating."

There wasn't anything Mortimer Potts wouldn't do for his grandsons. And it suddenly occurred to him that the purchase of his own little Pennsylvania town could help in that respect, too. "You are aware that if I proceed with this, my grandsons are certain to come try to rescue me from my folly."

Roderick nodded ever so slightly.

"Morgan is preparing to fly off on some assignment for *Time* magazine. And Michael is doing something quite mysterious, which he referred to as 'deep undercover' work."

That left Max. The rascal. Who would, without doubt, come to Trouble determined to save his grandfather.

Instead, Mortimer hoped, Max would be saving himself.

CHAPTER ONE

PILOTING A TWIN-ENGINE Cessna Citation CJ2+ out of Long Beach Airport in California, Max Taylor was prepared for a lot of things. Bad weather, low visibility, turbulence. He'd dealt with the wind shear off a low-flying commercial airliner. Equipment failure. Hell, even the odd seagull going *splat* on the windshield or getting sucked up into an engine.

But not this. Not a scene straight out of a bad porn movie. Nothing in his wildest dreams—or darkest nightmares—could have prepared him for a seventy-year-old passenger bursting into his cockpit. Naked. Completely, *shockingly* naked. "Wha—"

"Mr. Taylor, induct me into the mile-high club!" the gray-haired woman exclaimed, her arms wide, emphasizing the, uh, length of her bustline.

Max's first thought was to dive back below five thousand feet so they wouldn't be a mile up. His second was to think that all her millions hadn't managed to make Mrs. Rudolph Coltrane look as young from the neck down as it had managed to deal with her tightly Botoxed face. And his third was to realize that he was being attacked in his own plane. By a woman old enough to be his grandmother.

"Mrs. Coltrane, what do you think you're doing?" he

asked, somehow managing to keep his voice steady, his hands on the controls and his gaze straight ahead. Not that it was going to do much good—he'd already gotten an eyeful.

Still in shock, Max suspected he was going to have nightmares tonight. Nightmares about the unattractiveness of breast implants going south, and sags that couldn't be lifted by a crane, much less the best plastic surgeon in L.A.

"I was going to wait until we were higher up, but I can't," the woman said. "I've waited too long as it is. I know you're used to a slightly younger woman…"

Decades.

"…but we're alone now and I'm willing and a man with your…appetites probably can't go for long without giving in to his carnal urges."

Currently, Max's only urge was to jump out of the plane.

"I've paid good money for this trip, and I fully expect you to be my in-flight entertainment."

"That's what the DVD player is for," he whispered, shaking his head in bewilderment.

This couldn't be happening. Not along with all the other weird crap he'd been experiencing lately. A constant stream of women had been driving him nuts for weeks, almost sending him into hiding. He seemed to be the latest fad among the "ladies who lunch" of southern California.

Max had always enjoyed relationships with his fair share of females. Probably the next guy's fair share, too. He certainly wasn't going to apologize for liking women.

And he did. Oh, he really did. He liked how they smelled and how they looked. Liked the tender bit of skin at the nape of a lovely neck and the feel of soft hair against his bare chest. Liked tangled sheets, steamy nights and slow, deep kisses.

Careful not to get snagged in any commitment nets—not after his one disastrous experience with marriage and the major screw-up he'd made of his life following his divorce—he only got involved with women who were looking for the same things he was. Intelligent conversation, a few nice meals and, occasionally, scream-like-a-banshee sex. No strings.

Which meant, he supposed, that the strange abundance of propositions coming his way the past few weeks should have been a good thing.

It wasn't.

Because Max had become much more careful and circumspect about his sex life in recent years. Besides, he had always been the *pursuer,* not the pursued. He liked flirtation and seduction. A shared glance and the not-completely-innocent brush of a hand against a soft female arm. Charming his way into the good graces of even the most cool and unattainable ice queen gave him a great deal of satisfaction, whether sex was involved or not.

Lately, though, he'd been like a lame zebra being stalked by a pride of hungry lionesses.

He was being felt up by women in line at the bank, and having notes and drinks delivered to him in restaurants. One brunette with about ten carats of diamonds glittering from her fingers had been sitting on the hood of his Porsche last week. He'd been so concerned about possible dents in his car that at first the woman's lack of panties beneath her short dress hadn't registered. Once it did, his only reaction had been annoyance that he was also going to have to get the car washed.

"It's gotta be the cologne," he muttered, wondering if he was the subject of a secret scientific experiment. Maybe Calvin Klein was slipping some kind of animal secretion into his aftershave. Something that made Max give off irresistible pheromones that turned women into sex-starved vixens.

"Mr. Taylor…"

Or sex-starved bovines.

"Return to your seat," he said from between clenched teeth. He didn't look around, focusing instead on the blue sky spread in a brilliant panorama outside the windshield. Not on the age-spotted lady in the doorway spread in an Eve-old invitation. "Get dressed and sit down or I'll return to the airport."

"You can't mean to tell me you're refusing." The spoiled, rich socialite wasn't used to being told no. And as the owner of a young private charter company that was still struggling under last year's expansion from a four-jet fleet to a six-jet one, he wasn't used to saying it—not when it came to business.

Max had worked his ass off in the past three years, determined to get himself out of the quagmire his life had become after he'd left the Air Force. After a brief, year-long bout of drunkenness during his divorce, he'd pulled his shit together and had launched his small, regional airline. It was something he'd dreamed of doing since his teenage years when he first learned to fly over the African desert, taught by one of his grandfather's cronies.

Since then, his airline had become one of the fastest-growing private carriers in Orange County. Especially with customers like Mrs. Rudolph Coltrane, who freely shelled out major dollars to grab a ride to Vail or down to Cancún.

Of course, he'd always thought he'd be living this life *after* he finished a career as an Air Force pilot. That hadn't exactly gone as planned. *Don't go there*, he silently reminded himself.

"Look, I'm willing to fly you wherever you want to go," he said, trying to sound reasonable. "As long as it's within the safety parameters of the aircraft. And sex in the cockpit is *not*."

He didn't go into the whole "I'd rather poke my liver out with a burning pogo stick than have sex with you" bit. Hopefully the woman cared enough for her own skin to sit down.

"Rubbish."

Okay, apparently she didn't.

"I know you have autopilot," she added. "Everyone knows about this airline and your new planes."

Yeah, they did. Word had spread about Taylor Made until they could barely keep up with demand. So the idea of merging with a large outfit trying to break into the lucrative southern California market had seemed perfect when he'd been approached by a New York executive a few months ago.

The merger was progressing nicely and would be wrapped up later in the year. Determined to make it happen, Max was working double time to keep the business lucrative. He could take a vacation *after* he had a partner.

Mrs. Coltrane put her hand on his shoulder. "Now, set the autopilot and turn around."

Pleasing the customer was a top priority in his business, and he didn't want to alienate someone with as powerful a reputation as Mrs. Coltrane. But despite the special extras and level of excellence he advertised in his promotional material, flying the twin of the "I've fallen and I can't get up" lady to the heights of passion was not in his job description.

"You've got to the count of five, then I radio the tower

and we make an immediate landing," he said, trying to shrug off her hand.

"Don't be coy. I know all about you."

He stiffened, having no idea what she meant. "One."

"Surely you can at least do me the courtesy of a quickie."

The woman's indignance would have been laughable if Max's laughter hadn't been sucked out of him like spit through a dentist's tube. "Two."

"But I thought…"

He reached for the radio handset. "Three."

"Well," the woman said with a phlegmy harrumph, "if I don't have a thing or two to say to Grace Wellington."

The word *four* died on Max's lips as he focused on the name his passenger had uttered. *Grace Wellington*. What on earth a woman he'd gone out with a few years ago could have to do with Grandma getting naked in his Cessna, he had no idea. But he'd very much like to find out. Especially because he couldn't help wondering if all the other strange experiences he'd been having with women were also connected to Grace, whom he'd dated briefly after the death of her scandalous politician husband.

"What about Grace?" he couldn't help asking.

"She's a liar, that's what I think," Mrs. Coltrane said, her tone nasal.

He didn't have to look over his shoulder—and *wouldn't* have for the single winning lottery ticket in the biggest Powerball jackpot in history—to see the woman's chin jutting up and out, and her nostrils flaring with patrician arrogance. He was familiar with the expression, having seen it on the faces of a lot of his rich, female clients.

Of course, most of them were clothed when they got all haughty and pretentious. Wrinkly nudity probably ruined the effect—not that he wanted to find out.

"I never was certain whether the stories she wrote about you were true—that any man could be as sexually potent and addictive. Now I'm quite sure they're not." The woman grunted. "Some sexual fiend you are—a naked woman standing a foot away and you couldn't even manage a quick game of hide-the-joystick."

He didn't know whether to be relieved that she'd given up her seduction attempt, or offended that she thought him incapable of, uh, *playing* her game. But since the only place he wanted to hide his joystick was behind his own zipper, maybe her interpretation wasn't such a bad thing.

Then the rest of her words sunk in. *Sex fiend?* "What stories? What, exactly, are you talking about?"

She was silent for a moment. If he had had a whole lot more nerve, he would have turned around to see if she was wearing a guilty expression at spilling some kind of secret. He wasn't that brave, however, so he settled for prompting her. "Mrs. Coltrane?"

"You'll know soon enough, I suppose." Her voice sounded farther away, meaning she was back in the passenger cabin, hopefully getting dressed. "The book comes out this fall. And there's talk of a story in the *Star* or the *Globe* or something."

"*Book?*"

"Grace's autobiography. Huh! As if that woman is interesting enough to need a whole book. If not for the scandals, it would be nothing more than a page."

An autobiography. Grace Wellington—spoiled socialite turned scandalous widow after her bribe-taking politician husband had eaten the muzzle of a gun—had written her memoirs. And included him. *Damn.*

Almost afraid to hear the answer, he asked, "What exactly did Grace have to say about me in this book?"

The woman snorted an inelegant laugh. He realized she'd returned to the cockpit and was right behind him. When she moved her arm within view, he saw the sleeve of her designer blouse and breathed a deep sigh of relief.

"There's a whole chapter devoted to you, my boy, and it's been making the rounds. The lurid details are enough to make even the most risqué piece of erotica look tame."

His stomach rolled over. It hadn't done that in a cockpit since the first time he'd sat in an F-15 during his Air Force days…the *early* ones, before an unplanned pregnancy and a fucked-up marriage had derailed his plans to complete the pilot training program. "I can't believe this."

He didn't *want* to believe it, but Mrs. Coltrane seemed sure of herself. Grace had written a bunch of raunchy stuff about him and circulated it among her highbrow friends. Which explained why he'd become the flavor of the month among the Beverly Hills set.

"The book's coming out in hardcover in November."

His temple began to throb as the full implication hit him. A book with a chapter full of sordid stories about him was about to go public. Now. Right when he was entering negotiations to take his company to the next level with a major merger.

God, how he wished he'd never laid eyes—or hands— on Grace Wellington.

"This is wrong."

His passenger seemed unaware of his dismay. "If the rumors of an accompanying tabloid article are true, I imagine the book will sell well."

Tabloid article. He felt like throwing up.

"Well, if you're really not going to provide me with any form of entertainment, you may as well turn around.

I want to go home," Mrs. Coltrane said, her voice sharp with annoyance.

Max didn't have to be asked twice. Within a half hour they were on the ground and Mrs. Coltrane was flouncing toward the terminal used by the private airlines. Max, meanwhile, stood on the tarmac, cell phone in hand, dialing a familiar number.

His brother Morgan—who lived in New York managing the family assets when he wasn't off on some wildlife photographic safari—would know what to do. Or at least, who to call. But the minute Morgan answered the phone, Max heard a surprising note of excitement in his normally calm and collected older sibling's voice.

"Max. You heard?"

"I heard." He covered his free ear as a small Lear roared to life nearby. "Who's the best literary attorney you know?"

"Literary?" A crackle of static interrupted, then Max thought Morgan said, "…a real estate attorney!"

Jogging toward the terminal entrance to get better reception, he spoke loudly so his brother could understand. "I don't want to buy the woman's house, I want to stop her damn book." Speaking as he stepped inside, his raised voice garnered the attention of a number of people. This was *so* not his day.

"A book? Max, I'm talking about Trouble."

Max strode into the private pilot's lounge, which was, thankfully, deserted. "Tell me about it. I know I'm in trouble."

"You are? You're there? Then you've seen him?"

"Seen who?"

"Grandfather."

Grandfather. Ah…that explained Morgan's excited

mood. If anything could send his level-headed older
brother into a tailspin, it was their wildly flamboyant
grandfather, the elderly man who'd raised them after their
parents died. "Where is he and what has he done now?"

"I just told you, he's in Trouble."

"Yeah. I got it. He's gotten himself into another mess."

"No." His brother's voice was impatient. "You *don't* get
it. Grandfather is in a small town called Trouble."

Max had to laugh. Because if there was anywhere
Mortimer Potts was destined to be, it was in a town with
that dubious name. "Okay. So he's visiting a weird town.
That's nothing new."

"He's not on vacation," Morgan said. "He owns it,
Max."

"Huh?"

"Our grandfather has purchased an entire town. He now
officially *owns* Trouble, Pennsylvania. One of us has to fly
there right away to get him out of this mess."

One of us. Max could tell by his brother's voice which
one of us he meant. And it sure wasn't Morgan—or their
younger brother, Mike.

He was about to refuse, knowing there was too much
at stake with the merger to take off on an unexpected
vacation. Then he thought it over. Maybe getting out of
town for a while would be a good thing. He could disappear—away from more crazy, horny old moneybags like
Mrs. Coltrane. And in the meantime, get the best attorney
he could find to stop publication of Grace's book.

Besides, his grandfather was always a lot of fun. Right
now, he could use some fun…not to mention the distraction. A false identity wouldn't hurt, either, at least until this
book thing was taken care of.

Neither would a sip of alcohol.

Forget it. He didn't do that anymore—*couldn't* do that anymore. Not ever.

If the eccentric old man who'd raised him was in a bad way, well, there wasn't much Max wouldn't do for him. Wasn't much his brothers wouldn't do for him, either. They were family, after all, the four of them. Had been for eighteen years, since Max, Morgan and Mike had lost their dad to the first Gulf War and their mom to cancer.

"All right. I'll do it," he said, trying to look on the bright side. "It's not a bad time for me to get out of Dodge."

"What's wrong? Is there a problem?"

Max suddenly didn't want to talk to his brother about the Grace Wellington situation. Considering his older sibling had been hounding him since they were young about the scrapes Max got into with women, he couldn't give the other man the satisfaction.

He had to laugh at the irony. His grandfather's new town was aptly named for Max, too. Though he'd done everything he could to stay out of trouble for the past few years, he just seemed destined to keep landing in it.

"I'm okay," he finally replied. "After I make some arrangements here, I'll be getting the old man out of trouble. Figuratively *and* literally."

Two weeks later

SABRINA CAVANAUGH had heard the old saying about a place being so small you'd miss it if you blinked. But she'd never realized it could really be true of an entire town.

She *couldn't* have driven through Trouble and not realized it, could she? That awkward conglomeration of falling-down houses, boarded-up businesses and doleful people hadn't been her destination, right? Because she came from a dinky little Ohio town, population twelve, and it *still* seemed bigger than this.

Pulling her rented car over, she parked on the side of the dusty, two-lane road on which she'd been traveling since leaving the interstate. The road that had none of the shady trees, rolling hills or charming scenery she'd seen since leaving Philadelphia this morning. Then she reached for her map.

"Darn." She *had* missed it. That small cluster of buildings she'd barely noticed out of the corner of her eye must have been the town she was looking for.

Maybe it wasn't so surprising. The closer she'd gotten to Trouble, the more her mind had filled with doubt. The whole idea for this trip had seemed ridiculous when she and her senior editor at Liberty Books had conceived it, and it was much more so now.

"Yeah, right," she muttered, "a rich, hot pilot is really going to fall down with desire for a small-town minister's granddaughter turned junior book editor."

Why on earth had she ever gone to her boss and convinced her that she could do this? That she could stop a womanizing playboy from suing them for libel by *proving* he was a womanizing playboy?

She really needed to stop watching old movies—this was *so* Rock Hudson/Doris Day. Maybe it would have worked for Doris, but no way was it going to for Sabrina Cavanaugh.

She was in way over her head. Unless *wanting* it to happen was enough. Because Sabrina did. She desperately wanted Max Taylor to fall crazy in lust with her. Not so she could have wild, passionate sex with the man—*liar, liar*—but so she could nail him for the womanizing deviant

Grace Wellington's book made him out to be. The book that was right now in jeopardy since the rich, slimy playboy had hired a shark lawyer to threaten a lawsuit.

"What man wouldn't want to have his wickedly erotic sexual exploits glorified in a well-written memoir?" she mused.

Okay…*sort of* well written.

Apparently not this man. He, it seemed, had pulled out an angel costume and hired the best lawyer he could. Taylor's lawyer was demanding that publication be stopped, threatening a libel lawsuit over Grace's descriptions of their wild and kinky affair, her subsequent heartbreak and Max's jaded lifestyle. And in the post–James Frey era of memoirs, Liberty was threatening to pull the book altogether.

"Oh, no, you will not ruin this for me," Sabrina muttered, determined all over again to out the man for the reprobate he really was.

It was only because of the book—because of how important the success of that book would be for Sabrina. It had absolutely nothing—zero, zilch—to do with the man himself.

Keep telling yourself that, kid.

Sabrina never had been able to lie well, despite having a lot of experience with it as a kid. Lying had been a necessity for a troublemaking rebel trapped in the body of a small-town minister's granddaughter who wasn't allowed to wear jeans and had been called a harlot by her grandfather the first time she wiped a streak of pink lipstick across her mouth.

God help her if the old man had ever found out Sabrina was the one who'd put twenty packets of red Kool-Aid mix in the fountain outside his church. And had thrown one of her grandmother's old wigs in with it so the whole thing resembled a murder scene.

She'd had a vivid imagination as a child.

Glancing in her rearview mirror, Sabrina noticed the buildings a few hundred yards back—a gas station, and a sagging, cone-shaped hut that had once either sold ice cream or developed film. Farther back, she *thought* she remembered driving by a restaurant, a drug store and a small courthouse supported by a ring of dirty cement columns, pitted with age spots and faintly green with mildew. There had also been an overgrown playground with swings that would require a child to get a tetanus shot before climbing aboard.

It seemed exactly the kind of place that would be called Trouble. Especially considering that the barren landscape surrounding it was too marshy for farming and too rocky for developing. Reportedly there was no coal in the three mountains ringing the small valley or even a decent slope for skiing.

Just one sorry little town with a cocky name, her home for the next week or two. Or as long as it took to track down Mr. Taylor and get him to come out of hiding as Prince Charming and put on his Hugh Hefner robe.

She was about to swing the car around and head back when she got a welcome distraction. Grabbing her cell phone out of her purse, she recognized the number on the caller ID.

"Nancy, I don't know anything yet, I just got here," she said. Her boss, senior editor Nancy Carazzi, had called for hourly updates all morning.

"Are you sure he's there?"

"How could I be sure of that when I'm still in my car?"

"By the trail of women lying in satisfied puddles of lust around the town square?"

Sabrina chuckled at Nancy's droll tone. She wasn't surprised by the question. Though her boss—and friend—had no use for men, in or out of the bedroom, even *she* had been intrigued by the stories about one Maxwell Taylor, the stud of southern California—at least according to Grace Wellington's book.

Neither of them had seen a decent picture of the man, since his airline Web site only featured a group shot taken from a distance. Posed beside a fleet of planes, the owner of Taylor Made Air Charters had been indistinguishable from his staff. All of them wearing dark glasses against the sun, they had formed a solid block of blue-uniformed flyboys.

But Grace's descriptions had been evocative to say the least. And Sabrina could picture him in her mind.

He was suave. Sophisticated. James Bond in a pilot's cap, with an elegant, lean body and smoothed-back dark hair. He had high cheekbones, a strong chin, and deep, knowing eyes. She just knew it. Because she'd seen him in her dreams. A lot.

"You still there?"

Sabrina cleared her throat and pulled her thoughts off the book. *That* part of it, anyway. "I haven't spied any women stripping and throwing themselves naked at a man's feet."

"Is that *your* plan?"

"I'm not the least bit…"

"Can it," Nancy said. "You think I didn't notice the dreamy look you got on your face when you were reading the Max chapter of the book? You were intrigued, Sabrina. Hell, I haven't had any use for a penis since I decided as a kid that Betty should end up with Veronica instead of Archie, and *I* was intrigued."

Laughing, Sabrina mentally admitted she'd been *more* than intrigued. She wouldn't say so out loud, but in her mind she could acknowledge that her curiosity about Grace Wellington's former lover had become all-consuming.

"It's just curiosity," she insisted, not sure which of them she was trying harder to convince. "Plus a lot of skepticism. And a little bit of disgust." Okay, she could mentally admit it was *titillated* disgust when it came to some of the seedier details of the wicked pleasures Max had introduced Grace to.

Wiping her brow with the back of her hand, she wasn't surprised to find moisture there. Even with the car's air-conditioning, memories of those scenes made her break out in a sweat. But she gamely declared, "I'd never get involved with someone like that."

"Who said anything about getting involved? That man was born to inspire clothes to drop, not dreams of wedding rings."

Unfortunately, sex *did* mean getting involved for Sabrina—she couldn't help it. Some fire and brimstone had remained burning deep inside her long after she'd shaken off the dust of her hometown and upbringing, and taken off to the big city to go to college. Her single one-night stand a few years ago had left her feeling so guilty that she'd thrown out the sexy pair of slut shoes she'd worn to the bar that night.

Racked with guilt…hmm, her grandfather would be so proud. *After* he condemned her for the one-night-stand thing.

She shuddered at the thought of the old man with whom she, her mother and her younger siblings had lived since Sabrina was twelve. But, hey, she was lucky. Only one-third of her childhood had sucked. Her first twelve years had been wonderful. Her sister Allie had also been old enough to remember the good times, and they'd talked often about how fortunate they were because of that.

Sadly, their brother and youngest sister had never even known what their *real* family life had been like, back when they'd lived in New York and Dad was alive. Since he died when they were babies, all they'd ever known was the judgmental narrow-mindedness of their mother's father. Which might explain why Sabrina and Allie were so much alike—rebellious and anxious to escape—while the younger two were the models of proper youthful behavior.

God, she felt so sorry for them.

"You're supposed to be tempting the man into misbehaving. At least that's what you said when you came to me with this whole harebrained scheme."

"Don't remind me," Sabrina said, shaking off the dark thoughts. "I'm still wondering if I had some kind of psychotic break."

Nancy snickered. "Don't sell yourself short. You can do it…you're just his type."

"Alive and breathing?"

"Yes. But also beautiful, vulnerable… So why not misbehave yourself while you're at it?" Nancy asked.

"I'm not looking for a fling with a playboy," she insisted.

"Yeah, yeah. You want someone *nice*."

"Exactly. Decent, funny. A combination of Jimmy Stewart, Tom Hanks and every father from every old 1950s black-and-white family sitcom on TV Land."

"Boring."

She went on as though Nancy hadn't spoken. "The kind who'll be loyal and faithful."

"Get a Labrador."

"Gentle," she added.

"Get a girlfriend."

"Well hung."

"Get a dil—"

"Don't say it," Sabrina ordered. "I prefer male sexual organs that are actually attached to a body."

"Strap-on?"

Groaning helplessly, Sabrina muttered, "A *male* body."

Nancy sighed. "Picky picky."

One thing was sure, whoever the next serious guy in her life happened to be, he would *not* be the type who'd get so angry when a woman broke up with him that he'd seek cruel revenge. Like seducing her innocent younger sister, getting her pregnant and walking out on her.

Her sister Allie was currently waiting out the last two months of her pregnancy in Sabrina's apartment. Allie's entire life had been ruined as part of the stupid revenge plot concocted by a guy Sabrina had dumped.

Yes, she'd had enough scumbags to last her whole life. It was nice, decent men from now on. No wicked studs need apply.

So her almost overwhelming need to see this Max Taylor in person had to be about curiosity, that was all. She simply couldn't believe any man could be a modern-day combination of Valentino, James Bond and a porn star—as Grace claimed.

Skepticism and curiosity, she reminded herself. *Not interest. Not in a million years.*

She was about to continue arguing that point, but a noise distracted her. A metallic banging split the quiet afternoon air. It came from beyond a small stand of scraggly trees right off the road. Just after it came the loud, familiar tones of a calliope—the plaintive call to come to the circus.

Glancing that way, she caught the sparkle of something brilliantly shiny—a beautiful gleam of light that seemed entirely out of place in this gray-washed landscape.

Sabrina liked shiny things—bright lights, big city, loud music, fun. Just one more holdover from an early childhood with her funny, doting father that life with Grandfather hadn't been able to extinguish.

Which, she supposed, was why she ended the call, dropped her phone in her purse and stepped out of the car. The music and the colors were calling to her.

And her curiosity wasn't going to let her head back to Trouble without finding out where they were coming from.

CHAPTER TWO

TROUBLE MIGHT be the name of this town, but as far as Max was concerned, a better one would be The Mental Ward. After two weeks in the Pennsylvania community his grandfather called his kingdom, he was ready to run screaming off a bridge. Anything to escape the sounds of people calling him a savior—or a villain, the rattle of cars on their last piston, or—worst of all—the excruciating chirp of dozens of cuckoo clocks, all cuckooing their black little hearts out when the minute hand struck twelve.

The clocks. *They* were the tormenting fiends who'd convinced him he was one inch from insanity. At least one—usually more—of the vile things decorated every room of Max's grandfather's house, where Max was staying. And his grandfather loved them as much as he loved the dusty old furniture that had come with the place.

A lumpy couch he could live with. A few dozen cackling birds he could not. They'd driven him out early this morning, seeking both peace and quiet and a distraction. *Any* distraction.

Only not a female one, which was the biggest frustration of all. He was here to live down his reputation. Not add to it.

Coming to Trouble had been about more than talking his grandfather into unloading this bottomless pit he'd dumped a mountain of money into. The man did have a thing for lost causes and a sob story—apparently this tiny town being bankrupted by an embezzling crook had tugged at Mortimer's heartstrings.

Max couldn't forget his second objective, however— to lay low and stay out of the limelight while his lawyer took care of this Grace Wellington nonsense. Which was why he'd been here for days and had so far not given so much as a second glance to a nicely curved feminine ass.

Not that he'd seen any. Which was probably a good thing, even though it felt like a bad one.

There were only two things Max liked as well—or *did* as well—as women. Piloting. And tinkering with machinery.

He'd gone flying this morning, and, as always, the freedom and beauty of an endless blue sky had helped. Zipping and soaring between a few fluffy white clouds provided the kind of mindless delight he otherwise only got with sex. But once back on solid ground, the feeling had quickly disappeared. He was still tense…restless.

Which was why he was now cussing and coaxing the rust-covered engine of an ancient carousel back to life. He'd stumbled across the glorious ruin in the falling-down remnants of what had been Pennsylvania Kiddie World during one of his daily get-out-to-stay-sane walks earlier this week. Something about the place had appealed to him, unlike anything else in Trouble. Certainly unlike the moldering, cuckoo-clock-infested ruin in which he was currently residing with his happy-as-a-pig-in-mud grandfather.

He supposed there were benefits to being the grandson of a town owner, because he'd been able to get the power to this park turned on. Not that it seemed to have done any good. The poor carousel motor hadn't made so much as one long groan of agony in the days he'd been tinkering with it, even if he had managed to get a few wailing notes of the calliope to belt out.

"Come on, sweetheart, I know you're tired and old, but you must have one more go-round in you, merry or not."

"Excuse me?"

Jerking his attention from the control panel, which had required a good quart of WD-40 before even allowing itself to be opened, Max swung his head around and stared over his shoulder. A woman had come up behind him in the tiny, weed-encrusted, abandoned amusement park, which had once been the cubic zirconia jewel in Trouble's dubious crown.

And speaking of jewels…good Christ, was the woman standing in front of him one. A blonde. She was a blonde. His absolute weakness.

She was also tall, curvy and had the kind of lips that'd make a man howl to the night in pure, primal hunger.

No. No howling. No wolfing at all, remember?

Swallowing his libido, he offered her a smile. "Sorry. I guess you caught me talking to myself." He stood and brushed his hands off on his jeans, leaving a smear of grease on one thigh. Stepping closer, he forced himself to keep this encounter friendly, neighborly.

When what he wanted was sexy and suggestive.

She smiled back, also noncommittal. Cordial but not flirtatious. Unfortunately. "I didn't mean to interrupt your work." Pushing her sunglasses up onto the top of her head, she revealed a pair of bright sky-blue eyes.

Damn. A blue-eyed blonde with a pretty smile and a pair of succulent lips. A smooth-skinned face with soft cheeks and the tiniest jut in her jaw that said she was stubborn. A bright, smiling angel appearing in this private corner of perdition just like the sun coming out on a cloudy, overcast day….

He felt like groaning out loud. Who, he wondered, had he wronged in another life to have such temptation presented to him when he couldn't—simply could *not*—give in to it?

She looked him over, head to toe, with that calm, innocent glance women always hid their interest behind. A tiny hint of color appeared in her creamy cheeks and she licked at her lips—*those lips*—to moisten them.

Just throw a lightning bolt at me and be done with it.

"Talking to yourself—that can be a dangerous thing," she said, her voice throatier than he'd have expected from such a soft-looking female.

"So can cutting a hand on some of this sharp, rusty metal." Max grinned. "I feel like I ought to sweet-talk her to make sure she doesn't scratch me." Hmm…had that sounded suggestive? He hadn't meant it to.

Like hell. Knock it off, Taylor.

Her full lips twitching, she gazed at his hands. "Are you hurt?"

"Not yet. But I have the feeling I will be by the time I coax this old sweetheart into action."

The blonde glanced toward the carousel, one fine brow lifting as she studied the decrepit wreck. The only intact portion was the mini-carousel perched on the top, its mirror-tiled roof still sending out flashes of light when the sun hit it the right way. As for the rest…the once brightly colored circus animals were now mostly a uniform gray, with spots of red or green occasionally showing through. The zebra was missing its front legs, and two jagged shards were all that remained of the lion's mane. Behind each animal, old-fashioned mirrors—dingy and cracked—

provided a distorted, fun-house reflection of the washed-out menagerie, duplicating and emphasizing the sadness of each pitiful creature

He had no doubt what the stranger was looking at—but *did she see?* He couldn't help wondering if the blonde saw the same aching, sad beauty that had captivated him the first time he'd spotted this place, set back off the road in a tangled, forgotten clearing.

"I can't believe this thing hasn't been torn down." She kept her words in close, as if talking to herself.

"Me, either," he admitted. "From the service records on it, I'd say it's been closed since seventy-eight." Which meant it was probably almost as old as this woman. Just the right age.

For ignoring. He forced himself to focus on the book. And remember he was here as the boy next door. Not the wolf beneath the porch.

"I caught the sparkle of it out of the corner of my eye and couldn't resist exploring. I bet a lot of kids around here have had the same impulse."

"I would have when I was a kid."

As she met his gaze, her blue eyes sparkled. Her chuckle was as throaty as her voice as she admitted, "Me, too."

Their smiles and immediate mental connection to mischievous childhoods provided an instant rapport, one that took Max by surprise.

The blonde carefully stepped over the toolbox, which lay open on the ground, a smattering of hand tools jumbled inside.

Not Max's—it was from his grandfather's house. Max's toolbox was immaculate. Some things a man just couldn't mess around with. Like his tools.

And this woman.

"I guess the clang of metal I heard from the road was you doing some, uh, *coaxing* with your hammer?"

"Is that all you heard?"

"That and some music."

"Whew. Glad you didn't hear me yelling, so you won't be reaching for the soap to wash my mouth out."

Her gaze shifted to his mouth. Which made his blood grow one degree hotter and his jeans grow one size tighter.

"Don't tell me you were cursing at your *sweetheart.*"

"Guilty. Patience isn't my strongest attribute."

He'd like to tell her what his strongest attribute was, but that seemed like a dangerous idea. Besides, if she liked danger, she'd know exactly what he was talking about and would continue the subtle innuendo of their conversation.

She stepped closer to the carousel, focusing only on it, obviously not a danger-seeker. That was probably just as well.

"It is a ruin," she murmured, running a hand over the flank of a shabby horse whose braided tail was now merely a stump. "But somehow, it's…it's almost pretty in spite of that."

She *did* see. And just like that, Max realized he liked her. Didn't know her name or a thing about her, but the woman had vision. He liked a person with vision.

Especially when she also had incredibly long legs nicely hugged by sinfully tight jeans, and a mouthwatering hint of cleavage peeking from the scooped neck of her sleeveless top.

Stop.

"Yeah." He cleared his throat. "It tells a story."

"A wistful one."

"I was thinking more along the lines of pathetic, but I guess 'wistful' works."

"She's not pathetic. She's majestic…but worn. Weary."

"Very weary. I can't even get a moan out of her, much less a ride."

Bad choice of words. The blonde's lips parted as she breathed over them.

He tugged his attention off her mouth. Off her face. Off anything that could make him think things he should not be thinking. Which pretty much left the ground.

Nope. Flat, open surfaces suitable for rolling around on didn't work either.

"Not going to make it easy on you, is she?"

He lifted his eyes from the soft grass circling the perimeter of the park. "No way. She's stubborn. Keeps herself tight as a drum—dry—no matter how much I try to lube her." He almost groaned. This was going from bad to worse. Mentally kicking himself, he gave it another shot. "I can't loosen her up and get her going."

God, he was out of control. Blathering suggestive comments without any mental volition whatever. Like his mouth was on flirtation autopilot. It was just…second nature.

The woman kept watching, silently. Something that looked like amusement might have been dancing in those blue eyes of hers, but he couldn't be certain. Because her expression remained merely curious—friendly—not the least bit sexual or inviting.

"I mean," he said forcefully, almost dragging appropriately inane words from the un-sexed corner of his brain, "this thing might be too much for me to handle."

Not great. But acceptable.

He hoped.

"You keep insulting her and she's definitely going to scratch you," the blonde murmured as she stepped around him to examine the junction box. She bent over, her jeans pulling tight against the finest hips and backside he'd seen in months, and Max had to send up a prayer for strength.

"You actually think you can get it working?" she asked. She crouched down, shoving a long strand of fine, blond hair back and tucking it behind her ear.

No, he really didn't. But damned if he wasn't going to try. "What can I say? I like to tinker and I don't like having to give up on anything."

Merry-go-rounds. Sex. Marriages.

"Are you a mechanic?"

In the early days of his business, he'd been a jack-of-all-trades. Mechanic, pilot, reservations clerk. Flight attendant. Anything to keep Taylor Made in the air and in the black. "On occasion. I definitely know my way around a toolbox."

"I don't think even Mr. Goodwrench could get this old beauty going again."

"I don't think he works on merry-go-rounds. And I'm pretty sure he doesn't make house calls." Crossing his arms, he leaned against a striped carousel pole, which was a muddy brown and gray color, rather than red and white. "So I guess I'm all you've got, baby."

The woman tilted her head back to look at him from beneath her wispy bangs, as if she thought he'd been talking to her.

He hadn't. Well, maybe he had, just a bit. He couldn't help it. Flirting with women had come naturally to Max since childhood, when he'd realized his older brother Morgan was always going to be known as the smart, determined one and his younger brother Mike was a fearless daredevil who also had the whole baby thing working in his favor.

Max had his charm. He'd been using it since third grade, when he sweet-talked his teacher out of calling his parents after he'd been caught on the playground organizing an enthusiastic game of Han Solo Kisses Princess Leia.

He'd been Han Solo. Little girls had been standing in line waiting for their turn to play Princess Leia.

Even at age eight the middle Taylor son had understood the appeal of the bad-boy. Let Luke Skywalker get the glory—the Han Solos of the world were the ones who got the girl.

But not this *one.*

No. He couldn't afford those kinds of games right now. Not until he got some good news from his lawyer that his threats to sue Liberty Books had succeeded in halting— or altering—Grace Wellington's book. Until then, he had to be on his best behavior.

"Well, I guess I'd better get back to work," he said.

Perfect. His voice had held a combination of down-home friendliness and sincere work ethic while also silently telling her to move along.

Having to play Mr. Squeaky Clean was ridiculous at this point in his life. It seemed impossible that a tiny publisher he'd never even heard of might be so desperate to keep their book project going that they'd go after him personally. Would any legitimate publishing company really try to get some tabloid to do an expose on Max, showing him as the Don Juan he was made out to be in Grace's book?

Outrageous.

Though he came from a wealthy family—and his grandfather was pretty well known—there was absolutely nothing about Max's life that would garner the interest of a national magazine. His marriage had been pretty crazy, but not headline worthy. And he'd done some stupid shit following the breakup—but again, nothing to write about in the papers.

Grace, however, was another story. The woman had been the Paris Hilton of her decade before she'd married an up-and-coming congressman. When he'd become a down-and-out congressman and had committed suicide after getting his hand caught in a publicly funded cookie jar, she'd gotten even more attention.

So, yes, it could happen. There were a lot of jaded people out there who got off on reading about the rich and scandalous, so Grace's book might grab some attention. And if the chapter about *him* really had gotten most of the rich women of southern California talking, he supposed the publisher might be pretty desperate to keep it.

His lawyer sure seemed to think so. Suspecting the publisher might try something extreme now that Max had threatened to sue, he'd warned Max to keep himself out of trouble. So Max had dug out his dented halo and would be wearing it from here on out—if it killed him.

And it might.

Playing nice and proper was bad enough on a regular day, but with a female like this one—with a body made for silk sheets, sighs and sin—it was proving torturous. He hadn't expected to come to Trouble and stumble over a woman who made him stupid with lust, but here she was.

Which seemed almost too convenient, didn't it? He hadn't met an unattached, attractive woman between the ages of fifteen and forty since he'd shown up in town, and now here was one who'd tempt the *Queer Eye* guys to go straight. Out in the woods…alone…smelling so damn sweet and looking so damn delicious. What were the odds?

Not very good.

Suddenly, Max began to wonder if his lawyer might have been on to something. Maybe somebody out there was trying to set him up, to put his ass over the flame and see if he cried "Fire!" before being barbecued.

Could this blonde be some kind of reporter? Some tabloid shark using herself as bait?

All of his senses on high alert, he found a well of determination deep inside that enabled him to put on his best "I'm a trustworthy guy" face. That look—and the matching attitude—would stay there, too. At least until he found out exactly who this woman was. And why she was here.

One thing was certain—no matter how much she attracted him, Max Taylor's business meant a whole lot more to him than any woman. So from this moment on, this one was strictly hands-off.

Which was exactly the silent message he sent her as he smiled, nodded goodbye and murmured, "Well, have a nice day."

Then he bent down and returned to work on the engine, praying the blond sweetheart would leave before he forgot he was supposed to be a nice guy.

SABRINA HAD NO BUSINESS being out here on the outskirts of town drooling over the hottest male she'd ever seen. But somehow, she couldn't make herself walk away. Instead, she wandered around the old abandoned amusement park, surreptitiously watching him work.

If there were such a thing as an orgasm in a box, this man would be the spokesman for it. That smile, that husky voice, that knowing look—*oh, yeah, $29.95, ladies, flip the lid and start moaning.*

She'd buy a case. That was for sure.

His face had sent her heart into overdrive at first sight, and his playful smile had made her stomach roll over about ninety-four times. The body—whew, that big, massive body—had awakened all her most feminine parts and started them zinging. Sparking. Melting.

He had her tense with excitement, hyper-reactive, on alert. Wondering what to say to make him drop his wrench, rise to his feet and get back to paying attention to *her* rather than the merry-go-round.

Which didn't make any sense.

He wasn't her type. Not at all. A muscle-bound hunk wearing dusty jeans that clung to lean hips and solid thighs was *not* on her list of acceptable men. He certainly wasn't the nice, Tom Hanks type she'd been telling Nancy about earlier.

No. This brown-haired mechanic with his second-skin black T-shirt that clung to a pair of arms thick enough to burst its sleeves was definitely not for her. His shoulders looked broad enough for a lumberjack—as if he bench-pressed the cars he worked on. His thick, blond-streaked brown hair was windswept, and a little too long for "nice." It was also much too tempting for finger-curling.

Everything else was wrong, too. His face was too lean, his jaw too square, his eyes—those incredible green eyes—were much too bright and knowing. His mouth was too wide, his smile too confident, his laugh too enticing. His hands…his big, strong, rough hands… Oh, God help her.

No, no, *no*. He would not do at all.

So why in heaven's name couldn't she make herself leave? Even when she should have—given his provocative comments. Then again, he'd looked so innocent, so friendly-but-not-slimy when he'd made them, that she wasn't entirely sure he'd been coming on to her. Every word he'd said had made perfect sense in the context of the carousel.

And sex.

So which, exactly, had he been talking about?

The carousel. It had to be. This guy was too simple— too openly friendly, blue-collar working man—to play the kind of word games she'd been imagining. He was a small-town mechanic who saw the prettiness in a broken-down old carnival ride and was spending his spare time trying to revive it. Generous, sweet, gorgeous.

Perfect.

Could it be that simple? Could he just be the kind of nice, fabulous man women talked about meeting but never did? A good, honorable guy, despite his rock-hard, sex-on-two-legs appearance?

If only.

He had to have a flaw. Have the IQ of a rabbit or like to scratch his crotch and drink cheap beer while watching monster truck rallies on weekends. Something.

He was married. A chauvinist. A gambler.

She didn't for a moment suspect gay. No way would any woman think that. The female half of humanity would never stand for it—they'd stage a billion-woman protest march at the very idea.

But there had to be *something*—some imperfection she wasn't seeing. Because no way could he look this good *and* be the man of her dreams.

The man of her *nice* dreams. Her happily-ever-after dreams.

Not her wild, erotic, do-me-'til-I-can't-move dreams about smooth-talking, Mr. Suave playboy, Max Taylor.

The idea that one man could be both was simply too far in the realm of science fiction to seriously consider.

Sabrina had to admit one thing. She somehow suspected her Max Taylor dreams were going to be supplanted by big-hot-hard-mechanic dreams, at least for the time being.

So, go! She shouldn't be out here, wondering about this man, not when she had a job to do. But something wouldn't let her leave. Maybe it was curiosity. Maybe even a hint of cowardice about her real mission in Trouble, since she had about as much in common with a femme fatale as she did with Queen Elizabeth.

Whatever the reason, she suddenly wanted to take a few minutes for herself. Just a little longer to try to get to know this stranger who was apparently obsessed with bringing a sad old ruin back to life.

She'd begin her "mission" soon enough—dressed in the expensive knockoffs and playing the part of a rich, bored woman visiting a quaint American village. Trying to tempt Satan's sexy henchman into revealing his wicked seducer tendencies.

Hmm.

Tough job. But somebody has to do it.

But until she threw herself into some incognito role, she just wanted to be herself for a while longer. Why not, for a few more moments, enjoy the company of this simple mechanic, who probably had never *seen* the wife of a congressman—much less gotten her naked in the ladies' room of a trendy Los Angeles restaurant?

Enough with the book.

She really needed to stop thinking about it, to stop remembering the way her whole body had gone warm and moist when she'd imagined being wildly seduced into a debauched life of sensuality by a predatory Max Taylor, as Grace Wellington had been.

Somehow, this stranger with his big hands and his strong shoulders seemed just the person to help her do that.

"So, is there anything I can do to help you?" she asked, once she'd worked her way all around the park and had run out of sad, broken attractions to look at.

He glanced up, eyes widening, displaying the flecks of gold breaking through the green in his irises. *Beautiful eyes.*

"No, thanks, I think I have it covered."

Sabrina squatted next to him, anyway, wondering if the warm summer day felt even warmer down here close to the ground because of the man's overall hotness. "Your hands are pretty big. I'd probably have better luck reaching behind that panel."

His gaze dropped to her hands, which, hopefully, prevented him from seeing how avidly she was staring at his. *Big hands—big everything else?*

"Know a lot about engines, huh?" he asked, sounding amused.

He might be surprised. Her uncle, back in the tiny Ohio town where she grew up, owned an auto repair shop. She hadn't been allowed to spend a whole lot of time with her father's brother—mainly because her mother got so much grief from Grandfather whenever she allowed it—but she knew a thing or two. Not that she was about to get into her background with this stranger.

Especially since she almost certainly would never return to her hometown again. Not unless her little sister was welcome, too…which didn't seem likely. Not after the way their grandparents—and even their mother—had reacted to Allie's out-of-wedlock pregnancy. And to Sabrina's so-called culpability in the affair. After all, she'd been the one who'd brought that vermin-in-sheep's-clothing into their lives.

She hated Peter Prescott for going after her sister to get even with Sabrina for breaking up with him—and for turning him in to their employer for his dishonest activities. But she positively *loathed* him for costing both sisters their family. Judgmental and old-fashioned or not, they were the only family Sabrina had. And she truly missed them.

Well…*most* of them.

"I know enough about engines to know you're never going to be able to get to that green wire." She pushed his hand out of the way and slipped her fingers into the crevice, catching a frayed wire between the tips of two fingers. She might not always be able to walk in big-girl shoes, but she knew how to use her hands.

And she'd sure like to use them on him….

"Excellent," he murmured. "I scraped the rust off the receptor—can you reattach it?"

She did so, pretending she didn't notice the warmth of his breath against her hair. Nothing, however, could make her forget feeling it.

Once she'd accomplished the task, Sabrina leaned out of the way, allowing the stranger to get back to work. He focused on the motor for a few minutes, until she almost thought he'd forgotten she was there.

Then, under his breath, he asked, "Are you from Trouble?"

"No. You?"

He shook his head. "Just visiting."

"Hot time in the big city?" She didn't bother keeping the dry tone out of her voice.

"What can I say?" he said with a small laugh. "I love life in the fast lane."

"I think a horse and buggy would be too fast for this town, so I don't imagine you're going to stumble over any Hooters restaurants or wet T-shirt contests."

His lips twitched as if he was about to laugh at her quip, but he didn't. Instead, a slight frown tugged at his brow and his mouth pulled tight with disapproval. "I can't imagine such a thing. It's awful to think women would degrade themselves in such a way or that men would enjoy it."

Surprise made her jaw drop. He was *shocked* by the idea?

Wow, this had to be one amazing guy if he thought bouncing breasts in wet cotton were utterly shocking when she, Reverend Caleb Tucker's oldest granddaughter, did not. For a man who looked like this one, even Sabrina might forget that a wet T-shirt wouldn't look so great over the push-up bra she wore when she needed to pretend she had some cleavage.

"You know, I hear the old movie theater opens once a month," he offered, his eyes wide and innocent. "Third Saturday…that's coming up. Better keep your calendar clear."

"Are you asking me on a date?"

His eyes widened in surprise. "But, well, I don't even know you, ma'am."

She almost gnashed her teeth, embarrassed as hell. He wasn't being insulting and she hadn't shocked him. He simply sounded a little surprised, as if he wasn't used to such a forward female.

Ha. Nancy had been telling her for four years—since she'd hired Sabrina right out of college—that she was about as romantically aggressive as a guppy. Why this man—who had obviously in no way been making sexual comments earlier—was making her behave in such a way, she had no idea.

"I was just joking," she mumbled, wondering if the heat in her cheeks had made her face flame red. And if there was any way he'd interpret such redness as her skin crisping under the bright sun. One could hope.

"So why are you here, anyway?" he asked.

She thought of her cover story, the one she and Nancy had concocted. From all reports, Max Taylor's eccentric—some said mad—old grandfather had just purchased this entire town. And his grandson was here trying to get the man out of the deal, or else resell the property.

She didn't like carrying on the charade when Taylor wasn't around to hear it, but since she needed to maintain the facade for as long as she was here, she stuck to her story. "I'm just looking the place over, for possible investment purposes. This is the town that was advertised in the *New York Times*, isn't it, with lots of potential for investors?"

His eyes flared and the man reared back, almost tumbling to his butt on the dusty ground. Then a broad smile brightened his face, setting those green eyes to sparkling and sucking the last coherent thought right out of Sabrina's head.

"You bet it is, and you won't regret making the trip. Do you need a tour guide? I'd be glad to show you around." Rising to his feet again, he reached down to help her up, as well.

She shouldn't have taken his hand. Shouldn't have let skin touch skin. At the feel of his rough, warm fingers against her own, she mentally crossed the big giant *T* in her brain that reminded her she was in big trouble. And it had absolutely nothing to do with the name of the godforsaken little town.

No. She was in trouble because now, when she could least afford it, she'd stumbled over the kind of male distraction she'd almost given up on finding. A distraction who was looking at her like she was his guardian angel and *Playboy* fantasy woman all rolled into one.

She yanked her hand away, clenching then unclenching her fingers to get them to stop tingling.

"I can't tell you how happy I am that you're here. Have you seen all the public buildings yet? Been inside that movie theater? There's a huge amount of potential there."

Sabrina, still reeling from the way she'd reacted to his simple touch, remained silent.

"What a fortunate coincidence that we met," he added, his enthusiasm so boyishly charming that she couldn't help smiling in response.

"Why is that?"

"Because I'm exactly the man you need to see."

She *did* need to see him. Naked. And soon. No matter what her brain was telling her about why he was the wrong kind of man, her sexual self wanted nothing more than to watch his clothes come off piece by piece, to reveal that incredible body under the bright, sunny sky.

But he couldn't know that…she hoped. Which meant he was referring to something else.

"How so?"

"Because I happen to have an 'in' with the owner of this place and I can guarantee he'd love to meet you."

The owner. Max Taylor's grandfather. The one who lived with the spoiled, sexpot pilot himself.

Though shaking inside, Sabrina maintained a calm expression. It was time to focus on her mission—getting Grace's book into print *as written*—and to forget about handsome mechanics with laughing eyes and killer chests.

Time to get into character and do what she'd come to this lousy town to do: pretend to be an investor. Pretend to be rich. Get Max Taylor to come after her and prove himself as big a fiery sex maniac as Grace made him out to be.

Without getting herself burned in the process.

Maybe she should just call this Mission: Impossible?

Too bad she'd put on a simple pair of jeans and sneakers for the drive here today—she certainly wasn't dressed for seduction. But she wasn't about to let this opportunity slip away, not when she was finally so close to Max Taylor she could almost smell him.

"Okay," she forced herself to say to the dusty mechanic, who she could no longer afford to lust after, even mentally, "that would be wonderful. Can we go now?"

She held her breath, and almost groaned in frustration when the man shook his head. "He's not home right now, but if you want to come by tomorrow, I promise I'd be happy to introduce you. You can't miss the house—it's right there."

He pointed through the woods toward a small hill. She could just make out the top floor of a three-story monstrosity looking like something out of a Nathaniel Hawthorne story. A famous millionaire lived *there?*

Sabrina hid her surprise. "Okay. What time?"

He shrugged, looking at the carousel and at the hammer in his hand. "I have the feeling I'll be here all day. So come on by whenever you want and I'll walk you up."

"Perfect," she said, meaning it. That would allow her the chance to find the B&B where she'd made a reservation, get settled in and prepare to accomplish her objective.

A good night's sleep would be helpful before going on a clandestine sex campaign.

Hopefully, by tomorrow, Sabrina would have gotten a grip on her libido and would be able to shove her attraction to this sweet, sexy mechanic aside. And focus only on the wicked, soulless playboy she'd come here to expose.

CHAPTER THREE

IDA MAE MONROE AND Ivy Helmsley—better known as the Feeney sisters—had been fighting over men since they were two willowy slips of girls. It had started way back in forty-three when Ida Mae was fourteen and her sister Ivy only twelve and Ida Mae's beau, Buddy Hoolihan, threw Ivy's lunch pail down the well at his daddy's farm. Ida Mae laughed, though she did feel a bit bad for Ivy, 'specially since their mama had made corn bread for their lunches that day.

But sisters were only sisters and boys were better. So, deciding she'd give Ivy her pretty new yellow hair ribbon later that night, Ida Mae cheered Buddy on during his tormenting.

Then Ivy began to cry like her heart would break. Just like that, Buddy went all gooey-soft. He apologized to Ivy, put his arm around her and looked at a still-laughing Ida Mae like her heart was black as coal. Ivy batted her lashes at him, stuck her tongue out at Ida Mae…and silently declared a war that lasted for more than half a century.

The sisters had battled over Buddy throughout grade school, but moved on to other boys—and men—as the years progressed. Usually bloodlessly. But not always.

Eventually, after their mama had died, they both left town, married fellas from the outside, and each tried to keep her husband away from her man-stealing sister.

They'd realized, however, somewhere around 1980 when they'd both been widowed—Ivy more than once—that life just wasn't as much fun without a sister around to love to hate. So they moved back to Trouble and promptly resumed their feud.

Ida Mae called Ivy the black widow spider.

Ivy called Ida Mae the cold-hearted bride of Satan.

But God forbid anyone else call one of the sisters as much as miserly, for the other one would let loose a razor-blade tongue to defend her.

They lived next door to each other, on the north side of town in two ramshackle old houses that had once been Victorian but could now only be called sorry. Some days they sat in Ida Mae's kitchen drinking tea while arguing over who Buddy Hoolihan had loved more. And some evenings they sat on Ivy's front porch drinking bourbon while arguing over which of them had the tinier waist back in the day. Sometimes they merely sipped daisy wine and reminisced about the men they'd killed.

Most often, though, they talked about Mama. How she'd laughed. How she'd made the best pumpkin bread. How she'd tanned them when they were bad. How she'd taught them which poison to use on a man who was a little too free with his fists, or who couldn't keep his man-parts safely buttoned in his own trousers or between his wedded wife's legs.

This would inevitably lead to arguments about their daddy, whom both of them had loved to pieces when they were children. Whether Mama really murdered him, and whether Daddy truly had deserved it.

Ida Mae thought she did and he probably *had*.

Ivy thought she did but he definitely had *not*.

The argument—or any number of other ones—would

eventually lead one of them to steal the beautiful Sears, Roebuck urn with the glossy faux mother-of-pearl handles—which was full of Daddy's ashes—and hide it so the other one couldn't say good-night to him. Which was why Ida Mae was currently tugging all the flour, sugar, stale chocolate chips and dried-up boxes of prunes out of Ivy's dusty pantry.

"It's not your turn to take care of Daddy, it's mine. I have him until tomorrow night, sundown!"

Ivy was smiling as she watched from the other side of her kitchen. Curling her fingers together and resting her hands on the cracked linoleum surface of her faded, yellow kitchen table, she merely watched, a satisfied gleam in her eye. "Seems to me that he was feeling a little ignored."

Ida Mae glared at her sister, knowing by Ivy's expression that she wasn't even close in her hunt for Daddy's ashes. Ivy wouldn't be smiling like that if she were. If her sister had put Daddy on the roof again and Ida Mae had to climb out the third-story window, she was going to snatch her bald.

"I haven't ignored him."

"You were gone for two hours yesterday," Ivy replied. "Two whole hours and heaven only knows where you were. I thought we were going to start talking about the next book we're going to write."

Ivy had it in her head that the two of them could be the next Agatha Christie, even though the one murder book they wrote a few years back never had gotten sold anywhere. "Nobody's been killed around here in years, so we don't have anything to write about," Ida Mae retorted, hoping to change the subject.

It didn't work. "We'll discuss that later. Now, tell me what sneaky things you were up to yesterday."

Ida Mae felt hotness in her cheeks, the kind of heat she hadn't had rush through her since she'd gone through the change twenty-five years ago. "I don't know what you mean."

Her hawk-eyed sister noticed. "You're blushing."

"Where's Daddy?"

"Why? Where were you? What aren't you telling me?" Ivy braced her hands on the table. Pushing herself up with her strong, wiry arms, she rose on her spindly legs. She tottered over on those ridiculous high-heeled shoes that her vanity kept her from tossing into the trash heap where they could rest with Ivy's youth.

The heels put her nose to nose with Ida Mae—another reason Ida hated them—and Ivy took full advantage. Staring so hard her eyes almost bugged out, Ivy pasted on that mulish expression that said she wasn't going to give up until Ida Mae came clean with her secret.

But, no. Not this one. She wouldn't.

Unfortunately, as it turned out, she didn't have to.

"It's a man!"

Damnation, her sister was a know-it-all.

"Who? Who? Who?" Ivy chirped, like a greedy baby hoot owl opening its mouth for a still-wiggling worm dangling from its mama's beak.

"Don't be so foolish…"

Ivy grabbed the front of Ida Mae's blouse—her favorite one, with the little birds stitched on the collar. She knew how much Ida Mae liked birds because Ivy had stitched the thing herself as a Christmas gift. "Bye-bye, black-bird," she whispered in a singsong voice as she began to pluck at the threads with the long tips of her nails.

"Stop it."

"Who is he?"

Ivy wasn't going to stop. She'd tear the delicate birds right off her blouse, then move on to something else Ida Mae loved, until she got what she wanted. *The name*. Ida Mae knew it…because she'd have done exactly the same thing.

"All right," she snapped, determined that one day she would learn to keep a secret.

A joyful smile took ten years off Ivy's face. Ida Mae made a mental note to not tell any funny stories around her sister when eligible bachelors were in the vicinity.

"Really? You'll share?"

She'd rather share a bowl of rat pellets. But there would be no stopping Ivy now. "Yes."

"Who?" her silver-haired sister asked, almost bouncing on her toes like a debutante.

Ivy always had been man-crazy. Unlike Ida Mae, who simply liked men so much she sometimes felt the need to marry one for a while. "Just a stranger."

"A handsome one?"

"No."

"Liar. Where'd you meet him?"

She wasn't lying. The stranger hadn't been what you'd call handsome. More like, startling…striking. *Vivid*. That was a nice word for Mr. Potts.

"Where?" Ivy pressed, reaching for Ida Mae's collar again.

"He moved into Stuttgardt's old house."

Ivy wrinkled her nose. "That one…he was a nasty bad man."

"I know. Remember when Mama threatened him with a rifle if he didn't stop coming to pester her into selling that land between his place and hers?"

"Those clocks…"

"The scandal…"

They met each other's eyes, sharing a quick, unspoken memory. Ida Mae half hoped her sister had gone off the scent and would forget all about the stranger. Ivy was almost as fascinated by murder as she was by men, and Wilhelm Stuttgardt's had never been solved. The old German clockmaker had been dead and buried for five years but he was still talked about nearly every day. His villainy—and the money he'd stolen from the town, not to mention the pension funds he'd taken from his own employees at the clock factory—was fresh in everyone's minds. Even her sister's.

Stuttgardt had lived in Trouble for more'n thirty years, but most folks still called him "the German." Or "the Clockmaker."

Or just "the Thief."

He might have moved here at the age of twenty, planning to bring his silly, fussy clock-making business into their quiet, small community, but to Ida Mae's mind, he'd never been one of them. She hadn't been surprised that he'd eventually stolen anything he could get his hands on, bankrupting Trouble so that a few short years later it'd had to prostitute itself like a cheap street whore to stay alive.

And she most *definitely* hadn't been surprised that someone had made him pay for his crime. Pay *hard*.

"Oh, yes, he was a bad one. Someone took care of him, though, didn't they?" she said, hoping Ivy would now be good and distracted.

Today, however, wasn't her lucky day. Ivy wasn't distracted for long. "Now, tell me everything about *him*. This newcomer."

Sighing, knowing she had no choice, Ida Mae began the

tale. She told her sister about how she'd met the latest resident of their small hometown while picking over the badly wilting lettuce at Given's Grocery in town.

His name was Mr. Mortimer Potts. And despite his long, wild white hair, he was a gentleman. A true, noble, old-fashioned gent the likes of which hadn't moved to these parts in many a year.

And Ida Mae knew, by the gleam in her sister's eye, that even though she, herself, was seventy-seven years old and Ivy seventy-five, they were once again about to embark upon their favorite pastime. Competing for a man.

Maybe to the death.

SABRINA COULDN'T DECIDE which was worse: staying in a tiny old B&B called the Dewdrop Inn, or the fact that it was run by a pseudo-nudist. At least the innkeeper, who had introduced himself as Al Fitzweather when she'd arrived yesterday at the crusty old house pretending to be an inn, was only a nudist on the weekends, and only in the backyard. Unlike the Dewdrop Inn, which was *always* as nauseating as its name would imply.

She was still hearing Nancy's laughter through the cell phone a full minute after she'd described the first day of her assignment in Trouble. While waiting for the laughter to stop, she concluded that the inn was worse than its owner. His dangly bits probably couldn't compete in grossness with the fake grape arbor complete with Cupid statue, the heart-shaped bed and mirrored ceiling in her room, and the eight-person hot tub that probably contained the DNA of the last eighty people who'd been in it.

The Dewdrop obviously longed to run off to the Poconos to be a star in the honeymoon biz.

"So have you seen Mr. Hot Stuff yet?"

Sabrina dropped the curtain and stepped away from her window. No longer distracted by the sight of her landlord—who, since it was a weekday, was mercifully clothed while doing yard work—she was able to give her full attention to her boss.

She almost tossed out a quick, instinctive reply that, yes, she definitely had seen Mr. Hot Stuff, and he was an adorable mechanic who liked merry-go-rounds. One whose name she hadn't even asked for, though she supposed she could excuse herself for that—the man had been attractive enough to make a woman forget her *own* name.

But for some reason she wanted to keep that encounter to herself. "I haven't. But I have made a connection and am going to get introduced to his grandfather today." She threw off the instinctive dismay the word *grandfather* brought to her mind. "Max Taylor is staying with him, so I should have him directly in my line of sight within a few hours."

"Okay, but what about in the meantime?" Nancy said. "Have you learned anything that could be useful in defending against a possible lawsuit brought by the loverboy? That is still the objective, right?"

Oh, yes, it definitely was. Sabrina ticked the whole plan off in her mind: stop the lawsuit, get the book into print so it could make a big splash, earn a promotion *because* of that big splashy book, and make more money so she could take care of Allie. Should be simple—four little steps to her goal.

Too bad they suddenly seemed huge and insurmountable.

"Yes, it's still the objective."

"So what *have* you found out?"

She perched on the edge of a desk, on which sat a greasy phone book blackened with graffiti drawings of bearded men and enormous phalluses, and a Bible blackened with graffiti of bearded Jesuses and enormous crosses. "I've heard people talking about him. According to my waitress last night, he's Saint Max, the new benevolent lord who's come to help his grandfather save them from disappearing off the map."

Huh. More likely he was working on making the panties disappear off every attractive young female in the vicinity.

"From the sound of it, if there's a town that should disappear from the map, it's that one."

"Trouble, Pennsylvania, has definitely been hit with some hard times."

Not just hit with hard times, it'd been smacked about the head and shoulders with them. Then dipped in a tar of misery and feathered in dismay.

"Makes the city look a little more appealing, huh?"

"Philadelphia, Pennsylvania, sounds like heaven to me right now. I swear, the buildings here are only being held together by decades' worth of dried-up paint."

Not to mention everything else that was wrong with this place. The potholes on the main road had jarred her so hard during the drive in, she seriously thought she'd cracked a tooth. There were more businesses closed and shuttered than open. And the ones that *were* open appeared to have been sucked through a time warp—when she'd seen the old movie theater advertising *Smok y and t e B nd t,* the effect had been complete.

The theater unbelievably had seemed like the newest building, every other place having signs that looked original to the 1950s. From the pharmacy/drugstore, to the hardware shop that needed some of its own products to repair the front awning, the town wore its aura of abandon and weariness the way a tired old woman wore a housecoat—with lazy, haphazard helplessness.

Then there were the people...

"Okay, but what about the people, are they cheerful despite living in a rust bucket? Is everyone just as cloyingly friendly as they are in every TV small town?"

Sabrina thought about the small towns she'd seen on television and tried to find one that might compare. Finally, with a sigh, she admitted, "I can think of one or two episodes of *The X-Files* that could come close. Every single time I go down the street, I see this one man wearing a gray sweatsuit sitting on the same bench, in the exact same position. If his skin was gray, too, I'd swear he was dead and nobody in this place was interested enough to find out."

Uninterested. Gray. Dead. Three words that described Trouble and its residents very well. Except for the few bright, splashy colorful ones...like her landlord.

And one amazingly hot mechanic.

Nancy snorted. "Your choice, honey. You're the one who wanted to catch the guy in the act."

Wanted? No. Sabrina didn't *want* to catch Max Taylor schmoozing his way through every woman within range of his overactive hormones and the laser-precision missile between his legs. She *had* to. So much depended on it.

"I'll get him, Nancy. The next time that shark lawyer of his calls, we'll be able to hit him with *proof* his client's a reprobate and practically a gigolo and just dare him to try to sue for defamation."

And then the book would go to print as written—complete with the titillating, attention-grabbing details of

Grace's shocking sexual affair with Max Taylor. Sabrina would get a lot of attention…and hopefully a promotion. Not to mention a raise, which she would need if she was going to be able to help her sister pay for the baby she was expecting.

No, it wasn't her fault Allie had had unprotected sex and gotten pregnant. But it *was* Sabrina's fault that an older, sophisticated man had intentionally targeted the innocent college student for seduction and heartbreak.

She was responsible for her sister's situation. Even her mother believed it. And now that she and Sabrina's grandparents had turned against Allie—cut them *both* out of their lives in shame—Sabrina was all she had. She owed her.

"Okay, kid, it's your game. Let me know if you need anything else. I expect daily updates."

"You bet. Remember, if Allie tries to reach me at the office, I'm at a book expo." Her little sister had seemed suspicious about the sudden trip. Sabrina knew the twenty-year-old might call the office and try to find out exactly where Sabrina's "business trip" had taken her. Considering how bored and lonely her unpredictable sibling had been lately—now that she could no longer work as a waitress due to her advanced pregnancy—Sabrina wouldn't put it past Allie to try to follow her.

After finishing her phone conversation, Sabrina began to prepare herself for her visit to Max Taylor's grandfather, Mortimer Potts. She needed to get in character—to get her mind around her mission—since she might very well be meeting her quarry in just a few hours.

And you'll be seeing him.

She thrust that thought off. Sabrina couldn't afford distractions like small-town mechanics right now. Not when there was so much at stake. She had to get to work, focus on the real reason she'd gone shopping on a Philadelphia street corner to buy knock-offs of expensive-looking clothes and had rented a car that probably cost as much as she'd make for the next two years. It had seemed silly, but Nancy had insisted that she look the part. Because her whole purpose for being in Trouble was to validate every word Grace Wellington had written about playboy pilot Max Taylor. The man addicted to rich, vulnerable women.

Which meant she had to look like one.

Hmm…small-town girl who'd never seen a real pair of Gucci shoes, much less worn them…social klutz who'd once fallen facefirst in a giant bowl of cocktail sauce at a writers' conference—how tough could it be?

"This is ridiculous," she muttered. Then she shook off the doubt because she *had* to make this work. And she *would*.

Once she'd caught Taylor in the act of being exactly the heartbreaking, sex-addicted loverboy Grace had made him out to be, she'd cut his legal legs out from under him. Nip his lawsuit to stop publication of Grace's book in the bud. And laugh all the way to the bestseller lists.

Piece of cake.

She just had to remember one thing—this was *only* about the book. No matter how curious she was about Max Taylor, the world's greatest lover, her clothes were staying on.

Because if they didn't, all bets would be off.

IF MAX WERE A PSYCHO serial killer or a cannibal or something, the pretty blonde walking beside him through the woods would be in serious trouble. She'd shown up at the old, abandoned park this afternoon, and Max had no sooner said he was ready to take her to meet Mortimer than she'd started walking—away from the main road and possible witnesses. He'd fallen into step beside her, leading her toward the path going up the hill to hell. Er…home.

He wondered if she was a black belt. Or if she was armed. Or simply very, *very* trusting. Like a certain little girl with a red riding cape complete with hood.

"Why did you come with me?" he asked, unable to contain his curiosity. "Weren't you the least bit concerned that I could be dangerous?"

Her curvy lips twitched. An invisible string in his chest tugged his heart until it twitched along with them. Either that or his empty stomach was reminding him he hadn't eaten breakfast.

Had to be hunger. Max's heart hadn't been involved in any relationship with a woman in years.

"I'm prepared. I have something in my pocket…."

He shifted away a bit, giving her more room on the dirt path that led to his grandfather's new white elephant. "Please don't mace me, I was just asking a question."

She pulled her hand out of her pocket, and he saw her cell phone.

"Were you going to ring-tone me to death if I turned out to be Freddy Krueger in disguise?"

"I'm pretty sure I'm awake—not dreaming—so you can't be Freddy," she murmured, tucking her phone back into the pocket of her white slacks.

Considering they were delightfully tight, he wondered how she had the room, but quickly figured it out. *God bless spandex. Spandex is my friend.*

"I had my finger ready to speed-dial my friend Butch."

"Butch?"

Color rose in her cheeks and she cleared her throat before explaining. "The ex-Marine turned bouncer."

It was all he could do not to tsk, knowing she was lying.

She might have made a flip comeback, but she had also stepped away from him on the path. He hadn't intended to scare her. Honestly, he found her openness and trusting spirit incredibly attractive...if a bit naive. "There's no Butch."

"Says you."

"If there's a Butch, he's a five-foot-six engineer trying to counter his geekiness and ninety-eight-pound physique by having a tough nickname." Her audible sigh of defeat told him he'd hit home. "Sorry if I just offended your... boyfriend?"

Shaking her head, she reluctantly laughed, and little sparkles of delight seemed to spill out of her and bathe him in her good humor. "No, no boyfriend."

Hallelujah. He'd already noticed there was no wedding ring.

"But there really is a Butch..."

"Oh, yeah?"

Instead of meeting his eye, she glanced down at her feet, kicking a small branch away with one sneaker-clad foot. "He's my dog. A toy poodle."

"Is his name really Butch?"

She tugged one corner of her lip between her teeth before slowly shaking her head. "It's Giorgio."

Max snorted. "Who named him?"

"Me."

Shaking his head, he mourned for poor old Giorgio. "That should be against the law. Saddling a completely hideous name on another living creature."

"I like Giorgio. It's very...Mediterranean."

"Bet he gets the snot beat out of him by the other pups at the doggie park."

"He's got a bit of a Napoleon complex," she admitted. "So he does tend to get in trouble with some of the bigger dogs. That's why my younger sister decided to start calling him Butch once she moved in with me."

A sister who lived with her. He filed the information away for future use. Not that he knew for *sure* that he'd ever be invited in for coffee and an all-night sex-fest after one of their inevitable dates. But he was hoping. And a live-in sister could make things a little…crowded.

Now, however, wasn't the time to be thinking that way. Not until he was out of this whole book jam. *Best behavior,* he reminded himself. *You're Mr. Boy Next Door.* Because, though he wanted to believe this woman was in Trouble for exactly the reasons she claimed, he wasn't ready to completely discount the possibility that he was being played.

A player was always on the lookout for anyone who wanted to play him. And once upon a time, Max had been one of the best players around.

"So whose speed-dial number *did* you have your finger on?"

"The Trouble Police Department. They are programmed into my cell phone." She shuddered lightly, though the day was warm and comfortable. "I put them in there when I arrived and found out my landlord likes to get naked and prune the rosebushes in his backyard on the weekend. Which, to me, seems like a dangerous combination—thorns, hedge clippers and nudity."

"Ah. You're staying at the Dewdrop."

"Yes."

"Could be worse. You could be staying at Seaton

House, which used to be open as a hotel just north of Trouble."

Cringing, she admitted, "I saw pictures on the Internet of that place, hulking over the town like a gargoyle hovering over its still-bleeding prey."

Good visual.

"I had this image of a nightmarish version of Satan's Hotel where demons turn down your bed and you realize it's full of snakes. You check in and you never check out. It looked as if Norman Bates and his mother lived there."

"They might. Or so says the Trouble gossip mill. The hotel closed down a month ago, leaving the Dewdrop as the only lodging option within twenty miles of here." He grinned. "Nicely worded description by the way."

"Thanks. I guess I've got a lot of practice trying to paint pictures with words."

"Ah. You're a writer?"

She didn't answer right away, staring at the ground in front of them as if afraid she'd trip and fall over a jumbled mound of brush. Finally, though, she said, "I've wanted to be a novelist since I was a kid."

Though he had no fondness for writers lately, he admitted, "Well, you're good. As long as you stick to fiction and none of that tell-all crap."

Like Grace. But this blonde was nothing like Grace, who wasn't really a writer at all. She was merely a spoiled brat who was never happy if she wasn't messing with someone's life.

His companion stumbled a little and Max grabbed her arm to steady her. "Careful."

"Thanks," she said, her voice low.

They walked in silence for a few yards, then Max said, "Just so you know, I'd read your books. You've got me convinced to never set foot in Seaton House, much less sleep in it."

He wondered if she'd believe him if he told her there was somewhere she could be staying that was even *more* frightening—the house where they were heading. The one where he currently resided.

Because hearing a few dozen screaming cuckoos every hour had to be worse than sleeping one thin wall away from the owner of the Seaton House, a man most of Trouble apparently considered a murderer. Or from Al Fitzweather, whose goods, one would hope, would at least be hidden by his beer gut whenever he was walking around the house in the buff.

"Remind me to do a narrative passage on Al Fitzweather and the Dewdrop Inn, just to keep you safe from that place, too," she said.

"If there's a law against bad pet names, there should also be one against unattractive people getting naked in public," he said, inwardly cringing at the mental picture of the inn owner, and then of the old lady in his cockpit a few weeks ago.

"I think there already is."

"In Trouble? One can never be sure…"

"Good point."

Thinking about her comments regarding her cell phone, he added, "You know, even with your speed dial, I don't think any of the three officers on the Trouble P.D. could get here fast enough to save you if I turned into Jason or Pinhead."

"You have a thing about horror movies?"

"You obviously do, too, since you know exactly who I'm talking about, including Norman Bates."

They were passing beneath an enormous elm and a bit

of sunlight peeked between its leaves to bathe her hair in a warm, soft glow. He wondered if the color was natural and thought it might be—a cascading jumble of golds, blondes and light browns, it probably couldn't have come from a bottle.

His body chose that moment to remind him of that lack of breakfast again, because Max felt something roll over, deep inside. *Definitely food related.* Not female related. Uh-uh.

"I think I've seen every horror movie ever made, even though we weren't allowed to watch them in our house growing up," she explained. "My friends would have terror marathons whenever I slept over. I was a bad influence."

Oh, right. This soft, curvy-looking woman was probably about as bad as Mr. Peanut.

"A couple of times I'd go to the movies to see something PG rated but sneak into *Child's Play* or another bloody flick."

She had a naughty side. He wouldn't have predicted that—though he should have, given the sarcastic, earthy wit that she exhibited at unexpected moments. "How very shocking," he said, sarcasm heavy in his tone.

"Anyway, I learned enough to know that the girl who fights back is the only one who makes it out of the dark and scary house alive, so when I moved to the city I took a self-defense course from an ex-cop. I could hurt you... just so you know."

That he *wouldn't* have predicted. "You telling me another Butch story?"

Shaking her head, she lifted a golden brow, as if daring him to find out. That gleam in her blue eyes told him he'd better not. So maybe the pretty blonde wasn't naive at all—just confident of her ability to defend herself.

Not that she needed to. Max had never so much as yelled at a woman, much less lifted a hand to one. Seductive whispers or sweet, playful words were so much more effective than shouted ones, in his experience.

Except with his ex-wife. And with her, his lawyer had done all the yelling.

Max had stuck to drinking.

He'd spent a good year completely intoxicated following their shocking breakup. Which was why he currently had a twelve-step card tucked safely in his wallet. And why he hadn't had anything more alcoholic than a Butter Rum Lifesaver near his lips in three years.

"He said I was the best student he ever had," she said. "And I liked it so much, I went on to become an instructor at a local community center."

Hmm…a self-defense instructor at a community center? Didn't sound like the monied type—the type who'd be able to take this albatross called Trouble off his grandfather's back and let Max and his brothers return to their regularly scheduled lives. Then again, maybe she was an eccentric, altruistic rich person.

Max certainly was acquainted with a few of those. Some of whom were related to him. Like the one who'd bought this monstrosity of a town to try to breathe financial life into its carcass before rigor mortis set in.

"You know," he murmured as they crested the hill, reaching the edge of the tangled, overgrown yard surrounding his grandfather's new house, "it wasn't the girl who fought back who survived a night with Freddy, Jason or Norman." Hiding a smile, he continued. "It was always the good girl. The virgin."

He gave her a look of complete innocence, remembering at the last moment that he was not allowed to tread deep into dangerous, sexual waters with any woman just now. Frankly, he thought he'd been doing pretty well at keeping things light, friendly and above the waist with all this talk of blood, murder and psycho killers. But that last comment had shot his good intentions straight to hell.

He somehow didn't think she'd mind. He had the feeling that despite her angelic looks, this woman was not the sweet type. Which was good. Max didn't much care for sweet girls. Not when bad ones were so much more… entertaining.

"Well," she replied, "I guess it's a good thing you're not a Jason or a Freddy, then, or my guts might be hanging from a tree back in the woods right about now. Because my virginity was history long before Jason killed his hundredth victim."

Sassy comeback. Damn, he really liked that. On top of everything else he already liked about this stranger, who'd popped into his mind several times the night before when he'd been trying to sleep. "Considering he probably hit a hundred by the second movie, I somehow doubt that. You would've been in preschool."

"Thousandth victim, then. At least five movies ago."

"Okay." Since they were now discussing her virginity— Lord have mercy on his wicked soul for *those* mental images—he figured introductions might be good. "What's your name, anyway? We never did the how-do-you-do stuff. Some self-defense expert you are."

"It's Sabrina. Sabrina Cavanaugh."

He stuck his hand out. "Mine's Michael. Michael Myers."

She rolled her eyes, instantly recognizing the name of the psycho from the Halloween movies. Smiling, Max opened his mouth to offer his real name, but before he could, Sabrina—*pretty Sabrina*—cut him off with a surprised gasp.

"Oh, my God."

Wonderful. The woman had obviously seen Hell House. Sighing, Max steeled himself for her obvious dismay when she realized just how bad it was. She'd run as fast as she could when she saw the kind of accommodations the owner of this crazy little town would get to live in.

And there was more. He simply couldn't *wait* until she met Mortimer.

CHAPTER FOUR

ASIDE FROM GETTING lots of attention and feeling the baby moving around inside her, being pregnant sucked the big one. Not that Alicia Cavanaugh knew much about sucking, big ones or little ones...her single sexual relationship had been short-lived and pretty straightforward. Vanilla. None of the icky stuff.

Just a three-week game of wham, bam, thank you ma'am, and here's an up-yours to your sister, too. That pretty much described her one and only grown-up romance with Peter "the Prick" Prescott, who'd screwed her over but good, all to screw over her big sister, Sabrina.

Frankly, Peter the Prickface was the reason Allie was feeling especially yucky today. Well, Peter and the extra twenty pounds sitting squarely on her bladder. And the... other stuff.

It was beyond awful. Twenty years old and she had stretch marks and hemorrhoids. Unbe-freaking-lievable.

All of which Peter had provided. God, she wanted to kill him, especially after last night.

"It's okay, Lumpy, he was just being a jerk. He didn't mean it." She didn't know who she was trying harder to convince—the lump wriggling around on her kidneys, or herself.

He couldn't have meant it. Could not *seriously* be considering fighting her for custody of this baby once he or she was born.

"Never in a million years," she muttered as she scoured Sabrina's refrigerator, dying for something chocolate. It was nearly noon and any reasonable person would assume that a pregnant woman would want chocolate for lunch on occasion. But was there any to be found? Nooooo.

No chocolate. Not even any chocolate sauce lurking behind the nauseating fresh fruits and vegetables and high-protein shakes.

"My kingdom for a Yoo-hoo," she whispered, staring at all the healthy junk her sister had stocked up on before leaving town yesterday. "Bailing out, more like it," she added as she slammed the door shut, feeling tears well up in her eyes.

She knew it was stupid to feel this way. Sabrina hadn't bailed, she had a book expo to go to, a business trip. Her sister hadn't wanted to leave Allie alone this close to her due date. But she'd had no choice. Now that she was supporting not only herself but her freeloading, knocked-up sibling, Sabrina had to work extra hard.

She probably hated Allie.

A fat salty tear fell out of her eye, slid down her face and landed on her big belly. Quickly wiping it off, she blinked a few times, not wanting the baby to know she was crying. Again. Poor little thing might get a complex before he was ever born, thinking his mommy was a basket case who didn't love him.

"I do," she whispered. "And Aunt Sabrina loves you, too. She loves *both* of us."

In her heart, she knew her sister didn't resent her, but her whacked-out hormones had been calling the shots for a good seven months now. So Allie couldn't stop the tears.

She cried over being a burden to Sabrina.

Over being a single parent.

Over the scene with Peter the Prick-face.

Over the birthday coming up next month that would include no card from her younger sister or brother, no small bottle of cologne from her mother. No sermon disguised as a birthday greeting from her grandfather. No word from home at all.

Most of all she cried over the major screwup she'd made of her life.

Peter made it...

"No," she said, her voice firm, her tears drying as quickly as they'd burst forth.

Peter had used her and hurt her, but he hadn't forced her to open her legs and say *aah*. Or to trust him with the birth control issue. That was all on Allie's shoulders. And, oh, they felt mighty small these days.

"I need to tell Sabrina that we ran into him," she whispered. She was still cursing her decision to take the bus out to an upscale mall last night to window-shop for cute baby clothes she could never afford. Department store jammies were out of the question. Her baby was starting out life as a true American, clothed by Wal-Mart from head to toe.

"Should've just gone to the secondhand shop," she muttered, knowing she never would have run into *him* if she had. Him...the snob who'd never be caught dead in a non-designer suit. The man she'd hoped to never see again. Her ex. Her sister's ex. The six-foot-tall pile of shit in Versace known as Peter Prescott.

Sabrina's gonna kill me.

Disgusted by the very thought of Peter ever entering their lives again, Sabrina had warned her to stay close to home.

But figuring Peter was long gone, Allie hadn't seen the harm in going out for a little while. The apartment was too quiet without Sabrina in it, talking about how adorable the baby would be and what a great job Allie would do as a mother.

She'd thought her sister was being overprotective about Peter. Because once he'd quit his job at the publishing house where he'd worked with Sabrina—quit because of some big hush-hush scandal her sister wouldn't tell her about—Peter had supposedly left town. Sabrina figured he'd gone to New York. Allie had hoped he'd gone to a back alley in Tijuana and been jumped by some horny drug traffickers who'd kidnapped him and put him to work in a slave labor camp picking corn and cleaning toilets with his tongue.

Or something like that.

But, no, apparently not. Because he was here, in Philadelphia. So either he'd never really left, or he'd come back with his tail between his legs.

Whatever the case, the cat was out of the bag—or more appropriately, the pregnant belly was out of the maternity smock.

Remembering the initial shock on his face when he'd seen her—*all* of her—she couldn't prevent a small stab of righteous pleasure. But because her own heart had tumbled at the sight of him, she hadn't been able to enjoy his obvious dismay.

Allie wished it hadn't hurt to see his handsome face and experience that familiar rush of want she'd felt from the minute she'd met him on campus at Tyler College. Back when she'd had no idea the man had, until recently, been her sister's colleague—and *boyfriend*—and was carrying a grudge wider than an elephant's butt.

What an absolute idiot she'd been to fall for his line.

Easy pickings. And, oh, had he picked her over. Flirted with her, teased her, made her feel like a beautiful woman instead of an awkward, small-town girl.

Made her fall in love.

Then he'd dropped her flat. Not even sticking around to see just how much of an *impression* he'd left behind. A seven- or eight-pound one, she suspected.

Not even twenty-one and she had already disgraced her family, lost her scholarship to her Christian college and been forced to quit her job, move out of the dorm and crash with her big sister. No money. No insurance. No future.

All of that was *worse* than stretch marks. Or even hemorrhoids.

"Here lies Alicia Cavanaugh," she whispered. "Her grave marked with nothing but a great big *L*. For Loser."

Tears welled up again but this time they wouldn't stop. She wouldn't have been able to stop them if she tried, not even for chocolate. Not for Hershey's. Or Dove. Or Godiva. Or even those crunchy See's toffee candies.

"Mmm…toffee," she whispered through a hiccupping little sob.

Not having the toffee candies made her cry harder. Not even thoughts of how much she was going to love her baby boy or girl and how good a mother she was going to make helped.

Because Peter was threatening to take *that* away from her, too. Once he'd recovered from his shock last night, he informed her that there was no way he was paying child support. And that *she* might end up paying it to *him* because he could decide to sue for custody, and since she was an immature college dropout barely out of her teens, he would probably get it.

What if he was right?

He didn't want to raise this baby, she knew it. He was being hateful. That expression of amusement in his eyes, as he'd informed her he had to *think* about it first and would be in touch, said it all.

He didn't want to be a father. He just wanted to be cruel, which seemed to be what he did best.

"I have to tell Sabrina. She'll know what to do."

This wasn't something she could share over a cell phone, however. She needed to see her big sister face-to-face. Which might prove tricky, since Sabrina hadn't told her where she was going.

Fortunately, however, Allie knew a secret about Jane, Sabrina's secretary at Liberty Books—a secret Peter Pecker had revealed during their last phone call so many months ago. He'd told her about his affair with Jane, hoping she'd tell Sabrina…and hurt her some more. Allie had kept it to herself. Until now.

Allie wasn't fond of blackmail, but she'd learned a lot of hard lessons at the school of Peter. Jane would know where Sabrina was, and Allie had ammunition against Jane.

Now, it appeared, was a very good time to use it.

"WHAT ON EARTH is that?"

Hearing the shock in Sabrina's voice as they reached the top of the hill beside his grandfather's new home, Max steeled himself to explain. His own first closeup view of the house had been much the same.

The three-story mausoleum had been built about a hundred years ago and it wore every one of those years on its face. With missing tile shingles on the roof, shutters that couldn't be closed dangling outside most of the windows, peeling layers of varying colors of paint, and a sagging porch that had begun to separate from the front door—requiring a little hop to go inside—the place was silently begging for a wrecking ball.

Max was loudly begging for one.

Especially to maim, kill and annihilate the clocks. The former occupant had apparently owned a clock factory and had liked to sample the wares. Blue ones, red ones, open-billed ones…cuckoos with glittering emerald eyes and shiny black ones, with carefully detailed feathers or fake-looking plastic talons. With open wings or military epaulets or garland wreaths dangling from their beaks.

Two dozen of them, at least, though it seemed more like a thousand. The noise was enough to make a man lose his mind.

And the clocks weren't the beginning and the end of the insanity, oh, no. The inside of the house was, itself, a crazy maze, with oddly shaped rooms, doors that opened to interior brick walls, chimneys rising from no fireplaces. Like it had been built little by little—piece by piece—with no thought given to the finished product.

Grandfather loved it—right down to the last cuckoo and threadbare rug. No big surprise.

Max supposed that with a few million dollars, the cast and crew of *Trading Spaces* and that wrecking ball, it could be made into something inhabitable.

"I guess you're wondering about the house." But as Max followed Sabrina's stare, he realized she was not looking at the building. She was looking at the enormous structure *beside* the building. The one he hadn't noticed until right now, probably because his brain was used to blocking out the more impossible sights a life with Mortimer Potts often provided.

He closed his eyes briefly, but, unfortunately, the mirage hadn't disappeared when he reopened them.

Rising from the tangled brush, brambles and honeysuckle vines—which had grown from beyond their original perimeter against the falling-down stone fence to encroach all the way to the side patio—was a monstrosity. A gigantic *thing,* swaying in the light morning breeze.

Standing twenty feet high and covering most of the side yard, it was an enormous mass of colors all swirled together on a billowy fabric. A tent…but not a garden variety camping-in-the-backyard one. This was like something out of an old *Arabian Nights* film. Emblazoned with brilliant splashes of red, green and gold, the thing stood like an enormous jewel beneath the bright summer sky.

"Damn."

Mortimer was in one of his Middle East moods again. His grandfather had spent a number of years in Egypt after the Second World War. He liked to claim he'd been granted an honorary sheikhdom from a Bedouin tribe with which he'd spent one winter, cut off from the rest of the world in a secret, sand-battered camp.

As with many of Mortimer's stories, Max wasn't certain if this one was true or not. All Max knew was that whenever Morty had walked like an Egyptian, he and his brothers had been stuck drinking goat's milk and eating camel tongue.

"Is there a circus in town?"

There was almost always a circus in town when his grandfather was around. And the memory of all those circuses, all those towns—all that adventure—made him smile, despite his fears that the potential investor was about to be scared off. Any sane woman would be.

Especially if Mortimer came out brandishing his sword.

"Not a circus. But there could be animals."

She merely gaped.

"I don't think there would be any dangerous ones," he quickly added. "Though you can never be entirely sure. He did once rescue a tiger headed for the dinner table of some sick, twisted millionaire."

"He? Are you talking about Mr. Potts?" she asked, her eyes wide, as if she wasn't sure if he was pulling her leg.

He wasn't. Though he'd like to, if it meant he actually got to touch one of those long, beautiful legs.

"Es salaam aleikom!"

He tore his attention off Sabrina Cavanaugh's slender thighs and braced himself for introductions. This could be tricky.

"What did he say?"

"That's hello. I think. Though he could be offering you some camel tongue," Max muttered. Then he fell silent, watching Sabrina absorb Mortimer Potts.

A mane of thick white hair blew around his grandfather's shoulders, which were still strong and straight despite his age. His face was smooth, nearly unwrinkled, but dark and leathery after years in the blazing sun of Africa or South America. Even from several feet away, his blue eyes shone brilliantly—alight with intelligence and a genuine love of life—as he approached. His steps were firm, his legs never hinting that they'd been walking the earth for eight decades. Or that they suffered terribly with arthritis.

Clothed in a traditional long, white tunic with a red sleeveless coat draped over it, and a colorful cloth resting lightly on top of his hair, he looked just like the Bedouin sheikh he imagined himself to be. The garb flowed around his tall, lanky form, each gust of wind molding it against his skinny legs.

Max sent up a quick prayer that Mortimer was wearing something underneath this time.

Sabrina stared, saying nothing, not even when his grandfather reached her side. She looked stunned—as robbed of speech as if her prissy poodle Giorgio had started singing "Like A Virgin."

He understood the reaction. His grandfather was a little…startling, at first. But he was not truly crazy—just a bit eccentric.

And he was definitely not laughable.

In fact, if she laughed at him, he'd let her find her own damn way back to town and she could take her money with her.

Max, Morgan and Mike could laugh *with* the old man as much as they wanted. But heaven help anyone who laughed *at* him.

If, however, she saw the man Max and his brothers saw— as she'd seen the beauty in the carousel—he might fall in love and propose. Not marriage—God, no. But…something.

Probably something indecent.

"You've arrived just in time. I'll have my manservant fetch my pipe. Come smoke with me."

Max frowned. "You know you can't do that anymore."

"What do the doctors know?"

"I'm not talking about your health, I'm talking about the stuff you put in that pipe. It's illegal in most countries, especially this one."

Mortimer rolled his eyes.

"And," Max added, "you don't *have* a manservant anymore. Roderick spent one night with those clocks and hightailed it back to New York, remember?"

His grandfather waved an airy hand, completely unconcerned by such banal things as his health, flighty butlers with superiority complexes, or his stature as a law-abiding citizen. That last part was questionable, anyway.

"Did you put that thing up yourself?" Max asked, unable to figure out how Grandfather could have gotten this whole Middle Eastern scenario set up in the few hours since he'd left. Grandfather wasn't, after all, a seventy-year-old anymore.

Shaking his head, Mortimer explained. "Hired a few of the townies for the morning."

Oh, joy. Word was likely spreading already. *Our new town patriarch is a wingnut. Hide the good china, stash the children and lock up the virgins.*

"Now, tell me, who have we here?" Grandfather asked. A smile that could only be described as wolfish appeared on the old man's face, and a recognizable, flirtatious twinkle appeared in his eyes. Twenty years dropped off his age. Someone who didn't know him would peg him as a man of sixty. A virile one.

Oh, did Max ever want to be his grandfather when he was that old!

"My name is Sabrina Cavanaugh," she said, sticking out her hand and smiling at the old man. She appeared friendly, admiring.

Grandfather had a way with women. And judging by the light in his eyes, he'd noticed that this particular woman had a smile that could bring a man to his knees. Even aged arthritic ones.

"I am—"

"Mortimer Potts," Max interjected, nipping the long sheikh title in the bud.

Grandfather offered him a slight, condescending smirk. "I suppose that will do for now."

Max watched closely as Mortimer and the newcomer took stock of each other. His grandfather was, as always, regal and proud in his eccentricity. And so far, Sabrina wasn't running. In fact, she looked intrigued. The same way she'd looked at the carousel.

He *knew* he was going to like this woman.

"Mr. Potts, I am not a smoker, but I would very much like to see inside that tent. I've often wondered what they're like."

"They're so comfortable. Mountains of pillows, cool, silk draperies. Quite the thing for this dry, desert climate."

Not batting an eye, she offered him her arm. "I can't wait to see it."

"Good. Then I'll brew us some tea."

Max cleared his throat and shot the old man a warning glance, knowing Mortimer sometimes liked to get creative with what he put in his tea. "No weird *spices*."

Sabrina shook her head. "Oh, I'm so disappointed."

Great, just what Grandfather needed, a partner in crime. But Max knew how to scare the woman into behaving. "And none of that aphrodisiac powder, either."

This time she kept her mouth shut.

Grandfather rolled his eyes. "My grandson can be tiresomely pedestrian at times. Too bad, he really needs to stop that. He has such promise, you know, being the most like me."

And that truth terrified him almost as much as it excited him. To think he might really be like his grandfather…it was also another reason Max was glad he no longer drank. Because, even sober, he could probably have far too much fun with the idea if he let himself go with it.

Sabrina nodded her agreement. "He's very…" Then her words trailed off as she looked back and forth between the two of them. "Grandson?"

Mortimer nodded. So did Max.

The color disappeared out of the blonde's face so fast it was as if someone had doused her with a giant puff of talcum powder. Her mouth hung open, working a bit, but no sound came out. She stared at both of them, looking genuinely stunned, then began to shake her head.

"Sorry, I never did tell you how I knew this old codger, did I?" he said, figuring she was just confused. Maybe puzzled, thinking he'd been keeping his relationship with Mortimer secret for some reason. He hadn't. Max might think his grandfather a little nutty, but he was in no way ashamed of him.

In fact, he considered Grandfather one of the finest men he'd ever known. Not every man would have taken in three rowdy young grandsons and raised them himself, dragging them around the world with him wherever he went when he could easily have written a few checks and sent them away to expensive schools. He could have washed his hands of them when his daughter and son-in-law died. But he hadn't. He'd made them his own and he'd made them believe—truly, genuinely believe—that they were loved and safe and secure. And he'd even provided something of a mother figure, with prissy Roderick making them wash behind their ears and finish their peas while Mortimer plotted their next adventure. What more could any kid ask for?

Their upbringing may have been unconventional and eccentric, but the Taylor brothers had had both childhood and family from the moment they were orphaned. All thanks to this man.

Sabrina was still staring, silent, so Max shook off the introspection. "My name's Taylor. Max Taylor."

He stuck out his hand for the formal introduction, but

the blonde didn't take it. She simply stared at his fingers, slowly lifting her gaze to his face. Finally—wondering- ly—she said the strangest thing.

"As in *Bond*. James Bond?"

Confused, he simply stared at her, waiting for the punch line. Because he was so focused, it was easy to catch her reaction. Like water bursting through a dam, the blood returned to Sabrina's face. Her pale cheeks filled with color as rapidly as they had emptied of it. She jerked her chin up and licked her full, pouty lips.

And he saw it. *The* look. The suggestive, heated, *take me* expression he'd seen on women's faces from the minute he'd been both mature enough to inspire it and old enough to understand what it meant.

Unfortunately, at that time, he hadn't had the third key ingredient—being skilled enough to take advantage of it.

That had changed, though, round about age sixteen. The mother of one of his classmates at his multinational high school in Cairo had helped him develop his…skills. And he'd been utilizing them ever since, more during some periods of his life than others.

For the first time since he'd met her by the carousel, the blonde was finally looking at him the way he'd *wanted* her to look at him. The way he'd want any gorgeous, intelli- gent, witty woman to look at him. Not merely with spec- ulation, interest and friendliness. Not even with attraction and flirtatiousness.

No. Sexy Sabrina's blue eyes sparkled with excitement. Her breath exited her lips in choppy, audible exhalations. Though she didn't step away, or come any closer, her whole body slowly moved. Curving sinuously, like a cat stretching in the sun, one shoulder going back, one hip tilting to the side to highlight the indentation of her waist.

Yeah. He knew this look. Her stance, her expression, the heavy-lidded stare exuded one thing: pure, sexual want. A blatant, no-questions-asked invitation to sin.

He didn't know why he was getting it *now*, while his elderly grandfather watched wide-eyed with interest, but he had no doubt he was being silently propositioned by the blond stranger. He'd been propositioned by enough women to know.

It was just his damn bad luck that it was an invitation he could not, under any circumstances, accept.

MAX TAYLOR, SABRINA DECIDED late that night when lying alone in her bed at the inn, was a fiend. A sadistic, twisted, manipulative monster. He *had* to be. How else had he been able to fool her so completely—to make her think he was nothing but a simple small-town mechanic, when, in truth, he was more like an oversexed Dr. Evil?

Addictive. Seductive. Overpoweringly sensual. All while smiling a you-can-trust-me grin and keeping that aw-shucks-ma'am tone in his voice.

"Monster."

Oh, the man was good. Talented. If they gave out Academy Awards to playboys in disguise, he'd be writing his acceptance speech now.

Because he *must* have been acting. That sweet, kind, friendly—oh, God, sexy—guy she'd met tinkering with the carousel had to have been a façade. Behind the mask lurked a polished seducer who could lure women down a dark path of eroticism with a touch of his hand, a whisper in the ear.

The promise of a five-hour, nonstop session of love-making.

Impossible. No man could…no matter what Grace Wellington said in her memoir.

After yesterday—and this afternoon—Sabrina had to add a few other possibilities to his repertoire. A friendly nod, a welcoming smile. A twinkle in his eye. Who could have known they'd be just as effective as a deep kiss, a tender caress or a mammoth hard-on at inspiring lustful thoughts?

"Not lust, damn it," she whispered, rolling over and punching the lumpy pillow. She kept her voice low, knowing there were only three other guests staying at the inn. The last thing she wanted was to arouse her landlord's curiosity and have him come investigate.

"Oh, great, it's almost Saturday," she muttered, wondering whether his nudey thing began at midnight or would be mercifully held at bay until dawn.

If anything could kill her hungry curiosity about Max Taylor, it was thoughts of a nude Al Fitzweather.

Actually, she should *easily* be able to control any sexual feelings whatsoever. After all, Sabrina didn't lust. Well, maybe she lusted sometimes—lusted for the kind of sex she read about in racy novels or imagined in her mind's eye after the end of a movie. Who, for instance, hadn't pictured Buttercup and Wesley doing the deed in a meadow full of daisies after the end of *The Princess Bride?*

She'd said that to her mother once, when she was a teenager. For about three seconds, the older woman's lips had twitched, as if a real laugh was about to spill out. But she'd quickly sucked it back in.

Of all the reasons Sabrina resented her grandfather, that was probably the biggest one. Because he'd stolen her mother's smile. By making her feel like the death of her husband in a robbery had been God's judgment for marrying outside her rigid faith, he'd used guilt and heartache to control all their lives. And she hadn't had the education, money or career prospects to do anything about it.

"I lust, Grandfather," Sabrina whispered, staring up at the ceiling. "Hear me? Lust, lust, lust! Naked, sweaty sex. Big, hard penises. I think about them all the time!"

Only, she needed to not *talk* about them out loud right now for fear Mr. Fitzweather would think she was issuing an invitation.

She definitely wasn't. Not to him—not to anyone. Because Sabrina had never made a habit of lusting after real, live men, not even anyone she'd been dating.

She'd always been able to separate sex out from her other daily requirements. Exercise, mental stimulation, a steady influx of cash, an orgasm or two, mechanically provided, if necessary— Ooh, how wicked, a vibrator— she was surely destined for hell. She hadn't cared, because the thing had come in handy, particularly after she'd wised up to the kind of man Peter really was and dumped him seven-and-a-half months ago.

Since then, her life had been compartmentalized, planned, normal. No men required. Not crazy—other than her involvement in Allie's situation. Never unexpected— uh, other than that Allie thing again. But certainly never dangerous or wicked, despite what her grandfather had direly predicted when Sabrina left home at eighteen. Black sheep or not, she'd done a pretty good job of living a "good" life. Being safe, respectable and completely sensible.

At least…until she'd started working on Grace Wellington's book and had begun to wonder what it would be like to let go of all her inhibitions. To be so caught up in a dark, passionate affair that she'd open herself up to all sorts of kinky possibilities like the ones Grace had described. Threesomes and bondage…pleasure and pain.

The idea had repulsed her. And yet it had somehow aroused her, too.

One thing was certain. She hadn't been able to put it out of her thoughts—or her dreams. Night after night her mind had filled with sultry images. And by day she'd found herself wondering what it would be like to do something wild with someone who was totally outside polite society. An intoxicatingly wicked bad boy. The kind about whom rock songs were sung and romance novels were written. The kind she'd flirted with back in high school and had brought home once or twice in order to get *some* kind of action going in their very sedate house.

The Max Taylor kind of bad boy.

Or was he?

Could he really be as bad as all that if he liked to volunteer his spare time working to repair broken-down relics like the Kiddie World carousel? Or exchanging kindly barbs with a sweet, funny old man who told the most wonderful stories of deserts and pirates, harems and spies?

It was hard to dislike Max Taylor when Sabrina already adored his wonderfully vibrant grandfather. She'd never—*ever*—have imagined liking anyone with that title. But Mortimer Potts still made her smile, just picturing him pouring their tea as they'd sat in his colorful tent, chatting about the weather in Borneo and the dangers of the Asian trade routes.

Max had been there, too. Being friendly…and nothing else, despite her best flirting efforts.

That's how he'd been the entire time. Nothing but helpful and nonaggressive with a woman who had practically thrown herself at him.

"I didn't really *throw* myself at him," she whispered, wishing the bed wasn't as lumpy as a bag of rocks.

Liar. That movie invitation thing had definitely been throwing herself.

But that was the whole point, the reason she was here in the first place. Talk about stepping outside the safety zone—the one she'd erected around herself once it had become clear that *she* had to be the responsible adult who handled Allie's situation. This entire trip was *definitely* not safe.

Sabrina had come to Trouble to entice Max Taylor into proving his wicked reputation. No, she hadn't gotten off to the best start, but she had to hand it to herself, she'd recovered rather quickly from the shock of finding out the nice, boy-next-door mechanic was in fact her targeted sex fiend.

Once he'd confirmed his identity, Sabrina had gone into action. She'd thrown off her surprise, pasted on a sultry look and gone all come-hither.

And he'd nearly come and hithered.

The flash of interest in his sparkling green eyes had been unmistakable when she'd given him the kind of look any man would understand. Though he'd quickly squelched it, she'd seen the answering heat.

"I can get him, I *can* do this," she whispered, telling herself the reason her heart was pounding was that she might actually be able to pull it off. She might prevent him from interfering with Grace's book.

Yes. Just the possibility of success…that was the reason she was feeling so wildly excited. Anticipatory.

And not, she reminded herself, because for a moment the man she'd been having secret, wicked fantasies about for months had looked at her as though he wanted her, too.

CHAPTER FIVE

TROUBLE BOASTED two official restaurants still in operation. That didn't count the sandwiches sold over the counter at the local gas station, or the fast-food joints huddled like predators around the interstate exit a few miles outside town. Two real, sit-down-and-order establishments with chipped plates and bent, tarnished silverware.

Max had dined at both of them over the past two weeks and had decided that the rubbery pancakes at Tootie's Tavern were moderately more appealing than the slimy eggs at the Trouble Some Café. So, on Saturday morning, knowing his grandfather was safely tucked away in his tent smoking a pipe loaded with something Max probably didn't want to know about, he decided to head downtown.

He moved quickly. It was ten minutes before nine and he simply couldn't stand the thought of dining with the cuckoos, all of whom were freshly wound and singing.

One of these days, he was going to get his grandfather to stop winding those clocks. But first, he had to catch him in the act of doing it. Because whenever it came up, the old man vehemently denied any involvement, swearing the ghosts in the house wound the cursed things every night. He even insisted he heard their whispers on occasion, and the creaks of the floorboards as they tiptoed through the halls.

Who knew ghosts had toes?

At least the clocks didn't disturb Max's nights. He'd claimed the highest spot in the house—a turret room on the third floor, which was blessedly devoid of cuckoos. At least it was once Max had taken the single one lurking above the doorway and drop-kicked it under the eaves of the attic.

Apparently he wasn't the only one to have done so, because the skeletal remains of another clock were already back there, nearly hidden in some puffs of insulation. But it couldn't have been kicked—it was too big. It was also decorated with the largest carved cuckoo bird he'd ever seen, a mahogany carved creature with spread wings and a long, wickedly sharp beak. Somebody had obviously gone to town on the clock, breaking the rest of the pieces off and scattering them who knows where.

He'd like to do the same thing with all the others in the house, only take them up in his plane and drop-kick them from ten-thousand feet. See if those birdies could really fly. But his grandfather wouldn't hear of it.

The one drawback to Max's new room was that it was devoid of heat or air-conditioning. But hot nights spent lying naked atop the sheets praying for a bit of breeze to blow in from the open windows were a small price to pay to escape an hourly mechanical serenade, so he didn't complain.

Mortimer's room was on the second level, and his snores were loud enough to block out any sound with fewer decibels than a freight train. Not that even a train could wake him, because he had to be nearly unconscious during the few hours of rest he got. Max didn't know how the old man functioned on the little sleep he could eek out after furtively winding the clocks every night.

He'd actually counted. There were twenty-six, not

counting the two murdered ones in the attic. This Wilhelm Stuttgardt, the former owner of the house—and of the Stuttgardt Cuckoo Clock Company—had really liked his products. Or else he'd had one sick and twisted enjoyment of self-torture.

When Max pulled his rented car into the parking lot behind the tavern and saw the blonde entering the restaurant ahead of him, he decided *he* must like self-torture, too.

If he were wise, he'd back up and drive away. Steering clear of Sabrina was the smart course of action, since the woman made him stupid with want. And since he couldn't be entirely sure of who she was and what she was doing here.

He had to avoid her, not only because of the book, but also because, if she truly was some angel of mercy who might free his family of this town, he needed to make sure he didn't do anything to piss her off.

As much as he liked women, Max did have a tendency to piss them off.

But something wouldn't let him leave. The thought of the clocks, perhaps. The growl in his stomach that would not be quieted by slimy eggs. Or camel tongue.

Or maybe the realization that he hadn't gotten Sabrina's address and phone number—for when all his troubles— and Trouble—were behind him.

Entering the tavern, he responded with a smile and a nod to several greetings from some of the townspeople he'd met. A lot of residents viewed his grandfather as Santa Claus, come to deliver presents. Which, he supposed, made *him* an elf.

"Morning, Mr. Taylor," said a man standing at the counter, waiting to pay his check.

He quickly recognized him as the chief of police, Joe Bennigan, and not just because of the uniform. The chief had been out to check on Mortimer a few times before Max had come to town, as if worrying the older man could hurt himself in that desolate old place all alone.

Max hadn't forgotten, and he'd genuinely appreciated it. "Good morning, Chief."

"How's your grandpa?" He smiled a little. "Hear he decided to do some backyard camping."

Max sighed. "Yeah."

The chief clapped his hand on Max's shoulder. "Hey, don't worry about it, son. He gave a few hours' work to some men who haven't had any in a while."

"That's right," said someone sitting at the counter—a skinny, fortyish guy in a flannel shirt with ripped-off sleeves.

Beside him, another man, lean and younger, but having that same fatalistic, tired demeanor that seemed common in everyone here in Trouble, nodded. "Good morning's pay and your grandfather's a real fine storyteller." He started to laugh, the sound creaky and dry, like he wasn't used to doing it too often these days. "I'd like to visit a country that still has harems."

A waitress behind the counter snorted. "You wouldn't know what to do with one woman, if you ever managed to get one." She smirked as she slammed a plate down on the counter.

"Why don't you let me show you how wrong you are one'a these Friday nights instead sitting in your place watching let's-all-hate-men movies on Lifetime?"

The man was trying to pick the waitress up, and she practically simpered in response. Max's jaw dropped at the realization that actual flirtatious banter was taking place right here at the tavern. Compared to the dark-and-dour groaning he'd heard nonstop when he'd arrived, this was practically like an episode of *Friends*.

Maybe the town really was changing. Perhaps his grandfather's arrival had been a shot of water on a parched flower—well, a parched, scraggly weed.

"Good to see you, Taylor," the chief said as he walked toward the door.

"Tell your grandpa hello and thanks again," added one of the tent workers, the other one nodding his agreement.

Murmuring his goodbyes, Max added three more converts to the Mortimer-is-good side of the equation. But judging by the glares, not everyone was convinced. There were definitely those who weren't happy to have had their town "sold out from under them" to some rich investor.

That included the big, frowning guy sitting at the far end of the counter, who delivered the mail. Dean something or other. The man was constantly scowling and muttering. Probably trying to come up with a way to keep Mortimer Potts's money while getting rid of Mortimer Potts.

"Good morning, Mr. Taylor," a pleasant voice said.

Max immediately recognized Ann Newman, the well-dressed, ash-blond woman who nodded at him from her seat. The newly elected mayor had reportedly been the one who'd come up with the idea of selling Trouble's assets to try to save the town. Max didn't know the whole story, but he'd learned a few tidbits about Trouble's history from his grandfather.

Apparently one of the former mayors had been a real piece of work. A thieving one who'd used the town's bank accounts as his own personal petty cash fund, embezzling money over a period of years, a little at a time, so no one knew what was happening until it was too late.

He'd paid for it, though. The man—Stuttgardt—had been murdered five years ago. Right in his house…the one where Max was currently residing.

"Good morning, Mayor," he said to Mrs. Newman. The woman had been kind to his grandfather, and had been the first to take Max on a tour when he arrived. "Nice to see you."

The other woman seated with her at the table stiffened ever so slightly, ignoring him completely. She, obviously, was from the other camp—the camp still resentful of Mortimer Potts's intrusion into their lives.

From the whispers he'd heard, the town officials had promised a "foreign" investor would bail them out of the mess their town had become following the embezzlement scandal, and not even bother to show up to check on his investment. Free money from an oil-rich sheikh or a land-rich duke.

If only Mortimer had been in his poor, lonesome cowboy mode when the ad had come across his desk.

Max couldn't imagine anyone had fallen for that b.s. in this day and age. But his grandfather had shown him the ad and he'd read the thinly veiled plea for free money himself. It might as well have said, *Calling all princes— since there are so many of you out there—give us your cash, then go away.*

"Hey there, honey pie," he heard. "I was hoping you'd come in today—pancakes are on special. I know how much you like them!"

Looking up, he hid a grimace as the owner of the establishment, Tootie herself, waddled over to greet him.

Tootie was about sixty in years and two-sixty in weight. Given her raw humor and her reputation as a belcher, he honestly didn't want to know where she'd gotten her nickname. He somehow suspected it was not from some old TV show.

"Set your cute ass anyplace you want," she added as she

grabbed Max's arm and tugged it close to her body for a pseudo hug. Since her mammoth breasts occupied a position from just under her second chin to her waistband, he had the feeling he was being molested in some way. But he could merely be paranoid, not yet having gotten over the Mrs. Coltrane incident.

Managing a tight smile, he retrieved his arm and beelined for a booth in the far corner, where he could see the back of a blond head. Max knew exactly where he wanted to set his cute ass, and it was in the seat across from Sabrina Cavanaugh.

"Morning," he said as he slid into the booth, glad he'd remembered to wear jeans this morning, rather than nicer pants. The first time he'd come here, his good trousers had gotten snagged on a ragged tear in the faux leather seat. And since there wasn't a single seat in this place that wasn't ripped and oozing with fluffy, grayish chair guts, he'd decided to never wear good clothes here again.

Sabrina apparently hadn't gotten the memo. Her filmy, flowered sundress—which tied around her neck, revealing soft-looking, slender shoulders and long, slim arms—probably wasn't much protection against the scratches. But the selfish s.o.b. in him couldn't bring himself to care, because she looked so utterly beautiful.

"Mind if I join you?"

Sabrina's eyes widened, as did her mouth, and she slowly shook her head. "No, not at all."

"Coffee," he said to the waitress, who he thought was called Scoot. He figured she was somehow connected to Tootie—daughter, granddaughter, former cellmate. Something.

"Is this your first time here?" he asked when Sabrina didn't make any effort to initiate a conversation.

She shook her head. "I had dinner here Thursday night, when I first arrived."

"Dinner. Impressive. I haven't gone beyond a BLT for lunch."

"Well, my host at the B&B offered me the use of his kitchen, as well as breakfast, so I've been eating in." She shuddered lightly. "But today's Saturday."

He immediately got it. "Thought he only did his nudist act in the backyard."

"I'm not taking any chances."

He didn't blame her. In fact, he thought it was also pretty damn brave of her to stay at an inn run by a guy who liked to get naked and tiptoe through his tulips. And this town thought his *grandfather* was nuts?

"I wish I could offer you another option in terms of housing while you're in town," Max said, leaving an unspoken suggestion hanging in the air between them.

No way was he actually going to *make* that suggestion, and it wasn't merely because he wouldn't inflict the clocks on anyone. He also wouldn't inflict the torture of having this lovely woman sleeping under his roof—knowing he couldn't go near her—on *himself.*

She reached for a glass of orange juice and sipped from it, licking her lips—*oh, the agony*—before setting the drink back down. "I suppose I could go knock on the door of the hotel up on the mountain and ask if they'll reopen for me."

"Don't you even!" This came from Scoot, who lowered Max's cup and saucer to the table so hard that coffee sloshed out. "He has lampshades made from human skin."

Max hadn't heard that one before.

"I was joking," Sabrina said.

"I wasn't." Scoot looked over her shoulders, one way

then the next, then bent closer to avoid being overheard. Fat chance, since the woman could outdo a professional cheerleading squad in sheer volume.

Scoot leaned close enough for Max to see the thin line of elastic skirting the roots of her bright red hair and the few mousy brown strands of real hair beneath it. Catching the combined scents of maple syrup and cigarettes, he figured she'd been sampling today's special, and found himself half wishing he'd gone for the slimy eggs at the café.

But then he wouldn't have bumped into his most charming dining companion. And he wouldn't miss getting to know Sabrina Cavanaugh better for an omelette whipped up by Emeril himself.

"He closed the hotel down as soon as he came back, when his uncle died. Stays up there all alone, prowling along the top of the cliff looking down here, but never comes into town."

"Who?" Sabrina asked, her voice lowered to a loud whisper, just as Scoot's was.

"*Him.* The owner of that place," the woman said. She made a funny little hand gesture, which might have been to ward off evil or could have been to wave off a fly. "He moved here to hide from the police after he killed a bunch of people down in South Carolina."

"Not much of a hiding place if everybody knows he's here," Sabrina pointed out as she lifted her glass again.

"No one'll squeal on him because he'll get his revenge, even if he's in prison. Simon Lebeaux is not one to cross." She instantly bit her lip, as if speaking the name of the devil would make him arise.

Max couldn't take it anymore. He nodded toward the door. "You mean *him?*"

Scoot lurched back, staggering a couple of steps and

bringing a hand to her heart as she stared wild-eyed around the restaurant. "Where?"

"Just kidding."

"You naughty man," the waitress said, shaking her head as she lifted a hand to her brow and wiped away a sheen of sweat that had appeared there. "I nearly soiled my britches I was so scared. Now, ready to order?"

"Well, who wouldn't be, after that lovely comment?" Sabrina muttered under her breath.

He liked her sarcastic wit. "Give me the special, will you?"

The server wagged her pencil at him. "I'll give you anything you like, honey, long's you don't scare me anymore, telling me there's murderers coming up behind me." Then she looked at Sabrina. "You still want just toast and the fruit cup?"

Sabrina nodded, apparently having placed her order before Max came in. After the waitress walked away, she whispered, "Mentally running down your list of serial-killer names right about now?"

He liked how she'd pegged him so easily. Maybe because they thought the same way. "Yeah. I'm glad we had that conversation yesterday. Has them fresh in my memory. If she ever cops a feel I'm going to tell her Hannibal Lecter is ready to order some fava beans."

Reaching for the sugar, he dumped a spoonful into his coffee, stirred it, then lifted the cup to his lips. Tootie might put rubber in her pancakes, but she did know how to serve a damn fine cup of coffee.

"Now, since my grandfather is not here to whisk you away with promises of aphrodisiac tea, how about we continue our conversation from yesterday?"

"Is that what you want to talk about? Because I don't

think we actually ever fully discussed aphrodisiacs." Her gaze was direct, her voice throaty.

Max silently begged for mercy. Shifting in his seat, he mumbled, "Uh, no, not that one."

"The one about horror movies?"

He shook his head. "No. The one about you wanting to invest in this thriving, gold mine of a town. You and Mortimer were so busy socializing yesterday, the topic never really came up, did it?" Crossing his arms on the table, he leaned over them—closer to her—and added, "But having been here for a couple of days now, do you still want it? Are you still in the mood to get in on the action?"

That was just a tiny slip into suggestive repartee. Not nearly as bad as the come-ons that had been bouncing out of his mouth like Ping-Pong balls out of a lottery machine on the day they'd met, so he didn't start any mental self-flagellation over it.

Fortunately, she didn't notice, anyway. She looked around the room, her gaze resting a little long on the weary-looking residents lazily stirring their coffee. Then she focused on the water-stained ceiling and the cracked and dusty linoleum floor, which was the color of dirty mop water—not that it'd seen any in a very long time.

"You seeing the potential?"

"For disaster?"

"Hey, is this the same woman who saw the beauty of that carousel?"

"Touché." She looked out the window. "The small park across the street is pretty."

"Yes, it is. I hear there is still a sliding board under that tangled mound of brush."

"And the old ice cream parlor looks like it was once very quaint."

"Probably still ice cream in the freezer, too. Cuts down on start-up costs. And it even has a working ice maker. You could be the ice cream queen of Pennsylvania."

She rolled her eyes.

"What, ice cream isn't your thing?"

"Not exactly."

"Do you have some other specific ideas? Some particular kind of business you're looking for?" he asked, wondering exactly what her background was. He'd been so interested in her as a person that he hadn't done a whole lot of prying into her life before he'd entered it.

She shook her head. "No, definitely not. My family isn't exactly the business type."

"What type are they?"

"The rigid, judgmental, Bible-thumping type," she admitted with a humorless smile. "My grandfather founded his own church in Ohio and would probably decide that this town had brought its troubles down on itself because of its own wickedness."

Max could have fallen out of his chair at that one, because Sabrina Cavanaugh sure didn't seem like any church mouse he'd ever known. "But you…"

"I left home at eighteen and never looked back." She curled her fingers around her water glass, holding it tightly. "I'm an entirely self-made woman."

Okay. Self-made. He liked that about her. Especially since Max, too, had chosen to follow his own path rather than take the easy route by letting his grandfather give him money to replace the trust fund he'd pissed away. Which was why he was in debt to his ass but still able to say he'd made it on his own, despite how badly he'd stumbled after his divorce.

Max was curious to learn more about her background—

wondering how a woman as warm, sexy and delicious as this one could have come from the kind of family she described—but he sensed she didn't want to talk about that. Still clutching her glass, her fingers looked white. So obviously she hadn't finished saying whatever it was she needed to get off her chest.

"What else?"

Sighing, she peered at him from behind her wispy bangs. "Look, I don't want you to have the wrong idea. I am not in the position to *buy* this *whole* town."

Few people *were* in a position to buy a town, so she wasn't telling him anything he didn't know. "Sabrina, my brothers and I have no illusions that some other fabulously rich, bored person is going to come take this whole thriving metropolis off Grandfather's hands," he said with a dry laugh. Even as he said it, he wondered why he was being entirely honest with her when he should be buttering her up for the sale.

He couldn't help it. Something about her—something about the way they were already reacting to each other, as if they both knew they were headed for something more than a business relationship, even more than friendship—made him want to clear the air. At least, as much of it as he could without throwing caution to the wind and revealing the truth about himself. Including the Grace Wellington crap.

But that would mean trusting her completely, enough to really be himself. And he wasn't quite ready to go there yet, no matter how blue her eyes and how great her smile.

"So you're okay with a smaller investor?"

He nodded, reaching for her hand and tugging her fingers away from the glass. "Yeah. That's why the ad in the *Times* said we were looking for forward-thinking busi-

nesspeople who wanted to rejuvenate Trouble's downtown. We weren't advertising for sheikhs or princes who
want to play king of the castle."

Though, hell, it had worked for the guy who'd reeled
his grandfather in.

She smiled slowly, looking relieved. "Okay. I just didn't
want you thinking…believing…"

Her need to be honest was both refreshing and attractive. "I didn't. There aren't many people in this country
with the bank balance of Mortimer Potts. A modest
investor is absolutely fine, all right?"

"All right."

Their eyes met and they were silent for a moment, each
of them acknowledging that they'd taken another step
forward. They were already knocking down the walls that
typically existed at the start of any relationship.

Personally, Max couldn't wait to blow them straight to
hell. But until he was certain it was safe to get involved
with any woman again, he knew he could not.

"So what exactly do you do?" he asked, realizing he'd
never asked her that. She'd mentioned liking to write, but
had never confirmed that's how she made her living. "I
know you live with your sister and Butch the Dober-
poodle in Philadelphia and that you're self-made…but
how'd you 'make' yourself?"

Her lashes lowered over her eyes, almost fanning her
cheeks as she played with the condensation on her water
glass.

"What, are you a secret agent? A high-priced assassin?"

She chuckled. "No. I'm more…in the arts."

So she *was* a professional writer. Probably a successful one, considering she had enough money to invest in
out-of-town properties, and to support her pregnant little

sister. His curiosity about what she wrote—if he'd read any of her stuff—was killing him. He'd often noticed writers were quick to talk about their books, figuring every person they met was a potential client. He couldn't imagine why this one was so circumspect.

Maybe she wrote romance novels. Hot ones. Sexy, wild ones.

He could hope, anyway. He was about to ask her, but she shifted gears, obviously not wanting him to know.

"So, back to the town."

He nodded, respecting her right to privacy. "How about the movie theater? With a few hundred new seats, a new screen, new carpeting, lighting, walls, floors, ceilings, projection equipment, snack bar, roof and foundation, plus busloads of moviegoers imported from other towns, you might really have a gold mine on your hands."

Grinning, she tucked one long strand of hair behind her ear. "Are you trying to talk me into investing…or out of it?"

"Oh, in. Most definitely. Do you allow yourself to be talked into things easily?"

That was not a sexually loaded question. Absolutely not.

She apparently didn't read that mental denial. Because Sabrina's eyes suddenly narrowed and she leaned across the table, her arms folded on top of it. The loose, filmy dress pulled tighter against her body, the plunging neckline shifting a tiny bit to one side to reveal a thin, pale strip of skin on the curve of her breast. Max's mouth went dry and a dull hum filled his head as everything and everyone else seemed to fade into the background.

"Why do you ask?" she practically purred. "What did you have in mind?"

Oh, what he had in mind. Grabbing her by the hand and striding out into the sunlight. Leading her to his car and driving like a bat out of hell to the regional airport where his personal plane—a smart little single-engine Cessna Skyhawk, the first he'd ever bought—was waiting for him. Taking off into the sky with her and leaving this crazy town and its sour people behind.

His mind filled with possibilities. Pulling her on his lap in the cockpit, settling her filmy dress over their legs. Untying the halter. Kissing the nape of her neck and feeling the soft brush of her hair against his face.

Filling his hand with her breast and sliding into her sweet, tight body. While they flew and flew and flew.

Forget it.

Grabbing his own glass of water, which the waitress had just deposited on the table, he gulped it down. He needed to thrust that idea right out of his head because it was never going to happen. Not now. Not *ever*.

Max was not that kind of pilot. He might be a daredevil and he might enjoy women, but he wasn't a damn fool. He'd never risk anyone's life, least of all his own, by doing something as irresponsible as having sex while at the controls. He didn't even know where the thought had come from.

Max had already come too damn close to losing his right to fly because of women. Bad enough he'd had to drop out of the pilot training program in the Air Force because of an unexpected pregnancy and a quickie marriage. But the threat of having the FAA yank his license because of his wild partying after the divorce had forever cured him of any desire to be reckless in the cockpit.

Yet the thought of flying with Sabrina—even *without* sex—was so incredibly appealing. Watching her beautiful eyes grow large as she leaned forward in her seat to see every sight, hearing her breath catch in her throat as they topped ten-thousand feet. She'd love it. The thrill-seeker in her would absolutely love every dip and roll.

"Too soon," he muttered, unable to believe he was even thinking this way.

Taking a woman into the sky was something he rarely did. In the past, he had only invited the few women he'd gotten serious with.

Hell, he hadn't even kissed this one.

Flying was personal. Not when he was ferrying clients, but when he was alone, in his own plane. He was entirely in the moment, his senses filled with blue sky above and green earth below. Everything else falling away as easily as the clouds did beneath his wings, he genuinely came alive when in flight. Every inch of him in the present, with no masks to hide behind, no defenses.

No bad memories. No fears of the future.

It was…intimate. Taking someone with him was like letting someone into his head. Much more intimate, in Max's opinion, than taking a woman home. Or even, strange as it sounded, into his bed.

So taking this woman to the skies was out of the question. Completely. Totally. No doubt about it.

But somehow his brain disconnected from his vocal cords. Because before he could even think about it, the words were leaving his lips.

"Come fly with me."

THE MOMENT IDA MAE realized her sister Ivy's favorite pink hat with the lavender pearls and long, swooping purple feather that curled around the face was missing from its honored place on the top middle shelf in her closet, she *knew* she'd been had. Hoodwinked. Snookered.

"That lying little bitch."

Ivy was a no-good, cheating, stinking sneak. She hadn't had any appointment to go get a bunion scraped off her heel. She would never—*ever*—wear her favorite hat to go to a doctor's appointment, else she'd be wearing the blasted thing three times a week.

Ida Mae had suspected all along that Ivy was fibbing about this morning's destination. Because Dr. Tarryton, the only G.P. still practicing in Trouble, didn't keep Saturday hours. Her younger sister had claimed she'd used some eyelash-batting to charm him into opening for her.

Ida Mae had always suspected Dr. Tarryton would rather have Jack Fennimore, the taxidermist, bat his eyelashes in his direction, so she should have been much more suspicious of her sister's boasts.

"Not this time, you don't," she snapped as she whirled out of Ivy's closet—where she'd been hunting for Daddy's ashes—and raced toward her own house next door.

She didn't have time to do a proper going-hunting preparation. Thankfully, however, she'd had her bath two days ago and she still smelled a bit like that sweet, rose-scented soap she'd bought for Ivy last Christmas. The soap she'd stolen back out of Ivy's closet a few months ago, when her sister had refused to loan it to her.

Plus she'd set her hair last night before bed, so it was nice and springy. She didn't need some frilly hat to hide any thinning spots like Ivy did, which was only fair. If Ida Mae had gotten the cursed thick calves of the women in her family, it was right and proper that she should also get the thick, lush hair.

Ivy hadn't gotten either one. So, to Ida Mae's disgust, she had nice slender legs. And to Ida Mae's delight, Ivy also had a bald spot that she hid with hats and hairpieces.

Ida quickly grabbed her prettiest summer dress—with the lilacs and the ivory satin trim—and pulled it on over her head, careful not to muss her curls. If her sister thought she was going to snatch up the first attractive, eligible bachelor to move into these parts in the past twenty years without a fight, well, she was most sorely mistaken.

Because Ida Mae would give her a fight all right. One this town would never forget.

So forty minutes later, when she arrived downtown and saw her sister looking up at Mortimer Potts with her false-tooth smile, and simpering with that same giggle she'd used on Buddy Hoolihan sixty-some years ago, Ida Mae charged right into battle.

CHAPTER SIX

FLY WITH HIM.

Sabrina sat completely still in the booth in Tootie's Tavern, staring into Max Taylor's handsome face, feeling as though the hook-nosed child catcher from *Chitty Chitty Bang Bang* was offering her a huge lollipop. A juicy one. A sour apple one—her favorite.

Oh, was she tempted. And, oh, she did want to accept the offer. *Because of the book*, a mental voice insisted.

Yeah. Right. Him trying to get her alone was probably his first step in seduction; he probably always got in a woman's pants by showing her his...cockpit.

She should go for it, strictly for the sake of her career. That was the only reason she would even consider it, she was quite sure.

Maybe if she kept telling herself that the good fairy would make it be true, too. Because it was complete bull. Wanting to lock herself in an enclosed space with Max Taylor and spend a morning soaring to the highest heights with him, plane or no plane, had absolutely nothing to do with any book. It was entirely to do with the man.

But right now, at this particular moment, she wasn't sure *which* man intrigued her more. The wicked playboy pilot she'd been secretly fantasizing about for months? Or the friendly, funny mechanic with his big, strong hands, that great laugh and those glittering green eyes?

"You want to take me flying on your private plane?" she asked, her voice trembling as she gave the idea serious consideration.

He tilted his head to one side, appearing curious. "Did I tell you I had my own plane?"

Whoops. He hadn't. To her knowledge, he hadn't even admitted yesterday that he was, in actuality, a pilot. So she should have acted surprised by his invitation.

Stupid, you're going to blow this.

Striving to keep her tone even, she replied, "Your grandfather must have mentioned it."

"Oh, right," he said with an unconcerned shrug. "Well, it's true, I do have a little beauty at the dinky airstrip in Weldon, which is about twenty miles from here."

The very idea, while exciting, also sent a shiver through her. Sabrina had never even seen the inside of a private aircraft, much less been invited to fly in one. "I've never been in a plane smaller than a 737."

"Can't compare. Commercial jumbos are so impersonal. You haven't really flown until you're soaring ten thousand feet above the ground, only a thin tube of metal separating you from all that open air."

She felt queasy. And it wasn't from the lousy food in this place, since hers hadn't arrived yet. "Maybe not."

"You aren't afraid, are you?" He leaned closer as if to reassure her. "Because you shouldn't be. Many more people die in car accidents every year than in plane crashes."

"But at least after many car accidents there are survivors. They can even walk away a lot of the time," she pointed out, her tone skeptical. "I somehow don't think somebody can brush off the dust and flirt with the cops to avoid a ticket after falling several thousand feet out of the sky and landing in a fiery heap of metal."

A puzzled frown creased his brow and he stared at her as if she'd grown two heads. "You're serious? You're *genuinely* afraid of crashing?"

"It's possible."

"I'm an outstanding pilot."

"So was Amelia Earhart."

"Do you honestly think I'd let you be hurt?"

He sounded…wounded, somehow. As if she'd truly offended him. Which gave her a glimpse into exactly how confident a man he was. Not cocky. He hadn't shown any signs of that. Just completely sure of his abilities.

"I don't know that I've ever met anyone so self-assured," she murmured, knowing it was true. And wondering how it must feel to be so good at something you never *ever* second-guessed yourself about it.

"Is that so strange? Aren't you confident of a few things you do really well?"

"Uh, not exactly."

Sabrina knew she was a good editor, and she had some talent with writing, too—a secret wish she'd never seriously pursued but sometimes dabbled with. But second-guessing yourself was a way of life when you grew up in a small town in a modest house full of modest people. Especially when you heard daily fire-and-brimstone speeches from a grandfather who didn't seem to like *anyone,* and more moderate ones from a mother who—while loving—had to walk a fine line between her longing-to-live children and her longing-to-suppress father.

Sabrina had grown up being told that congratulations and praise were a prelude to vanity, so she'd seldom heard them. It had been all Sabrina could do to hide her pride at landing a four-year scholarship to Penn State after high school, but she'd done it, knowing her grandfather had already been preaching against her going.

Her mother had, for the first time in as long as Sabrina could remember, stood up to him. Right when she'd begun to wonder if the woman who used to swing her in big circles by her feet in Central Park had ceased to exist, she'd found her mother again, and the discovery had given Sabrina all the encouragement she needed to fight for what she wanted.

Mom's support had helped, but Sabrina knew, deep inside, that she would have gone without it. She wouldn't have let him—*anyone*—stop her. At age eighteen, she'd had too many years of suppressing her need to be free and be herself, to live life to its fullest, to allow a thing like family disapproval stop her from getting the hell out of Bridgerton, Ohio.

What a fine example she'd set for her feisty, funny little sister to emulate.

God, Allie. I'm so sorry.

"I still can't believe you think I'd let us crash," he said, shaking his head in bemusement.

Before she could reply, the waitress returned with their food. Max's breakfast looked every bit as unappealing as she'd thought it would, but there wasn't much that could go wrong with toast and fresh fruit. Nibbling on a corner of her stale, crumbly bread made only slightly moist by a thin spread of lumpy margarine, she watched as Max smothered his plate with most of a bottle of maple syrup. He took a bite, grimaced, then gamely continued eating.

"I don't think you'd *let* us crash. I'm sure you're very skilled," she finally said, having thought about his words. "But things do happen that are out of anyone's control. That's why they call them accidents."

He still looked offended, and now surprised. "You mean you'd let the fear that something bad *might* happen keep you from doing something you really want to do?"

"Who said I really want to go flying with you?"

He smiled slowly, staring her in the eyes and silently daring her to deny that a big part of her did want to take him up on his invitation. She didn't even try.

"Aren't you afraid of *anything?*" she said, wanting him to understand, and wanting to understand *him*.

"Sure. The IRS."

"Who's not?"

"Scary movies."

What a liar. "You phony, you love them."

"Sure I do, *because* they scare me. Isn't that why you love them?" he asked.

"I don't think so," she admitted, never having thought about it. She'd always just sort of figured she had a morbid streak. Kind of an inherent need to have the bejesus scared out of her once in a while, since her home life had always been so…pure. Wholesome. Nondescript.

Like her?

"The reason those movies work is that they scare you to pieces but you still walk out of the theater feeling powerful and confident, knowing everything's okay in the real world," he explained. "You tell yourself it was just a movie, laugh it off and get on with your life."

True.

"Except," he continued, lowering his voice to a heavy whisper, his eyes twinkling, "that you jump when you see the huge shadow around the corner as you exit the building. And you're a little nervous about the guy wearing the hockey mask standing by your car with a butcher knife in his hand."

Oh, the man could make her laugh. Because he'd gotten that part right, too. "Okay, so, yes, on occasion I do like the thrill of being scared. And the moment of uncertainty that comes even after I think everything's okay."

"Flying can be like that." Then he added, "But not with me, because you'd have absolutely nothing to be afraid of."

Ha. She had a lot to be afraid of with him. Falling out of the sky in a tiny airplane was only the beginning. "There's that confidence again," she murmured. "Be serious. Isn't there anything that really, *truly* frightens you?"

He met her stare, his gaze steady. The smile slowly fading from his face, he thought about it. Finally, after a long pause, he admitted—perhaps only to himself—"I'm afraid of losing someone *else* I care about."

A universal fear. But his emphasis told her he'd already experienced such loss. Too much of it, given the dark expression that flashed across his face and was just as quickly gone.

Something else they had in common, then. *How can this man be so right, and yet so wrong?*

"I'm afraid of cancer."

She heard the unspoken admission in his voice. Whoever it was he'd lost, this was how the person had died. Given what she'd read about Max and his brothers being raised by their grandfather, she had to assume it was a parent.

She didn't ask for details. If he wanted her to know, he'd continue. Sabrina certainly didn't go around volunteering information about *her* father's death.

"Sometimes, I'm even afraid of myself."

Sabrina raised a brow. "Why?"

"Because I've had a few close calls in my life when I've nearly ruined it. Everything I had." Max pushed his plate away and continued, almost matter-of-factly. "I won't let myself get that close to the edge again, and I walk a careful line to make sure it doesn't happen."

"Make sure what doesn't happen?" she asked, wondering if he knew how much he was revealing about himself. And wondering if her desire to hear more was about the book she was supposed to be saving, or about how much she already liked Max Taylor.

She didn't have to wonder for long. Right now, Sabrina couldn't even remember the title of Grace What's-her-name's book.

He shrugged. "I won't ever let myself become so vulnerable to my emotions that I sabotage myself and nearly destroy everything I've worked for out of hurt or anger."

He spoke from experience—he'd felt heartbreak. The stab of jealousy that realization caused deep inside her surprised Sabrina. She hadn't felt this kind of resentment when thinking about Max's supposed womanizing. But Max actually in love with someone? Why, she wondered, did that thought hurt so much?

He met her stare evenly, as if watching for her reaction, and said, "One of my greatest fears is that I'll be fooled into letting down my guard with someone I should never have trusted. Someone who never really cared for the real me at all."

Oh, God, as she was trying to fool him now? Was she even fooling him at all? More importantly, did she really *want* to anymore?

She bit into her toast, hoping it would calm her suddenly upset stomach.

"Or that I'll be so disappointed when things don't go the way I want them to that I'll do something idiotic." Lifting his coffee cup, Max shook his head and sighed. "And blow it again."

All these hints at things that were important to him—things that had happened in his past—intrigued her. How had this man nearly 'blown it?' He seemed to have everything—wealth, power, a fabulous, successful business. Good looks, charm and intelligence. But he'd been hurt, he'd been reckless.

She wanted more than anything to know why, sensing Max was finally revealing the true man. Not the flyboy. Not the mechanic. But the real person existing inside that gorgeous exterior.

To her disappointment, he shifted gears on her, shutting himself back down as physically as if someone had turned a key and cut his engine. "Not quite serial-killer material, is it?"

He glanced out the window, obviously not wanting the conversation to continue, then closed his eyes, rubbed at the corners of them with two fingers, and opened them again. Shaking his head, he sighed. "Of course, there *is* one more thing I'm afraid of."

"What?" she asked.

"I'm afraid someday that's going to be me."

Pointing out the window, he directed her gaze toward the sidewalk running along the front of the restaurant. And Sabrina instantly understood what he meant.

"I live in abject terror that one day I will be the one with a bewildered expression on my face while two old ladies have a bitch-slapping fight over me on a public street."

TOM KING HAD LIVED in Trouble his whole life—all sixty-one years of it. And in all those years, he'd never imagined that someday his hometown would be sold out from under him.

The day that foolish old millionaire bought this place

had been one of the worst days of Tom's life. Mainly because it had come within just a few weeks of what he'd thought had been one of the *best* days of his life.

They said the Lord giveth and the Lord taketh away. Tom King, however, had been on the taketh-away side of the equation for far too long. It was time for something good to come in his direction. Time for *him* to take, to reclaim that which had been stolen and try to salvage what was left of his life.

He could have done it. He *would* have done it.

Imagine. After five years, he'd finally figured out the riddle—finally had something to go on. Five long years of waiting, wondering, worrying, muddling. Not to mention searching.

Then he'd been given the key. And to think those wicked old women had been the ones who handed it to him.

It was a good thing for him that neither of them had dropped dead—as he had often wished they would over the years, while in the grip of their delicate, oh-so-lady-like blackmail scheme. Because if they had, he'd never have come up with a new theory about what Wilhelm Stuttgardt's cryptic last words had meant.

What he *hoped* they'd meant. After so many false leads, it was getting harder to remain positive.

The old witches had put him on the right track, though, he felt sure of it. And wouldn't they hate it if they knew. The Feeney sisters were never happy unless everyone else was miserable. So he'd never let on that they'd given him a clue to getting at old Stuttgardt's money.

Everything would have been fine—he could have searched the old house to his heart's content—if that rich old fool hadn't come to Trouble. And now this, a grandson.

One who, perhaps, wasn't as whimsical and easily fooled as his grandfather. One who mightn't sleep as soundly during Tom's nightly visits.

It was unfair. From the ruin Wilhelm Stuttgardt had brought down on them all to this latest invasion by Mortimer Potts.

Life wasn't supposed to have turned out like this. All those years working in a dingy factory office surrounded by those stupid clocks were supposed to have been for *something*. He should have had some kind of support to look forward to in his last years. But now, look at him. In his sixties and he had nothing but an old house in a town that was breathing its last. No job, no future. Certainly no pension, since the fat old German bastard had stolen it from him, as he had from so many others.

I could find it. Fix it. Set things right for everyone. Maybe even be able to forgive himself for his part in it.

He was close, he felt it. "But the obstacles," he whispered. Obstacles like Mortimer Potts seemed insurmountable.

Driving his old car—which bounced hard enough to snap his neck because he couldn't afford to replace the shocks—toward Given's Grocery Saturday morning, he nearly ran off the road when he saw the object of his disdain standing outside Tootie's Tavern. The man had ventured from home, which hadn't happened often, to Tom's frustration. He was so excited he hardly noticed the ruckus going on at Mortimer Potts's feet.

Grabbing his cell phone, he ignored the changing of the stoplight from red to green and dialed a familiar number.

"Yes?"

"Potts is here, downtown, right now."

A pause. Before the response came the muffled sound of chattering voices. "The grandson is in Tootie's."

King nodded. Fortune, it appeared, was smiling on him this morning. This seemed too good an opportunity to miss.

His friend obviously agreed. "I'll keep watch and will call to warn you when they leave to go home."

"I'm on my way."

Yes, on his way to take advantage of whatever time he had. Because time was growing short. If he didn't find what he was looking for soon, this Mortimer Potts idiot might just stick around for good. Throwing his money around. Making changes. Bringing his big-world evil into Tom's hometown.

And that, Tom King wouldn't allow. After what Stuttgardt had done, *nobody* was ever again going to corrupt this quaint little place where everything was peaceful, perfect and kind.

HALF THE TOWN came outside to watch the old ladies brawl.

From what Sabrina could gather from the shouts and not-terribly-discreet wagering going on in the crowd, the women rolling around on the grass between the sidewalk and the street were regulars when it came to fighting. The expressions on the onlookers' faces ranged from amusement to excitement to bored disapproval. But not surprise.

Sabrina, Max and his grandfather appeared to be the only ones at all shocked by the sight of two gray-haired women rolling on the ground, slapping, scratching and punching one another.

Too bad Don King wasn't here. He could come up with a whole new class for professional boxing. Granny Weight.

"The Feeney sisters are always good for a few rounds," someone said.

Another voice piped in. "Miss Ida's going for the hair. Miss Ivy'll get her for that."

Beside her, more cash changed hands. So this was how a dead town got its kicks.

Miss Ivy, Sabrina assumed, was the one with her head twisted behind her like a giraffe doing the limbo, tugged into that position by the hand wound in her silvery curls. Sabrina wasn't certain how she was going to get her opponent to let go—until she saw the hatpin appear in her fingers. When it disappeared into the fleshy arm holding her down, the other woman shrieked and rolled off the one called Miss Ivy.

"Is anyone going to put a stop to this?" she asked, shaking her head but unable to look away. It was like watching an episode of *Fear Factor*—a little embarrassing, at times disgusting, but fascinating nonetheless.

Feeling a hand on her arm, she glanced over and saw a resigned-looking young woman whose empty eyes matched those of so many other people's here in Trouble.

"Honestly, it's best to let them get it out of their systems here and now, where there are people around to take care of them if they get hurt."

Sabrina couldn't believe it. Nobody was going to dive in to tear the two women apart before they murdered each other. Or broke a few hips.

"Grandfather, what did you do?" Max asked, his voice low. The two of them were close enough for Sabrina to overhear, and she immediately focused her attention on Mortimer Potts.

A suspicious smile lurked on his lips. He didn't appear at all displeased to have two women fighting over him. She somehow suspected his playboy grandson would have had the same reaction.

But would the mechanic? The man who had just admitted one of his deepest fears was this very scenario?

She honestly didn't know.

Potts was wearing normal street clothes today. A bit overdressed in his old-fashioned seersucker suit, but not as remarkable as he'd been in his sheikh mode. "I didn't do anything, my boy, not a thing. I am completely at a loss here. An innocent bystander, I assure you."

"Yeah, right," Max snapped. "Let's get out of here before they come after *you*."

Mortimer didn't budge. "I'm quite sincere. I was merely taking a stroll with Miss Ivy, and invited her to come to tea. When her sister arrived, I asked her to join us, and suddenly they were, well, engaged in fisticuffs."

The elderly gentleman looked at the two women, whose legs were entangled as they moved from slapping to wrestling. Both of them wore dresses, now stained and filthy with dirt and grass. Their new strategy of trying to pin one another had caused those dresses to ride up to the waist, revealing the seams of two matching pairs of support hose.

Sabrina had to admit, the skinnier one had nice legs.

Mortimer obviously noticed, too, because an unmistakable spark of interest appeared in his eyes.

The dog. Must run in the family.

"That is *enough!*" someone shouted.

The crowd seemed to melt back as a beefy, round man in a too-tight postal uniform pushed his way toward the center of the ring. "Miss Ivy, Miss Ida, you two should be ashamed of yourselves. You promised after the incident at the church carnival that this would never happen again."

The women stopped rolling, though the smaller one did get in one more sharp-knuckled punch to the other's hip.

"And you, you're a lunatic and a disgrace," the newcomer said, swinging around to face Mortimer, his tone dripping with malevolence. "Haven't you done enough damage here without inciting riots? Why don't you just go away and leave us in peace before you ruin *everything?*"

For the first time since she'd met him, Sabrina saw Mortimer Potts caught off guard. His mouth dropped open, but he said nothing. She'd swear that was hurt in his eyes, genuine dismay that someone so obviously disliked him.

A wave of anger rolled through her body until her temples pounded, and Sabrina suddenly understood the appeal of a little bitch-slapping. Though she had no idea where the protective instincts came from since she'd known Mr. Potts for only a short time, she wanted to reach out and smack this hateful-sounding stranger right across his jowly face. She settled for smacking him with some righteous indignation. "Why don't *you*," she said, pointing her index finger at his pendulous belly, "stick to getting these two back in their cages and leave this gentleman alone?"

Beside her, she heard Max make a sound that was half laugh, half cough. "It's all right, I'll handle this," he whispered, flashing her an amused but grateful smile.

Feeling a hand slip into hers, she glanced down. Mortimer's fingers were wrapped around her own, and he squeezed them lightly, expressing his silent thanks. And also, she suspected, telling her to let Max deal with it.

It wasn't easy to do, but she knew, deep down, that Max wouldn't allow anyone to get away with hurting Mortimer, so she forced herself to relax. But she still stayed close to the old man.

Strange. She'd only known these two a few days, yet right now, she felt they were a threesome facing down an enemy army. Or a crowd of superstitious, torch-bearing villagers ready to burn out the strangers.

Max stepped closer to the obnoxious man, who was about his height but probably outweighed him by forty pounds due to his chunkiness. Not that it seemed to matter. The man shuffled back a couple of inches and his belligerent expression faded a bit.

Though Max's face appeared calm and relaxed, as usual, there was a spark of energy that practically made his words snap and sizzle. "Say one more vicious word to my grandfather and I'll break you in half. Got it?"

A few people nearby must have overheard. A flurry of whispers—and a few laughs—told Sabrina a great deal about how this mean-spirited bully was thought of in the town of Trouble. Gave her a little hope for the humanity of the rest of them.

One fiftyish woman, an ash-blonde who'd been eating in the tavern when Sabrina arrived, put her hand on the man's arm and pulled him back, obviously a lot stronger than her slim appearance would indicate. She was also tough, glaring the postman into silence. "Don't you have mail to deliver, Dean Wilson?" Turning to Max's grandfather, she murmured, "I'm so very sorry, Mr. Potts. You mustn't think we all share those sentiments."

Mortimer waved a hand unconcernedly. "That's quite all right, Madame Mayor." He smiled pleasantly, though a hint of mischief made his blue eyes gleam. "Madness comes in many forms, not the least of which is pure mean-spiritedness."

Ooh. Score one for the old man.

"Cages?" one of the women on the ground suddenly asked, her voice shrill. "Did she say *cages?*"

The exclamation diffused the situation going on above the lady's head. The chunky-legged one—who'd apparently just figured out Sabrina's implication from a few moments before—looked up at her with an expression of offended surprise. It really didn't go well with the rest of the woman's appearance, since she was sitting in the dirt with one sleeve ripped off her dress to reveal a two-inch-wide bra strap, her granny panties peeking out from the waistband of her support hose, grass in her hair, a scratch on her arm and a big smudge of dirt on her cheek.

Disreputable, to say the least.

"Did you imply my sister is an *animal?*" the other Feeney sister asked, sounding every bit as affronted. Ladylike—as if she'd found an ant in her soup.

Sabrina couldn't believe it. The two women looked like they were about to turn on *her* now.

"Ladies," Max said as he pushed past the obnoxious postal worker, who was probably grateful for the interruption, since it allowed him to back down yet save face. "Please let me help you up. And do forgive my friend, she is as protective of my grandfather as I am. I'm sure you understand."

He leaned over and offered each of the women a hand, carefully pulling them to their feet then stepping between them. "I don't know what caused this misunderstanding, but it appears to be all over now." Glancing at the crowd, he waved them off. "Nothing more to see, everyone can just move on."

The two old ladies shifted, straightened, smoothed and sighed. But they didn't touch each other. And the crowd, for some unfathomable reason, obeyed. Max never even looked away from the old sisters, obviously fully expecting everyone to do as he had asked, not for a moment doubting they would.

Sabrina could only watch, more interested in the man than she'd ever been before. Because in the span of a half hour, he'd revealed so much about himself. Including depths and quirks of his personality that Sabrina would never have expected.

His uncertainties. His fierce protectiveness. His charm. His skill as a mediator.

Which left her wondering one thing—where, exactly, did the womanizing playboy fit into the mix?

CHAPTER SEVEN

A SHORT TIME LATER, Max stood with Sabrina in the parking lot of the tavern, watching as his grandfather left to escort the Feeney sisters home. If not for the crushed hat with the broken feather on one sister's head, the broken heel on the shoe of the other and the torn, stained dresses, one might never have known the two old ladies had been trying to rip each other's throats out ten minutes ago.

As they strolled off, the three of them smiled and chatted lightly, commenting on the mildness of the day and the pleasant chirp of the summer birds nesting in the tops of the dogwood trees lining the street.

These days, Max equated the chirping of birds with the swish of a falling guillotine, but who was he to argue. "This place is certifiable," he muttered under his breath.

Sabrina simply nodded in silent agreement. Which was when he cursed himself for opening his big mouth. Talk about scaring off any potential buyers—this morning's activities must surely have done it. First his big lapse in discussing ancient memories that had no business being thought of, much less talked about. Then a fight that nearly rivaled Foreman versus Ali.

"Your grandfather seems to have a way with the ladies. He's a real bad boy at heart." She didn't look at him as she added, "Does that run in the family?"

Oh, if she only knew.

"Can't really say. My brothers are both single but they're also workaholics."

"And you?"

"I'm a choirboy," he said, not even hesitating. It was scary how easily that lie came to his lips. Her light peal of laughter told him just how much she believed it, too.

And here he thought he'd done such a good job of being the guy any woman would be proud to bring home to the folks. Well, except for that sexual rambling he'd been unable to control when they'd met by the carousel. Since then, however, he'd been on his best behavior.

Pretty much.

But the more he got to know Sabrina Cavanaugh, the more he wondered if the effort was worth it. It almost seemed pointless to continue to pretend to be something he wasn't. Because if this woman with the big blue eyes and bright blond hair was a reporter for the *Globe* or the *Enquirer,* he'd surrender his entire *Playboy* magazine collection.

Hell, he'd been himself *most* of the time he'd been with her, anyway. Which was, in itself, strange. He usually didn't open up to people he'd just met—especially not about things like his own fears and regrets.

She had an unusual effect on him. And for some reason, he found himself wanting to explore it more. Not as much as he wanted to explore the body under that soft-looking dress, of course, but close.

Okay, then, let it go. He could be himself, take the risk. No matter what Grace Wellington's book might say, he wasn't *that* different from any other guy—at least not anymore. Maybe a little more experienced. A little more successful with women. But not heartless, not even during his darkest days when he'd done some pretty stupid shit to try to wash away the humiliation of his divorce.

So why not take her up on the silent invitation she'd made with her eyes yesterday at his grandfather's house, and see what happened?

Could be risky. Because even if Sabrina wasn't a reporter, that didn't mean she hadn't been sent here as some kind of decoy. Or that someone hired by the publishing company wasn't lurking around the corner, trying to get some womanizer dirt on him. Trouble could be a hotbed of dishonest, incognito activity. The very idea was so incongruous, he had to chuckle.

"Funny, I can't picture you as a saintly kid. I somehow see you as the cautionary cartoon bad boy in the young man's puberty handbook. The one with the cigarette in his hand."

"Don't smoke."

"The beer can, then."

"Don't drink, either."

Her eyes widened. "You really have no vices?"

He smiled. Slowly. Deliberately. "I didn't say *that*."

Oh, would he like to show her what a sinner he could be. Starting by pushing her up against the wall of the restaurant and kissing the taste out of her mouth.

She caught his expression, parted her lips and waved a hand in front of her face, as if fanning herself to cool off.

It wasn't that hot.

Hell. He'd done it now. The awareness—the heat—was back, drifting between them as if it had physical form. A living entity of awareness and desire that they'd both been dancing around—or hiding from—since the moment they met.

"I happen to have one serious addiction," he said, keeping

his voice low, intimate. Then he stepped closer, until the tips of his shoes nearly touched her pretty pink toenails and he could feel the wispy softness of her dress against his forearm.

"What's that?" Her words weren't spoken. They were breathed.

He leaned closer, close enough that he could inhale and almost taste the sweet scent of her perfume and feel the brush of her blond hair against his cheek. Finally, his lips close to her temple, he asked, "You really want to know what turns me on more than anything?"

A choking little whimper came from her throat. Her eyes drifted closed and she nodded. "I do."

He could tell her the truth. Tell her *she* turned him on, that he'd wanted her since the first second he set eyes on her. Then invite her to his car and drive the twenty miles to the next town, which had a decent hotel. Take her to bed and not let her up until…

Only one thing stopped him. Thoughts of the merger—and the book.

Though it almost killed him, he bit back his initial response and answered her question with a half truth. "Flying. Flying turns me on."

Her eyes flared wide, in almost visible disappointment. As if she'd been prepared for another answer, and had been considering how to respond to it.

He might have told himself he couldn't seduce her, but damned if he could refrain any longer from touching her. Because she was so close, because it was such a sultry day, because her skin smelled like strawberries and her lips were so lush, because he *wanted* to and could no longer fight the urge—he lowered his mouth to hers and stole a kiss.

He took nothing more than she offered, keeping the kiss

sweet, soft. A gentle introduction to pleasure. A how-do-you-do and a how-well-we-would-do rolled into one.

She tasted good. He'd known she would. Like spicy, delicious woman. Warm and welcoming.

Sabrina was the one who took things further, tilting her head and parting her lips on his. Her hands crept up his chest until she looped her arms around his neck, pressing her slender, soft body tightly against him.

Max wasn't about to deny himself the chance to taste her and he offered no resistance when she licked into his mouth. The slide of her tongue against his made the sidewalk roll again. And started that crazy, dizzy sensation in his head.

Each thrust was lazy, seductive. Her body began to sway slightly, brushing against his in an instinctive female dance that had every Y chromosome in his body standing up and begging.

He slid one hand into her hair to cup her head, letting the silkiness trap his fingers. Dropping his other hand to her hip, he caressed her, soaking in the warmth of her body. The halter dress was delightfully accessible and he took full advantage. Exploring her bare back, he trailed his fingers across her waist, savoring the silky skin, delicately brushing his thumb against the tiny protrusions of her spine.

"Max," she moaned into his mouth.

He honestly didn't know if she was about to say they should stop or beg him not to. Choosing option two, he tugged her closer, splaying his hand across her lower back until his fingertips brushed the curve of her ass.

She whimpered, writhed a little, rocking back against his hand as if wanting more, then pressing forward until her soft thighs outlined his rock-hard sex. Even through her filmy dress and his own pants he could feel the heat of her and knew she was wet, ready and hungry. Tight. Sweet—so sweet. The image of plunging into all that liquid warmth with his cock, his fingers, or his tongue sent every other thought out of his head. There was only want.

Cupping her backside, he tugged her up onto her tiptoes, pulling her closer until she was almost riding him. Her soft breasts were crushed against his chest and her fragrant curls brushed his face. "Fly with me," he muttered, before capturing her mouth again, sliding his tongue deep the way he wanted to slide into her body. Slowly. Deliberately. Savoring every intimate stroke.

Whimpering, she twined her fingers tightly in his hair and kissed him back. She ground against him, her sighs telling him exactly where his rigid erection was pleasuring her, tormenting them both with the knowledge of how good—how very good—it could be if not for their clothes.

Pulling away to draw in a ragged breath, she whispered, "We shouldn't…"

"To hell with shouldn'ts."

Sabrina groaned in surrender and he ate the groan up, not about to let her go, not without another deep thrust of his tongue and hungry exploration of her mouth.

He wanted to continue tasting and exploring her all afternoon, but the loud beeping of a horn reminded him he could not. Remembering they were standing on a public street, Max regretfully ended the encounter, removed his hand from her delightfully curvy butt and stepped back.

Watching her staring at him with a ravenous look in those baby blues, he forced himself to back up even more. He had to, if only to avoid giving in to the temptation to kiss her all over again. Or to push her against the nearest building, yank that dress up and sink his fingers into her hot, creamy crevice to see if she really was as ready as he thought she was. Figuring the customers watching them through the front window of the small grocery store had had enough titillation for the day, he resisted the urge.

Sabrina lifted her hand to her throat as she drew in a few slow, deep breaths. Her chest rose and fell with her inhalations and her silky, flimsy dress highlighted the tight nipples topping those delicate breasts beneath the fabric. Max closed his eyes briefly, willing away the tingle in his hands—which would fit so nicely around those soft mounds—and the sudden desperate hunger he felt to taste them.

"Flying, huh?" she finally asked, still sounding breathless. "Flying is what turns you on?"

Max nodded, feeling his heart finally slow down and return to a regular rhythm. "Yeah, Sabrina. Flying. It totally turns me on."

Sabrina stared at him, then shook her head once—twice—visibly trying to clear it. The warm, lazy lust in her eyes faded away, replaced by a confused uncertainty, then a small frown of regret.

Damn. He didn't like that confusion and he sure as hell didn't like the regret.

Finally, her shoulders squaring, she cleared her throat and tipped her chin up. "I have to tell you something. If just a kiss makes me ready to rip my own clothes off on a public street and completely lose control of myself, then there's one thing I know for sure."

Clothes ripping off…losing her mind—those were good things. But he could tell by her tone that he wasn't going to like whatever it was she knew *for sure*. "What's that?"

"I'm *never* going up in a tiny little airplane with you, Max Taylor."

And without another word, she turned and walked back to the entrance of the tavern.

Max watched her go, not trying to stop her. Noting a slight wobble in her step, he couldn't prevent a smile. He apparently wasn't the only one who'd been left weak-kneed by the unexpected heat of their encounter. Judging by her confusion, he wasn't the only one who'd been left a little stunned by it, either.

"You're wrong about one thing, angel," he whispered as he saw her reach for the door handle of the restaurant. She peeked over her shoulder, saw him watching, but ignored him and marched inside.

Laughing softly, Max said, "You *are* going to fly with me sooner or later."

THE BUS DIDN'T go all the way to the town of Trouble. Allie hadn't worried too much about that when she'd boarded it shortly after dawn on Sunday morning in Philadelphia, figuring she'd work it out when she got to the end of the line, twenty miles or so from her destination. She'd grab a taxi or find a local commuter bus or something.

But there didn't seem to be any taxis or commuter buses in the town of Weldon, Pennsylvania. At least, none she could see as she stood on the curb outside the bus terminal, her small suitcase in one hand, and a dog leash in the other.

Speaking of which… "Butch, no, wait until we get to some grass," she hissed when she realized the dog was doing his business right on the sidewalk.

Of course, he had been holding it for several hours, so she couldn't entirely blame him. But she had the feeling he was doing it to mark the area as his own, since a Labrador was loping up the street toward them with a friendly doggy grin.

Butch bared his teeth and growled, bouncing on all fours like a cartoon pup, as if daring the bigger dog to approach his newly claimed territory. The lab gave the poodle a condescending sneer as he and his owner ambled by.

"You're a big brave boy," she said, not wanting Butch to feel hurt at having his fierceness so casually dismissed.

"He sure doesn't act like a specially trained rescue dog," someone said from behind her.

Allie glanced over her shoulder and saw an elderly woman with short, curly grey hair, who'd been on the bus with her. The woman—dressed in the brightest, loudest purple blouse Allie had ever seen—had been kind, sharing her sweet, juicy grapes during the four-hour trip. Her eyes twinkled with amusement. As if she knew Allie had been lying about Butch's abilities as a seizure-sensing companion.

"He's very smart," Allie insisted, tilting her head up. "Poodles are, you know."

He probably was smart enough to *really* be trained to react to medical emergencies. Besides, he looked so adorable in his tiny vest, which identified him as a special assistance dog. Good thing she'd thought to quickly make it last night, once, knowing where Sabrina *really* was, she had made the decision to come after her.

No way could she leave Butch behind—not only because she had no one to care for him, but also because she was right in the middle of training him as an attack dog. Ever since running into Peter the other night, she'd been working with Sabrina's pet on one trick: how to bite Peter Prescott right where it counted if he ever showed up again.

Butch was a good little leaper. And he'd gotten really skilled at snatching the two kiwi fruit off the string she'd dangled down the front of a life-size, cardboard stand-up poster of a man. Sometimes he even managed to get them without bringing down the banana, as well.

Not that Allie really cared if Peter's banana got nipped, too, but she was trying to teach the dog precision in his attack.

"You're a good boy, Butch, and I'll get you to some grass, I promise," she whispered. She was desperate to find some facilities for herself again soon, too, courtesy of the bladder-bashing creature living inside her uterus.

"For a minute, I thought the driver wasn't going to let him on," the older woman said, still staring curiously—though not unkindly—at Allie, and the dog.

"You and me both."

As she'd expected, the bus driver had given her trouble about bringing Giorgio—*Butch*—along this morning. But with a pair of moist eyes, a shaky hand lifted to her forehead while another went to her belly and a tiny bit of a wobble in her step, Allie had convinced him not to argue with her.

The threat to call the ACLU if he didn't let her travel with her special assistance animal had helped. So had her asking the man if he really wanted to be driving down the highway with a seven-months' pregnant woman having a grand mal episode.

Allie was a big fan of *Grey's Anatomy* and *E.R.*

Goodness, how her family would frown if they could see the dark, deceitful path the middle Cavanaugh daughter was traveling these days. Lying, scheming, blackmailing. They probably wouldn't recognize her.

A tiny bit of her—the old Alicia who'd been a small-town girl fresh to the big city less than a year ago—was bothered about that. The new Allie, who was about to be a mother and had been completely cut off by nearly everyone she'd ever cared about, didn't give a damn.

"We made it this far," she whispered. All three of them. Allie, baby and poodle.

Now they just had to make it the rest of the way to the town of Trouble—where her sister had a lot of explaining to do. A whole lot. Like why she'd lied about a book expo. Why she hadn't been there to stop Allie from doing something stupid like going out and running into Peter.

Why she'd left.

Was Sabrina abandoning her, too?

The older woman bent down and patted Giorgio on the top of his head. Then she offered him a few little bits of a Slim Jim she'd had tucked in her pocket.

Mmm. Slim Jim.

Her mouth watering, Allie wondered if she should go find a restaurant before setting out for Trouble. Seemed like she was always hungry…or the baby was. But her money was limited, and she'd had a sandwich during a fuel-stop just an hour and a half ago. That'd last her for a while.

But mmm…Slim Jim.

"You were very nice to me," Allie said to the lady when she straightened up. Glancing at the woman's hands, she wondered if the dog had eaten every bit of the treat or if the meat stick had been part of a two-pack.

"You looked so young, and so tired," the stranger said.

She *was* tired. And young. But she wasn't helpless, and she knew when it was time to own up to her actions. "I'm fine. But I have to be honest with you—he's not really a seizure dog. I made that up so the driver would let him on the bus."

One side of the woman's mouth curled up and her tone

was dry as she said, "Well, gee, you don't say. Who would ever have imagined that?"

"Obviously not that bus driver," Allie said, liking the older woman's friendly smile and hint of sarcasm. She obviously hadn't been fooled.

"Lucky for you."

"Lucky for all of us," she said, rubbing her hand on her big belly.

"Is *that* real, or a pillow?" the woman asked, her brown eyes twinkling.

"Definitely real. Couldn't you tell by how often I had to get up to use the facilities on the bus?"

"Yes. I could." The lady reached a hand out, and for a second Allie tensed, thinking she was going to touch her belly. It was so weird how people felt completely comfortable putting their hands on her body, like she was some fluffy chair at a department store. One of these days, she was going to pat some touchy stranger right back, just to get the rudeness across.

But the woman lightly touched her shoulder instead, as if offering a bit of comfort and support. "My name's Emily."

"I'm Alicia."

"Pleased to meet you," Emily said. "Now, tell me, dear, is anyone coming to get you?"

Allie sucked her bottom lip into her mouth. The last thing she wanted was to be a burden on this very nice lady. She was tired of being a burden on everyone. But she could use a little help—like, at least, the phone number of the local cab company.

"Not *exactly*."

"How far are you going?"

"To a town called Trouble."

"Well, this is your lucky day, then, isn't it?" Emily said

with a huge smile, which made her cheeks puff out in two rosy circles. She reached over and took the small suitcase out of Allie's hand, waving off any protest. "I live in Trouble. Just went into the city to do some shopping. Can't get a decent pair of underwear within fifty miles of here, much less a dress to wear to a wedding."

Allie's heart skipped a beat. "Do you have a car? Can you give me a ride?"

The woman shook her head. "Nope, I don't drive, that's why I took the bus."

Allie's hopes shrank. "Oh."

"But I might be able to help you with that ride. My nephew—my brother's boy—is visiting me this week. He's been staying at my house the last couple of days while I was gone, and he's coming to pick me up any minute now."

Allie opened her mouth to reply, unable to believe her good fortune. Before she could get a word out, though, a small sedan pulled up to the curb with a cheery beep of the horn. As she watched, a young, dark-haired man stepped out of the driver's side.

He had a nice smile. A very nice smile. His wasn't a particularly handsome face, but a nicely-put-together one. Plus he had an average-height body—that could be on the cover of *Sports Illustrated*…

Forget it. You've had enough experience with men to last a lifetime.

"Here's my Joey," the woman said. "Now just hand your things over to him and get yourself all buckled in the back seat. We'll get you where you're going. Joey, we've got a couple of traveling companions today."

Joey gave his aunt a surprised look, then Allie a curious one. But it quickly faded when he saw her big stomach, the leash in her hand and, perhaps, the flash of fear on her face.

A nice smile? She didn't know how she could have thought that. Because the one he flashed at her as he took her suitcase from his aunt was *heavenly*, complete with dimples.

"Pleased to meet you."

She was pleased to meet him, too, on top of having met his kind aunt. Things were definitely looking up. Allie couldn't help feeling better about today, like she'd made the right decision in coming here.

How funny—on Friday, when she'd found out where Sabrina had gone, she'd had a few misgivings about following her. The name of the town had seemed like a bad omen. But really, if Trouble, Pennsylvania, boasted of such lovely, old-fashioned, kind-hearted people, how bad could it be?

CHAPTER EIGHT

TALKING TO A BALD, naked, middle-aged guy about a problem with leaky pipes wasn't high on Sabrina's list of favorite things to do. But since the sink in her private bathroom had started leaking this morning, getting water all over the bath mats and threatening to float into the bedroom, she really had no choice.

Why, oh why, couldn't the thing have broken tomorrow morning, Monday, instead of now, the weekend—his *special* time. But it hadn't, which meant she had to track down her landlord immediately.

Eyes front. Chin up. Head back.

She found Mr. Fitzweather in the backyard of the Dewdrop, trimming the tangle of vines that grew on the trellises around the large hot tub. The thick, flowery hedge provided a nice screen for the spa, giving it an air of privacy and the feel of being in a secluded grove. If not for the cheesy-looking, naked cupids dangling fake grapes overhead as they squirted water into the spa through their tiny peepees, it might actually look elegant.

Not that she'd use the thing in a million and a half years. Not unless Mr. Clean and a hundred Merry Maids came and worked on it for a week and the Culligan Man himself declared the water fit to use.

"Um, Mr. Fitzweather?" she said, spying a bare shoulder

on the other side of the thick vines. Maybe she'd get lucky and he'd stay there.

He took one step out from behind the trellis.

Damn.

Fortunately, though, he didn't come any farther, so only his side—a lumpy, rolling flank the color of a dead mullet—remained in her line of sight. "Good morning, Miss Cavanaugh! Beautiful day to be out and about, enjoying the sunshine, don't you think?"

It was hotter than Johnny Depp out here. Even though she'd just come outside, her brow already dripped sweat. Still, she wasn't going to argue with a fat, naked man holding a pair of hedge clippers. "Yes, wonderful."

"Ah, one moment, let me get this one," he said.

Sabrina's hope that the man would remain mostly hidden deserted her. Al Fitzweather stepped completely out from behind the green screen and leaned up on tiptoe to snip at one protruding vine.

Don't look down. Don't look down. Don't look down.

"That's better. Now, what can I do for you?"

She stared directly into his round face. If a sexual or suggestive expression had been there, she would have stormed off and taken her chances with Norman Bates up at the hotel on the hill. But there wasn't. The middle-aged man just appeared friendly and completely comfortable.

She was about as comfortable as a pair of spike-heeled shoes. But she swallowed away her anxiety and pretended she was talking to a fully clothed, *normal* person. "I'm having a problem in my room," she explained. "I think one of the pipes broke, because there's water all over the bathroom floor."

Mr. Fitzweather frowned in disapproval. "Did you flush anything…unseemly?"

Eww. This coming from the small-town exhibitionist. "No. It appears to be coming from the sink beneath the cabinet."

"Did you *wash* anything unseemly down the drain?"

Okay, the man was a fruitcake. What, exactly, did he imagine she'd shoved into the tiny drain opening, her drug stash? "Nothing unseemly, I assure you. I turned off the valves under the sink, so the leaking has stopped, but I assumed you'd want to take care of it before the standing water causes any damage."

He waved a hand, obviously forgetting the pair of clippers clutched in it. Sabrina took a quick step back to avoid having an ear cut off. He didn't seem concerned about cutting anything else off.

"Very well, I'll deal with it later. I've a lot of work to do just now. The ladies Garden Club is coming over to view my hedges this morning, and I must get ready."

Hmm. A ladies garden club. Seemed to Sabrina that getting ready for such an event might include tidying up, making cucumber sandwiches.

Putting on some damn clothes.

But before she could say anything—not that she knew what to say, other than, *Gee, you going to leave your Wee Willie Winkie out when you welcome the mayor?*—she heard someone calling from the side gate.

"Sabrina? You back there?"

She recognized the voice. *Max.*

If she'd thought she was hot and steamy before, that was nothing compared to how she felt now. A rush of heat washed over her and her face probably turned as red as Mr. Fitzweather's shiny bald head.

She couldn't face Max. Not after what had happened yesterday. Not after she'd totally blown her chance to do exactly what she'd come here to do—seduce the man into some serious misbehavior—by practically running away after a little kiss.

Okay, it hadn't been little, she had to admit that much, at least to herself. It had been huge. Enormous. A galaxy of a kiss.

Sabrina had had a few lovers—even one or two good ones. But she'd never been involved with a fabulous kisser.

Max Taylor was one fabulous kisser.

Just the right amount of pressure, just the right amount of tenderness. Not too dry, not too wet. The way he'd slid his hands in her hair and cupped her face had made her shiver. A lot of men liked to squeeze the breath out of the woman they were kissing as if physical control would be a turn-on. But that simple curl of Max's hand around her jaw had been much more sexy and possessive than any full-frontal embrace Sabrina had ever experienced.

She'd loved the stroke of his tongue, the pressure of his lips, the maple sweetness of his breath. Then there was his huge…oh, Lord, she was getting all shaky merely thinking about it.

"Is that someone calling you?" Mr. Fitzweather said.

Okay, she could pretend it wasn't and stand here trying to look everywhere but at the Fitzweather family stones, or she could remember why she'd come to town and march over to the gate to greet Max Taylor.

He was infinitely more appealing in every way, even if her so-called mission was not. She didn't know exactly when the idea had become so *un*appealing to her. It had always sounded stupid to think she could fool a playboy into trying to seduce her and show his true colors. But now, since she'd started getting to know Max, she honestly had to question everything she thought she knew about him.

Could he be the absolutely amazing lover Grace Wellington had written about? Yes. No question about it. That
kiss yesterday had confirmed it for her beyond all doubt.

But was he also the kinky sexual predator and heartbreaking love-'em-and-leave-'em dog Grace had described?

Hmm...

"Sabrina?"

"I'm coming," she called, smiling pleasantly at Mr.
Fitzweather—*don't look down, don't look down, don't
look down*—before walking away.

The backyard was enclosed by a high, wooden fence,
which afforded Mr. Fitzweather privacy for his naked frol-
icking, at least from everyone *except* his paying customers. Max, however, was tall enough to peer over the top of
it. When he saw her, he smiled, but quickly looked side to
side—as if making sure she was unaccompanied.

"The coast is clear," she said, jerking her head toward
the spa. "He's busy working on the hedges."

"Whew," Max said as he opened the gate for her,
closing it as soon as she'd joined him on the gravel
driveway just outside the fence. "I couldn't believe it when
the maid said you were out back. You've got guts. Believe
me, I have had enough of seeing people naked who I don't
want to see naked to last my whole life."

His vehemence was almost funny. And if Sabrina hadn't
been feeling like she had to go wash her eyes out with
soap, she would have laughed at it. "What are you doing
here?"

"Came to invite you to go flying with me."

Her heart dropping somewhere in the vicinity of her
heels, she opened her mouth to reply. Then she saw a
sparkle in his eyes that said he'd been teasing her.

Before Max, no man had teased her for a very long time. She wasn't sure whether she liked the fluttering sensation it brought.

Bull. She liked it. A lot.

"What do you *really* want to invite me to do with you?"

A boyish grin tugged at his lips, and Sabrina almost kicked herself for handing him that line. But he played the gentleman and didn't lob it back with a sexy response to her unintentional innuendo.

She told herself she was not disappointed.

"I actually came by to ask if you want to tour the town today. We seem to keep getting interrupted by sheikhs, fighting grannies and…unexpected kisses, whenever I'm about to offer to show you around Trouble."

The way his voice lingered over the words *unexpected kisses,* caressing them almost, made Sabrina shift a little. She was dressed in perfectly adequate clothes, with a really stylish pair of knockoff gaucho pants that looked just like some she'd seen in a fashion magazine, and a sleeveless blouse that was so simple it looked like it had to be expensive.

Why, then, did the silky fabric of the blouse feel so scratchy against her sensitive nipples? And why, in heaven's name, did the loose pants suddenly feel so tight in the most intimate of places?

It wasn't hard to figure out. She was turned on—het up, as her mechanic uncle would say. Crude description, but true. She was reacting as strongly now, to Max's simple words, as she had to his kiss yesterday. Stronger, really, because she'd had twenty-four hours to remember that kiss and build up a whole lot of anticipation for another one.

Not to mention whatever came after it.

That, she suspected, was why today she'd put on this sinfully sensuous top with nothing underneath. Sabrina didn't particularly need one, but she always wore a bra. Always. But this morning, after a long night of dreams that had left her frustrated and restless, she'd wanted something silky and seductive touching her with intimacy. Even if it was nothing more than her own damn blouse.

"What do you say? Will you spend the day with me?" he asked.

He stepped closer. Sabrina stepped back, until she hit the closed-gate and was left with nowhere else to go.

"You don't have any other plans, do you?"

She managed one slow shake of her head.

"Is that no, you don't have any other plans?" he asked, lifting his hand to her face and rubbing the side of his thumb across her jaw.

Oh, Lord, she loved the way he touched her face.

"Or, no, you won't spend the day with me?"

She couldn't answer. His touch had effectively sucked the vibration right out of her vocal cords and they were incapable of making any noise. She could only stand there and exist.

"I promise I won't try to tempt you into—" he leaned even closer, letting his fingertips drift to the hair at the nape of her neck and sift through it "—flying."

Flying. Oh, she *wanted* to fly. Wanted to soar with him.

Playboy or not, she wanted Max Taylor. Wanted him badly. Much more than she had when he'd been merely a wicked character in an erotic book. Now that she'd tasted his mouth and felt his hands on her skin, she could no longer deny the truth…even to herself.

She'd come here to nail him—and she didn't mean legally.

This whole trip to Trouble—despite the explanations

she'd made to Nancy, and to herself—had always, deep down, been about the heated fantasies she'd had about Max. Fantasies she'd had since the first time she'd read his name on Grace's manuscript and pictured being the one he'd tied up and sensually tormented for hours.

She'd told herself she could expose him, stop the lawsuit and save the book—all while being careful to keep her heart guarded and her panties on. But after that kiss yesterday, she wasn't so sure she could. Or that she wanted to. At least, wanted to keep the panties on part, not the heart part. Because she'd never let herself actually fall in love with a guy like Max.

But sleeping with him, now *that* sounded pretty much okay.

Are you insane? a little voice in her head asked.

Maybe. Probably. Given her track record, the last thing she should even be considering was a fling with a playboy. But, oh, it had been a long time since she'd had a man's rough hands touching her. And his were so very, *very* tempting. Her body had tingled all day yesterday whenever she'd thought of the warm scrape of his fingers across her spine and the strength of his hand cupping her bottom.

"What do you say?" he asked. He stepped close, so that the front of his body brushed against hers. Suggestively... not threateningly. Just a gentle slide, a casual stroke.

A silent invitation to pleasure.

"If you don't say you'll go sightseeing," he murmured, his warm breath touching her temple, "I might have to convince you to come fly with me."

"I don't think that's a great idea." Her voice sounded about as firm as a kindergartner's saying no to a cookie.

She cleared her throat and tried again. "I mean, after what happened yesterday…"

"When we kissed?"

She nodded.

"You didn't like it?"

"Does the Pope like praying?" she murmured back before she could think better of it.

He laughed softly. His lips were now touching her skin, so his laughter turned into a series of tiny kisses pressed along the top of her cheekbone. She sighed, the gentle sound turning into a moan when she felt his hand touch her hip.

"I doubt the Pope likes praying more than I liked kissing you." He toyed with her hip, his fingers drawing tiny lines on her waist, then her midriff. His touch remained light, almost teasing, which only built the hunger more.

Almost breathless with anticipation, Sabrina waited for his hand to move even higher so he could continue those maddeningly delicious caresses across the sensitive tips of her breasts. She'd been aching for just such a touch yesterday, when they'd practically made love on a public sidewalk.

Yesterday—think of yesterday. The thought raced through her brain as she tried to find some well of inner resolve against letting this happen again. Letting *him* happen again.

After their encounter, she'd been angry at herself— furious at how easily he'd gotten around her defenses and at how utterly wanton she'd become with a mere kiss. That was the real reason she'd told Max she'd never go flying with him—not that she didn't trust him, she didn't trust *herself.* He made her crazy and reckless and she'd already proved she had no willpower around the man. So she needed to keep both feet on the ground. At least until she found out for sure whether he was the swinging playboy or the fabulous, funny, adorable and sexy guy she was falling for.

Falling for. Oh, you fool.

But, like yesterday, none of those protestations seemed to matter a damn when he was so close and so big and so perfect. When he whispered such sweet words and his tone was so playful, and his masculine smell so heady. Just as it didn't seem to matter that they stood outside, only partially blocked from view by the house and the thick honeysuckle hedge running along the fence.

Because she wanted him. Was dying for him. This man made her forget everything else, even her promises to herself. Made her long to say yes to any wicked thing he suggested, to indulge—to take—whatever she wanted.

Just as he took whatever he wanted—like that kiss yesterday. And now…another one?

Lifting his hand to cup her face, Max tilted her head up until they shared a breath. "You know you taste like strawberries?" he asked.

And *he* tasted like heaven.

So she tasted him, slid her arms around his neck, pressed against his body and opened her mouth on his for a deep, wet, lazy kiss. It was as if they were picking up where they'd left off yesterday after only a brief pause.

Kissing Max was like stretching out in the sun, slowly soaking up physical delight. There was nothing frenzied, nothing demanding. Just a sweet, languorous mating of lips and tongues and breath.

Wanting to feel that strong chest, she lowered one hand and scraped the backs of her fingers across his shoulder.

Max was so solid, so muscular, and she was dying to see him without his clothes, knowing he had the kind of body women fantasized about but usually never saw in real life.

Well, that wasn't entirely accurate. Because seeing him naked wouldn't be quite enough. No. What she really wanted was to feel him, stroke the man, smear him with massage oil and roll all over him.

Max reacted to their kiss in the most elemental way. Sabrina felt him, big and hard against her hip. Oh, so big and hard. And she could think of something else slick and wet—something other than massage oil—that she wanted to rub on him. On *that* part of him. She was drenched. Aroused enough not to protest if he yanked her clothes off and made sweet, wild love to her right out here in the sunlight, Trouble be damned.

"I have to have your hands on me, Max," she groaned. Drawing him back into the shadowy corner where the fence met the house, she quickly realized they were completely hidden from view. This private spot was blocked from the street not only by the fence but by the trees and shrubs the landlord spent so much time taking care of.

Max apparently realized just how secluded they were, too. His eyes glittered in the shadows of the leaves and his playful smile had faded into one of pure sexual desire. Which somehow fit, in the dangerously public yet somehow private setting. Because the anticipation was enormous and the danger of exposure real. But she didn't give a damn. And neither did he.

The air was thick and ripe with the scent of earth from the garden and the sweet perfume of honeysuckle vines cascading over their heads along the fence. Sabrina breathed in, wondering how far they could go. How much they could risk.

Bending to press a hot kiss against the side of her neck, Max tugged at the bottom of her blouse. She shifted and let him pull it free of her loose pants, wanting his touch more than she wanted the sun to keep on shining.

Hissing as her skin was bared to the coolness of the shadows—such a contrast to the hot, sunny day—she arched toward him. When his hands brushed against her flesh, she cried out, indulging in sensation as Max played a melody on her stomach with the tips of his fingers.

He continued to kiss her neck, her throat and her jaw. Though his warm mouth skimmed close to her own, he wouldn't kiss her, which only built the tension more.

"Please, Max," she whispered, reaching up to twine her fingers in his hair. Tugging his lips toward hers, she added, "I've got to taste you."

He brushed his mouth across hers, not giving her the deep, carnal kiss she hungered for. "And I've got to feel you," he replied, as if he wanted her focused purely on his touch.

And she wanted to be felt.

Sabrina cried out in pure satisfaction when his hands slid a path from her waist up her midriff to cup the bottoms of her breasts.

"You feel amazing," Max muttered as he caressed her, tweaking her nipples with his thumbs. "Tell me you're not wearing anything under this blouse because you wanted me to show up." He kissed her jaw, the tender spot below her ear. "You wanted *this*."

Closing her eyes and leaning her head to the side to give him access to her neck, she nodded. "Yes. I wanted this. Your hands." He nipped at the tender spot where neck met shoulder. "Oh, please…your mouth."

He gave her what she wanted, kissing and tasting his way down her throat, then dropping to his knees in front of her. Sabrina opened her eyes, wanting to see, to imprint every moment on her brain. She held her breath, enjoying the caress of her silky blouse—and his strong rough hands—as Max slid it up her body.

His every move was slow and deliberate. He was savoring it.

She wanted to rip the damn thing off. She was dying for it.

"Beautiful," he murmured as he uncovered her. Once she was bared to him, he stared at her breasts, a slow smile of satisfaction making him appear almost predatory. Sabrina shivered, loving that hungry expression, thrilled that he'd seen her admittedly average curves and wanted her anyway.

"You are absolutely perfect," he whispered as he toyed with one puckered nipple.

His touch was firm, not tentative—there was nothing tentative about this man. He stroked her with just enough pressure to make her gasp, causing a molten, lava-flow of pleasure to wash through her body. When Max leaned closer and covered her nipple with his mouth, that lava flow erupted with volcanic insistence between her legs.

She tangled her hands in his hair, dropping her head back against the wall as he sucked the sensitive tip of one breast while stroking and plucking the other. The intensity built, spiraled, and she wanted more…more pressure. More roughness. More insanity.

As if knowing that, he plumped her breast with his hand to suck even deeper, devouring her. She felt every pull of his mouth like a rocket shot to her wet, hungry core.

Sabrina began to shake, wondering if she'd be able to remain standing—knowing without a doubt that he could make her come by doing little more than moving his face lower and breathing on her hard.

"You ready to fly with me now?" he whispered against her skin as he moved over to pay deliberate attention to her other breast. "Because if you're not, I'd be happy to try to...*persuade* you some more."

Oh, yes. She was ready to beg and thrust and give and take right here and now. Anything, everything, as long as he just...didn't...stop.

"I think you could talk me into just about anything right now," she admitted, nearly sobbing out the words. "I'd probably strip naked and take you on a table in Tootie's Tavern."

But at that moment, with the image of how easily she could let herself go with him—how easily she *had* let herself go with him, twice now—she remembered a passage of Grace's book. Where the woman had described a man—*this man*—seducing her in the bathroom of an expensive restaurant.

Cold reality flooded her as if someone had doused her with ice water. Her whole body stiffened, growing frigid where it had been warm and pliant.

Max appeared to sense her change in mood. Without a word, he stood, reaching for her to draw her into his arms, but Sabrina put a hand on his chest to stop him. Stepping to the side, almost to the point of risking exposure to anyone on the street, she stared at him. Physically unable to prevent the image of Max with Grace Wellington—or some other woman susceptible to his charm and his kiss—from invading her brain, she felt like crying.

"I think that's enough," she said, wishing her voice didn't sound choppy. Weak. She managed to yank her blouse back on, covering herself and grabbing a moment to think.

"Sabrina?" He sounded confused, but instantly serious,

as if he knew something important had just happened but wasn't sure what.

Something important *had* just happened. For a moment, Sabrina had allowed herself to forget everything she knew about this man. Or thought she knew.

Max was doing what she'd hoped he'd do when she came to this crappy little town: trying to seduce her. Only, the objective was to make him *try* it…not to let herself fall for it. Yet she had come so close to falling.

Is that such a bad thing?

She honestly wasn't sure. Before meeting him, she'd been certain she knew who he was. In the past few days—before he'd kissed her—she'd begun to revise her opinion.

But now, with proof positive of the man's abilities as a seducer, she just didn't know what to believe anymore.

The sexy sweetheart she was getting to know? Or the near-reprobate Grace described in her book?

"What's wrong?" he asked. "Tell me what you're thinking."

The words rushed to her mouth, almost spilling out. *Who are you really?*

Before they could escape, however, the sound of a voice—a voice that she simply could *not* be hearing—interfered.

"Sabrina? Is that you?"

Her heart stopped beating. Her mind stopped working. Because it wasn't possible—that could not be who she thought it was.

"Oh, my God," she muttered when an absolutely unfathomable sight came into view.

She blinked a couple of times, but the apparition did not disappear. Despite everything she'd done to keep her location a secret, her very pregnant sister, Allie, had followed her to Trouble.

PETER PRESCOTT hated being back in Philadelphia.

When he left this miserable city several months ago, he'd been determined he wouldn't return until he'd become famous for discovering the next *Da Vinci Code*. He'd confidently predicted he'd be heading up the acquisitions department at a major New York publisher before he turned thirty. Then, and only then, would he come back to gloat over those who'd doubted him.

But it hadn't happened. Despite the fact that Liberty Books had allowed him to resign quietly rather than be fired, word had gotten out in the publishing industry. Every door in Manhattan had been firmly shut against him, and he'd knocked on enough to know it.

He'd been blackballed. Silently by the big boys and blatantly by the little ones who personally knew his old colleagues.

Including the woman who'd caused all of this.

"Sabrina," he muttered as he walked down Broad Street on Sunday morning, hating the taste of her name in his mouth.

He had thought he'd gotten over his need to pay his ex-girlfriend back for what she'd done to him. Maybe if she'd *only* dumped him—something *no* woman had ever done— he would have been able to let it go at nailing her sister. Since Sabrina had never stopped talking about Allie the whole time they were dating, Peter had known exactly how to cause her as much pain as she'd caused him by ending the relationship before he was ready for it to be over.

There'd been a few unexpected benefits to his plan, too. Finding out Allie had been a virgin had been one great final fuck-you to her big sister.

He probably could have left it at that and moved on,

having taught her a lesson about who, exactly, was supposed to have dumped who. But, as it had turned out, Sabrina had done more than humiliate him personally. She'd cost him his career.

Ducking under a covered doorway across the street from his old office building, he stared up at the tenth-story window, which had once been his. His own window. His own office. He'd been a senior editor, the right hand of the editorial director and in line for that job when the fat old bastard retired next year.

If he'd gotten it, his financial problems would have been over. Peter wouldn't have needed the money he earned on the side—money given to him by authors desperate to see their name in print—to supplement his income. All of that would have ended and he would have been set—two years as a manager at Liberty and he could waltz right into a job in the big leagues.

And Sabrina had thought he would give that up voluntarily?

Unbelievable. When she'd found out about his less-than-honest dealings—right around the time they'd broken up—she'd urged him to invent some reason to resign. She'd even believed he'd do it. The woman had actually convinced herself that her appeals to his honor and code of ethics would be enough to make him give up everything he'd been working toward. *Everything.* As if the fact that she'd already broken up with him would somehow turn him into some schmuck who'd mourn what he'd lost—namely her—and decide to do the right thing by throwing himself on his sword like a damn martyr.

Looking back, he realized that's what he should have done. Either that or killed the bitch. But he simply hadn't believed she'd do anything about it if he didn't do as she asked, nor that she could prove it if she did.

Oh, had he been wrong. Because after giving him a final warning, which he'd again ignored, she had gone to their boss. Armed with letters from authors who'd paid Peter to get their books on Liberty's publication schedule, she'd skewered him. She'd put him in the line of fire and he'd had to either resign or face public character assassination by being thrown out.

He'd been too numb with shock to do much more than head out of town after one final sneer at Sabrina and her sister. Confident he'd land on top, anyway, he'd headed to New York and…failed. Nobody would even talk to him. Broke and relying on his family for money, he'd been forced to come back to Philadelphia. He'd been home for a week, trying to figure out what the hell to do, beyond trying to come up with another way to pay Sabrina back.

And then he'd seen her sister. Her very pregnant sister.

"Just call me Daddy," he said now with a humorless smile, ignoring a passerby who gave him a curious glance.

He had no doubt the kid was his. While at first he'd been panicked like any guy in that situation, he'd quickly realized he was being handed an opportunity. A weapon. He simply had to figure out how best to use it.

Allie had been an effective weapon the first time— as he'd known she would be. When he'd been dating Sabrina, she'd talked of almost nothing else but her brilliant, beautiful little sister who was moving to the big city to attend college. The two of them, Peter knew, had been incredibly close, bound together by their rough childhood.

Boo-fucking-hoo. *Cry me a river.*

Allie had been easy to track down, and even easier to

seduce. But he'd played that card. Which was why it was so nice that fate had given him another one—the baby.

"Excellent," he murmured, already knowing he'd start with fear. Scaring the hell out of Sabrina the way he had out of Allie when he'd threatened to try to take the kid away would be effective. Not that he wanted any brat in his life, but he liked the idea of her worrying about it.

Just one problem—he couldn't find Sabrina. He'd staked out the office since the middle of last week—even before he'd run into Allie—and hadn't seen her. Desperate, he'd even gone to her apartment this morning, very early, to avoid being seen by a nosy neighbor. But he'd only spotted her fat sister leaving with a suitcase and Sabrina's yappy mutt.

Wondering if perhaps Sabrina was out of town and Allie was leaving to join her, he'd followed the girl to the bus station and had watched her board a bus for western Pennsylvania. But he had no idea of her final destination.

Which was why he'd called Jane, his former secretary, who now worked for Sabrina. The wary tone in her voice when he'd called told him she knew he was probably going to be trying to get information out of her when they met for lunch today.

She was right. He'd be willing to bet the woman wouldn't want her new boss to find out she'd been messing around with Peter while he and Sabrina had been involved. Hopefully, Jane would be so anxious to avoid that, she'd come up with some information on exactly what Sabrina was up to.

And where she'd gone.

CHAPTER NINE

MAX WASN'T ENTIRELY certain who the pregnant girl getting out of the white sedan in front of the Dewdrop Inn was, but he had no doubt she knew Sabrina. Because right at the moment he'd thought for sure the beautiful blonde was going to tell him why she'd gone from molten angel to aloof stranger, she went pale. Her whole body jerked and her jaw worked, opening and closing, no sound coming out. She stepped completely out into the open, staring in shock toward the street.

Once he'd gotten his body back under control, he joined her. As he watched the newcomer, he heard Sabrina's tiny groan. He couldn't resist reaching out and grabbing her hand, knowing that whoever this girl was, Sabrina was not entirely thrilled to see her. She squeezed back, giving him a quick look of appreciation before turning her full attention on the newcomer. Interesting. She'd been icy cold toward him a moment before, yet she now seemed grateful to have him by her side.

Which gave him hope that she might want him to stay there.

After what they'd just shared, Max knew he was not going to be satisfied with a stolen interlude in the bushes. He wanted to make love to her, to take all her clothes off and fill his senses with that delicate body. To stare at her soft skin and the perfect breasts he could still taste on his tongue. To smell the musky scent of her arousal and the flowery scent of her hair. To caress her arms and stroke her thighs and slide his tongue inside her. Then bury himself in her tight body and lose his mind completely.

"I can't believe this is happening," Sabrina said, interrupting his heated memories of what had happened—and more heated fantasies of what was yet to come.

The young woman waved at the people in the car as they drove away. Struggling with a suitcase and a dog leash, she walked up the uneven driveway. Max instinctively stepped forward and grabbed the luggage.

When she flashed him a grateful smile, he pegged her as a family member. The smile was the same. So was the sparkle in the bright blue eyes.

Her hair was much darker, her face rounder. She looked young—not much beyond her teenage years. And she was obviously very pregnant. But he'd be willing to bet he was looking at a sister or a cousin of the woman he'd been about to make love to in the shadows.

Then he focused on the dog at her feet and figured he was at last meeting the infamous Butch. So, this had to be the sister.

"Hi," she said, her smile fading as Sabrina continued to stare. "I guess you're probably wondering what I'm doing here."

"You could say that." Sabrina frowned. "How did you…?"

"Jane told me where you were."

"She wouldn't have done that."

"I had something on her."

Ah, blackmail. He began to like this girl.

"You strong-armed my assistant?" Sabrina asked. Then

she quickly glanced toward him, her lips rounding into an O of surprise, as if she'd forgotten he was there.

"I'll get out of your hair, I guess you're going to be busy this morning." Smiling, he added, "Too busy to go...fly-ing."

"Flying?" the girl said, sounding like a kid being offered a ride on an elephant. "You're going *flying?*"

"No. We're not," Sabrina said. "You're going to explain what you're doing here. You followed me? You have got to be kidding me. What were you *thinking?*"

Max didn't hear anger in Sabrina's voice, but a confused disappointment. A resignation that he absolutely did not like.

In the time he'd known her, he'd seen Sabrina Cava-naugh in varying moods. Friendly and helpful at the carousel. Snappy and caustic when they'd walked to the house. Flirtatious with his grandfather. Thoughtful and concerned at the tavern. Even suggestive on occasion. And oh...absolutely sinful in his arms.

But he hadn't seen this. This weariness that seemed to pull her shoulders down and put a stark sadness in her eyes.

Her unhappiness made him instantly stiffen. Where this protective instinct had come from, he had no idea. He hadn't felt protective toward a woman in years. If ever, considering what his first wife, Teresa, had been like.

"And Giorgio? You brought the dog on this wild game of hide-and-seek?" Sabrina asked.

Ah, Giorgio the Doberman stuck in a poodle's body. Max smiled as he stared at the dog, who was jumping up onto Sabrina's leg, looking for attention. She crouched down to scratch him beneath his fuzzy beige chin, rubbing her nose against his and burying her face in his fur.

It was a telling moment. A quiet one, but an interesting one nonetheless. She stayed bent down, hugging the dog like she couldn't bear to let him go. Couldn't bear to stand up and finish the conversation she'd been having with the young woman. As if wanting to prolong her freedom for just a little bit longer. He could almost see her mentally dealing with this situation, which, he had begun to suspect, was not a happy one.

Sensing she wouldn't appreciate the attention, Max strolled a few feet away, giving them some privacy. But not too far, because he wanted to keep an eye on the pair. Maybe to lend a hand if the pregnant woman needed it. Maybe just to be a silent support system for Sabrina.

He leaned against the porch railing. Crossing his arms, he feigned interest in the stupid sign Al Fitzweather had had painted for the front of the inn—a drop of moisture falling off a rose. Such subtlety. He could hardly stand it.

"We probably shouldn't talk now," the girl said. "We'll talk later. I think Butch has to go. He needs some grass. Why don't I take him for a walk?"

Max was about to offer to take the dog off their hands, when Sabrina's head jerked up and she rose to her feet. "Uh-uh. You and I have some things to discuss. We can let Giorgio in the backyard." Swinging around, she opened the gate, unleashed the dog and gently shooed him in.

"He's such a good boy. He's an angel to travel with."

"Why is he traveling at all? Allie, why are you *here*?"

The girl—Allie—continued as if Sabrina hadn't even spoken. "And he's smart, too. Very smart. No silly speak or play dead tricks for him. I've been teaching him to be a guard dog."

Guard dog. Right. The fuzzball could guard against any ants who threatened to invade Sabrina's kitchen. Or guard against bigger dogs, who'd laugh themselves to death the minute this one tried to act threatening.

"I *had* to teach him to be a guard dog, you see," the girl said, her voice growing louder—more shrill.

And, Max suddenly realized, a little bit hysterical.

"Because of Peter. In case Peter…"

Even from here he could see the expression of dismay that flashed across Sabrina's face. She instantly stepped close, putting her arm around her sister's shoulders. "He's gone ,honey, he's never going to bother you again."

Max somehow maintained his seemingly indolent position leaning against the railing, though every muscle in his body had tensed. He had a sudden suspicion that this Peter character could be the father of Allie's baby. And given her youth—and obvious fear of him—he had to wonder if she'd been the victim of rape.

Jesus. The girl looked barely twenty. He'd never laid eyes on her until now, but Max still felt like going after the man who'd done this to Sabrina's sister.

Allie sniffled, hugged her sister back, then glanced at her own feet. "You never know, it's a small world. Anything can happen." She opened her mouth, closed it.

Hell, even from several feet away Max could tell she was hiding something. He wondered what it was the girl was afraid to tell Sabrina. And how it would affect Sabrina when she did.

Instead, Allie was evasive. "So, because of that, I've been working with Butch on his attack skills." She smiled, though the sheen in her eyes remained. "I took that big cardboard standing-poster of Fabio that you got as a gag gift from work last Christmas and tied a string around it, with a banana and two kiwis hanging down between his legs."

Unable to stop it, Max let out a bark of laughter. He didn't know what amused him more—the thought of Sabrina having a life-size Fabio stuffed in her closet, or the image of Butch going after his, um…fruit.

Allie glanced at him, looking surprised, as if she'd forgotten he was nearby. So did her sister, who nibbled on her lower lip, obviously embarrassed.

Max couldn't help it. When Allie turned her attention back to Sabrina, he lifted one brow and mouthed *Fabio?*

She shot him a glare.

"When I say *sic,* well, Butch, he just goes crazy."

Picturing the rabid little furball, Max couldn't help smiling. Talk about your ultimate stupid pet trick—he wondered if Butch had a future on Letterman.

A yappy string of barks indicated that the furball had heard Allie's command. The dog was barking, growling and practically bouncing off the fence in excitement, judging by the thumps Max heard even from a few feet away.

The thumps were suddenly drowned out, however, by a loud male voice. "What's that noise? Whose dog is this?"

Max and Sabrina met each other's stares. The way her eyes flared and her mouth dropped open, she had the exact same thought he did, at the very same moment.

That the mutt wasn't alone in the backyard—the owner of the inn was there, too.

And it was Sunday.

Before he could so much as call out a warning, the morning air was split by a high-pitched shriek. Several more echoed it.

Max didn't think, didn't plan. He merely sprinted toward the gate, his hand touching the latch at the same instant Sabrina's did. They opened it together, burst into the yard, and were greeted by the kind of sight you just didn't see every day. Not even in a town called Trouble.

Standing a few feet away, screaming like a young girl being chased by one of the knife-wielding movie psychos Sabrina so loved, was Al Fitzweather. Red-faced, sweaty and naked. A typical weekend look for the man, or so he'd heard.

Except for one thing—the small poodle dangling between his spread legs, its jaws clamped on the man's... kiwis.

IDA MAE WAS WORRIED. Deeply concerned, even. She'd sat on her fears for almost twenty-four hours now, but couldn't make them go away. Because something she'd seen yesterday was eating at her. And all the Milk of Magnesia in the world wouldn't ease the tight feeling in her stomach.

Usually when she spied a person doing some skulking, she was able to find the silver lining. That silver lining sometimes even involved cold, hard cash when the skulkers didn't want to be exposed. Like the last time she and Ivy had seen some people lurking around the old Stuttgardt place five years ago.

But *this* time, she was afraid. Not for herself, but for Mortimer Potts.

She'd tried to brush off her fears. Why, after all, would anyone want to harm that kind, handsome gentleman? He was nothing like Wilhelm Stuttgardt, whose death, everyone agreed, had been proof of the expression "what goes around, comes around."

Ida Mae preferred to think of it as "an eye for an eye." She snickered at her own wit. Clever, she thought, considering how the man had died.

But even her certainty that Mr. Potts could not have an

enemy in the world couldn't rid her of this feeling of dread. She felt queasy with worry whenever she thought of the way she'd seen Tom King racing away from the man's house yesterday.

After the *unfortunate incident* downtown, Mortimer had walked her and Ivy home, then headed toward his place. Ida Mae had, naturally, followed, to make sure Ivy wasn't following.

Ivy *was* following, of course. So the two of them had stood guard on each other to guarantee one sister didn't get an advantage on the other by stealing extra time with their shared beau.

They'd crept up through the woods on the east side of the house, watching as Mortimer had come walking up the driveway out front. So they'd seen Tom King run out the back and down the hill toward the road, and had heard a car start up a few moments later. Mr. Potts had not.

The question remained: what had the sour-faced man been doing there? If he'd just come to visit, why hadn't he parked in the driveway like any good, decent neighbor? And why had he run away before Mortimer had even come into sight of the house?

Not that she considered King good and decent, no, sir. That man had dark secrets—and he'd been right generous in paying to keep them that way. Secret.

If it had been anyone else, she might not have gotten so worked up. Worked up enough that she'd had to get up during the night and sip a few glasses of bourbon to help her fall back to sleep.

The only thing that had given her any bit of comfort in the midnight hours—as she'd finished off her bottle—was sitting in her living room staring at her coffee table, thinking of how she'd fixed Ivy but good this time. From now on when her sister tried to hold on to Daddy's Sears, Roebuck urn longer than she was supposed to, Ida Mae would have the last laugh. Oh, yes, she would.

Her smile over that quickly faded as her thoughts returned to today's dilemma. "Tom King was a nasty little boy who picked his nose and wet his bed until he was in secondary school," Ida Mae whispered as she dropped the curtain back down over her front window. She'd been standing there, gazing up the hill over the trees, at the roof of Mortimer Potts's house, barely visible from here. "But even nasty little bed-wetting boys can grow up to be dangerous men and thieves."

Tom's past certainly proved that.

Though she hated to think of sharing anything with her sister, she knew Ivy was the one person who would understand—and maybe even come up with an idea of what they should do. Ivy did have some good ideas—she was sneaky that way. Ida Mae had, therefore, called her sister a few minutes ago and asked her to come over to tea.

Ivy had immediately asked if she was spicing one of Mama's *specially* flavored teas. *Almond for Abusers, Coriander for Cheaters, Orange for Overnighters*—they'd learned the lessons at their mother's apron strings.

Ida Mae had fantasized about it for a moment, then agreed not to. She'd play nice this morning, even though it galled her. Especially considering just yesterday Ivy had stabbed her with a hatpin, causing an ugly cut that Ida Mae had considered going to have stitched up.

She hadn't. Because doing so would have required a trip to the walk-in clinic in Weldon, which was open on Sundays. Ida Mae was not about to let Ivy out of her sight for that long—not when Mortimer Potts was sitting in his house, just like a lamb to the slaughter.

"He *is* a lamb to the slaughter," she muttered as she filled a kettle and put it on for tea.

Only, not just *their* lamb. She and Ivy might be the shepherds, but she had the feeling a bad wolf was out there circling their flock.

And while the shepherds might quite enjoy a plate of juicy spring lamb with mint jelly, under absolutely no circumstances would they allow anyone else to harm a hair on their sheep's head.

"I CAN'T BELIEVE we're going to have to stay with Norman Bates."

Sabrina sat in the expansive driveway of Seaton House, an old hulk of a hotel hovering near the edge of a cliff, right above the town of Trouble. It was about as welcoming as a terrorist camp. Unlike Mortimer's house, which had a certain charm despite its strangeness, this place looked straight out of a horror movie.

Though she'd put the rental car in park a full minute ago, she hadn't cut off the engine. Instead, she sat inside, wondering why she didn't turn around, get on the highway and drive back to Philadelphia. There seemed no point in staying. Her so-called *mission* had already misfired even before her pregnant sister had shown up, attack-poodle in tow.

Allie, who sat next to her in the passenger seat, was probably also wondering why they weren't heading out of town. But she hadn't said it. Sabrina had the feeling Allie was remaining silent out of fear that if she started talking, Sabrina would start talking back.

Good call. Because, oh, did she have a lot to say to her sister. Especially after learning a bit more about Allie's travels. She'd heard the words *bus* and *nice lady and her nephew offered me a ride* and had instantly seen red. It was as if her sister was so sheltered she'd never even thought about the danger she might have put herself in by taking off without a word to anyone. She could have been kidnapped, hurt, and no one would even have known where she'd gone.

So, yes, she definitely had some things to say.

Not now. Her questions had to wait. She couldn't have that conversation while she was still so upset about not only Allie's recklessness, but also the trouble her arrival had caused.

Trouble like Sabrina being kicked out of the Dewdrop Inn.

Because as Al Fitzweather was being carried off by the paramedics, he'd spied Sabrina holding Giorgio—who'd let go of his prize only after Allie had offered him a Slim Jim. Her former landlord had screamed for Sabrina and her "hound from hell" to be out of his house by the time he returned.

Poor Giorgio. She really needed to find a pet store around here and get some kind of doggie mouth sanitizer.

"Do you honestly think we should stay *here?*" Allie asked in a loud whisper. Her sister was staring out the windshield, her eyes wide, her lower lip disappearing between her teeth. Instead of looking merely guilty and uncomfortable—as she had since Sabrina had stormed into the inn, packed her bags and marched back out—she now looked a little afraid.

Sabrina couldn't blame her. The former hotel was gothic. In her job at Liberty Books, Sabrina had seen a few gothic novels come across her desk. This looked like just the kind of place where a young, virginal governess would arrive to care for the estate owner's children. Finding his mad, murderous wife locked in the attic, and bodies of her victims hidden in the crumbling walls, she'd run along the stormy cliffs only to fall into the arms of the handsome, mysterious owner. Wife buys it. Happiness ensues. Fade to black.

Hmm, Sabrina didn't like the fade-to-black part. If she was going to read a juicy romance, she darn well wanted to see the action in all its blazing glory.

Then again, this place wasn't exactly happily-ever-after material. She couldn't imagine *any* woman being happy in this setting, no matter how hot the fictional hero might be, and she definitely couldn't see any sexy love-nest potential.

Even the grounds were bare and stark. Bleak. Though it was August and the weather had been lovely for days, most of the grass was dead. Only a few scraggly puffs of green emerged through the dirt here and there.

The massive oak trees closest to the house were fully clothed with summer leaves. But they hadn't been pruned in so long, the branches grew in all directions, creating strange shapes like great green snakes writhing toward the sky. Many of the other trees had died long ago, remaining as mere skeletons to complete the message that practically screamed in neon: *Go back!*

A voice in her head replied, *O-kay!*

But she couldn't do it. Couldn't put the car in drive and pull out of here because there was nowhere else in town to stay. And she wasn't leaving Trouble. Not when so much was still left undiscovered about Max Taylor.

Even though the reason for her initial desperation to push Grace Wellington's memoir through to print was sitting right beside her in the car, Sabrina couldn't fool herself that her job—or the book—had anything to do with her desire to stay.

She wanted to stay because of *him*. Period.

Not merely because of her intense attraction to the man, but also because she now had a deep, insatiable curiosity about who Max really was.

She'd already decided he was not the bad-ass, heartless playboy Grace had made him out to be. Sure, he'd kissed her, flirted with her, but not until after they'd spent a good bit of time together—shared some serious moments as well as some light ones. Thinking of the old ladies fighting, she had to add *weird ones* to the list.

But he hadn't crossed the line. In fact, he'd behaved like any other guy in the world.

Only, he was more attractive to her than any other guy in the world. And that, at the end of the day, was why she wasn't going anywhere. Not until she found out whether that attraction—connection—they shared was something unique and special. Or, to him at least, merely a fling.

"Sabrina? I thought that hot guy at the B&B said this place wasn't even open."

"That's what the locals say. But before I came here, I did an Internet search and the Seaton House still had a Web site." Of course, the pictures on that site had inspired her to decide immediately to stay at the Dewdrop Inn, instead. But that was no longer an option.

"Elvis still has a Web site," Allie retorted.

"Look, it's at least possible they *are* open and the residents in town don't like the new owner of this place so they try to discourage people from coming here."

Just as Max had when she'd been about to drive away from the Dewdrop Inn an hour ago.

He'd remained calm and in control during the whole Butch-sic-kiwis crisis. Racing inside to call 911, he'd emerged with an armful of towels for Mr. Fitzweather to hold against himself. He'd kept calm and focused, in charge during the frenzy.

But when Max had seen Sabrina pack up her car to leave, he'd look almost panicked. Which had been kind of nice, even though it was possible he was more concerned about losing a potential investor than he was about not seeing her anymore.

She preferred to think it was the latter.

When she'd told him she was going to take her chances at Seaton House, he'd tried to talk her out of it. But he'd offered no alternative.

One possible thought about where she could stay had flashed through Sabrina's mind like a wicked fantasy masquerading as possibility: Max's place.

Of course, she hadn't told him that, but she'd certainly thought about it for about half a second. Until she'd chickened out, figuring staying with an alleged murderer was safer than sleeping next door to a man she wanted to jump on and ride like one of those horses on the carousel he'd been fixing up.

She shifted in her seat as a hot barrage of images rolled through her mind. Knowing, however, that she couldn't do it, she snuffed the images out. Because she wasn't going to act on this attraction again. She couldn't—not until she knew for sure who he was and what she was going to do about it.

If he *was* just a nice guy who'd been wronged by a woman he'd scorned a few years back—which, knowing Grace, was possible—Sabrina also knew she'd have some damage control to do. Starting with salvaging Max's reputation.

No matter what he was—*who* he was—Sabrina couldn't hide from the truth. She was getting to know him under false pretenses. And sleeping with him while she was still on the fence about whether or not she was going to let the man be crucified in print went against every one of Sabrina's principles.

Making out with him...well, she'd give herself a break on that. What woman would have been able to resist at least a little sin?

But no more. That was the end of it until she'd made her decision about him, one way or the other.

"You researched this place before you came. So just how long have you been planning this trip?" Allie asked.

Seeing an expression of angry confusion on her sister's face, Sabrina told her the truth. "A couple of weeks." Since the minute her boss, Nancy, had used her sources to find out where Max Taylor was hiding out while his lawyer threatened lawsuits.

"And you couldn't be honest about where you were going?"

"I told you I was going away on business."

"To a book expo. I didn't see any books at that inn." Allie's voice grew louder. "Plus, look at your clothes, not to mention this expensive car, which I assume is a rental. What do they have to do with a book expo?"

Sabrina took a deep breath, trying to stay calm and reasonable when she really wanted to yell at her sister. Not for sabotaging Sabrina's "mission" but for getting on a bus while heavily pregnant, telling no one where she was going and trusting complete strangers to drive her to the inn.

Had Sabrina ever been that young and trusting? If so, she certainly wasn't anymore.

"Well?" Allie prompted.

"It's complicated."

"So explain it."

Sabrina was tired of explaining things to people. As much as she loved Allie, there were moments when she really longed for her life to return to what it had been a year ago. When she'd been a hardworking single woman with a job she loved. When she'd lived in the city in her own pretty little apartment where she could walk around naked if she wanted to and never have to explain herself to anyone.

Your fault. It's your fault.

She swallowed the resentment, knowing if it weren't for her, neither of them would be in this position. Her bad judgment had led her to date Peter even though he was a colleague—that was before she'd realized he was also a pig. Yes, her *good* judgment had also led her to break up with him when she'd really gotten to know him. But the damage had been done. She'd invited a serpent into their lives and he'd bitten her sister. Hard.

"Look," she finally said, trying to figure out what to say without hurting Allie's feelings. "This is a really strange job I'm doing. I can't explain it except that I needed to present myself a certain way."

"Yeah, yeah, I get it, you had to look like a rich woman. Something to do with that hunky pilot you were hiding in the bushes with when I showed up?"

Wow, she *did* get it. And not just the job, but Sabrina's obviously physical relationship with Max.

"I figure maybe your company's competing for his book or something. But why couldn't you *tell me?*"

She didn't correct Allie's mistaken assumption. "Maybe because I knew if you found out the whole story you'd harass me into bringing you along."

Allie's brow shot up in indignance. "I wouldn't have—"

"You're here, aren't you?"

"That's different. I'm here to tell you something."

"And if I'd told you everything up front," Sabrina added, not even pausing, "you wouldn't have begged and pleaded to come with me because you're so bored and so lonely and *so* can't stand to be on your own for a few days?"

Her sister's pretty face fell and Sabrina instantly regretted the words. "I'm sorry. I shouldn't have said that."

Drawing in a deep breath, Allie slowly nodded. "Yes, you should have," she replied. "Because you're right. I guess there's a part of me that would have come after you, anyway, even if I didn't have something important to talk to you about." Her voice lowered to a whisper. "To tell you the truth, the closer it gets to the big day, the more convinced I am that I can't deal with this."

Sabrina grabbed her sister's hand. "You can. *We* can. There is no way I'd let you go through it alone, you know that."

"I know. In my brain I know." Allie paused. "But my heart isn't always so sure."

Allie's heart—the one that had been trampled on. First by Peter, then by their family. Their grandfather, who'd declared her immoral and unfit to know. And their mother, who *hadn't* told her father to go to hell and come to stand beside her daughter.

"Look," Sabrina said, remembering, finally, what was most important in her life, "we can go back to Philadelphia if you want. We'll leave now."

It hurt to say the words, to think of leaving, not knowing…always regretting.

No. Max was a fantasy. She should end that fantasy now and be done with it. Go back to work, call Grace and question her thoroughly to see just how much fiction she'd inserted into her "memoir." That certainly wouldn't be a first—something to which Oprah's book club could attest.

And if Grace *had* used a lot of authorial license, Sabrina would tell her to start revising. The book could still proceed, though the watered-down version might not be as attention-getting as the scandalously sexy original. But on the bright side, removing the stuff about Max should at least ensure it wouldn't get shelved in the erotica section of the bookstore.

Then Sabrina could move on. And wonder. Always wonder...

"I don't know if that's such a good idea. Maybe staying away isn't a bad thing," Allie said.

There was that note of trepidation in her sister's voice again, and this time Sabrina zoned in on it. "What, exactly, did you come here to talk to me about?" When Allie looked down at her hands, clenched tightly in her lap, Sabrina added, "Come on, I'm not really mad—just scared-mad." Laughing softly, she added, "Like Mom was the first time you and I ran away from Grandpa's."

Allie immediately remembered. "I was seven."

"And I was twelve."

"We got as far as the bus station that time, too."

"I asked for two tickets to New York."

Allie's eyes grew bright. "And I asked for two to heaven so we could see Daddy."

Then someone who knew their grandfather had called him and he'd dragged them back. Their mother had been frantic—angry because of her fear, but so relieved she'd kept kissing them over and over. At least until their grandfather had put a stop to it, demanding to oversee their punishment.

They'd been on their knees repenting for eight hours,

until poor little Allie's legs had given out and Sabrina had tried to rub them back to life.

"Tell me what's going on so we can deal with it together," she murmured. "Like we always have."

Their heavy silence fell in the car, the only sound the low hum of the engine and the hiss of cold air streaming through the air-conditioning vents. Finally, though, her sister admitted, "I did something really stupid."

"Call out the media," she said with a rueful chuckle. "One of the Cavanaugh girls has done something stupid."

Allie finally smiled.

"Go ahead. Just say it."

Allie opened her mouth to do exactly that, but instead of words, a tiny shriek emerged.

Startled, Sabrina jerked her head around to follow her sister's horrified stare. And echoed Allie's scream. Because right outside her window—his nose almost pressed to the glass—was a dark-eyed, angry looking man.

"Go, go, back up and get out of here," Allie yelled. Her hand clutched her big belly and her eyes bugged out in pure, unadulterated fear.

Sabrina couldn't do a thing. All her horror-movie training and she could only sit there, frozen, like a deer being confronted by a pair of bright headlights. She half wished the psychotic killer would start up his chainsaw right now—maybe the noise would startle her into action.

Staring into the man's face, she was able to grasp a few details—the eyes so brown she couldn't tell the pupils from the irises. The dark, slashing brows tugged down in a severe frown. The jut of his chin and the clench of his jaw. Not to mention a scar running from his temple down beside the corner of his eye to his high cheekbone.

Then he lifted his hand, which, she saw to her immediate relief, wasn't holding a butcher knife or a chainsaw. Rapping his knuckles on the window, he stepped back, obviously waiting for her to open it.

"Don't you dare!" Allie snapped when Sabrina reached for the window control.

Taking a deep breath, she pushed the switch and watched the window descend an inch. "Yes?"

The stranger, clad in black from his head to toe, stared at her from a few feet away, his gaze both fierce and mesmerizing. "Aside from arguing, may I ask what the two of you are doing sitting in a car in my driveway?" he asked, his voice silky smooth. As smooth as his jet-black hair—windswept, though it was a calm day—looked to be.

"Uh, we're…"

"Lost. We're just lost. Turning around now," Allie said, reaching over to grab Sabrina's leg.

Almost wincing at the pinch her sister gave her, Sabrina worked up her nerve and offered the man a weak smile. "We were wondering if perhaps you were open for business. We're looking for a place to stay."

His eyes flared; the man had obviously been caught by surprise. Maybe he wasn't used to his victims landing on his doorstep like this. Sheesh, some serial killer *he* was. Then again, maybe he'd never even seen *Psycho*.

But before she could ask—before she could even grab her sister's fingers and get them off her leg before Allie drew blood—Sabrina saw a welcome sight. Coming down the front steps of the forbidding inn like a welcoming ray of sunshine was a man dressed in an old-fashioned African-safari–looking outfit, complete with knee-length jodhpurs and high boots. Even if she couldn't see the bright white hair cascading out from under the broad-rimmed, beige hat, she would have recognized the man immediately. As he, from his jaunty wave, recognized her.

Saved by the sheikh. Or, judging by his appearance today, the big-game hunter.

She sighed in relief. Because it appeared Mr. Potts had been visiting the resident serial killer. And even if Max Taylor was a danger to women, she knew in her heart that his grandfather was not.

CHAPTER TEN

MORTIMER POTTS WAS NOT only *not* insane, he was also not blind. Some people in this town might have decided he was a bit dotty, particularly after he'd plunked down an exorbitant sum of money to lay claim to a motley assortment of buildings and properties. But nobody had ever questioned his vision.

And he could easily see what was going on right in front of his eyes.

Max was falling fast, falling hard. Probably not in love, but at the very least into infatuation.

Having seen all of his grandsons involved in various romantic entanglements throughout their lives—from Morgan's unrequited love for the most popular young lady in eighth grade to Michael's scandalous affair with a witness to a murder—he'd come to recognize the signs. He'd seen them in Max more than a few times. The boy did enjoy dancing his way in and out of the arms of attractive women. Especially during the past few years when he seemed to think he had something to prove.

Probably not surprising, given what had happened with his wife. Mortimer still hadn't gotten used to that situation. Things were *so* different today than they'd been in his time.

But Max had survived it. And his fancy footwork had

kept him carefully waltzing his way out of any possible entanglements.

Only, he didn't seem to be dancing now. In fact, if Mortimer had to guess, he'd say Max was standing very still, trying to determine just what he felt for Miss Sabrina Cavanaugh.

Interesting. Particularly since his grandson seemed to have shaken off the dark mood that had kept him quiet and unusually morose for the first two weeks of his stay here. Mortimer could only attribute that to the lovely blonde.

Which was why, when he'd heard the woman mention her predicament to the owner of Seaton House—an interesting fellow, that one—he'd immediately come up with a suggestion. There was absolutely no need for Sabrina and her prettily pregnant sister to leave Trouble.

They could simply come stay with him.

Sabrina had demurred, of course, but Mortimer hadn't been willing to take no for an answer. Besides, though her mouth had declined, something in her eyes told him the young lady was every bit as keen to stay in town as he was to have her here. And not, he was willing to venture, for any investment reasons.

Seemed to him that Miss Cavanaugh hadn't even mentioned her interest in "investing" since the day she'd arrived. Which led Mortimer to suspect her reasons for remaining in Trouble were personal rather than financial. Personal reasons with his grandson's name written all over them.

"So you're sure that guy's not a killer?" the younger sister—Allie—said from the back seat of the car as they rode toward his home. "He looks like a vampire or something."

Mortimer snorted. "It is my belief that Mr. Lebeaux's reputation has been greatly exaggerated." Mortimer was certainly acquainted with that experience and had great tolerance for anyone in such a situation.

Though, to be honest, he hadn't quite believed his new neighbor's entire explanation as to why he was currently living in a drafty old hotel in the middle of nowhere. There was more to the story, Mortimer would wager on it.

Fortunately for Mr. Lebeaux, Mortimer was rather adept at minding his own business. At least when it didn't involve a member of his own family.

"You're very nice to let us stay with you," Allie said.

"You're sure Max won't mind?" Sabrina murmured. Her voice was a bit thin, as if now that she'd finally agreed to his plan, she was having second thoughts.

"Certainly not. Besides, it isn't as if you'll be underfoot. He'll barely know you're there, for the most part. You should be quite comfortable in the tent."

"I like camping," the one in the back seat said, her words slow, as if she feared offending him. "But I'm not so sure in my current condition that I'll be up for roughing it for too long."

Mortimer laughed. So did Sabrina. She shifted her gaze toward him and their eyes met in companionable commiseration.

He liked this girl. Had liked her since the moment she'd stepped into his tent and decreed it one of the most beautiful things she'd ever seen.

"My dear," Mortimer explained, "there's no such thing as roughing it in one of my tents. They come from Shari Khayyamiya—the Street of Tents—in Cairo. And I've added a few modern conveniences."

"Like a generator with lights and air-conditioning," Sabrina said dryly. "Not to mention the mountains of pillows. I've seen less plush rooms in four-star hotels."

Exactly, and quite the point. Mortimer hadn't minded *roughing it,* as the youngster had called it, when he was in his twenties. Now, however, his aching bones weren't up to being rolled in a scratchy blanket smelling of horses and sweaty men and laid on a dirt floor.

"I can't wait to see it," the girl said, then she covered her mouth in an attempt to hide a yawn.

So young to be in her condition. Mortimer had, of course, noticed the lack of a wedding ring on her finger, but he was no prude. He merely wondered what the girl's situation was, and whether her sister had taken on the role of weary caretaker for good or merely for the duration of the pregnancy.

He'd like to think she'd be free and unencumbered soon. And that she liked the idea of pregnancy and babies. Because ever since the moment he'd had the fleeting hope that Max's problems involved getting a woman in trouble, he hadn't been able to stop thinking about having a great-grandchild.

A little girl. One just like her grandmother.

Though he'd deny it—especially to Roderick, were he around to see—Mortimer was aware of the quick rush of moisture in his eyes as he thought of his own Carla, the boys' mother. No one should ever have to outlive their child. No one.

The grief of it would probably have done him in if it hadn't been for Carla's three sons, who'd stared at him from across her flower-laden coffin, alone in the world and wondering what was to become of them.

Mortimer had become of them. And what a time they'd had.

She'd be proud. Somewhere, he felt quite sure, Carla *was* proud of the men they'd become. Except for one thing—the lack of families, wives, children, of their own.

"Well," he said, clearing his throat and thrusting the

sadness out of his mind, "I'm sure you'll be quite comfortable and you're welcome to stay as long as you'd like."

He meant it. He rather hoped this young woman driving a bit too fast up his driveway would stay long enough to bring some excitement—perhaps even happiness—into his grandson's life. If Mortimer had to pull a few strings to make that happen, well, so be it. After all, he'd already bought himself a town, knowing full well his middle grandson would show up sooner or later to try to get him out of the deal. So cajoling a young woman to be his houseguest didn't sound nearly as meddlesome.

Whether Max would see it that way, however, remained to be seen.

WHY MAX HAD EVER for a moment thought the idea of Sabrina Cavanaugh and her sister staying at his grandfather's house—er, his grandfather's tent—was a good one, he'd never know. Because now that he'd had a couple of days to get used to the arrangement, he was in agony.

It was absolute torture to know the woman he'd been wanting since the moment they'd met was sleeping a few yards outside his door and he couldn't do a thing about it. And not just because of the stupid book. A wide-eyed, big-bellied chaperone had been glued to Sabrina's side for forty-eight hours. Plus, Max's own grandfather had been playing the role of host to the hilt.

He hadn't seen Sabrina alone since Sunday morning when he kissed her outside the Dewdrop Inn.

"That was mistake number eighty in the hundred mistakes you've made since you met that woman. Never should have kissed her," he muttered as he strode down the hill into the woods that separated Mortimer's property from the old amusement park. If he couldn't do what he really wanted to do—make something hot and intense happen with Sabrina—he figured he might as well pound the crap out of some metal.

That damn carousel was going to go around again if it was the last thing Max ever did. The thing had become a personal challenge and he was going to fix it or blow it up. He wasn't sure which.

Fix it. You can make it work.

The carousel. He meant the carousel. Not his relationship with Sabrina.

He was still telling himself that two hours later as he kicked the junction box with his boot, then started cussing because it hurt.

"Now I *am* going to have to wash your mouth out with soap."

Jerking his head, he spotted her watching him from a few feet away. He should have been surprised, but he wasn't. He'd known Sabrina would show up here. That if she found out where he'd gone, she'd find a reason to come after him, and not just because of the lure this tired old spot held for both of them.

Strange, this certainty, and he wondered if she felt it, too. But there was something between them—a connection. Now that they were practically roommates, it had only grown. Especially because for the past couple of days, when they'd shared friendly conversation and meals with her sister and his grandfather, and walks around town, he'd been silently asking a question: *when?* And she'd been silently answering it: *soon.*

"Déjà vu all over again, huh?"

"But this time I heard everything." Shaking her head, she tsked, though the disapproving expression couldn't disguise the smile lurking around her full lips. "Such language."

YOUR OPINION POLL
THANK-YOU FREE GIFTS INCLUDE

▶ **2 ROMANCE OR 2 SUSPENSE BOOKS**

▶ **A LOVELY SURPRISE GIFT**

OFFICIAL OPINION POLL

YOUR OPINION COUNTS!

Please check TRUE or FALSE below to express your opinion about the following statements:

Q1 Do you believe in "true love"?

"TRUE LOVE HAPPENS ONLY ONCE IN A LIFETIME."   ○ TRUE   ○ FALSE

Q2 Do you think marriage has any value in today's world?

"YOU CAN BE TOTALLY COMMITTED TO SOMEONE WITHOUT BEING MARRIED."   ○ TRUE   ○ FALSE

Q3 What kind of books do you enjoy?

"A GREAT NOVEL MUST HAVE A HAPPY ENDING."   ○ TRUE   ○ FALSE

Place the sticker next to one of the selections below to receive your 2 **FREE BOOKS** and **FREE GIFT**. I understand that I am under no obligation to purchase anything as explained on the back of this card.

Romance

193 MDL EE5Z

393 MDL EE3Q

Suspense

192 MDL EE6D

392 MDL EE32

0074823 | FREE GIFT CLAIM # **3 6 2 2**

FIRST NAME   LAST NAME

ADDRESS

APT.#   CITY

STATE / PROV.   ZIP / POSTAL CODE   (TF-HQN-06)

The Reader Service — Here's How It Works:

Accepting your 2 free books and gift places you under no obligation to buy anything. You may keep the books and gift and return the shipping statement marked "cancel." If you do not cancel, about a month later we'll send you 3 additional books and bill you just $5.24 each in the U.S., or $5.74 each in Canada, plus 25¢ shipping & handling per book and applicable taxes if any.* That's the complete price, and — compared to cover prices of $5.99 or more each in the U.S. and $6.99 or more in Canada — it's quite a bargain! You may cancel at any time, but if you choose to continue, every month we'll send you 3 more books, which you may either purchase at the discount price...or return to us and cancel your subscription.

*Terms and prices subject to change without notice. Sales tax applicable in N.Y.
Canadian residents will be charged applicable provincial taxes and GST.

Rising to his feet, Max brushed off his hands on his jeans and shrugged. "Ex military."

"Is that where you learned to fly?"

"No. I'd been doing that since I was a teenager. I always wanted to fly for the U.S. Air Force." He paused before quietly adding, "Like my father."

"But you didn't?"

"I could have, but life interfered. Staying in for the years pilot training would have required seemed to have too high a cost."

"What did you think it would cost you, that shaggy haircut?" she asked, her eyes twinkling.

"And a family."

She blinked. "You wanted that?"

"Sure. I wouldn't have gotten married if I hadn't."

Max hadn't planned on letting those words come out of his mouth. Honestly, he didn't talk about his marriage very much, and they certainly weren't having some deep, intense, let's-share-our-shit conversation. But something made him want to be honest about that much, at least. Maybe to make up for the fact that he'd been trying to act like he was an angel when devil's horns had been growing out of his forehead since birth.

"I had no idea you were married." Her gaze shifted to his bare left hand. "And...divorced?"

He nodded, noting her surprise. With today's divorce rate, it really wasn't that shocking, but Sabrina seemed genuinely taken aback. "Is that so unusual?"

Shaking her head, she quickly said, "No, it's not. I just...hadn't realized."

"It's not like you get to wear a divorce ring to let every new person you meet know about it," he said with a small smile, wondering how far to go with this friendly chat.

Considering how comfortable he already felt with Sabrina, he suspected it could be far. Farther into Max's private life and history than he'd gone with any woman in a long time.

Not about everything, certainly. He wasn't interested in talking about what it had been like to watch TV coverage of his dad being blown out of the sky over the desert, or to see his mother being eaten from inside by disease. But his marriage had always made for some interesting conversation. And once Max had stopped feeling the need to punch his friends—who had gotten a good couple of years' worth of jokes out of it—he'd begun to see the whole thing for the learning experience it had really been.

He'd definitely learned one thing: people could make you believe *anything* if they really tried hard enough. His wife certainly had. He'd believed she loved him. He'd believed she wanted him. He'd believed she wanted a normal, happy marriage.

He'd believed she'd been pregnant when he married her. Uh…no.

"I didn't mean to pry," Sabrina said as she stepped over his toolbox and moved closer.

"You're not prying. You didn't ask, I told you. It's not a big deal, I just thought you should know."

Maybe because something deep inside told him they were going to take a step forward, and soon. Physically, emotionally—didn't matter, really. Either way she probably deserved to know a little more about him. And he'd definitely like to know more about her—like why she was responsible for her pregnant sister who looked like a teenager and where the hell the rest of their family was.

The plastic bottle of water in Sabrina's hand reminded Max that he was thirsty. It was a hot summer day. She'd thought ahead, he had not.

Without much thinking about it, he reached for the bottle. Twisting off the lid, he lifted it to his mouth, pausing for a second when he saw the small smear of pink lipstick on its rim. God, he wanted to kiss her again. And her lips would only be the first of many places he'd kiss once he got started.

As he drank, Sabrina murmured, "Sure, help yourself."

When he was finished, he wiped off his mouth with the back of his hand, then screwed the top back on the bottle. As he handed it back to her, their fingers brushed—his cool and moist with condensation, hers warm and soft, kissed by the sun.

Together they were just about perfect.

"Thanks, I was thirsty."

"Funny, you don't seem the type to reach out and grab what you want," she said, staring at him intently, her big blue eyes holding a question.

She was talking to the nice guy she'd met that first day. The one shocked by the idea of waitresses in tiny T-shirts.

Hell, Max owned stock in Hooters.

This farce was getting old. He just couldn't pretend to be what he was not. So maybe it was time to stop even trying, the book be damned and Grace along with it. "That's something you ought to know about me," he murmured. "I sometimes don't wait to ask when there's something I want."

Max half expected her to lick her lips, to step closer, to melt into him. Put one slender hand on his chest and twine the other in his hair and draw him down for a sultry kiss.

Instead, she shifted back. Color rose in her cheeks and her gaze moved down so that she no longer met his stare.

He'd increased the stakes and she'd pushed away from the table. Though he knew he should be relieved, since they were in an only partially secluded place in broad daylight, he couldn't help feeling disappointed. Because the Sabrina who'd gone after that fat postman who'd mouthed off to Grandfather Saturday morning didn't seem like the type who'd back off of anything.

He thought about the way she'd abruptly ended their crazy sexy encounter Sunday morning outside the inn. Something had made her back off then, too. Which, looking back, had been a good thing, since her sister had showed up. Though, at the time, it had felt like someone had put a vice around his nuts and a rope around his neck and pulled both of them tight.

"So how long were you married?"

Ah, she wanted details. That explained the reticence.

He really felt like telling her to be careful what she asked for. Too much 411—at least in the case of his marriage—could be a pretty uncomfortable thing. "About a year. Just as long as it took to get divorced."

Yeah. It had been two days shy of a year from the day he caught his wife in bed with someone else to the day he'd held the signed divorce decree in his hand. Max knew the date of the decree by heart. Because that night had been the last night of his old life.

His *new* one had begun the next morning, when his brother, Morgan, had showed up at Max's beach house, which he'd purchased with his trust fund when he turned twenty-five. It was the only remaining asset from the family money Max had inherited. The rest had gone through his fingers like sand through a sieve—or liquor through a bottle.

Morgan had taken a good look around at the crowd— the empty bottles, the girls, the professional revelers who'd been using Max's beautiful house as a party palace—and kicked Max's ass.

"You must have been young when you got married."

"Barely twenty-four. I was in the Air Force, stationed in Germany when we met."

"She was a European?"

He sighed. "No. Actually, she was a lesbian."

It was amazing how that statement caught people off guard. Saying it out loud still shocked *Max* sometimes, and he'd been living with the knowledge for several years now.

Sabrina went through the quick succession of reactions that everyone did when a man admitted something as… unmanly as the fact that his wife had preferred other women. Her eyes got so big they could have been used as headlights. Her mouth fell open, though she quickly snapped it shut. And she shook her head back and forth rapidly, as if trying to force the mental images out of her mind, as well as making sure she'd heard him correctly.

Kind of like his reaction when he'd found out. All except for the "storming out and going on a twelve-month drunk" part. So far, Sabrina wasn't taking off for the nearest bar.

"I can't believe you just said that."

"You get used to it," he said with a shrug.

"But, to come out and say it like that, with no build-up…"

"What, was I supposed to start out slow by saying I noticed she liked to wear ugly shoes and watch reruns of *Ellen?*"

Sabrina came closer—close enough for him to smell the light fragrance of fruit and flowers that he would forever associate with her hair. Especially when he pictured her dressed as she was now, in a pair of tight white cropped jeans and a reddish pink top scooped low to reveal the top curves of her pretty, delicate breasts, which he so wanted to taste again.

Soon. Very soon.

"You're joking, right? I mean, you're pulling my leg. You didn't really mean…"

"Oh, yeah, I meant it."

He'd figured he might as well get this conversation over with. If Sabrina had cooled off because he'd been divorced, this could cinch the deal. Better to find out now. "You okay?"

She leaned back against the carousel, then slowly slid down against a pole until her butt landed on the dusty floor. He almost warned her about the effects of twenty-five years' worth of dirt and rust on her white jeans, but figured it was too late. Besides, there was something wickedly arousing about standing beside her when she was sitting, her face about even with his hip.

That thought brought such a sharp, sexual image into his head that he had to shift to the side, so she wouldn't see the way his body had reacted.

Christ, he'd only kissed the woman twice, hadn't touched her in two days, and he was as hard for her as if they'd been rolling around naked in a tub of Jell-O.

She finally spoke again. "Was she *insane?*"

He appreciated the note of incredulity in her voice. "Nope. Just greedy. And a liar."

Her brow lifted.

"She fooled everyone about who she was and what she wanted," he explained. "Lied to me and her family and her friends. Even to herself, I think."

"You're actually fine about this?" Sabrina asked, still sounding disbelieving.

He shrugged. "*Fine* is a strong word. I dealt with it in one way or another." Some self-destructive, some less so. "But I moved on. Trusted karma, 'what goes around'—all that Dr. Phil shit."

"Did it come around?"

"Oh, yeah."

He fell silent, not seeing the need to get any further into the details. What was the point in telling Sabrina that he'd been married for his trust fund, which some of his buddies had told his ex about? Or that Teresa had claimed she was pregnant to get what she wanted—his ring on her finger. His money in her bank account.

Mostly he didn't need to tell her about the stupid things he'd been thinking about family and children, which had led him to make one of the biggest mistakes of his life— he'd dropped out of the Air Force pilot training program. All so he could be an around-the-house dad, not an around-the-world one.

And so no child of his would ever be eating his Cheerios and catch sight of the morning news repeating and repeating the image of his father's plane exploding out of the sky.

Only there wasn't any baby. He'd eventually found out there never had been one.

While Teresa might have fooled herself into thinking she could change who she was for the sake of the money Max stood to inherit, she hadn't been able to make it through the first year of their marriage—to Max's twenty-fifth birthday, trust fund day—without getting what she truly wanted: a girlfriend.

When it all blew up, she lost Max *and* his money, thanks to his excellent lawyer. The girlfriend, who'd also been counting Max's pennies before he'd inherited them, dumped her, as well.

Teresa had ended up alone and broke. So, yeah, what she'd sown, she'd definitely reaped. Not that he was vindictive anymore—he might never entirely forgive his ex-wife, but at least he didn't hate her the way he once had.

And she'd certainly left an impression on his life, one he'd never forget. Some things couldn't be forgotten and some lessons, once learned, would remain imbedded forever. Like his intolerance for liars and people who claimed to be one thing when they were really another.

Which made him feel even crappier about having pretended to be something he wasn't when he first met Sabrina.

Not that he'd been very good at playing Mr. Squeaky Clean, but he had tried. Whether he'd had a good reason or not, he'd disliked the deception and was glad it was over. He'd be himself from here on out. Hell, he'd pretty much *been* himself for the past several days, anyway, and she hadn't gone running.

Someday maybe he'd even work up the nerve to admit the whole thing to her, once all this book crap was over with.

"How did you find out?" she finally asked.

Realizing she wasn't going to let this go without a few more details, Max sighed and sat beside her on the floor of the carousel. His thigh brushed against hers and his mind instantly went down *that* road. But he still managed to answer her question. "I walked in on them."

"Them?" Then she gasped. "Oh, God, *them?*"

"Yeah." With a wicked grin he added, "And since it wasn't my birthday I figured out what was going on pretty damn quick."

Sabrina rolled her eyes. "You're such a guy."

"Exactly."

Just an average guy with sex on the brain, and it was nice to be able to act like one—like himself—instead of pretending he was some kind of lame-ass choirboy who didn't have a dick much less know what to do with it.

"You're so calm about this."

"I wasn't at first. Especially when my buddies started with the 'eating at the Y' comments."

She shuddered. "I can't believe you're joking about it."

He hadn't at first, not for months. But that was another conversation, one he wasn't ready to have with her. One he'd only had with a few other people—those closest to him. The ones who'd done the intervention and made him realize his drinking and wild lifestyle had gone from a brief crutch to a potential lifelong problem. Grandfather and his brothers.

Nobody else knew why he hadn't shared in a celebratory glass of champagne when they'd christened the new jets Taylor Made had added to the fleet last year. Nor asked him about the club soda with lime that was in his hand at every cocktail party. Or demanded to know why he always killed off an enormous bottle of Coke during a ball game, rather than a beer.

It was his problem. He'd dealt with it. End of story.

"Did you...did you try to do anything about it?" she asked, sounding tentative, as if she realized his mind had suddenly gone far, far away.

"What was I supposed to do? Force her to become something she wasn't?" Then, because Sabrina still seemed so stunned, he added, "You want to hear something really twisted?"

"More twisted than a woman married to one of the sexiest men on earth deciding she'd rather sleep with women?"

Laughing, he nodded. "Yeah."

"Sure."

Sliding off the merry-go-round, he squatted in front of her so they were eye level. Then he told her something he'd realized several years ago but had never shared with anyone else. And had never expected to. "It was better that it was a woman."

Now her jaw really dropped. For a second he wanted to ask Sabrina if she was a big milk drinker, because she had great teeth, not a filling in sight.

"You're kidding."

"Nope. After I calmed down and could think straight again, I realized it would have been worse if she'd been cheating with another man. That would have been head-to-head competition. And losing to a man would have made me, well, a loser."

She slowly nodded. "But you couldn't compete with a woman?"

"You got it. Can't go head to head, so to speak, when you don't have the same equipment."

She smiled a little. The first time since he'd dropped the gay-bomb on her. "Which made it all okay?"

"As okay as it can get," he said.

"Did it— Never mind."

"What?"

Seeing the way her chest rose and fell as she drew in deep breaths, he was prepared for another uncomfortable question. He simply hadn't realized quite how uncomfortable it would be until she put it into words.

"Did it make you hate women?" Her words stumbled over each other. "Did you want to punish them or something?"

"Hell, no," he said with a bark of laughter. "I love women."

Couldn't get enough of them in fact.

"But what about the long term? Marriage?"

He caught her drift. What kind of self-respecting female wouldn't want to know right up front if a man was a lost cause in terms of commitment, happily-ever-after and all that stuff they put so much emphasis on?

Max could have lied. Maybe a few years ago, he would

have, just to ensure he was going to get into her pants. But he didn't. Whoever he might have been in the past, deceiving her wasn't who he was now. "I don't see that happening again, Sabrina. I'm not exactly marriage material." Shaking his head, he added, "I come with too much baggage."

She continued to stare at him, her blue eyes clear, her gaze steady. He'd thrown the ball back into her court. Now she had to decide whether she wanted to pick it up and keep playing, or figure there was no way she was going to win and walk off without letting either one of them score.

Damn, his mind did turn in sexual ways.

"Okay," she said with a nod, not appearing disappointed or confused in any way. "I can understand that."

Rising to his feet, he reached for her hand to pull her up, as well. She took it and started to stand. With the backs of Sabrina's calves pressed against the carousel and Max standing right in front of her, she had nowhere to go but straight up.

It was a long, slow slide. And she ended up a few inches from him. Close enough for him to see the shine on her pretty pink lips when she licked them. Plus the warmth—and compassion—in her eyes.

Not rejection. Not pity. Not amusement. Not greed. Thank heaven. He'd had enough of those to last his lifetime.

"Oh, God," she whispered, her eyes narrowing and her head tilting as she stared at him, "that explains it."

"Explains what?" he asked, a little wary.

She opened her mouth as if to answer, then closed it again like she didn't know what to say. But she had something on her mind—the woman looked stunned, as if someone had just proved to her the world was flat instead of round. Though it made no sense to Max, it somehow seemed the pathetic story of his love life had knocked down whatever barriers Sabrina had erected against him and made her see him in a new light.

He wanted to find out if his theory was right. Intended to find out, in fact. It would be easy to do, just by pulling her closer, wrapping his arms around her and kissing any remaining words right off her tongue.

Then he'd ask her to fly with him.

But he didn't have to. Because suddenly Sabrina grabbed the front of his shirt in both her hands and pushed him around until he was the one leaning against the carousel pole. Before he could ask what was going on, she was diving onto his mouth like it was an oxygen mask and the aircraft was losing pressure.

He kissed her back, thrust his tongue deep and hard against hers, feeling in her slim body all the hunger they'd been dancing around since the day they'd met. Something had snapped, crackled and popped and she was all demanding, devouring woman.

Their tongues tangling and mating, he reached for her hips and tugged her closer against him, until she could feel the rock-hard response of his body. He groaned when she responded by lifting her legs and wrapping them around his waist, arching against him until he could feel the dampness of her through her jeans. She jerked, took the pressure she needed, and a low, keening cry emerged from her throat. Like she could get off just by rubbing him the right way.

"Sabrina, yes…" he muttered against her mouth as he tugged her legs tighter, dying to release his cock and plunge into her right here and now.

He was about to do it—was reaching toward his zipper,

in fact—when he heard a woman's voice calling. A familiar voice.

And the barking of a spastic dog. A familiar dog.

Damn.

"You have got to be kidding me," Sabrina muttered with a frustrated groan.

Somehow managing to disguise his own groan as a sigh, he slowly let Sabrina down, feeling her frustration in the stiffness of her shoulders and arms.

"I'm going to kill her," she muttered.

"Stand in line."

Shifting to straighten out his jeans, he cleared his throat and watched Sabrina's sister emerge from the woods. Allie bounced along as jauntily as a heavily pregnant young woman tugging a reluctant dog behind her could.

Allie Cavanaugh might not be a five-year-old, but she had the timing of a classic bratty little sister. Once again, her arrival had come just in time to stop Max from doing what he most wanted to do with Sabrina: make love to her until neither one of them could think.

Before she got within earshot, he whispered, "Do you suppose we could ditch her the way I used to ditch my kid brother when he was being a pest?"

"How are you at climbing trees?"

"Excellent. Had a lot of practice at running away and hiding as a kid."

"Me, too."

He chuckled. "So you were a bad kid, too? I knew there was something I liked about you."

"What's that?" she asked, crossing her arms in front of her chest and lifting a brow. "That I remind you of you?"

"Yeah." His smile slowly fading, he lowered his voice to say, "Though I think I like you better."

She didn't look away—not immediately. And for that one long second, when they stared at each other, they both acknowledged what would have happened if her sister hadn't shown up.

Finally breaking the stare, Sabrina nodded toward her sister. "Tempting as it sounds to run away, she's my responsibility."

Yeah, he got that. He just wanted to know *why*.

"And maybe it's for the best."

"You're kidding, right?"

Sabrina's eyes were wide and shiny and her well-kissed mouth tight with tension. "I need to think," she whispered, keeping her focus on Allie, who was coming closer with every step.

"Think about what?"

"About whether that was a good thing or not."

Her sister showing up? Or what had almost happened between them on the floor of that carousel?

He had no idea. Before he could find out, Allie had walked within earshot. And Sabrina had put that invisible wall firmly back in place.

CHAPTER ELEVEN

It had been hard enough for Tom King to sneak into the old Stuttgardt place at night when just the old man and his grandson were living there. Now, with the two women and that stupid dog staying in a tent right outside the back door, it had become nearly impossible.

Parked on the side of the road running behind the property late Tuesday morning, he saw a car approach, and slid down in his seat. Fortunately, Tom did not recognize the driver.

But his luck wouldn't hold out forever. Sooner or later Chief Bennigan was going to start wondering why Tom's car was often parked, half hidden, in the woods behind the infamous house. Especially late at night.

"It might be time to give this up," he muttered aloud, wanting some sound, even if it was just his own voice. The radio had given out in this old piece of junk long ago. Another reminder of the penniless hell his life had become—all thanks to his former employer, Wilhelm Stuttgardt.

That man hadn't only stolen a lot of folks' money, he'd stolen their futures, Tom included. By embezzling every hard-earned dollar his employees had contributed to their pension funds, what the fiend had really stolen was their golden years.

Which was why it was only right and proper that the clockmaker had paid for his crimes. And why no one in this town had much cared that whoever killed him hadn't been caught.

If only Stuttgardt had revealed a useful bit of information before he'd died instead of some foolish, cryptic riddle.

So go home, it's pointless.

Whatever Wilhelm had done with the money he'd stolen from this town during his term as mayor—and from all his employees at the factory—someone else would have to find it. Tom was getting too tired and frustrated to look any longer. Creeping through that house in the middle of the night, he'd begun to feel his age. He'd also started thinking the so-called *clue* the Feeney sisters had helped him figure out had been a false one.

For five years, everyone who was anyone in Trouble had been scratching their heads, speculating over what old Willie had meant by his final words, "The money will be found in time."

Had he put it in some kind of secured account until a set date? Hidden it in a place so obvious that someone would find it eventually? Left it with a lawyer who'd return it to the town once the old scoundrel died?

No one knew. And no money had turned up. Not in five years.

Even Tom had stopped wondering, until Ida Mae made a joking comment about Wilhelm's famous last words. "Maybe the treasure was hidden in the courthouse clock," she'd said one day last month, smirking with malicious glee at the very idea, since the bat-infested clock tower had burned down a few summers ago.

But Tom hadn't laughed. Oh, no. Instead, something had clicked in him. *The clocks. Stuttgardt's clocks.*

No, they weren't large enough to hold a few million dollars in cash, but they certainly could hold a key to a safe deposit box. Or a map. Some kind of clue on this treasure hunt.

So he'd gone hunting. Had *been* hunting for weeks now, but time was quickly running out.

If only the hag had made the offhand comment long ago, rather than just days before Potts had moved into the old house. All that time the place had been standing there empty, everything exactly as it had been on the day Stuttgardt died. Well, pretty much as it had been. Some treasure hunters had combed through there in the early days after the murder, until the police had locked the place up.

Not, of course, until after the chief had searched it himself.

Eventually, no one had even seemed interested in looking for the stolen money anymore, except drunk teenagers who sometimes threw rocks through a window to get in. But for the most part, folks around here had come to believe Stuttgardt had deposited his ill-gotten gains in some foreign bank account where it would never be found. That his final words were one last malicious trick—a final thrust of the knife to the heart of the town he'd killed with his greed.

But Ida Mae's spiteful comment—made when he'd been delivering the hush money she demanded to keep his most shameful secret—had aroused Tom's curiosity again. It had been enough to make him want to do some searching.

A year ago, he would have had lots of privacy to do it. He probably would have finished up in a matter of days.

Unfortunately, it wasn't to be. Because now the house was occupied again, by a rich busybody who thought he could lord over all of them just because he had some money to throw around.

So for the past few weeks, Tom had been confined to treasure hunting primarily during nighttime hours. Even working furtively under the cover of darkness, he'd managed a basic inspection of most of the clocks—enough to make him think he'd now wasted even more of his life on a lost cause.

But a suggestion from a friend had made him wonder if it was possible the clue could be accessed only at a certain time of day, when the hour and minute hands were in a certain position. He wouldn't put it past the wily old German to have made a special device with a hidden cubbyhole to hide his dirty secret. One that could only be accessed when the hour struck two or some such nonsense.

So each night he set the cursed things, wound them and sat there watching them tick. But he'd found nothing. And every time he went back he grew more afraid that one day the old man or his grandson would come down the stairs and mistake him for a burglar. Which was why he had a gun tucked into his belt.

The gun was currently digging into his back, so he shifted on the seat. Peering out the streaked window, he waited to see if Potts really was going out today, as he'd heard he would be. While keeping a close watch on the house this morning, he'd seen all of them leave—all except the old man.

Glancing at his watch and noting the time, he shook his head. His information must have been wrong—Potts was sticking close to home. He'd come out here for nothing.

Not sure whether he was relieved or disappointed, he reached for the ignition key. But just then, Mortimer Potts exited the house. Tom hunkered down again, watching out the passenger window as Potts strolled along the driveway and walked off toward downtown. For a rich old geezer, the man sure liked to walk a lot. He rarely drove around in his big Cadillac, which was parked in the garage gathering dust.

If Tom had that car, he'd be cruising all over town even if he just needed a roll of toilet paper. Of course, if he had Potts's money, he'd have a driver to move him from his front door to his mailbox, as well as getting said toilet paper.

"The house is empty," he muttered, not sure whether he was glad for this new opportunity or not. It was risky—he couldn't be sure Potts or one of the others wouldn't come back and catch him in the act.

Part of him had been hoping for an excuse to take the day off, something he hadn't done since the demand he'd gotten from Ida Mae Feeney last week. The demand had reminded him of what was at stake—why he could not let this go without fighting a little more. Because money didn't grow on trees and he had to come up with some soon or else risk Ida Mae ruining him by opening her mouth.

Besides, Trouble might not be much, but it was his home. His family had lived here for generations. Rumor had it his own ancestor had been the one who'd started calling the odd assortment of buildings out here in the middle of nowhere a town. Treble Town, at first, since it sat at the base of a trio of rocky mountains. Then, eventually, just Trouble.

He couldn't let it be turned into a playground for a rich old man with time to kill any more than he could afford to ignore the danger from Ida Mae.

If only someone would come along and drop a house on that old witch. Of course, *he* couldn't do it—Ida Mae had told him she and her equally wicked sister had hidden away some proof that would come out if anything happened to them.

Not that Tom would go around killing old ladies, no, sir. But a man couldn't be blamed for wishing the right hand of God would come down and slap those two women like it had Wilhelm Stuttgardt.

Someday he'd be free of them one way or another. Either one of them would drop dead, or he would.

Right now, he couldn't say which he wished for more. Because even in his most optimistic of moods, he found it more and more difficult to believe he might ever actually fulfill his dream: find Willie's stolen money, give most of it back to the town...then take what he was owed and disappear.

ALLIE LOVED TROUBLE. She'd only been here a few days but she already felt more at home in this small town than she had the entire two years she'd lived in Philadelphia. Or the ones she'd lived in Bridgerton, Ohio.

It could have been because she'd already made such nice friends here—like Mr. Potts, and Max, who was so far gone over her sister Sabrina he was almost on another continent. And Emily Baker, the nice lady she'd met on the bus, who had invited Allie to come over for lunch Wednesday afternoon.

She'd had a passing curiosity about whether Emily's nephew, Joey, the one with the nice smile, would be there, but she hadn't asked. It just hadn't seemed an appropriate question considering she was seven months pregnant with another man's child.

Peter. She'd managed to put him out of her mind for a couple of days now. Out of mind...and out of conversation. Somehow, that whole talk she'd planned to have with

Sabrina about how funny it had been—funny *ack*, not funny ha-ha—to have run into the man like that, when they all thought he was long gone, uh, just hadn't happened.

They'd both gotten caught up in other things—like supposed serial killers and a sweet old man who told funny stories and brewed the most delicious spiced tea. A sexy pilot who had the broadest shoulders Allie had ever seen and who was practically a walking erection around her big sister.

Not that Sabrina seemed ready to believe that. Which made Allie laugh. Though Sabrina was the older one, she didn't see men as clearly as Allie did these days and had shrugged off the idea that Max Taylor was dying for her.

Of course, Sabrina wouldn't admit she was dying for him, either, which made them both pretty entertaining to watch.

So, yes, there were lots of other things to talk about. So many other *nice* things that a nasty topic like Peter Poophead hadn't even seemed worth bringing up.

Chicken. There had been plenty of opportunities for her to come clean with her sister, even though Sabrina had not come completely clean with her. For instance, she'd sworn Allie to secrecy about what Sabrina really did for a living. She'd also ordered her to say nothing about their lives that would reveal as much as a hint that Sabrina did not have money to invest in this town.

Money to invest? That was the biggest laugh of all. Because if Sabrina had an extra dime, she'd have spent it on a baby rattle, of that Allie had no doubt.

But Allie hadn't argued. In fact, when wandering around town on Monday, she'd quite enjoyed dropping hints that she was the sister of a rich woman. Everyone she met had just been so impressed and kind. The manager of the charming little tavern where Allie stopped for lunch had told her she was so pretty she ought to compete in the Miss Trouble pageant at the Founders' Day carnival this weekend.

Not that she would in her condition—but it was awfully nice to have someone think of her as Miss Trouble rather than Miss *in* Trouble.

"So you're sure you don't need a ride home this afternoon?" Max asked from the front seat of his car on Wednesday as they drove toward Miss Emily's house.

"I'm sure. Your grandfather said he'd come by and pick me up," she answered. Mr. Potts hadn't exactly offered—Allie had asked, mainly because Miss Emily was such a nice old lady and Mr. Potts was such a nice old man, and nice old people deserved to be nice together, didn't they? She had asked for the ride precisely so she'd have the chance to hook them up.

Allie might not be able to make a love connection for herself, but she liked the idea that she had some skill as a matchmaker. She only hoped Mr. Potts wouldn't forget. She'd asked yesterday morning and he'd kindly agreed, but he'd also been scarce since then. She hadn't seen him at all and hoped whatever was keeping him so busy wouldn't make him forget his promise.

She wasn't about to tell Max and Sabrina that, however. Knowing her overprotective sibling, Sabrina would insist on coming to get her, cutting short whatever plans Max had lined up for this afternoon. "I feel bad enough about having to ask you for the ride there," she added. "I'm sure you have lots to do."

That was another reason Allie had accepted Miss Emily's invitation—to give these two a chance to be alone. By the time she'd realized what they were up to yesterday at that broken-down old park, it had been too late to turn around and pretend she'd never been there. Besides, having seen a dirty, dingy car parked half hidden in the woods on the other side of the house—away from the park but in sight of the tent—Allie had felt the tiniest bit nervous about going back to the house alone. She could have sworn she'd seen someone sitting in the driver's seat, hunkered low. Considering there were no other houses anywhere near Mr. Potts's, she couldn't understand why someone would have been hovering around like that.

Probably, though, her imagination was just playing games with her head. It did that a lot. Especially now that she was pregnant. She had, in fact, begun suspecting that there was a secret message saying, "Go eat ice cream" flashing every two-point-eight seconds during *Entertainment Tonight*, because she was always digging into the Chunky Monkey by seven-thirty p.m. these days.

"It was no problem," Sabrina insisted. "It's nothing important. As a matter of fact, you're welcome to come with us if you'd rather not go to lunch."

Ha. She was making excuses, as if trying to avoid being alone with Max.

Well, *that* wasn't going to happen. If Sabrina needed a little push out of the nest, baby bird was ready to shove with both wings and her beak.

"No, thanks. But again, Max, I really appreciate you giving me a ride," she said. "I know you two probably have tons to do. Miss Emily offered to come get me, but it seemed like such an imposition after she'd already invited me to come over."

"It's nothing, Allie," Max said.

"You're sure you don't want to come with me? She did invite all of us," she said, knowing full well Max would never let that happen.

He didn't disappoint her. "Sorry, I'm planning on dragging your sister out with me all afternoon."

"To go flying?" she asked with a tiny smile.

Allie wasn't stupid. She'd caught the sexy innuendo between these two and knew what Max was *really* asking for every time he asked her sister to fly off into the sky with him.

Frankly, Allie wouldn't have been able to say no if a man like Max Taylor asked her to go shop for antifungal cream. So she had absolutely no idea how Sabrina was resisting a blatant invitation to the kind of sex most women only dreamed about.

Max met her eyes in the rearview mirror and winked, even as Sabrina glared at her from the front passenger seat.

Allie didn't care. She hadn't seen her sister this happy in a very long time. Not since long before the ruthless bastard who'd hurt them both so badly had come into their lives.

Which reminded her…she really did need to talk to Sabrina about Peter. But not now. Not today, when it was so lovely and sunny and she had a lunch invitation with a kind lady with a cute nephew.

No cute nephews for you. You're going to be a mommy, she reminded herself.

"So where *are* you two going?" she asked.

"To the theater," Max replied.

Boring. "Like, a musical theater with the nine-thousandth touring company of *Cats?*"

Max grinned. "Nope. To the dusty theater with the ninety-thousandth rerun of *Smokey and the Bandit.*"

"What's that?" she asked.

Sabrina and Max exchanged a quick glance, both of

them laughing. Just like two parents ignoring the chattery kid in the back seat. Even though the chattery kid was the one who was about to become a parent.

Allie didn't mind. Seeing Sabrina this happy and full of excitement made anything okay. Even holding on to the secret of Peter Prescott's return to their lives for just a little while longer.

MAX HADN'T BEEN EXAGGERATING about the condition of the Trouble Movie Emporium. When he unlocked the door and led her into the abandoned place, Sabrina immediately waved a hand in front of her nose to try to clear away the musty odor of age permeating every molecule of air. And promptly sneezed.

"Sorry, it's pretty dusty," he said as he reached around the door and flipped a wall switch.

She half expected the lobby to remain dark and shadowy, illuminated only by whatever sunlight managed to sneak through the warped, discolored panes of glass in the front windows. But a weak, yellowish glow slowly flickered to life above them, bathing the tired old lobby in equally tired old light. "I'm surprised the power's on."

"It's good to be the owner's grandson," he said.

"Ah. Throwing your weight around?"

"Hey, they were happy I wasn't bitching about the power to the old amusement park this time. And the local utility company is used to lighting this place up, since it opens for business one Saturday a month."

He'd mentioned that the morning they'd met. "So, does this mean we are on a date?" she asked, remembering more of that conversation.

He obviously remembered, too. "Why, ma'am, we hardly know each other."

"Save that innocent boy-next-door act for somebody else. I'm not buying it," she said, swatting his upper arm.

Sabrina ignored his start of surprise—as if he hadn't realized she'd figured out he was not as harmless as he'd appeared to be at first—and walked across the dusty, cracked linoleum floor. Dingy green and dented with the impression of shoes that had probably ceased to exist twenty years before, it looked like the skin of an enormous, pitted lime.

The place was standard 1960s issue movie-theater with none of the charm of an old-fashioned movie palace and none of the slick glass-and-brass look of more recent years. It had a basic lobby with a caged-in ticket window and a squat, plain glass snack bar long emptied of Sno-Caps and Milk Duds. Sad, decrepit and abandoned. Just like the rest of the town.

"What killed this place?" she asked softly.

"*Ishtar? Gigli?*" he said. "Wait...I know this one. DVD players."

About to swat him again, she saw the laughter in his eyes. Warmth rushed through her, making her quivery inside. She liked being teased by him. Liked seeing him laugh. Liked the way his eyes crinkled up at the corners when he smiled.

Damn. She liked him. *Really* liked him. On top of wanting to wrap him around her whole body and wear him like an overcoat.

Realizing he was watching her stare at him, she quickly glanced away. "I mean, it's like all of Trouble shriveled up and died of ennui."

"Big words, ma'am," he said as he rubbed a plate-size clear spot on the dirty glass countertop. "I'm just a flyboy, remember?"

A flyboy who'd been on nearly every continent on the planet and was the grandson of a famous millionaire. He wasn't fooling her with that self-deprecating act. "Yeah, right. Seriously, tell me what happened to Trouble."

Turning, he leaned one elbow on the counter, his arm and shoulder flexing attractively beneath the tight blue T-shirt he wore. Sabrina forced herself to focus on his words. Not on his thick shoulders and strong arms. Not on that chest. Not on the memory of the way those shoulders, arms and chest had felt pressed against her twenty-four hours ago.

She still couldn't believe she'd thrown herself into his arms like that. Not that she regretted it—but it hadn't exactly been planned. And once in his arms, she hadn't known what was going to happen next, though her legs being around his waist had been a pretty strong indication.

Remembering the massive bulge that had given her such intense pleasure, even through their clothing, she shivered. She couldn't even fathom how it might feel skin to skin.

"I don't know the whole story," he said, obviously not noticing her trip off to lust-land. "From the rumors I've heard, and from what Roderick—my grandfather's right-hand man—was able to find out, it appears a lot of public money was stolen by a former town official. It was never recovered and they had to keep mortgaging their assets to keep going. Eventually there was nothing left to mortgage."

"Sad."

"People lost their jobs, couldn't afford to stay, so they moved away. Businesses closed."

"And the town died."

He nodded.

"Until your grandfather decided to bring it back to life."

As always, an expression of rueful amusement crossed Max's face when his grandfather was mentioned. "Mortimer does like lost causes."

Curious about something the old man had said during dinner one evening, she had to ask. "Did he really save the life of a Saudi prince? And is there really a private palace reserved for him whenever he goes to visit there?"

"Who knows? Anything's possible. Just as he might really have shared a few cigars with Churchill after the war. And perhaps really was supposed to have dinner with Marilyn Monroe the week she died. With Grandfather, you just never know."

Somehow, that seemed a good thing. "I think I like not being sure."

Max's eyes crinkled and that genuinely pleased smile brought out a glorious dimple in his cheek. "Never being sure is what makes it so damn fun."

Their stares met and she sensed something—approval? Appreciation? Admiration? Something...

Max seemed pleased that she liked the old man. But how could anyone not? She wasn't the only one, either. Considering Mortimer's social calendar, he appeared to be quite popular among the remaining residents of Trouble.

"Now, shall we?" he asked. He tapped on the counter, nodding toward an invisible worker behind it. "Large popcorn, with butter, one Coke and two straws." Then, glancing at Sabrina out of the corner of his eye, he asked, "Lemonheads?"

Playing along, she shook her head. "No, thank you. And no butter, either."

Glancing at her, he narrowed his eyes and rolled a steady, appreciative look from the top of her head to the tip of her feet. "Make that *extra* butter. With her figure, this woman has not one thing to worry about."

"You get everything you want with that charm?" she asked, laughing in spite of herself.

Max shrugged. "Not everything, Sabrina."

Oh, she liked how he said her name. All sweet and sexy, like the man himself. As if he knew he was too hot to resist but it hadn't made him cocky. Just so incredibly confident. Playful. Irresistible.

"I wonder how many couples had their first dates in this place," he mused.

"Thought this wasn't a date. After all, you don't even know me, so it's merely an investment field trip, right?"

Not that she and Max had even talked about the whole investment nonsense for the past few days. No, since Saturday in the tavern their relationship had been strictly personal— playful, flirtatious, at times serious and sensuous. There'd been no business at all since before their kisses. Before she'd moved into his backyard. Before that strange but revealing conversation they'd had at the carousel the day before.

The conversation which had explained *everything* about this man.

"Okay, not a date," he agreed, his tone steady. "If that's the way you want it."

It wasn't. Definitely wasn't. But she couldn't find the words to admit that now. She'd been trying to find those words—to figure out how to make her next move—ever since their talk about his divorce.

The revelations at the carousel had cleared up all of Sabrina's confusion, and erased many of her doubts regarding Max's character. Because hearing about the crazy soap-opera ending of Max's marriage had made her understand so much more about the man.

What red-blooded American male *wouldn't* have tried to erase the bitter memories of his awful marriage by going out and proving his manhood with as many women as he could? Max might laugh now, saying he couldn't have *competed* against the person his wife had cheated with. But Sabrina would lay money he hadn't realized that right away.

She was only speculating. But it made perfect sense. Sabrina didn't know a woman who wouldn't have done the same thing. Either that, or eaten so much chocolate she wouldn't have wanted anyone to see her naked ever again.

"I've got to go up to the projection booth," he said. "I have the instructions on how to run the equipment, but it might take me a couple of minutes."

"You're sure about this?" She looked at the rickety stairs leading to the upper floor of the building. "There could be just about anything lurking around in this place."

"Zombie ticket-takers?" he asked with a laugh, looking amused. "I'll be fine. I'm a big boy."

Oh, a *very* big boy. One who could definitely take care of himself. So why did Sabrina feel so protective of the man all of a sudden?

Maybe it was because she knew he hadn't told her everything. Sabrina knew there was more. A shadow in his eyes, a regretful tone in his voice—they told her there was something about the divorce he didn't want to talk about.

Which *had* to be his womanizing, and regrets about his past.

According to Grace's book, she'd met Max a few years ago, obviously after his marriage had fallen apart. And he must still have been in some kind of need-to-prove-himself mode. So, though it killed Sabrina to think of the vivid details, she knew Grace *had* been telling the truth, at least about the affair.

She'd always known Max was sexy enough to be the kind of lover Grace had described, she just hadn't been able to put this man's face to that callous, heartbreaking character. Or the, um, somewhat raunchy one.

Now she could—at least a little bit. Now she understood.

But somehow, Sabrina couldn't blame Max for it anymore. In fact, her heart broke for him. To be married so young—obviously seeking a normal family. Like the one he'd been denied as a child, perhaps? Because judging by some things Mortimer had said over the past few days, Max and his brothers' lives had been anything but normal.

He'd grown up, reached out to someone, tried to create something he'd never had—and been smacked in the face by a double betrayal. His wife's infidelity and her dishonesty about who she really was.

Who she really was.

Sabrina acknowledged a quick flash of dismay. Because she hadn't been entirely honest, either. He had no idea what she was doing here in Trouble.

Keeping that secret was wrong.

Telling him would be worse.

Not merely because of his anger—and the cost it would have for *her*—but because she just didn't want him to experience that again. She did not want Max to feel he'd been made a fool of for a second time, tricked by a woman who'd claimed to be one thing when she was really something else.

No. She couldn't come clean with him entirely, but deep inside she was already deciding on ways to make amends.

Before she could decide exactly how to go about that, her cell phone rang. Grabbing it, she answered, keeping an eye out for Max on the stairs.

"What's going on? I haven't heard from you in days!"

"Nancy, I'm sorry," she replied, almost wishing she hadn't answered. Sabrina hadn't been keeping her boss in the loop for a couple of reasons—first, because she already knew she was letting her growing feelings for Max interfere with her judgment. And second, because Nancy was her friend and would almost certainly get overprotective if she thought Sabrina was doing something stupid. Like losing her heart to a playboy.

But Sabrina just didn't want to hear any "all men are scum" lectures right now.

"What's going on? Have you got the dirt on him? What do we do about the book?"

At last, something she could respond to. Sabrina definitely knew how to answer the last question. "Grace is going to have to revise it."

After a pause—and a sigh—Nancy said, "So it wasn't true, huh? He's not really the sexual stud of the western world?"

"Well, yeah, he sort of is. But he's *not* the heartbreaking reprobate she made him out to be."

Another pause. Then, her tone careful, Nancy asked, "Sabrina, are you doing something reckless?"

"If by reckless you mean am I letting myself fall for a twisted sex fiend, the answer is no." Because he *wasn't* one.

"That wasn't the question."

She hadn't thought so.

"Is there something going on between you and Taylor?"

Sabrina wished she could explain. But Max wasn't the kind of man who could be summed up in a phone conversation. A *short* conversation—which this would have to be, since he could return at any moment.

Too bad she couldn't tell the truth about his past, because if anyone would understand and empathize, it was Nancy. She loathed sexual posers and had ever since she'd had her heart broken by a woman who couldn't decide what she wanted.

But Max's confidence had been private, and Sabrina had to respect that. "Look, I think the affair happened, but I also think Grace invented a lot of the more sordid stuff…and the aftermath—his supposed cruelty and callousness. She wanted him. They had a fling. But I believe he was the one who decided to move on and she is trying to punish him for it."

"You're sure?"

No. She wasn't sure at all. She just knew Max was not the kind of man who'd have slept with Grace for weeks, then seduced her best friend—and her *maid*—and invited Grace to join them all in a group sex-fest. Or the kind who'd have been cutting and cruel when ending their affair. If anyone had been vengeful at the end of that relationship, she'd lay serious money it was Grace Wellington. Because she was still going after Max—in print—a few years after the fact.

"It is my professional opinion that she did some serious padding of her memoir purely as payback and to titillate her readers."

Nancy responded with a dry laugh. "Well, stop the presses, imagine an author doing that."

"And," Sabrina added, "that we could damage this man's reputation and bring serious legal ramifications on the publisher if we proceed as written."

"So what are you going to do about it?"

"First I'm going to have a talk with Grace."

And she would. Because while she had no doubt Max

had had a fling with the woman, and that he'd probably waltzed off with someone else as soon as he'd lost interest, she simply couldn't believe he'd been the cold heart-breaker Grace had made him out to be. Not even shortly after his divorce when he'd been a lot angrier than he was now.

It just wasn't in him. He had no cruelty. No deceit. He was simply a charming, playful guy—who was too sexy for his own good. A flirt who'd once been so badly wounded he was never going to let his heart be vulnerable to a woman again.

Max loved women—Sabrina knew that as surely as she knew she was never going to miraculously wake up one morning and be a D cup. Unfortunately, Sabrina suspected he loved *all* women a little but would never love *one* woman a lot. It simply wouldn't be possible for him. And woe to any woman who didn't figure that out before being stupid enough to lose her heart to him.

Which, perhaps, was what Grace Wellington had done. If she'd gotten her heart broken, it was probably because she'd mentally built her relationship with Max into something it wasn't. Something he'd never intended it to be.

Like she *was doing?*

"Okay, that's good enough for me," Nancy said. "When are you coming back?"

Good question. If only she knew the answer. "I have some vacation time coming."

"Sabrina…"

"I know, I know. I'm an idiot. But he's really not the man we read about in that book, Nancy." She quickly clarified, "I mean, he is every bit as sexy and desirable, but he's also adorably sweet and charming. I've never seen a moment of cruelty in him, and he's never once suggested anything inappropriate, much less obscene."

"Your call, kid," Nancy said. "I told you from the get-go that you were due for a fling, so you're not going to hear any argument from me. Just don't let your heart get tangled up in any of this."

"No chance of that happening," she said, then ended the call and disconnected.

Even if she'd ever entertained the slight possibility that she could allow herself to develop feelings for Max, his honest assessment of how unlikely he was to trust a woman again—or commit to one—had put that out of her head. When it came to Max Taylor, she expected nothing—no long term, no happily ever after.

No love.

Because though Max was obviously the kind of guy a woman could easily fall head over heels for, Sabrina wouldn't allow that. She liked him. She *wanted* him. But loving a guy like Max—a sweetheart, a free-spirit, a heart-breaker—would be the stupidest thing she could do.

That didn't mean she was ready to walk away from him, to go back to Philadelphia and forget they'd ever met. Not yet. There were a few things she wanted to take care of first, a few more moments to steal with the man. Moments of fun and laughter…

"And sex," she murmured, acknowledging it out loud for the first time. She watched the stairs for his return, wondering if he'd see her red cheeks and instantly know what she was thinking.

What she was thinking was that she wanted the man desperately. Wanted crazy wild hot sex.

"So have it. Take it," she whispered, wondering why the good-girl voice deep inside wasn't screeching an enormous *No!* at the very idea.

Heck, maybe even good girls knew when it was time

to stop fighting something that was inevitable and would be so damn good.

So do it. Take what you can. Then she could go home, straighten Grace out and proceed with the project. Without allowing it to ruin Max's reputation. Without regrets.

Without him.

"You ready for the feature film?"

Sabrina jerked around, not believing he'd come back down the stairs and caught her standing there mentally lusting over him. But his friendly smile told her he hadn't read anything into her pink face and ragged breathing. Perhaps he hadn't even noticed the way her blouse draped over the rigid points of her nipples.

Then she looked again, saw the hungry, aware expression on his face, and knew there was not a single thing Max Taylor didn't notice.

He reached the bottom step and came closer, moving slowly, and her imaginative mind suddenly saw him as a sexy predator—the man Grace had seen.

But that man didn't exist. She knew it down to her toes.

He extended his arm, maybe to lead her into the abandoned theater. Maybe to lead her somewhere else. "Shall we?"

She didn't take it. Instead, she simply stared at him, wondering why her throat was so tight and her middle so empty.

It didn't take much wondering.

Sabrina didn't know how much longer she had, and suddenly this cat-and-mouse game of flirt and retreat, kiss and push away, just seemed foolish. Wasteful. For whatever time she had left in Trouble—however much longer she could justify being away from work now that she knew what she was going to do about the book—she wanted to spend it the right way.

And that definitely wasn't sitting in a dusty movie theater watching a thirty-year-old film and eating imaginary popcorn.

"Max?"

He lowered his arm.

"Maybe I do want to call this a date."

One brow lifted and his eyes glittered in the half light. "You're sure?"

She nodded.

He hesitated for one long moment, during which he silently asked her a number of questions. She answered as many of them as she could with her eyes, knowing he knew exactly what she meant and exactly what she wanted.

Him. Them. *Now.*

Then, instead of kissing her, pulling her into his arms, throwing her on the counter and pounding into her until the whole thing gave way beneath them, he grabbed her hand and strode toward the door, tugging her after him.

"Wha—"

"There's something you should know about me," he muttered over his shoulder. "I don't take dates to the movies."

Oh, boy. "So where are we going?"

He didn't even pause as he pushed the door open and blinded them both with the bright sunshine.

"Flying."

CHAPTER TWELVE

PETER HAD BEEN in the piece-of-shit town of Trouble, Pennsylvania, for two days. And not only had he not seen Sabrina Cavanaugh or her sister, he still had no idea what the hell they were doing here. He was beginning to curse his crazy impulse to follow them, still not knowing exactly what he could accomplish now—here—that he couldn't do whenever they returned to the city.

But something wouldn't let him wait. His need to hurt her some more, probably. Because every day he spent in Philadelphia was another day he remembered how he'd been driven away. All because of Sabrina. Besides, it wasn't like he had anything tying him to the city; there was no reason to hurry back.

One positive thing was that this town—which had sounded familiar to him for some reason when Jane, his former secretary, named it—was small. So he had no problem finding out where the Cavanaugh sisters were. His landlord at the inn had been happy to fill him in.

The man, Mr. Fitzweather, wore a long women's-style sarong and walked on crutches. He had had a lot to say about Peter's ex-girlfriend, and it was easy to get him talking on the subject. By, for instance, saying something like, "So you're really telling me that this woman allowed her fierce dog to maul you?"

Fitzweather's frown—a constant expression since Peter had arrived on Monday afternoon—deepened into scowl of pure dislike. "She did. The wretched creature nearly ruined me for life."

Remembering Sabrina's fussy little poodle, Peter had to wonder exactly what he'd done to this big, solid man. But the innkeeper hadn't volunteered details.

Fitzweather shifted on his crutches, making his way around the living room, which was open to his guests. It was crowded with tacky furniture, from fuzzy gold velvet upholstery to glue-together prefab crap. Peter hated sitting on it, much less watching a crippled bald guy maneuver around it, but he kept a pleasantly sympathetic expression on his face.

"I can't believe the authorities didn't take the animal into custody," Peter said, still mentally scrambling for a way to get at Sabrina. Maybe the mutt, which she loved, would do.

"If not for that rich, crazy old man she's living with, I'd have had the monster put down. Potts used his clout to make sure the foul beast wasn't taken away. And since that female was able to produce proof of the animal's shots and medical records, there was nothing more I could do." Fitzweather went on to mutter something under his breath, a word that sounded like *humiliating*.

Well, yeah, he'd guess being brought down by a ten-pound ball of fuzz would probably be pretty embarrassing. Had he nibbled at Fitzweather's ankles? Peter just couldn't envision what had happened.

"And people are talking, oh, yes, they are," Fitzweather said, shaking his bald head. He smacked his palm flat on the sofa in visible frustration. "That Ivy Feeney whispered and laughed right behind my back at the bank this morning."

"Ivy Feeney," Peter murmured, wondering why the name sounded familiar.

"Yes, she and her sister know everything that goes on in this town—and don't think they'll ever let anyone forget it, either."

"They've been here for a long time?"

"Forever. Together they're older than the Liberty Bell and more dangerous than a pair of armed felons."

A memory twisted in Peter's mind. The names. The image.

Feeney. Sisters.

And suddenly it clicked into place. Why he'd heard of this town before.

It had only been two years ago that he'd corresponded with two authors with the strange address of Trouble, Pennsylvania. They'd been sisters. Sisters named Feeney. Sisters who'd written an awful book about a murder by means of death so ridiculous it could only be considered a broad comedy.

He'd offered to have Liberty Books publish it. For a price.

"These sisters sound interesting," he said, trying to remember bits and pieces of the story they'd been peddling. It was, if he remembered correctly, set in the town of Problem, Iowa, and it had involved the murder of a wealthy councilman who'd embezzled all the town's money.

How fascinating. Because in the two days that he'd been buttering up Al Fitzweather to try to get any information he could on Sabrina, he'd been listening to the man's incessant stories about his hometown. An embezzlement scandal. A murder.

All very familiar, including the cause of death. Which was too bizarre to be real.

Then again, sometimes reality was stranger than fiction.

Which left him wondering about the Feeney sisters' book. And whether it had really been fiction at all.

SABRINA WAS either about to burst into peals of delighted laughter…or throw up. Glancing over at her from the cockpit of his Cessna Skyhawk XP, Max saw a flurry of expressions cross her face as they topped six thousand feet and banked left to skim over the mountains.

She'd been holding her breath during their taxi and takeoff from the long dirt landing strip at the Weldon airfield. Fortunately the well-oiled runway was smoother than some pothole-pitted tarmacs at major airports and they lifted into the air easily.

Since his private plane was a small four-passenger one, the leather seat in which Sabrina sat was so close to his that he could hear her breathing—at least, he would when she finally started doing it again. He could probably have heard her heart beat, too, if he hadn't been focused on his instrumentation during takeoff.

Finally, her choppy breaths normalized and evened out. Not that she'd relaxed. Her hands were clenched tight on the armrests, her fingers white with tension from her death grip. She'd let go only a few times since they boarded— to check and quadruple-check her seat belt, and to put her hands across her stomach with a groan when she'd actually looked out at the ground as it fell away beneath them.

"You doing okay?"

She nodded slowly.

"Sure?"

"No."

At least she was honest. "Stop thinking about what *could* happen and enjoy what *is* happening."

"How can I enjoy what is happening if all I *think* is happening is that tiny pieces of metal are breaking apart on the wing and an electrical fire is sparking in the engine?"

Max couldn't help it, he chuckled softly.

"What? You find my abject terror funny?"

"You're not terrified, Sabrina. You're a little nervous. Just like when you hear the clack of Freddy's razor-blade fingernails or the chick-chick-aaah sound that says Michael Myers is coming close."

"I think I'd rather hear chick-chick-aah than the explosion of the single engine on this thing."

"Pessimist."

"Cocky bastard. This is some first date."

That made him laugh out loud. Which made her finally smile a bit. And ease up her hands.

"Would knowing I've had a few thousand flight hours help?"

She stared through her bangs. "How many crashes?"

"Zero."

"Emergency landings?"

He hesitated. "Does a client's sudden need to stop in Vegas to play some slots while en route to a Colorado spa count?"

"I guess not."

"Okay, then, also zero. I have had to do a few RTAs over the years—return to airport—for various reasons." Like naked grannies in his cockpit. "But none that I'd classify as emergencies." Other than naked grannies in his cockpit.

But Sabrina didn't need to hear that story. The last thing he wanted to do was tell her about the stupid rumors circulating about him in southern California, and the book that had spawned those rumors. Especially given the content of that book.

Max hadn't read it—he hadn't been able to bring himself to do so yet. But his lawyer had gotten a copy and had summed it up with two words: *outrageous* and *damaging*.

"Okay, I'm calm," she whispered. "This is me being calm."

Reaching over, he covered one of her hands with his, gently stroking her fingers until she let go of the armrest.

"Don't you need both hands on the controls?" Since she was twining her fingers in his as she said the words, he suspected she hoped the answer was no.

"Forget everything else and just look. Breathe in and out, keep your eyes—and your mind—open. And let it fill your senses. Can you do that for me?"

She tried. He saw her try. Staring straight ahead into the blue, she visibly steadied her inhalations. She turned her head neither to the left nor the right—apparently not ready to glance down at the ground. But forward was a good start. Because who could look toward the infinite stretch of cerulean sky and not feel certain that miracles did exist and nothing bad could possibly happen in this perfect world high among the clouds?

"It's lovely," she said, her voice low.

"Serene." His awed tone matched hers.

"Yes. Eternal. Like you could keep going and never reach the end."

"With a big enough gas tank, that's exactly what would happen. Clean, unadulterated freedom in front of us."

"With none of the garbage below us."

She got it. She absolutely understood.

"Grandfather often says he found his utmost freedom racing stallions across the desert. I think the sensations must be the same. That you can go on forever, not stop moving. Allow nothing to catch up with you. Nothing to touch you."

Realizing he'd been speaking out loud—not just mentally going over something he'd thought many times before—he glanced at his passenger. She was no longer stiff and tense, nor was she focused on the front windshield. Instead Sabrina was watching *him,* her full lips parted, her blue eyes filled with emotion.

"What is it you're running from?"

Right. Like he was going to have that conversation here, now, with her. Max himself hadn't figured out what had been driving him—what he'd been running from—most of his life.

Probably the whole big boiling stew of it. His parents' deaths. His own reckless lifestyle. Losing his Air Force dream. The baby. The marriage. The alcohol. The book.

He should just open up a vein and bleed all over the cockpit; it'd probably take less time and be less messy. So instead of even trying to answer her question, he gave her a quick wink and a crooked smile. "Have you made the other instant association yet?"

She appeared confused.

"I mean, most people associate flying in a small plane—the vibrations, the danger, the freedom and thrill of it—with something else."

Licking her lips, she asked, "What else?"

Instead of replying, he began to stroke her hand, which was still tucked in his. He ran the tip of his fingers over the fleshy pad of her palm, then higher, so he could touch the delicate skin of her wrist. Her pulse was beating wildly. "You *know* what else."

An intimate vibe rolled between them again; the same one that had been there since they met. Thick and sexual, aware and certain that they would, sooner or later, come together. He had the feeling it was going to be sooner. Much sooner.

"Maybe I do know what else," she admitted. Her voice throaty, she went on. "It's like making love."

"Uh-huh. Like making long, slow, erotic love. Sliding, climbing, gliding. Free and mindless delight overwhelming every other emotion."

She was almost panting. He didn't stop.

"The physical satisfaction feels like it'll go on forever if you just hold on, don't head back to earth. Don't let it end. Every other thought leaves your mind until you are focusing only on the pleasure of the moment and trying to capture the memories for the future, knowing they'll never be as good as the reality."

Swallowing hard, she slowly nodded. "Yeah. You're right. It's like that."

The air in the plane grew thicker. Warmer. It smelled like sex. It *felt* like sex.

Sabrina curled to her side, shifting to face him as she brought her legs up and tucked them under her curvy butt. She'd moved closer—close enough for him to catch the intoxicating floral scent of her perfume. And to feel the warmth of her breath on his skin.

The warmth was soon much, *much* closer. Because without a word, Sabrina leaned over and pressed a hot, openmouthed kiss on his neck. She tasted him there, licking delicately, then nibbling her way to his earlobe.

"Sabrina…"

"Shh. Pay attention to what you're doing, Captain."

Oh, right, that'd be easy when a woman he was dying for was filling his every inhalation with her scent and his brain with images of what he was going to do to her the minute they landed.

"You taste so good to me, Max," she said as she continued to kiss him. "I've been dreaming of the way you'd taste."

He was going to stop her. Absolutely. Soon.

"The way you'd feel." Her hand dropped to his thigh. Soon. Any second now.

"I've been wanting you for a long time," she whispered as she scraped her lips across his jaw.

Her silky blond hair caressed his cheek and the weight of her hand on his leg sent every one of his senses supersonic.

"I want you to make love to me in every way two people can make love."

"And you pick now—*here*—to tell me this?" he choked out.

Her laughter rolled over him as she shifted again. Closer. Close enough to press her lips to the hollow of his throat. A flick of her tongue had him ready to come out of his seat.

"I've been telling you all along. Surely you noticed."

"I noticed," he muttered. "But you chose a hell of a time to act on it. We have to land."

"What about the mile-high club?" she asked, moving her hand up his leg.

A few inches more and she'd have control of the stick and they'd both go for one hell of a ride.

"I've always wondered about it."

"That's not for pilots, babe. Not for good ones, anyway. It's only for when somebody else is flying the plane." He immediately forced thoughts of Mrs. Coltrane out of his mind.

Unlike her, Sabrina was a serious temptation. He totally understood her sudden, driving urge to have hot, passionate sex right now while they were wrapped in this sensuous cocoon, separate from the rest of the world. He shared it, and would love nothing more than plunging into Sabrina's body while the two of them hurtled toward the horizon, thousands of feet in the air.

But he wasn't about to kill them both for the sake of a few minutes of pleasure, when he could have them safely back on the ground in less than half an hour. Which was exactly what he told her.

"Fine," she said, sounding disappointed as she threw herself back in her own seat. "But I want you the minute we land."

"Can I cut the engines first?"

Frowning, she continued. "Okay, but that's it. I want you inside me so much I'm not going to be able to wait any longer than that, Max."

Amused and incredibly turned on by her aggressiveness, he said, "So I guess we'll save the foreplay for next time?"

"The foreplay's been going on since the minute we met." Her challenging expression dared him to deny it.

He didn't even try. Reaching over to run his fingers through her golden hair, he said, "There's a condom in my flight bag. In case you want to save a few more seconds after we land."

Her catlike expression told him he'd given her an opening even before she said, "Want me to put it on you now?"

She was relentless. And he loved it even though it was driving him stark raving nuts. "No. I meant we can have it handy and not waste time looking for it."

The bag was behind his seat, and she unbuckled to go after it. So much for her fear of flying. It seemed to have been erased by pure sexual want. Though, damned if he could understand why, since they'd done nothing more erotic than *talk* about sex since they'd taken off.

But he wasn't complaining. He'd seen this side of Sabrina yesterday, at the carousel, when she'd aggressively demanded a kiss, taking the situation into her own hands. She was feisty and determined to get what she wanted. That she wanted him—*now, right this second and immediately*—was both his greatest pleasure and his biggest frustration.

Rising to her knees, she reached around Max's seat to get the bag, coming so damn close to his face that he could have taken a bite out of one beautiful breast. God, it was tempting. He couldn't resist scraping his teeth across the taut tip, protruding saucily against her blouse.

"Mmm," she groaned as she retrieved the condom and dropped it on her seat. "More." Reaching up, she unfastened her top button, tugging the silky fabric aside so he could get a better taste.

He *had* to have that taste. Just a sample—an appetizer to last him the twenty minutes it would take to get on the ground.

"You are perfect," he muttered. Rolling his tongue across her puckered nipple, he savored her for a moment. Then, knowing they were both building things to a frenzied peak that was going to abso-fucking-lutely erupt when they landed, he sucked her into his mouth. Deep. Hard. Demanding surrender and promising satisfaction.

"Oh, Max," she whimpered, twining her fingers in his hair. "I could...it would be so easy to undress, then slide across your lap and straddle you."

He pulled a refusal out of his gut, using every bit of willpower he had to focus on the gauges and the cartographic map on the LCD display in front of him. "No."

"I'm dying to be touched."

He knew that, he could hear it in her voice. His mind already filling with the image, he ordered, "So lean your seat back and touch yourself." He liked this idea. "While I watch."

She stiffened the tiniest bit, studying him with uncertain eyes. "That's a little…"

"Intimate?"

She nodded.

"Exactly. We're about to become intimate, in every way."

Judging by the way her teeth were holding on to her bottom lip, she wasn't convinced. So Max cajoled her. "Let me become familiar with your body, Sabrina. What you like, where you like to be stroked, how tender or rough you want it."

He shifted, a warm need rolling through him and settling in his groin. "Let me see the hungry look on your face when you have to have it fast." His own heart started to race. "And hear the way your breath catches when you want it slow and easy. I'll learn so much, all before I even put my hands on you."

Moaning, she tugged at her khaki pants like they were too tight—too confining. "When we land…what if someone sees?"

"Impossible. That's a one-man operation down there and mine's the only bird that's been in or out for days. Besides, I'm going to be buried inside you right after we land—don't you think you're going to have to take some clothes off?"

He could have reached over and touched her, taken the decision out of her hands. But he didn't, wondering why she was suddenly skittish—almost shy—even though a few minutes ago she'd stuck her beautiful breast in his mouth.

She didn't answer, but the tiny, wicked smile told him she'd come around. When she tilted the handle and reclined her seat, then moved her hands to her blouse, he knew it for certain.

"Talk to me," she murmured as she slowly slipped the remaining buttons free. The sleeveless top soon hung open on her shoulders, her breasts peeking from the edges of the pink fabric. Just as pink. Just as soft…other than her two taut, puckered nipples. "Tell me what to do."

"Lose the blouse."

She tipped one shoulder then the other, and it fell away, puddling around her on the seat. Cocking a brow, she waited for further instruction.

"Show me how you want me to treat those nipples."

Sabrina covered one breast with her hand, her fingers spread, then she slowly closed them, puckering that pink tip tight. "The same way you sucked them. Gentle. Then hard. Pleasure…and just the tiniest bit of pain."

His mouth went dry as he shifted his gaze back and forth between the siren beside him and the controls in front of him. He kept an eye on the ground, too. Both for safety reasons, and because the sooner they were on it, the sooner his would be the hands on Sabrina's body.

Hearing the sound of a zipper, he glanced back in time to see her slipping out of her pants. Beneath them, she wore a tiny pair of pink thong panties, one lacy strap over each hip.

"You want these gone, too?"

"Unless you want me to touch you through the fabric," he muttered hoarsely. "To close my mouth over you and inhale you through that silk."

Some inner well of sensual determination apparently outweighed her residual embarrassment. Because, licking her lips, she twined her finger in the elastic and tugged the panties down until her body was completely bared to his gaze.

It was hard not to stare. The woman was perfect—all long, delicate lines and gentle, inviting curves. Her skin appeared smooth and supple and every inch of her looked soft.

Max had sampled her breasts, and now longed to kiss his way down her midriff, over that flat belly, then to the hollow below. He wanted to bury his face in her golden curls and lick into her wet folds. To indulge in her, drink from her.

"Show me how wet you are."

His hands tightened reflexively on the controls when Sabrina slid her palm across her stomach until the tips of her fingers tangled in the tuft of curls between her legs. When they slid lower, growing slick and juicy with her body's moisture, Max nearly came out of his seat.

Sabrina's eyes drifted closed, her lips parting as her breathing grew deeper. A low moan emerged from her throat as she stroked herself, showing him—as he'd asked—what she liked.

He was a good pupil. And he could hardly wait to prove to her just how carefully he was paying attention to the lesson.

Soon. Almost there. A few minutes…

"Max?" she whispered, close—she'd leaned over toward him again. "Hurry, okay?"

"Ten minutes," he said as he reached for the radio. As he informed the dinky tower at the Weldon airstrip—nothing more than a corrugated metal shed run by some local yokel—that they were returning so shortly after takeoff, he steeled himself to remain strong for a little while longer.

But she made that impossible.

"I think we can do a few other things to prepare," she whispered, nibbling his ear as she slid her hand up his thigh. Into very dangerous territory. "I mean, we've got the protection ready to go. And *I'm* certainly ready to go." She was nearly purring in his ear when her hand moved even higher, the tips of her fingers tracing the outline of his bulge. "All that's left is to make sure *you're* all ready to go."

"Oh, I'm ready. Trust me on this."

Her laugh was purely feminine, made confident by his desire for her. Her fingers did some walking. "I can tell."

"Please, you're killing me here."

"So die happy," she said, her tone pure evil as she moved even closer and wrapped her hand around his hard-on.

Absolutely incapable of resisting, he arched into her grip, wanting her to grab him tight, squeeze and steer him right down the runway.

Unable to do anything but breathe and keep the plane on course, he didn't try to stop her when her fingertips moved to his zipper and slowly began drawing it down. She was careful, her breathing labored. His was even more so.

"Don't go too far," he cautioned, wondering where his willpower was coming from. And just how far was *too* far.

"Oh, of course not," she said. "I know you're very busy. Very focused. So I'll stay out of your way."

He somehow didn't equate Sabrina sliding her fingers into the opening of his briefs and stroking his erection with staying out of his way. "Whoa…"

"Oh, my, you *are* ready," she said as she pushed the cotton out of the way, freeing his rigid cock and catching it in her hand.

If her touch had been good with his clothes between them, it was absolutely mind-blowing skin to skin.

"I, uh, had been wondering…" Her voice trailed off as she stared at his cock. He saw the way her throat moved as she swallowed hard, and *knew* what she'd been wondering.

She looked pleased at what she'd discovered. *Very* pleased. Her next words confirmed it. "Oh, yum."

With a laugh that was half groan, Max put his head back against the headrest and stared at the ceiling, wondering how the hell he'd gotten himself into this situation. At the controls, in flight, with a gorgeous naked woman holding his dick in her hand.

Sounded like something out of a teenage boy's pilot fantasy.

"Holy shit," he yelped when she made her next move. Because now she'd *definitely* moved into fantasy territory. He hadn't even realized her intent, but now Sabrina's sweet, wet mouth was wrapped around the head of his shaft.

Her blond head looked gorgeous in his lap. Those silky strands spread over his jeans as she sucked and licked at him. The pleasure was like nothing he'd ever experienced, particularly as he gave himself over to the sensations, and the view out the windshield.

Needing to touch her, he slid his fingers through her hair, gently rubbing the back of her neck, then gliding his palm down her back. Not stopping what she was doing, she wriggled that gorgeous ass a little, and he couldn't resist reaching just a bit farther to cup it.

"You know I'm going to get even with you for this," he growled. "I fully intend to torture you when I have a whole lot of time to do it. Do things to make you scream and not take you until you're begging for it." He started to even out the torture by curling his fingers farther, between her cheeks, and sliding them into her wet crevice.

"Oh," she moaned, her back arching, her hips bucking up in welcome.

He gave himself a few seconds to enjoy the slick softness of her skin, dipping his finger once—twice—into her tight channel. Each time, she groaned and ground against his hand. And each time she groaned, she sucked him harder.

"Enough," he said, seeing the small airport up ahead. Though it killed him, he pulled his hand away. "I mean it. Please, honey, sit up and put your seat belt on."

She looked up at him, her eyes big and dreamy, her mouth wet and red. "You're sure?"

"I'm sure." He ran the pad of his thumb across her lower lip. "Give me five minutes to land and then I'll do you until you can't remember what century it is."

WHAT CENTURY WAS IT, anyway? She *already* couldn't remember. Completely out of her mind with excitement, Sabrina leaned back in her own seat, somehow feeling absolutely no embarrassment that she sat here in a tiny airplane, completely naked beside the pilot.

The pilot whose most impressive erection was sticking out of his pants.

Oh, she wanted that. She wriggled in the seat, the leather cool against her bottom and her legs. Still tingly from the way he'd touched her, she almost whimpered at how badly she needed more. Wanted more.

Wanted *him*.

She wanted to make love with Max Taylor more than she'd wanted anything in her entire life—more than she'd wanted to escape from her hometown, or to succeed at her job. More than she wanted to pursue her secret passion for writing.

Right now, absolutely none of that mattered. The only thing that mattered was that the man she'd been fantasizing about for months and the man she'd been getting to know for days had blended together into one amazing package. And she was dying for them both.

Toying with the condom packet, she tore the corner of it off. No sense wasting a moment once they were on the ground. Max was watching her out of the corner of his eye and she saw him start to laugh.

"There are only two minutes left of your five," she said, warning him. She was also playing with him.

She *liked* playing with him. Sexy word games or sexy sex games, she just liked the way she felt when she was around Max Taylor. All the inhibitions—her initial doubts—had fallen away. She'd known when she left the theater with him how this "date" would end up—with the two of them finally doing what they'd been wanting to do since they met.

What she hadn't expected was that she'd fall a little deeper, get her emotions a little more tangled up, all because of the way they'd shared sensation and emotion. The way Max had eased her fear of flying with his sweet, vivid verbal seduction, turning her concerns into something else entirely. Something hot and wicked and hungry.

Sabrina also felt as though he'd opened another page in the private book of his life. About why he needed to fly—to stay ahead, out of reach of anyone who might hurt him. He hadn't liked that he'd revealed it, but it had been too late. She'd heard. She'd seen. She'd understood. Maybe she was the only one who understood this man. Or perhaps she just wanted to be.

"One minute," she murmured, glancing at her watch.
"We're taxiing."

To her surprise, she realized they were. Max's landing had been so smooth she hadn't even noticed they were on the ground.

Close now. Oh, incredibly close. And the anticipation was so incredibly good. It was like that second before she blew out her birthday candles, knowing it was time to make the wish she'd been waiting a whole year to make. Or the moment before she used to open her eyes on Christmas morning when she was very small, knowing whatever was about to happen would be magical.

This was going to be magical.

Knowing where Max's plane had been parked when they'd arrived at the airstrip, she realized immediately that they were heading toward another spot. Max pulled the plane to the very end of the tarmac, the farthest he could get from the teeny building where the airstrip manager worked, giving them that much more privacy.

Good thing. Because the second he pulled the plane up and killed the engine, Sabrina was leaning toward him. "Now."

"Condom." He grabbed it from her hand and pulled it on, then, without another word, reached over and lifted her off her seat. Moving her as easily as he would a doll, he separated her legs and opened her for him. Opened her wide.

"Now," he growled.

With one hard thrust, he buried himself deep, so deep she had to howl at it. She was stretched and gloriously filled—completely connected.

Max caught her cries with his mouth, kissing her ravenously as he tangled his hands in her hair and cupped her head. Kissing him back, she tugged at his shirt, needing it gone, needing to feel that bare skin and that amazing body. He let her pull her mouth off his just long enough for her to tug the shirt up and toss it away. Pausing for one second, she admired the thick ropes of muscle across his shoulders, the hard chest, the lean middle. He was absolutely beautiful to look at.

And beautiful to touch.

Digging her fingers into his arms, already slick with sweat, she started to move, sinking deeper, then pulling away. Every stroke was a new delight, every thrust a reminder of how empty she'd been before him.

He caught her rhythm, matched it. Still kissing her like he wanted to devour her whole, he thrust into her again and again, imprinting himself on her, somewhere deep inside.

It wasn't long—not long at all—before Sabrina felt the wild, rollicking tremors roll through her body in a powerful orgasm. She wailed against his mouth and he carried her through it, holding her in his arms as she collapsed against his chest, almost exhausted at the power of the climax.

"Oh, Max," she mumbled against his neck, liking the taste of his sweaty skin, "I *like* flying with you."

He grabbed her hips, shifting her again, grinding into her until she panted at how good it felt. "Good thing. Because we're just taking off."

CHAPTER THIRTEEN

ALLIE HAD NO WAY to get home. It was three o'clock—one hour past the time Mr. Potts had promised to pick her up from Miss Emily's house after their lovely luncheon. Only, he hadn't shown up. He'd apparently forgotten all about her.

"You're sure your phone is working?" she asked her hostess, who'd made the most yummy tuna salad, complete with pickles, as if knowing Allie had been dying for something salty and tangy today. She'd followed it up with fudge brownies—also knowing Allie would want chocolate?

"Joey checked and said it was fine."

Joey. The cute nephew.

He'd been here for lunch and had been so thoughtful—pulling out her chair, offering to refill her water glass the moment it fell an inch below the rim. He was a gentleman, which was unbelievably rare for someone probably only a year older than her. Most of the guys Allie had met in college had been horny boys anxious to notch their belts now that they no longer lived at home. Even in the Christian school she'd attended, the need for eighteen-year-olds to get drunk and lose their virginity had been huge.

Joey was different. Sweet. Earnest. A real Pennsylvania farmboy, born and raised.

With his thick, sandy-colored hair, heart-melting smile

and great body, she'd figured he had a girlfriend for sure. Some pretty dairy queen with big udders and blond braids. So she had been pretty surprised—and a little pleased— when he'd told his aunt that he did not.

Allie thought Emily had stared at her and wagged her eyebrows. But that didn't seem possible. What protective aunt would set her adored nephew up with a knocked-up twenty-year-old whose own family was probably cutting out scarlet letter *A*s to sew on her maternity dresses?

She hated that damn book. It had been hell reading it in English Lit last semester when she'd been trying to hide her pregnancy.

"Sorry, Allie," Joey said. "It is working. I just tried Mr. Potts's number again and got his voice mail. You're sure he's American? He sounded like a stuffy English guy on the recording."

"Must be his butler. I haven't met him yet but I've heard lots of stories."

Romantic stories, wild stories. Stories of countries she'd only ever read about and worlds she'd only ever dreamed of. Far removed from the reality of Allie Cavanaugh, Reverend Tucker's second-oldest granddaughter. As was any idea that she could still be a simple, fun-loving twenty-year-old and bask in the attention of a cute guy with a great laugh and strong shoulders.

The realization making her sad, she steeled her shoulders and gave Joey the most polite, nondescript smile she could manage. "Well, it's not too far, I can walk."

"Don't be ridiculous." Emily shook her head so hard her brownish curls flopped over her forehead. It made her look younger, prettier. Which Mr. Potts would surely have noticed if he had shown up. "Joey can take you home."

"Yes, of course I can," he said, sounding pleased by the idea.

Dear Lord, please don't let him see me as some poor fallen woman he needs to rescue. But he probably did.

Suddenly feeling very old—much older and wiser than Miss Emily's nephew—she let him help her to her feet, absently rubbing her belly with the palm of her hand. Catching him watching her, she bit back a smile as his eyes widened in surprise—as if he'd just remembered there was a whole other person living inside her.

Though he remained polite, she sensed a veil of formality drop over him. Once again, Allie began again to feel alone—far removed from Joey and his problems at the small community college he attended. They seemed so insignificant. Young. Like he still thought the number of imaginary friends he had on MySpace really mattered.

It wasn't only because she was pregnant—about to be a mother—while he probably hadn't had a whole lot of sexual experience. She wasn't older just in terms of sex. She was also far too experienced in heartache.

But Peter hadn't broken her heart. Her family had.

This attractive guy didn't know about that. Had no frame of reference. Neither did any of Allie's other college friends. She, alone, had been forced to grow up practically overnight, realizing you *couldn't* always go home again. And sometimes home was where you made it.

Like here, in Trouble…in a tent in Mr. Potts's backyard.

"I would appreciate the ride," she murmured. "Ma'am, thank you so very much for the lunch, I appreciate it. I'm sorry you didn't have the chance to meet Mr. Potts."

Miss Emily tucked her arm in Allie's and led her to the door. "That's quite all right. You let Joey take you home safe and sound, honey, and you put your feet up for a while. Give Butch a scratch under the chin for me, will you?"

Smiling, she agreed, then let Emily's nephew escort her to the car. He held the door open for her—playing at gentleman again—and then lent her a hand so she could lower herself into the passenger seat. She carefully buckled up, keeping the belt low, beneath her belly, as all her maternity books said she should.

Allie might not be handling all the other aspects of her pregnancy too well—the stretch marks, the discomfort, the isolation, the loss of her family. But she was doing very well in one area: loving her child. There was nothing she wouldn't do to keep the baby safe, even if his father was the biggest prick on the face of the planet.

As they drove through the town of Trouble toward Mr. Potts's place, Joey tried to make small talk. He asked her about her family, her education. But in her mind, every conversation ended in a silent question: *Who knocked you up?* So they soon stopped talking.

The silence heavy in the car, Allie withdrew deep into her thoughts, going over—as always—her plans for the future. A future that involved her standing on her own, relying on her sister to be not her caretaker but her confidante, her sibling. Her friend. She wanted to reach that point—wanted to free Sabrina from this hair coat of guilt she wore, as if she'd wound up the key in Peter's back and pushed him in Allie's direction.

"It's not your fault," she whispered as she looked out the window. Someday she'd make her sister believe that. And their family, too.

"Pardon?"

"Sorry. It's nothing." She didn't even look over, not wanting this boy who was one year ahead of her in age but light years behind her in experience to see the brightness in her eyes and realize they were filling with tears. Not *poor me* tears. But tears for her sister, who'd put her life on hold and had remained the one person in Allie's life she could depend on.

Suddenly, though, it wasn't so hard to keep her attention focused outside—away from Miss Emily's good-looking nephew. Because as they passed a couple of old, half-falling-down houses on the north end of town, she saw someone she couldn't *possibly* be seeing.

"Slow down," she snapped.

Joey hit the brake. The car didn't screech to a stop, but it immediately dropped below twenty. Slow enough for her to crane close to the passenger side window and study the dark-haired man getting out of a car and going up to the porch of one of those two houses.

"It can't be…"

"Can't be who?"

She shook her head. "*Can't.* It's impossible. He *couldn't* have known."

"*Who* couldn't have known? Allie, is something wrong?"

Risking a quick glance at Joey, she asked, "Whose house is that?"

He peered around her. "Not sure. I think it belongs to one of those old sisters. I remember them scaring the fear of God into me when I was a kid and we'd come visit Aunt Emily during the Trouble Founders' Festival." His brow scrunching, he added, "I think their name's Feeney."

Old sisters named Feeney. There could be no connection—she had to be mistaken. Allie was thinking that over, almost kicking herself for being so paranoid, when the dark-haired man on the porch of the house turned a little, almost in her direction. She sank down into the seat, unable to silence a gasp. Because she recognized that face and knew that profile. A slow boil of anger rolled up from her swollen feet all the way to the top of her head.

"What is it?"

She didn't answer. The name would mean nothing to Joey, unless she went on to identify the man as the walking six-foot-tall penis who'd fathered her child.

Only one person in Trouble would recognize the name. And she was the one person Allie most hated to tell— Sabrina. But there was no choice. She was going to have to tell her sister that Peter Prescott had, apparently, followed them to Trouble.

The bastard.

This time, when she'd seen him, there was no stab of regret, no secret sadness over one of those passionate moments they'd shared in the beginning.

He'd followed her. And she was so furious, she could hardly stand it. Reaching the house, Allie could barely find words to thank Miss Emily's nephew for driving her home. He looked disappointed, as if he'd expected something from her.

Like the pregnant chick was gonna put out or something as thanks for the ride? Knowing the thought was unkind—and a product of her rage toward Peter—she somehow managed a genuine smile before shooing Joey away. She mourned a little that she wasn't some free young girl who could take him up on his soft-spoken offer to grab a burger sometime.

But she wasn't that girl. Today, socializing with someone her own age and seeing how far removed her life was from his, had underscored that reality.

Funny, though, she didn't feel depressed about it. Or weak. Instead she began to feel better—stronger—than she had in a long time. Maybe because she'd finally acknowledged her life was never going to be the same and she could not go back. Maybe because she'd reacted with rage rather than fear when she'd seen the side of Peter's fat head today.

Maybe just because she was growing up.

"Yes. That's it," she murmured as she paced around the house a few hours later, waiting for somebody to get home. She'd been alone here with only Butch for company since Joey dropped her off. She and the dog by themselves in the big empty house with a big empty tent out back. Silent. Abandoned. As dead as it must have been before Mr. Potts had bought the place and moved in a few weeks ago.

At around five, she'd thought she heard someone in Mr. Potts's private office. Butch growled at the door; he'd heard something, too. But when she went in, she saw no one. Nothing out of place. Just the same dusty old furniture that Max's grandfather swore he'd have replaced one of these days. And all those nasty, loud clocks that he swore he would not.

"It was our imagination, boy," she said as she picked the dog up and tucked him under her chin so he rested partly on her big belly. He liked this position, as if he already enjoyed bonding with the baby. "Everything's fine," she added.

For some reason, though, she felt a chill despite the heat of the day. She hadn't been able to shake the memory of that dark, shabby car parked at the bottom of the hill yesterday. And the shadowy figure inside it.

By seven o'clock, when those clocks screeched their heads off again, Allie was staring at the shadows lengthening in the house, wondering why her sister hadn't responded to any of her calls. She didn't mind being alone…

usually. But tonight felt different. She was jumpy, her nerves stretched tight.

"Cool it," she whispered. "You've spent an evening alone before."

She could certainly fend for herself, despite what her sister thought. Doing as Mr. Potts had asked and making herself at home in his kitchen, she whipped up an omelette—protein for the baby—then resumed her pacing.

Where *was* everyone? Max and Sabrina she could guess—the way those two had been looking at each other, she figured they might have driven to the nearest no-tell motel and checked out every magic-fingers machine they could find.

But Mortimer? It wasn't like him not to show up. Not to return any of Allie's calls. And when she thought about the fact that he hadn't been at breakfast—she hadn't seen him at all since *yesterday*—she grew more concerned.

Allie had only know the old guy for a few days. But she already loved him with all the devotion she'd never felt for her own grandfather. Sabrina, she strongly suspected, felt the same way.

"He wouldn't just disappear," she muttered, talking to herself while pretending to talk to the baby. "He wouldn't have left me stranded, either. That's not like him."

And then there was that car…

Her imagination had gone so far into overdrive that when she finally heard someone pull up outside, Allie raced as fast as her pregnant belly would let her out to the front porch. Seeing her sister's blond head, and Max's dark one, she leaned to watch the rear car door. But nobody got out.

Now she was worried. As soon as Max and Sabrina stepped out into the driveway, she bounded down the stairs toward them, holding her belly with both hands and sending down a mental apology to the baby.

"Allie, what is it?" Sabrina asked, immediately hurrying to her side. "What's wrong?"

Max was right there, too. "Are you in labor?"

Ack! She didn't even want to think about that. "No, no, it isn't the baby."

Sabrina took Allie's arm. "It's okay, then, just calm down and we'll go inside. You know you can tell me anything."

Allie always had been able to tell Sabrina anything, which was the main reason she'd wanted to go to Philadelphia for college. She'd missed her older sister badly when Sabrina had gone away, and there was no one in her life she trusted more.

So, yes, she had a lot of things to tell her. Things like *I'm sorry* and *I forgive you* and *You're not responsible for me.* Not to mention, of course, the *I led that scumbag right to our door* thing. But instead she settled for the most pressing.

Grasping her sister's hand, she came to a stop and swung around to face her, as well as Max. "I think something's wrong."

Sabrina's eyes dropped to Allie's stomach and her face went pale, the washed-out color easy to make out even with the quickly fading light already dimming toward sunset. "With the baby?"

She shook her head. "No." Swallowing, she grabbed Max's hand, too, wanting him to believe her, though she knew she had no real reason for the near panic she felt. It was merely intuition…mother's intuition. She just had this feeling. A bad one.

"It's your grandfather, Max," she said. "I haven't seen him, he's not answering his phone and he didn't show up to pick me up today. When I thought about it, I realized I haven't seen him *at all* since yesterday." She stared search-ingly into their faces. "Have you?"

Sabrina shook her head. Max stiffened even more, his body tight, on alert.

"No. I haven't. I figured he was napping this morning when we left." Then, his eyes flashing fire and his jaw working in his cheek, he added, "Tell me what you know, Allie. Tell me everything."

So she did, including mentioning the strange car—everything except seeing Peter. She concluded by saying, "I have a bad feeling, Max. I think something's happened to your grandfather."

BY THURSDAY MORNING, Max had notified Roderick, the Trouble P.D., the state police and anyone else he could think of about Mortimer's disappearance. He'd had to leave messages for his brothers, both of whom were cur-rently unreachable—Morgan in the Middle East, Mike undercover. If they'd been reachable, both of them would have been here by now, he had no doubt.

Getting Roderick to stay put had been tough. He'd only agreed when Max had scared the hell out of them both by saying he needed to stick near New York in case a ransom call came in.

Don't think that way, he reminded himself.

"Mr. Taylor, we have flyers going up all over downtown and volunteers ready to go door to door asking questions. The state police have circulated the picture and descrip-tion. Don't worry, we'll find your granddad."

Nodding at Chief Bennigan, Max turned to the fire-place mantel and stared absently at it. A ceramic cuckoo—the things weren't even confined to the clocks—stared back at him, its beady black eyes adding to his dark mood.

"I know you're doing what you can, Chief. I appreciate you and your officers helping us search the woods last night."

The night before had been a long, sleepless one. Trouble's tiny three-man police force had responded immediately. They, along with Max, Sabrina and her sister, had scoured every inch of the property, wondering if Mortimer had perhaps fallen somewhere in the wooded acreage surrounding the house. But they'd found nothing. No sign of him at all.

In fact, there'd been no sign of him for two days, they realized. No one had seen him since Tuesday morning at breakfast. They'd figured he had another invitation from one of the locals for dinner that night and was perhaps sleeping in the next morning. And Max had been so caught up in what was going on in his own life that he hadn't even questioned it. Had never stuck his head in Grandfather's room to make sure his bed had been slept in.

Stupid. Thoughtless.

Typical. Max the playboy, thinking only of himself.

Never in the past three years had he wanted a drink more. The crystal decanter on the bar in the corner was filled with Mortimer's best scotch. The old man had offered to put it away when Max arrived. Max had refused the offer, which, of course, had pleased Grandfather. Mortimer liked a man strong enough to stick to his principles and resist even the most obvious temptation.

He hadn't been tempted in the weeks he'd been here.

Until now.

"You don't need it," he muttered under his breath.

It wasn't as if Max had always liked to drink. Even in the Service he'd never been known to finish more than two beers a night. No, the booze itself hadn't really been the crutch during the year of his divorce.

The lifestyle had.

The parties, the women, the drinking. He'd been addicted to all of it—anything to shut out the humiliation and the regret over how badly he'd fucked up his life.

Fortunately, the one vice he hadn't submitted to was drugs. A lot of the scumbag people who'd appeared out of nowhere—following the party—had offered. But something hadn't let him take that step—not just his upbringing and his basic values, but also the knowledge that mandatory drug screening could cost him the one thing he had left: his pilot's license.

So that, at least, had been one less thing to quit cold turkey the morning Morgan had dumped him out of his bed onto the floor of his trashed beach house. Which was exactly how he'd handled the rest—cold turkey—with some professional help and family support, of course.

When he'd sent that lifestyle packing, the alcohol had gone, too. He hadn't missed it—until now.

"Did you go through all his things and make sure nothing was missing?" the chief asked. "It's not unheard of for someone to pack a bag and take a personal skedaddle for a day or two. 'Specially someone with as much traveling experience as your grandpa."

Bennigan was an amiable, small-town man with a large head that didn't quite fit on top of his body. One of those smiling bobblehead dolls come to life. But he'd been friendly and concerned. And, surprisingly, quite effective at organizing a search. His suggestion was not unreasonable, either, considering Mortimer's globe-trotting background.

"His clothes are all in his room, along with his reading

glasses and medications. Besides, he would have told me if he was going away."

"Even if he wanted to do something risky and knew you'd try to stop him?"

Max couldn't help laughing. "I couldn't stop my grandfather from climbing into a volcano for his seventy-fifth birthday. After all these years, I know better than to even try. So there'd have been no reason for him to sneak away."

Bennigan nodded, appearing convinced, not beating on the possibility any longer. Which brought him up another step in Max's estimation. "Well, with his car being in the garage, we know he can't have gone too far."

"Unless someone picked him up," Max muttered. He hadn't stopped thinking about the car Allie had mentioned seeing. "Have you had any luck with the neighbors? Did any of them see anyone lurking around here?"

Bennigan rose from the lumpy sofa—looking relieved to be off it—and stretched his back. He'd had a long night, too, but hadn't uttered a word of complaint. "Well, with the house's reputation, there's always people lurking about."

"Reputation?" Sabrina asked as she entered the room, carrying two large glasses filled with iced tea.

Max's heart twisted at the sight of her. Was it really just twenty-four hours ago that they'd embarked upon that crazy-hot plane ride? Not to mention the hours of incredibly erotic sex they'd had in the cockpit once they'd landed?

He shifted a little, wondering if there would ever come a day when he'd be able to think about Sabrina Cavanaugh without his pants getting tight. Maybe when they were ninety.

Whoa. Where the hell had that *come from?*

Max hadn't thought of growing old with a woman in, well, forever. Even during his marriage there had always been something in the back of his mind that said it might not last. Probably the circumstances under which they'd gotten married. Not to mention, of course, the whole lesbian thing.

But with Sabrina, he was picturing all the things he had never thought he'd want again. Sleeping with her every night, waking up with her every morning. Family...

Insane.

"Thank you, ma'am," Bennigan said, taking the glass of tea from Sabrina's hand and nodding gratefully. "You folks do know about the murder, don't you?"

Max had heard about it when he arrived in Trouble, mainly from people who were unhappy about Mortimer's arrival and likely wanted to scare them off with tales about the house. But he'd never gotten the specifics. "I know who it was, and that it happened somewhere in this house."

Bennigan pointed through the open French doors toward the foyer. "Right at the bottom of those stairs."

Sabrina's eyebrow cocked, but she didn't seem jumpy or nervous. He almost laughed, thinking all her experience with horror movies had enabled her to remain blasé when a lot of people would have at least gone pale at the thought of walking over a spot where someone died. But he just couldn't muster up the laughter right now.

"Who was he?" she asked.

Bennigan sipped his drink appreciatively. The air-conditioning was not quite adequate for the hot Pennsylvania summer they were experiencing. "Former mayor of Trouble. The man who owned this house."

Walking to him, Sabrina handed Max his drink. Their fingers touched briefly and she met his eyes, offering him a warm smile. No shyness, no reservations. Yesterday had completely erased any possibility of that.

They already knew each other so intimately, Max could predict when she'd lick her lips or tuck a strand of hair behind her ear. After what had happened between them, he was completely in tune with her, the way he'd never been with anyone else.

They shouldn't have spent last night and today in a terror over his grandfather. If all had been right with the world, Mortimer would have been safely sleeping in his own bed. Allie would have decided she simply had to sleep inside the house. And Max would have been sliding all over the silk pillows in that tent, making love to Sabrina in every way known to man.

"He wasn't well liked around here," Bennigan said.

Max and Sabrina had been looking only at each other, both of them—he knew—reliving the wickedly delightful moments from the day before. Clearing his throat, he murmured, "Thanks," then stepped a few sanity-saving inches away from her and focused on the chief. "He stole some money from the town treasury, right?"

Bennigan's mouth pulled tight. "He'd been siphoning it off for years, a little at a time, probably waiting until he had enough to run. Only, I guess he never thought there was enough."

There never was for a man like that.

"Trouble's capital accounts were bad enough. But he also went after the pension funds of all the town's workers."

Damn. Max hadn't heard that part. Knowing Bennigan had been the chief around here for more than a decade, he felt a renewed respect for the man. Not everyone would have stuck it out.

"Plus," the chief added, "the funds of everyone who worked for him at that clock factory."

Sabrina's brow furrowed in disgust. "I hate these clocks."

"Join the club." Glancing at his watch, Max noted the time. Ten 'til twelve—almost witching hour, when all of them squawked the longest. He'd managed to stay outside for most of the morning, tormented only by the crowing on the seven o'clock hour when he'd come inside for a cup of coffee and a quick shower.

He suddenly paused, something strange occurring to him.

The clocks...they'd been working this morning, ticking away, counting down the minutes until the next torture session began. *But Grandfather hadn't been here to wind them.*

Max had already figured out that a few of the ones in the house were eight-day types that only needed setting once a week. But the others were only good for a day before the weights and chains had to be reset.

"Maybe there really are ghosts," he murmured, though he knew the more logical answer was that Allie had done it. She'd been following Mortimer around all week, the two of them egging each other on in their silliness like a pair of seven-year-olds.

They liked each other. A lot. Which made Mortimer's disappearance even harder to bear—*all* of them felt his absence. Not just Max.

Making a mental note to ask Allie about it later, he tuned back in to the conversation.

"So did someone push him down the stairs or something?" Sabrina was asking, the way someone might ask if it had rained the day before. He adored that bloodthirsty streak.

"Looked that way at first," Bennigan said with a shrug. "His head was all squished in, which could have come from a trip down that high flight of stairs. But there was one thing that didn't fit with that theory."

Curious, Max put his drink on the table. "What?"

"The cuckoo bird sticking out of his eyeball."

He was glad he'd put the drink down, because the words, despite the chief's matter-of-fact delivery, were pretty damn unexpected. "Are you joking?"

"Uh-uh. Thing was stuck in there but good, beak-first. A wicked-looking one it was, and big—not one of the little tweeties from inside. This was carved into the wood of an oversized mahogany clock. Beak was a good three inches long, and an inch of it was sticking in old Wilhelm's brain."

"Eww," Sabrina said, wrinkling her nose.

"Ayuh. Wasn't a pretty sight."

"I don't suppose he could have stumbled against it on the way down?" Max asked. "There are clocks above every other step."

"Nope. Everybody who set foot in this house knew that particular clock—it was his favorite. Used to hang right over that fancy gold-leaf table beside the front door."

Max glanced over to the empty space above the table, grateful no one had thought to wipe the blood off the bird and put the thing back up.

"Somebody hoisted it off the wall and bashed Stuttgardt in the face with it, then musta taken it with him during his getaway. Only thing left was the bird in Willie's eye and a few shards of wood on the floor." Sipping his tea, Bennigan then added, "The blow woulda killed him anyway, you known, even without the birdie. Took a few minutes, though."

"How do you know?"

"His secretary from the factory came by with some papers for him to sign and found him there, getting busy dyin'. He had time to say a few last words."

"About who killed him?"

Appearing disgusted, Bennigan shook his head. "You'd think that, but no. Right up to the end the old miser was thinking only about the money. Saying it'd be found *in time*." He glanced around the room. "Five years is a long time and a lotta folks have looked. Nobody's ever found a nickel."

Reaching for his hat, which he'd placed on top of the old-fashioned upright piano when he entered, he put it on, obviously preparing to get back to work. "So if the young lady saw someone lurking around, I'd expect it was somebody staring at the house fantasizing about finding the lost fortune."

Max walked him to the door. "Thanks for the update."

"We'll keep on it. Your grandpa'll be home by nightfall, Mr. Taylor, I feel it in my bones."

After the chief left, Max returned to the living room. His eyes shifted to the right—toward the crystal decanter. Then straight ahead. Toward Sabrina.

She stepped into his arms. Which was the moment he realized she could become more addicting than anything he'd consumed in his entire life.

CHAPTER FOURTEEN

THOUGH SABRINA TRIED to do what she could to comfort Max, she knew as the day wore on that he was ready to tear down the walls in pure frustration. Though just as concerned, she didn't want to let on. So she did what she could to keep busy—manning the phones, putting out messages on the Internet to local news agencies. Anything she could think to do.

Absolutely the *only* good thing that all of today's activities had done was to keep her thoughts from straying too long to what had happened yesterday in Max's plane. Because going over all of that again in her mind—remembering the sheer intimacy, the physical pleasure—would have her all hot and hungry to do it some more.

He'd been amazing. The most incredible lover—like something out of a fantasy. Attentive and powerful, tender and all-consuming.

They'd gone on and on—longer than she'd ever realized a man could go. Pausing to strip off the last of his clothes, they'd climbed into the back of the plane, rolled around, changed positions. At one point when the windows were completely steamed with their exertions, they'd grabbed some bottled water out of Max's bag. Guzzling some, they'd dribbled the rest on each other's naked bodies, letting the liquid blend with the sheen of sweat on each of them.

When it had finally ended, they'd talked. Not about life-altering things—divorces, betrayals—but stupid stuff. Movies and politics and which fast-food restaurant had the best fries.

Then they'd started all over again. "Oh, yes," she whispered with a deep sigh as she stood at the window of Mortimer's office, staring out into the backyard.

"What was that sigh for?"

Turning, Sabrina spotted Max a few feet away. She hadn't heard him come in. There was no point denying it, so she said, "Exactly what you think it was for. I was just…remembering."

His lips quirked in a tiny smile—his first of the day. "Believe me, memories of that are all that's kept me sane today." Dropping one hand to her hip and sliding another into her hair to tug her close for a kiss, he whispered, "That, and the thought of how much I'm looking forward to doing it again when we find Grandpa."

Rising to meet his mouth, she kissed him, a warm, sultry, lazy kiss of two people who were already lovers in every way possible. For a moment—a long one—that kiss was the only thing that existed. But it ended all too quickly, and he soon released her, the empty look returning to his eyes.

"Look," she said, seeing the worry rapidly return to his face, "we're not doing any good here. I'm tired of doing nothing."

"What do you suggest?"

"Let's at least go downtown and do some pavement pounding ourselves. Allie's here—she can keep watch and call us if there's any word."

Appearing relieved to at last have something to do, he

nodded his agreement. Grabbing his hand, she tugged him to the caddy and in a few minutes they were driving down Trouble's main street. They parked behind Tootie's Tavern, got out and walked from shop to shop, seeing the flyers regarding Mortimer's disappearance already on display but asking about him nonetheless.

Their efforts were fruitless. Though everyone—well, *almost* everyone—offered to help and expressed concern, nobody had a clue where the old man could be.

"Maybe it's an alien abduction," Tootie said late that afternoon as they stood at the lunch counter in the tavern, waiting for a couple of to-go soft drinks. "You know we had some of them crop circles a few years back, like in that Mel Gibson movie."

"They weren't crop circles," a woman's smooth, amused voice interjected.

Sabrina recognized her—the mayor, Ann something. The attractive middle-aged woman had just walked in the door, nicely dressed and calm. One of the few *normal* people she'd met here in Trouble.

"Tiny and Billy Walker were out there with their pickup trying to get themselves interviewed on the news."

Max stared at Sabrina and she'd swear a twinkle of amusement appeared in his eyes.

"That doesn't mean the aliens couldn't be here now," said Scoot, the waitress, siding with her boss. Shoving a tray full of dirty dishes laden with chicken bones and lettuce leaves through a window to the kitchen, she added, "But I bet it's more likely that your grandpa ran across one of those wild motorcycle gangs who come through once in a while on their way to Pittsburgh."

"Oh, I feel *so* much better," Max said, his voice low, for Sabrina's ears only.

"Not that they'd hurt him or anything!" Scoot said, looking suddenly embarrassed.

Sure. It was okay to speculate that the old man was having alien probes stuck into him, but black-leather-wearing thugs made her regret her big mouth.

"They're not all psycho killers—they donate toys for kids every Christmas," she mumbled, digging herself in deeper.

"Or," said Ann, clearing her throat and glaring at Scoot, "maybe Mr. Potts suddenly remembered an out-of-town business meeting and forgot to let you know." Patting his hand, she continued. "I'm sure he's fine. Just know the whole town's praying he'll come home safe and sound real soon."

"Thank you," Max murmured, his eyes narrowing. "Though I'm not sure the *whole* town is thinking such kind thoughts."

The mayor suddenly became all business. "Has someone given you problems?"

Sabrina followed Max's stare and noticed the burly jackass who'd been so spiteful toward Mortimer last weekend. He was sitting in a booth near the door, wearing his postal uniform, devouring a sandwich as big as his head.

"No problems," Max said softly, already walking toward the other man's table. His steps were firm, deliberate. And even from across the room, Sabrina could see the way the obnoxious stranger's face paled. Because while Max was a big guy, he usually gave off an air of casual grace and charm. Right now, anger rolled off him in great dripping waves.

Dropping some money on the counter and grabbing their drinks, Sabrina followed him. "Max, keep cool. Let's go out and walk down the next block."

"I'm quite cool, Sabrina."

Yeah. That's why the muscles in the back of his neck were all bunched up and his arms were as tense and straight as tree trunks. "Don't do anything crazy."

He finally looked at her, one brow shooting up in indignation. "Me? Do something crazy? You mean like ripping the man's head off if I find out he had anything to do with my grandfather's disappearance?"

The man in the booth obviously heard. He stood, mumbling, "Sorry about your grandfather. Me'n my wife are wishing him all the best."

Max stepped into his path before he could leave. "You mean you're not cursing him anymore for ruining your perfect utopia?"

Shaking his head quickly, the man said, "I feel bad about that. Didn't mean it. I hear he's done some real nice things for folks around here."

He sounded sincere, Sabrina had to give him that. Max didn't seem so sure.

"Mr. Taylor, we all know you're upset," a woman's voice said.

The mayor again, she'd come over to diffuse the situation. She was pretty good at peacekeeper—probably had a lot of experience with it in this place.

"But really," she said, "I don't believe anyone here wishes your grandfather ill." Casting a cold stare at the postman, she added, "Isn't that right, Dean?"

"Right! It sure is. Nobody wanted that old man hurt."

This came *not* from the postman but from the front of the restaurant. A skinny, nervous-looking man, probably sixty, with a little bit of hair and a whole lot of liver spots had just come in and was bobbing his head up and down. He didn't move from the doorway, simply stared at everyone inside, Max and Sabrina in particular.

"Well, come on in, Tom, don't stand there lettin' the flies in and the air-conditioning out," said Tootie. Even as she spoke she waddled over to shut the door herself.

After shoving it closed, she made her way back behind the counter, bumping into the man as she went by. He was light enough that the blow sent him staggering a little, right into Scoot, who was serving a platter of chicken wings to a couple of teenagers. Which just proved that chicken wings really *were* capable of flight, because they went everywhere, including all over Scoot, the man—Tom—and the mayor.

"I think now's a good time to get out of here before the rest of this comedy of errors plays out and one of us ends up wearing a platter of spaghetti," Max muttered.

She absolutely agreed. Noting that Max seemed to have dropped his belligerence toward the postman—who was watching, wide-eyed like everyone else—she edged closer to the door. Tom was babbling apologies all around.

"It's all right, Mr. King," said Scoot as she dabbed at her pink polyester uniform with a handful of paper napkins. "Accidents happen."

The mayor didn't look quite so forgiving. In fact, she was staring at Tom like he had two heads. "What did you *do*, Tom?" she asked, as if not quite believing there really were greasy red spots all over her pretty cream-colored slacks.

Sabrina didn't wait to hear the man's mumbled answer, though she hoped he'd work up the nerve to blame Tootie. But she didn't want to get involved. She just focused on getting Max out of here—away from the curious townspeople and their ridiculous speculations about aliens and Hells Angels. And away from any possible confrontation with the guy in the postal cap.

Taking his arm, she led him outside. Once in the bright sunshine, she couldn't hold back a laugh. "Remember how you said this town was certifiable?"

He nodded.

"You were right."

Dropping an arm across her shoulders, he pulled her close as they walked down the sidewalk. "Still want to invest?"

She snorted.

"Guess that's a no." Squeezing her, he added, "I'm glad you're sticking around, anyway. Today would have been a lot worse if you weren't here."

Which was about as close to a declaration of genuine feelings as Sabrina had ever expected to hear from him. Feelings for *her,* anyway. "I wouldn't dream of being anywhere else. I already love your grandfather."

And his grandson?

Oh, no, please, no, a voice whispered in her head.

Oh, God, she hadn't really lost her heart to Max already, had she? Yesterday was just supposed to have been about sex—about grabbing some great memories of a terrific guy before going back to her normal life.

Damn it, *when* had her emotions gotten tangled up in this?

"Wait, is that your car?" Max asked, looking up the block.

Sabrina immediately followed his glance, her heart rate kicking up a notch when she realized her expensive rental car was barreling up the street. "Allie," she muttered.

As they both watched her sister swerve the car much too close to a delivery truck parked outside the pharmacy, Max asked, "Can she even drive?"

"Barely. I wish I'd never taught her."

He laughed.

"You think I'm kidding? You should have seen me trying to get her ready to take her driving test when she came to Philadelphia to start college."

"Why'd she start driving so late?"

"We weren't allowed to get our licenses back home," she said, rising to her tiptoes to watch which way Allie turned on Roosevelt Avenue. "Wasn't seemly for a female to drive."

His jaw dropped. Sabrina would have been amused by his reaction if the truth weren't quite so pathetic—especially since her mother and little sister and brother still lived in her narrow-minded grandfather's house. She wasn't sure which scared her worse—her baby sister being crushed by him, or her younger brother turning out like him.

"You really were serious about your family? Your parents, they…"

"My father died when I was twelve."

He nodded slowly. "Mine when I was ten."

"I know," she admitted, having talked to Mortimer about his family in the past several days. "I'm sorry."

"I'm sorry for you, too. Your mother, did she…?"

"She took us back to her family home, the one her father had told her never to darken the door of again the day she married without his permission. Yours?"

He cleared his throat, glancing away. "She died eleven months after he did. Ovarian cancer."

Her heart ached for him—for *them*. Mortimer hadn't told her that—when the subject of his only child had come up, he'd gotten silent, misty-eyed, and had left the room.

"Something else we have in common, huh?" she murmured.

"I would've been happy stopping at our favorite ice cream."

She laughed a little, though inside she felt like crying, too. For both of them. For the kids they'd been. For the lives they'd led. For the moments they'd each missed out on.

"I guess we should find out where your sister's going before she wrecks your car," he said.

"I'm more worried about her hurting herself or the baby. Sometimes she just acts like she has no common sense."

Max put his hand on her elbow. "That's why you take care of her, isn't it. This thing with your grandfather—I don't imagine they reacted well back home to Allie's…situation."

Shaking her head, Sabrina bit back the urge to launch into that whole rant. But she wouldn't. Not now and certainly not with Max. She would let loose one of these days, but when she did it would be at her grandfather or her mother. "She's my responsibility."

"For how long?" he asked. "When did you sign on to become a parent to a full-grown woman and her newborn?"

The day she'd led Peter to Allie's door. That's when. But she wasn't about to tell Max that, not when there was so much else going on in their lives.

"We'd better go," she mumbled, walking toward the parking lot where Max had parked Mortimer's Caddy.

Max grabbed her arm. "Sabrina, you can't do this on your own. Are you sure your family won't help? Your mother—have you or Allie tried talking to her without your grandfather around?"

"That's impossible. Besides, it doesn't matter whether he's around or not, he's got her so convinced she has nowhere else to go that she won't stand up to him. Once in her lifetime was her quota, I'm afraid."

Sad, so sad. As angry as she was at her mother, Sabrina's heart also broke for her. Having grown up in that rigid household, it must have taken every bit of courage she possessed to run away to marry Dad. To lose him when she had four young children to raise, well, Sabrina didn't fault her mother for doing what she had to in order to survive. She just wished her mother had found the strength to get out and stand on her own eventually.

"All I'm saying is you have to try. Give her a chance to be the woman you want her to be," Max murmured, stroking her arm as if he could sense her inner turmoil. "Everyone deserves a chance to make things right, to make up for past wrongs." He lowered his voice. "And after today, I'm very aware of the fact that you can never be certain of *anything*. People you love can be taken from you in a moment."

Covering his hand with hers, she squeezed it. "We'll find him, Max."

"And you'll think about what I said?"

"I will." She only wished she could believe reaching out to her mother would make a difference. "Now, we'd better go find Allie. I don't want to lose her."

Fortunately, there wasn't much risk of that. Because within a few minutes, as they drove to the northernmost street of Trouble and turned onto it, Sabrina spotted her car right away. It was parked in the driveway of a sagging old monstrosity of a house—which mirrored the one next door to it. They were both more dilapidated than Mr. Potts's, the paint even thinner, the walls more bowed. Wondering if this was where Allie's friend—the older lady who'd given her a ride from the bus station—lived, she pointed it out to Max.

"I thought she was going to stay near the phone," she

said with a sigh, wishing her sister wasn't so damn irresponsible. "I'm sorry."

"It's all right. The chief has one of his men stopping by the house every half hour or so to check in. We'd hear if Grandfather came back."

Funny, Max's mood seemed better—he appeared less tense, less angry than he'd been before. She suspected it was because his focus had shifted—for at least a little while—off his grandfather, and onto her. Her life. Her family. Her problems.

He would deny it and a lot of people probably wouldn't believe it, but Max Taylor was a caring and deeply feeling man. The charm and sense of humor she'd taken for granted all along—she just hadn't anticipated the integrity.

They parked in the driveway behind Sabrina's car and got out. Walking by it, Sabrina suddenly realized Allie was still in the driver's seat. Her hands clutched around the wheel, she was staring straight ahead at the house. She was so deep in thought she didn't even notice their presence until Sabrina tapped on the window.

"Oh!" Allie exclaimed, whirling around with wide eyes and an open mouth.

"*Oh* is right. What are you doing here?"

Opening the door, Allie stepped out. Giorgio hopped out after her, immediately bounding over to the closest patch of dirt and grass to do his business. "And why did you bring the dog?"

Allie swallowed visibly. "I figured he'd be a big help. You know, a bloodhound."

"The only thing that dog can track is canned dog food."

"And fruit," Max offered, laughter in his voice.

She closed her eyes, willing the image of poor naked

Mr. Fitzweather out of her head. "Come on, tell me what you're really doing here."

Allie put her hand on her stomach and rubbed. She was not going for effect here. Sabrina knew her sister often stroked her belly as if already tenderly touching her baby.

She'd be a good mother. If she ever grew up.

Finally, after a long pause, Allie squared her shoulders. "I wanted to take care of this since it's my problem…and my fault. I didn't want you to have any more to deal with."

A feeling of dread began at Sabrina's feet and started crawling up her body like a spider. This was bad. She knew it. Still, there was a part of her that couldn't help admiring Allie's calm and confidence. This wasn't her hysterical baby sister here, it was an in-control young woman. One Sabrina suddenly wondered if she'd ever even met before.

"Tell me."

Allie nodded. "Peter followed me to Trouble. I saw him go in this house yesterday."

Sabrina froze, not believing she'd heard the words correctly. But Allie's unwavering expression and the clenching of her jaw said she wasn't kidding. Peter Prescott was here. In town. Now.

Which meant it hadn't been a spider crawling up Sabrina's body. It had been a snake.

PETER HAD NO IDEA why the local Deputy Dawg cops were hanging around outside the house where Sabrina and Allie had been staying, he just knew they were in his way. He sat in his car at the edge of town, watching the place, wondering why the cops kept cruising up the driveway every thirty minutes. The waiting was driving him nuts.

Figured—hadn't his luck run like this for months? *Since Sabrina.*

"Bitch," he muttered, lifting his foam cup of coffee to his mouth and sipping from it. He was tired, having sat here most of the night, watching all the activity going on up there—lights in the woods, the cops, cars going in and out.

But no ambulances. So he didn't figure anything had happened to Sabrina, Allie or her kid.

He didn't particularly care to think of it as *his*.

"So what the hell's going on?" His head was pounding with the tension of waiting.

He should have known something would prevent him from sneaking into that house. Because things had been going too well. He'd *finally* gotten those batty old sisters to admit their stupid fiction book—which they'd submitted to him at Liberty Books a couple of years ago—was actually based on truth. They'd also revealed their theories about what the murder victim, some clockmaker, had done with his stolen money.

It had taken some doing to get them to open up to him yesterday when he'd popped in on them unannounced. They'd been suspicious, one refusing to even come to the door, the other coming out on her porch and yelling at him to go away. But when he'd told them he was visiting to talk about their brilliant piece of fiction, they'd been much more accommodating.

He'd turned on the charm. They'd been putty in his hands.

He was good at charming women, no matter how old they were. He hadn't been there ten minutes before they were falling over themselves trying to get him to have tea and freshly baked almond cookies. They'd seemed terribly disappointed when he refused.

Women. All the same.

He'd promised he would come back soon to take them up on that offer and they'd said they couldn't wait. Which was a good thing, because it meant they had no idea that if he didn't find anything up at the drafty old house where the murder had taken place, he'd have to go back to plan B.

Blackmail.

Those two silly old hags wouldn't want the police finding out about their not-so-fictional book, which they said they'd written together a few years ago. Because they knew a little *too* much detail. Which meant, in Peter's opinion, they had to have been the ones who killed the guy.

Twenty-to-life in the big house would sound pretty damn long to a couple of seventy-year-olds. He'd be willing to bet they'd do anything—*pay* anything—to prevent him from bringing their crappy manuscript to the cops.

Of course, he didn't actually have a copy of the thing.

But *they* didn't know that.

It was good to have that piece of ammunition to use against them, just in case. But he hoped he wouldn't need to. Because ever since he'd gotten to town and heard his landlord talking about all that lost money—millions, he'd claimed—Peter had been able to think of nothing else but finding it.

And how perfect would it be if he took it right out from under the noses of his ex and her new boyfriend.

Oh, yeah, he knew about the boyfriend. Everyone in town talked about the pilot—the way he and Sabrina had been stuck together like glue for days.

"See how much you stick with him once you find out the money's gone," he muttered, figuring that's what Sabrina was up to. Why she was here, in Trouble, at *that* house.

Maybe she'd found an old copy of the Feeney sisters' manuscript. Or heard a rumor. Something had tipped her off to the money and she was here trying to get it herself.

He only wished he could see her face when she realized who had gotten to it first.

MAX DIDN'T KNOW Peter Prescott, but he knew within a minute of hearing about the man that he wanted to kill him.

A few things had become clear as soon as Allie had begun filling her sister in on what was happening. First—this Peter guy was the father of Allie's baby. Second—he'd been involved with Sabrina once, too. And third—he hated them both.

That was enough for Max. The guy was a pig. Filth. It was one thing to get pissed off at an ex-girlfriend. But to then take up with her virginal younger sister, that was scumbag territory.

"What does he look like?" he bit out, seeing both women flinch as if they'd completely forgotten he was here.

"Max…"

"Don't, Sabrina. Don't tell me to stay cool and relaxed. There's only one reason an ex follows a woman across the state. He's a goddamn stalker who is dangerous and needs to be dealt with."

"I'll deal with him," Allie said, her voice not shaking at all. As if she—all one hundred thirty pregnant pounds of her—could deal with any man with revenge on his mind.

"No, sweetie, you won't. I'll deal with him."

And he would. Not knowing where his grandfather was had built up a genuine frustration in Max—a worry, and even a rage. Sounded like this Peter Prescott dude would be the perfect way to work all that off.

"What are you people doing out here making all this noise?"

Max, Sabrina and Allie all spun around at the sound of a querulous voice. On the porch closest to them stood an elderly woman, her face tugged so deep into a frown that her eyes were almost invisible beneath her bushy brows.

He recognized her easily. This was one of the women who'd been brawling over his grandfather in the street last weekend. "Sorry to disturb you, ma'am," he said, stepping closer to the porch where the woman stood. Offering her his most disarming smile, he added, "I'm Max Taylor."

Her stiff stance didn't relax. Tugging her housecoat tighter around her shoulders, she pointed an index finger at him. "What are you doing out here with two women? Have you no shame? If that's your bun in her oven, what business have you got in a car with the blond floozy who called my sister an animal?"

He heard a gasp, and had to assume Sabrina didn't like being called a floozy. He almost had to bite the insides of his cheeks to prevent a laugh from spilling out. He didn't have to turn around to know what expression was on Sabrina's beautiful face.

"Actually, ma'am, we're all going door to door looking for a missing person."

The old lady—Ida Mae Feeney, someone had called her during the fight outside Tootie's Tavern—waved him off impatiently. "Nobody's missing around here. We're all just fine. Now off you go."

Determined old lady, that was for sure. She even crossed her arms, lifting up her sagging bosom, and stepped to the top of the stairs, blocking them from trying to come up.

Allie, however, thought on her feet. "Oh," she cried, clutching at her stomach. "The baby. I need to sit down!"

The old woman apparently had some kind of heart, because she immediately came down the steps, her hands fluttering about her head like a pair of birds. "Goodness, bring the girl inside. What's wrong with you people these days? Letting a woman with child go gallivanting about on her own?"

As they walked up to the porch, Sabrina and Max each holding one of Allie's elbows, the younger woman winked.

He liked Sabrina's sister—liked her a lot. Even if she did have the most horrible timing.

Reaching the front door, minding their hostess's order to wipe their feet, they stepped inside. The air in the old house smelled of rose petals and talcum powder. Thick. Cloying. Not an inch of fussily papered wall space was left clear of some heavy, dark furniture, and there wasn't even much room to walk around it. Maneuvering Allie between an enormous rolltop desk and a solid side table, they managed to get her to the couch, which looked like a lumpy corpse covered in worn, faded velvet.

When they sat down, he realized it felt more like a lumpy bale of straw covered in worn, faded velvet.

"Tea?" the woman asked.

Sabrina nodded. "That would be…"

"I was asking *her*," she said, nodding at Allie. "Not you."

Sabrina's lips disappeared into her mouth. Whether to keep from bursting into laughter or just to avoid telling their hostess she was a rude old shrew, he honestly didn't know. He suspected Ida Mae was holding a grudge about the cage remark.

"No, thank you," Allie said. "But water would be nice."

The woman nodded hard, sending her chins bouncing

beneath her face and her mammoth bosom bouncing beneath her housecoat. "Mind that dog," she said, pointing at Giorgio, who'd followed them inside. "I usually don't let dogs into my house." Then a reluctant smile curled her lips. "But since I heard what he did to nasty-bum Al Fitz-weather, I guess he's all right."

Cackling in audible schadenfreude over Mr. Fitzweather's humiliation, she left the room. Once she was gone, the three of them looked at one another. "What are we doing here again? I can't breathe without feeling like I'm being smothered by a musty blanket full of rotting rose petals."

"Nice description," Sabrina said.

"Thanks. From a writer, I'll take that as a compliment."

She quickly looked away, clearing her throat. "Now, Allie, you're sure Peter was inside this house yesterday?"

"Positive."

"Ah, so that's the mission, trying to figure out what he was doing here?" Remembering the way the old lady and her sister had been brawling over Mortimer, he murmured, "Plus we can ask her when she last saw Grandfather."

From the next room, he could hear the sounds of Ida Mae slamming cabinet doors and cracking an ice cube tray. He also suddenly heard a thump from upstairs, almost directly overhead. Exchanging glances with Sabrina, he noticed her concern.

When their hostess returned with two water glasses—one of which she handed to Allie, and the other of which she kept for herself—Sabrina asked her about the noise. "Does your sister live with you? If so, you might want to check on her—I think something fell upstairs."

The woman ignored her, smiling pleasantly at Allie. "Now, what did you say you're doing today? Looking for someone?"

Allie nodded. "Mr. Potts. You remember Mr. Potts?"

"Well, of course, what a kind gentleman. Sister and I just loved having him over for tea last week."

"So your sister *does* live with you?" Sabrina asked, obviously still worried, as was Max.

Frowning, Ida Mae finally deigned to turn her head slightly toward Sabrina. "She most certainly does not. She lives next door. I called her a moment ago and she's going to come join us."

"But the noise…"

"Rats. It is an old house, you know."

Must've been a pair of hundred-pound rats, by the sound of the thump. But they obviously didn't bother the old lady, who said the word as if she'd just mentioned having a niggling little problem with too many ladybugs in her garden.

Before Sabrina could reply—and judging by her wide-open mouth, she was also surprised by the lady's unconcern about having giant mutant rats in her house—the screen door opened. The sister came in, giving them all a languid wave. "Why, good afternoon, how lovely that you've come to call."

She was smaller than the other one—thinner and probably younger—and obviously dressed for company. Wearing a long, flowery dress and a wide-brimmed red hat, she smiled as though they were her audience and she an old-time movie starlet. The yellowed gloves—once white—completed the look that screamed "I'm living in the forties in my mind."

"Ivy," their hostess said with a frown. She also tugged at her housecoat, quite obviously wishing she was dressed to compete with her sibling.

"Ida." The newcomer's smile was tight. Then, almost floating across the floor and lowering herself onto the edge of a chair, she turned her attention toward Max. "Well, aren't you the handsome one. And so much like your grandfather. I was just telling that man he's the spitting image of Steve McQueen, if Steve McQueen hadn't died so young. And wasn't that an almighty shame…had the cancer, you know."

"Ivy…"

She ignored her sister's warning tone. "I imagine you have to beat the young ladies off with a stick." Then she glanced toward Sabrina and Allie. Quickly dismissing them, she leaned closer to Max, dropping her gloved hand on his thigh. *High* on his thigh, to Max's discomfort. Sotto voce, she added, "Might want to get a bigger one, though, looks like you missed a few."

He didn't dare look at Sabrina. "Speaking of my grandfather…"

"A delightful man."

Ida Mae piped in. "A wonderful man."

"A charming man."

"A…a well-cultured man."

Max interrupted. "Yes, indeed, he is. But I must ask, have you ladies seen him anytime since Tuesday morning?"

Ivy looked at Ida Mae. "Tuesday…hmm…"

"Of course not. Why would we have seen him? He came to tea over a week ago, at least."

"But you also saw him last Saturday," Sabrina said, her baby blues wide and innocent. "Surely you remember, when you were downtown with him?"

Oh, man, if old ladies could turn their eyes into laser beams and fry people, the woman he was crazy about would be a million floating particles of Sabrina dust. "I'm sure I don't know what you are referring to," Ida Mae said, her tone icy.

"Not a clue," Ivy added. Her forced, half smile emphasized the creases of heavy makeup on her cheeks.

Sabrina opened her mouth, but before she could say anything, another loud thump came from upstairs.

"The radiator," Ivy murmured.

On this sweltering summer day? That made sense.

Allie picked Giorgio up off the floor and lifted him onto her lap—what little of it there was. "Thought it was rats."

"Rats? Gracious what an unusual child you are," Ivy said.

"Ivy..."

"Now, Ida Mae, do tell me, have you offered our guests some tea and cookies?" Glancing hard at Sabrina, Ivy added, "You would probably especially like the almond-flavored ones."

"Ivy, will you be quiet!"

Rolling her eyes, Ivy leaned back in her chair and crossed her ankles. "Oh, all right, play hostess your own way."

Ida Mae stood. "Was that all you people wanted?"

Ida Mae's way of playing hostess left something to be desired.

As for her question? No. Frankly, Max wanted some explanation as to whether these two were for real. He was beginning to think he'd fallen into an old movie and Bette Davis and Joan Crawford were about to scratch each other's eyes out.

Another thump. This time, all five of them looked up. "I should go see about that," Ivy murmured, rising to her feet.

Ida Mae grabbed her arm. "Oh, no, you will not. It's my house. If anyone goes to see, it will be me."

The two sisters drew closer, nose to nose. Ivy's eyes

narrowed. "Maybe it's best for us to go together, sister dear. Remember, share and share alike."

And with those words, Max suddenly had a bad feeling. About what might be making those strange noises.

He and Sabrina exchanged looks over Allie's head. In that instant, he knew she'd had the same immediate fear. Her lips were parted, color rushing into her cheeks. "Wait," he mouthed.

Thinking quickly, he tried to come up with a plan—a reason to get the sisters out of the way so he could go upstairs and investigate. As it turned out, he didn't have to. Because Allie, either by design or by accident, suddenly slid Giorgio off her lap and onto the coffee table in front of her. The dog skittered on it, his nails slipping around on the highly polished surface.

"Watch out for that animal," Ida Mae yelled.

Ivy didn't yell, she actually shrieked. "Daddy!"

Max had no idea what the woman was talking about— not until poor Giorgio skidded to the far end of the table and bumped into an old-fashioned, lidded urn. It—and the dog—flew off, landing on the hardwood floor. As they landed, the urn broke, the dog yelped and a puff of fine gray powder sifted up from the chunks of broken ceramic.

This, he presumed, would be Daddy.

"Argh!" the one in the flower dress shrieked. Launching toward the broken urn, she almost slipped in her high-heeled shoes. The old lady landing on the floor and covering herself with her father's remains would certainly be the appropriate encore to today's surreal performance, but she managed to remain steady as she dropped to her knees beside the mess.

Sabrina jumped up, obviously realizing what Butch had knocked over. "Oh, ma'am, I am so sorry."

"Ivy…" said the other one, Ida Mae, who'd remained surprisingly calm.

"That beast, that monster," Ivy ranted, her slim body shaking as she reached for the ash.

Ida Mae just sighed. "Ivy…"

"Your dog is dead, do you hear me?" Ivy lunged at Butch, who'd stayed on the edge of the sooty ashes, but she stopped short of crawling through them to wring his poor little neck. So she settled for pointing. "Dead doggy, that's you."

As per his nickname, the dog didn't seem intimidated. In fact, he casually leaned down and sniffed at the mess, oblivious to the danger he faced at the hands of a deranged old lady.

Max knew he should stay here and sort this out. Help clean up. At least stand up for poor old Butch. But he was already edging toward the stairs.

"Giorgio, *come*," Sabrina ordered. "Ma'am, I am so sorry. Is there anything we can do?"

"Just leave," Ida Mae snapped.

"Oh, my God," Ivy shrieked, even louder than before. "His finger—that monster has Daddy's finger!"

For a millisecond, Max winced in shock. But common sense immediately made him realize the little hunk of fleshy colored meat in Butch's mouth couldn't possibly have come from the late Mr. Feeney. He knew enough about cremation to know that was impossible.

"Sister, it isn't Daddy. Calm yourself," Ida Mae said, finally showing some emotion.

"How can you be calm?" Ivy wailed. "Our father is being cannibalized."

Max didn't think it would be called cannibalism—even if it were truly Mr. Feeney's digit dangling from Butch's mouth—since Butch was a dog. But he wasn't going to argue the point.

The older sister shuffled over and bent down, dropping one arm over her sibling's thin shoulders. "No, he isn't. I swapped him with the ashes from my grill so you wouldn't hide him from me anymore. It's a bit of hot dog, that's all."

The younger sister looked up, her tear-stained face looking hopeful, relieved. But her expression quickly faded and she staggered to her feet. "You did what?"

He sensed it was now or never. The sisters were distracted, about to battle over their father's remains—as, apparently, they fought over a lot of things. So not wasting another second, Max dashed up the stairs two at a time.

What he was thinking seemed impossible. Ridiculous. But given the scene downstairs, the way they talked, the physical brawl last Saturday...anything was possible.

Running down the upstairs hallway toward the farthest door—which would be the room directly over the one he'd just been in—he grabbed the handle.

Locked.

From downstairs, the shouting grew louder, both sisters demanding that the other apologize. Apparently, they hadn't even noticed he was gone.

He tried the knob again, twisting harder this time, but it didn't budge. Hearing another muffled thump from inside the room, however, he whispered, "Fuck it," and threw his shoulder against the door, breaking it in.

The force of the blow propelled him into what appeared to be a bedroom, all draped with lacy white fabric and dimly lit with a few fringed lamps. Dominating the room was a large four-poster bed complete with mosquito netting and a bedspread which, if he was not mistaken, graphically illustrated the Kama Sutra.

But he didn't have time to process that. He was too busy processing what else he was seeing.

That would be his grandfather. Naked. Tied to the bed. And grinning like a fool.

CHAPTER FIFTEEN

"BUT I DON'T *want* to press charges," Mortimer said for the dozenth time as Sabrina tucked a blanket over his lap.

Allie hovered nearby, a glass of cognac in her hand.

"Don't worry about that now," Sabrina said. "Let's just make sure you're comfortable. Can I get you something to eat?"

The old man, who looked none the worse for wear after his kidnapping ordeal, shook his head. "That skinny one's a good cook. But they're teetotalers, so I do want *that*." He nodded toward the glass Allie was holding, and she passed it over.

They'd arrived back at the house a few minutes ago. Mortimer, who'd immediately gone to dress, was now calmly sitting in his favorite chair, a little smile playing about his lips as if he'd rather enjoyed all the fuss.

Max was in the other room, calling his brothers and friends to tell them his grandfather had been found safe. Sabrina and Allie remained with Mortimer, watching over him protectively as they waited for the arrival of Chief Bennigan.

They'd called the police from Sabrina's cell phone as they got in the car at Ida Mae's house. The sisters hadn't even seen them leave, hadn't noticed Max coming down the stairs, holding his blanket-wrapped grandfather against his side. Sabrina, seeing them, had grabbed Allie and the dog, and they'd all taken off as fast as they could go.

Sabrina hadn't gotten the whole story yet—as far as what Max had found in the bedroom in that crazy old lady's house. Other than Mortimer. But she'd sensed by the looks exchanged between grandson and grandfather that it had been bad. The fact that Mortimer had been wearing nothing but a blanket made her amend that to outrageous.

"They didn't… You don't think they…" Allie whispered.

"Shh." She didn't want to think about it. Or picture it.

"Bennigan's not here yet?" Max said as he entered the room, his gaze immediately focusing on his grandfather.

"I said there's no need for the police." Mortimer sipped his cognac. "No harm done, I'm just fine."

"Grandfather, you were kidnapped."

"Merely restrained." Chuckling, he murmured, "in more ways than one," then sipped his drink again.

Crossing his arms, Max leaned against the desk. "Are you telling me you went up to that room voluntarily?"

"No. I'd gone for tea, you see, on Tuesday. I was commenting to Miss Ida Mae that her spiced tea tasted so much like something I'd tried back in India, oh, years ago." He thought about it, tilting his head. "Orange blossoms—it was fragrant, strong. Exotic." Shrugging, he added, "The next thing I knew, I woke up exactly where you found me."

"So they *poisoned* you."

"*Poisoned* is a strong word." He chuckled. "Been a long time since anyone's slipped me a Mickey Finn."

Yikes, good thing she hadn't accepted the tea Miss Ivy had mentioned. Sabrina couldn't believe the old man was taking this whole thing so calmly.

His grandson, however, was not. "Good Christ, Grand-father, they could have killed you."

"Nonsense. They were protecting me."

Rolling his eyes, Max threw himself into a chair and stared at the old man in disbelief.

"It's true. They said they were concerned that someone wanted to do me harm. It was a public service, you know."

"Public service, my ass."

Mortimer finished his drink and set his empty glass on the table. "Gracious, you act as though I've never been tied up by two women before."

Oh, *that* was way too much 411.

"The Feeney sisters are harmless to everyone except each other," he added.

Sabrina wasn't entirely sure that was true. "Mr. Potts," she said, sensing Max's growing frustration, "did the... ladies say why they were worried about your safety?"

"Not specifically—just that they've seen someone skulking about up here and were afraid he meant to do me harm."

Guess the Feeneys hadn't much cared if she, Max or Allie came to any harm. Then again, thinking of how they'd "protected" Mortimer, that was probably a good thing.

"I wonder if it was the same person I saw," Allie murmured, sounding concerned. "You don't think...do you suppose Peter..."

"But why?" Sabrina asked. "Why would he?"

"Maybe to mess with your heads?" Max stood and paced the room, his angry steps pounding on the wood floor. "We never did find out from the sisters what the hell he was doing there."

"Oh, if you need information from Miss Ida and Miss

Ivy, feel free to go back. They're quite amenable," Mortimer said.

"To kidnapping and assault," Max muttered.

"I'm unscathed, I assure you."

Pounding his hand on the edge of the mantel, Max snapped, "Grandfather, they *molested* you."

The old man snorted. "Don't be ridiculous."

Allie mumbled, "Think I'll go watch for the police."

Sabrina was right there with her. "Me, too."

"No need of that," Mortimer said. "I have no secrets. I do not consider myself a victim. Imagine, at my age, having the kind of adventure I hadn't expected ever to have again. Kidnapped by two beautiful women and used as a sex slave? Why, that hasn't happened to me in years, not since that time in Singapore."

Okay, she had definitely heard enough. Grabbing her sister's arm, she led Allie out of the room, hearing Max's deep groan as he realized he, alone, would get to listen to the gory details.

Shutting the French doors to the living room behind them, Sabrina stood with Allie in the foyer, watching out the front window for the police to arrive. "I'm sure they'll be here soon."

"I just hope Mr. Potts has figured out what he's going to tell them when they get here. The truth is a little...wild."

That was putting it mildly.

"Sabrina," Allie said, "We haven't had a chance to talk privately about the Peter situation. I'm sorry I led him here."

Rubbing a weary hand over her brow, Sabrina shrugged. "You don't know that you did. He could easily have followed me."

"I doubt it. I ran into him the night you left town."

Her sister still had that unexpected note of calm in her

voice. A few months ago, she would have anticipated at least a hint of a whine. Something, she realized, had changed in Allie since she'd arrived in Trouble. "I see."

"I've been thinking about that a lot. He made some threats."

"He hurt you?" She grabbed Allie's shoulders.

Allie shook her head quickly. "No. He threatened that he might try to take the baby."

"That's ridiculous, he doesn't want the baby."

"I know. But it scared me enough to make me realize that I can't just keep coasting along, focused only on the day this child is born. I have to think about creating some kind of future for us, so no judge would ever think I can't be a good mother."

Wow. That was very un-Allie-like.

For the past several months, since the day her sister had come to her tearfully, confiding her pregnancy—and who the father was—Allie had said nothing about what would happen after the baby was born, beyond how cute he or she was going to be. So she'd *really* been thinking about this.

"Are you considering going back to school?" Something else occurred to her. "Or reaching out to Mom? Because Max has me halfway convinced that we should try talking to her again."

More than halfway convinced, really. During their conversation today, when Max had talked about how uncertain life was and how quickly you could lose someone you care about, Sabrina had realized she didn't want to let her family disappear from her life. Not without trying one more time to keep them in it. "Maybe we could call her together. Or show up on Grandpa's doorstep with a Baby On Board sign."

Allie's laugh was heartfelt and yet melancholy. It trailed off and she lowered her gaze, dropping her hand on her stomach. "Actually," she said, her voice soft, "I've been thinking, maybe instead of going back to Philadelphia, I'll stay here."

Sabrina's heart stopped mid-beat. "You're joking."

"No, I'm not. Mr. Potts has told me I could stay. We discussed it on Monday while I helped him organize his office."

Wondering if her sister realized she was talking about exchanging one type of dependency for another, Sabrina opened her mouth to reply.

But Allie went on. "*Not* as charity. He said he needs an assistant. Someone to help with his appointments and correspondence. To keep his schedule and help him manage his business day."

"The baby…"

"Miss Emily already told me that if I do stay here long term and ever need a babysitter, she's had experience in child care."

"You can't do this," Sabrina said, already shaking her head. "You're coming home with me. We have it all planned."

Allie squeezed her hand. "I know you've been working so hard to take care of me—*us*. But, Sabrina, you don't have to. I can take care of myself. When the baby's older, I'll go back to school. There's a college campus in the next town and they offer Internet classes. I checked."

She'd *checked*.

"With the credits from the community college in Ohio, plus the ones from this last year in Philadelphia, I only need a few more classes to get my Associate of Arts degree."

"This is ridiculous. You *can't*." And she meant it. Allie

couldn't leave. Not after all these months of planning—anticipating. Her sister couldn't just waltz out of Sabrina's life, taking the baby with her.

They were the only family she had left.

"I know this is hard for you to understand, but the truth is, I like it here. I never hated Ohio as much as you did—other than living with Grandpa. And Philadelphia never felt like home to me. *This* place felt like home as soon as I arrived."

Sabrina opened her mouth to argue some more, already picturing all the terrible things that could happen to her little sister alone in a new town. But before she could say anything, they both heard the sound of a car door slamming out front.

"It's the chief," Allie murmured, glancing out the window.

"We're not finished talking about this. You don't have to stay here, we can make it work. I'll take care of you."

Allie put her arms around Sabrina's shoulders and pulled her as close as she could, her belly pressed between them. "I love you. I don't know what I would have done without you."

Sabrina couldn't stop tears from welling up in her eyes. Allie meant it. She really, truly planned to stay here.

"I want you to be happy. But this is my life, and it's about time I start taking responsibility for it."

A sharp knock sounded on the front door, but before either of them reached to answer it, Allie whispered, "Sabrina, it's not your fault. None of this was your fault. I don't blame you and you need to stop blaming yourself."

Then she stepped away, opened the door and invited the police chief into the house. Offering Sabrina one more gentle, Madonna-like smile, she led the man into the living room where Mortimer and Max waited.

Sabrina stood there, staring at the group in the other room, wondering how her world could have changed so completely in the past ten minutes. Everything she'd thought she knew about how she'd be spending the next few years had just dissipated like a fine mist under the morning sun. When she left here to return to her real life, she'd be losing her sister, and her niece or nephew.

And Max.

IT DIDN'T TAKE Tom King long to realize someone else was watching the Stuttgardt house. And it wasn't the chief or one of his officers. Tom knew everyone in Trouble, and the young man with the black hair who'd been parked on the edge of town staring up at the house wasn't a local.

He was after something. Something that belonged to Tom.

The money.

"Oh, no, you don't," he muttered as once again he drove by the parked car, sitting in the same spot at eight o'clock that night as it had been at eight this morning. Like a predator.

If the old man hadn't been found—and wasn't the town whispering about what'n hell he'd been up to with those evil old Feeney sisters for two days—he'd have suspected this stranger of being involved in the disappearance.

But Potts was home again, the house had been full of people coming and going all evening, and still the stranger waited. Probably hoping he'd be able to sneak up there under cover of darkness. Just like Tom was doing.

He couldn't stand this. The longer those people lived in that house, the more likely it was that one of them would find something—a clue, even the money itself. The thought that he'd gone through all of this for nothing was unbearable. Just bumping into the grandson today at Tootie's had made him damn near start blubbering out a confession.

The ring of his cellular phone quickly distracted him from his dark thoughts. He recognized the number right away and answered. "I can't get in. There's too much going on."

"It's all right. Wait until Saturday."

He quickly thought about it. "The Founders' Day Festival?"

"Yes. They'll all be at the festival, the house'll be empty, and you can search then."

Sounded like a good idea. "You're sure they'll be there?"

"Mortimer Potts and his family are getting an award for the way they've helped the town. They'll be there."

"Okay, then," Tom said, relieved to avoid any nighttime hunting tonight. But that didn't mean his competitor would.

Which gave him an idea. "That fella I told you about is still there, waiting for his chance. But I think I know a way to fix him." He revealed his idea.

"That'll work. Keep me posted—you know I'll back you up."

"You might be hearing about some more activity going on up at that house tonight."

Disconnecting the call, Tom sat back in his seat, watching quietly, prepared for a long vigil. When the dark-haired man made his move, Tom would be ready. He just wondered how the stranger was going to like a stay in the Trouble city jail.

THOUGH HE TRIED, Max couldn't talk his grandfather into pressing charges against the Feeney sisters. Mortimer had bent so far backward trying to convince the police chief he'd been a willing participant in their weird games, even Max had begun to believe it.

He really wished he hadn't been there for the details, particularly when Mortimer started talking about how much he liked that newfangled Viagra stuff—not that he'd needed it at first. Even as he thought it, though, he couldn't help again hoping he'd be like the old man when he was that age. Loving and living and causing a fuss, with a woman on each arm.

No, just one woman.

Yeah. He was very much afraid there was just one woman. Just one he'd *ever* want. From now until the day he died.

He didn't quite know how, when or why, but he'd fallen in love with Sabrina. Maybe it was that moment when she'd taken off her seat belt on the plane, putting her trust in him to keep her safe. Or earlier—the moment she'd shown up at the carousel.

He couldn't be sure. And since he had never been in love before, he probably shouldn't have been sure that the emotion he felt for her was love. But he knew.

"So what are you going to do about it?" he asked himself late that night as he walked out the back door and down the steps. Sabrina was in the tent…by herself. As if knowing the two of them would want to be alone, Allie had offered to sleep in the house, in case Mortimer needed anything and Max couldn't hear him from up on the third floor.

Lifting the flap, he stuck his head inside. "Knock, knock."

He expected a laughing invitation, or at least a smile of welcome. But he didn't see Sabrina at all. The inside of the tent was shadowy—made cool and comfortable by the generator-operated air-conditioning unit. But all except one of the lights running off that generator were turned off.

His eyes quickly adjusting, he looked around, finally seeing a curled-up mound under the covers of one of the plush down mattresses. "Sabrina?"

A sniff was her only response.

Concerned now, he walked to her, crouching beside the bed, tugging the covers away. She was curled on her side, her hands clenched together, tucked under her chin. Her lovely face was stained with tears and her eyes red.

"What, honey, what is it?" He looked around, checking every shadowy corner of the massive, billowy structure. "Did someone hurt you?"

"I'm fine. But Allie…"

"Is something wrong with her?"

"She wants to stay here, Max. With your grandfather, who offered her a job. To live in Trouble and raise her baby here."

"Wow." Without another word, he crawled in beside her, sliding one arm under her shoulders so she could curl up against his chest. Sabrina wasn't a tiny woman, but she felt incredibly vulnerable in his arms, particularly because of the way her body was shaking as if chilled, though the tent was quite comfortable.

"I'm sorry. I know you feel responsible for her."

"She's my family. She and the baby are my *only* family now." Burrowing her face into his neck, she added, "I know it's Allie's baby, but I also felt like it was mine. And I wanted it, Max. I wanted them both in my life."

He ran his hand across her back, a comforting stroke, wondering if she would possibly believe him if he told her he knew how it felt. To want that—a family, a child. No, her situation was nothing like his, and yet, like him she was mourning something she'd thought she was going to have that had suddenly been taken away.

He understood her pain, would have taken it into himself if he could. Instead, he settled for trying to let her know she was not alone. "Have I ever told you why I got married?"

She shook her head, smearing the moisture of her tears on his neck. "No, you haven't."

So he did. Speaking slowly at first, he told her everything. How he'd grown up wanting to be just like his father. Had joined the military at twenty-one, right out of college and immediately applied for the Pilot Training Program. Two years later he'd met Teresa, and then came the supposed pregnancy. He remained stoic as he told Sabrina about how he'd chosen to let go of his dream and withdraw his application to be a military pilot so he could be a father—of a child that had never even existed.

"There was never any baby?" she asked, sitting up in the bed and staring at him, her eyes wide with disbelief and compassion.

"No," he admitted. "She lied. Heard I'd be coming into a lot of money at twenty-five and figured she'd marry some of it. I didn't know until after we split up. I'd thought she had a miscarriage while I was stationed overseas."

"I'm sorry," she whispered, lifting her hand to his face. She stroked his cheek, and he turned to place a kiss on her palm. "I'm so sorry that happened to you, Max. That you had to give up your dream—" Her voice broke. "That you were used in that way."

"I didn't tell you to try to play for the sympathy vote. I just wanted you to know."

Because of what she was going through now. And because of what Max hoped would happen between them in the future.

No, he wasn't ready to tell her all his secrets. Some things were too ugly—too dark and humiliating—and he didn't want to let her know how weak and stupid he'd once been. How much of a mess he'd made of his life.

But this he could share with her.

"Did you— Was there any chance of you getting back into the Pilot Training Program?"

He shook his head. "Nah. By the time I walked in on Teresa and her, um, *friend,* I'd already been discharged."

"Oh, I figured you were still in…"

He continued. "Being an Air Force pilot would have required ten years' service, but once I withdrew, I only owed a total of four. By the time I met Teresa, I'd already done two. Finished my last year after we got married, then headed home to try to make my marriage work. Try to have another baby to make up for the one I thought we'd lost." He laughed humorlessly. "Surprised her by coming home a day early. She was surprised all right. But not as much as me."

Sabrina muttered a foul curse under her breath, which made him laugh for real this time. "Thanks for the indignation on my behalf."

"I'd like to rip her lips off."

"Violent. I like that in a woman."

She settled back against him, the curves of her body fitting naturally to him, her head tucked against his neck, one leg lifted over his thighs. Dropping her hand onto his chest, she trailed her fingers down. Lower. Until she reached the waistband of his jeans and tugged his cotton T-shirt out of it so she could touch his bare stomach.

The touch tingled. Burned. Flared.

Rolling her onto her back, he slid one leg between hers before covering her mouth in a deep, hungry kiss. Sabrina wrapped her arms around his neck and her legs around his hips and ground into him in welcome. She was hungry and hot, but not desperate like they'd started out yesterday. This was slow and lazy.

Which was exactly the way he wanted to make love to her.

"I've been wanting you since the minute we left the airport yesterday," he mumbled as he moved his mouth lower to kiss her jaw, then the delicate skin of her throat.

"That long? I wanted you as soon as we got off the plane."

He chuckled softly, his cheek brushing her skin. Beneath him Sabrina shivered.

"Your face is rough."

"Sorry. Didn't have time to shave today."

She ran her fingers through his hair. "I like it." When he nuzzled lower, until his lips met the cleavage revealed by her low-cut top and his chin scraped against the top curves of her breasts, she added, "I *love* it."

Wriggling out of the top, she tossed it aside, rolling sinuously across the satin fabric of the bed. Her blond hair spilled around her face, bright and soft against a turquoise-colored pillow, which matched her eyes.

He looked down at her, admiring everything, from the fine line of her collarbone—which he tasted—to the taut, rosy tip of her breast—which he licked.

"Max…"

"I'm busy, Sabrina," he whispered as he continued working his way down her body, brushing his lips down over her belly, dipping his tongue into her navel.

She writhed. "Please."

He ignored her, watching in delight as a rosy glow of warmth washed over Sabrina's pale body. Wanting to see more of her, he unbuttoned her pants, pushing them off with her help. She wore just a tiny pair of panties like the ones she'd had on yesterday, but yellow. And he suddenly remembered what he'd wanted to do to her through those panties yesterday.

Shimmying down, he scraped his teeth along the elastic barely extending above her soft curls. She arched toward him, silent, both asking for what she wanted and giving him permission to give it to her.

Not that he was asking. And not that he'd have waited for her to say yes.

Blowing on the silky fabric, he shifted her legs farther apart. Her panties were damp and he breathed in, inhaling the musky scent of her arousal combined with the perfume of her skin.

"Please, Max, taste me," she moaned as she writhed against the silk bed, obviously liking the feel of it on her body.

He brushed his lips across the dampness even as he moved his hands to her thighs, slowly sliding them up each one so he could hold her still. Exactly where he wanted her.

"More," she ordered, sounding frustrated, trying to arch toward him.

She couldn't. He had her pinned in place, vulnerable, the want rolling off her until it made her shake. Finally, when he heard the choppy desperation of her breathing, he lowered his mouth over her, wetting the silky fabric even more with his tongue just as he'd imagined doing yesterday in the cockpit.

She moaned. Sighed.

But he wanted nothing separating his mouth from that sweet spot. He wanted to see her—much closer than he'd seen her yesterday. Make her come against his tongue, her legs shaking, her body heaving against the satin sheets, completely out of control.

Tugging her panties off, he licked her delicate skin, right above her pelvis. She tried arching again, and this time, because he wanted her even closer, he allowed it. Her curls brushed his chin, then his lips, and without any warning, he opened his mouth on her and slid his tongue deep.

"Oh, God," she said, her voice high-pitched and desperate.

She tried to move. He kept her in place. Dipping into her for taste after taste, he made thorough love to her, hearing by her cries when she was close to reaching her peak. Sucking her clit between his lips, he toyed with it, then finally let go of one of her legs. He needed to feel her wrapped around him—some part of him—so he plunged a finger into her tight channel.

Her release washed over her until she shook—just as he'd hoped—and she cried out in satisfaction. While she was coming, he took a moment to rip off his clothes and sheathe himself. He was back between her legs before she'd even opened her eyes or started breathing normally again.

"Sabrina?"

"Uh-huh?"

"Still with me?" he asked, laughter in his voice.

She still didn't look up. "Uh-huh."

"Good," he said, sliding his cock into her.

Her eyes flew open. "Oh, yeah. I'm with you."

"I'd hate to think you were somewhere else." He eased farther, driving deeper. Sabrina arched up, taking more, until he was buried inside her. "We're a good fit."

She tugged him close for a kiss. "We're a perfect fit."

Proving that, she rocked up, and he rocked down. They slid and rolled, thrusting, stroking, on and on until their bodies were slick with sweat and the air thick with sex.

Finally, when he couldn't hold it back anymore, he gave himself over to the spasms of pleasure. Groaning, he drove into her one last time, feeling her squeeze them both into release.

Rolling over onto his back, he took Sabrina with him, holding her on top of him, not letting her pull away. They remained that way, joined, for a long time, until the world started turning again and they were part of it. Passionate caresses segued into intimate strokes and the desperate raging of their hearts slowed into the relaxed comfort of a shared rhythm.

"That was amazing," she murmured, her breath tickling the hair on his chest. "I've never felt so—"

Suddenly, Sabrina's whole body jerked, growing stiff and tense. Immediately realizing something was wrong, Max pushed her toward the side of the tent and sat up, blocking her with his body. "What is it?"

"Somebody was there," she whispered, grabbing the sheets and drawing them around her naked body. "I just saw a shape standing there—not round enough to be Allie or tall enough to be Mortimer. Then the tent flap fell."

"Son of a bitch," he muttered. Diving out of the bed for his clothes, he stopped moving only long enough to yank off the condom and yank on his jeans. "I'll kill him."

He was out of the tent, pounding barefoot across the lawn toward the back of the house, within twenty seconds. Jeans zipped but not buttoned, bare chested and still wet and sweaty from the fabulous sex he and Sabrina had just enjoyed.

The sex someone had *watched* them enjoying.

But he couldn't think of that. Could think of nothing

except catching whoever it was the Feeney sisters had warned his grandfather about. And if it was Peter Prescott, so much the better. Because Max wanted to *hurt* the man.

"Max," Sabrina called in a loud whisper as she raced after him, the silk sheet the only thing covering her. "Don't do anything crazy."

Crazy? He wasn't going to do anything crazy. He was merely going to break the arms and legs of the bastard who'd been spying on him and Sabrina.

Seeing a shadow climbing through a window of Mortimer's office, he dashed up the steps. He ignored the shards of glass that dug into his bare feet—the bastard had smashed the porch light to disguise his break-in.

Max dove into the intruder from a yard away, dragging him out of the window and onto the planked floor. He was solid, tall, but no match for the force of an enraged man tackling him by surprise.

They rolled across the porch, Max immediately going for the arms to pin him. But the guy was wiry, quick, and he landed a glancing punch to Max's shoulder.

With three quick jabs to the dark-clothed, shadowy stranger's face, Max quickly subdued him and knelt, one knee on his chest, pinning him like a bug stuck to a display board.

Sabrina came up the steps. "Careful of the broken glass," he ordered. She paused. "Max, the police are coming, I see the flashing lights coming up the road."

Damn. He really didn't want the interference.

He especially regretted it when he turned the intruder's face toward Sabrina. The moonlight and other outside lights gave her a clear view and she gasped. "Peter."

A red, hazy cloud of rage filled his vision. "That's it, you bastard, you're dead."

He drew back his arm, ready to pound the guy through

the floorboards, but Sabrina grabbed his fist. "Let him be arrested."

"Your feet," he snapped, not even looking over his shoulder at her.

Peter's eyes bugged out, which was when Max finally jerked his head to look over his shoulder. Sabrina stood there, stark naked, the sheet bunched up on the deck floor beneath her, protecting her toes. But nothing protected the rest of her body.

Bare skin and rage looked really good on this woman.

But the fact that Peter was staring at her too made that red cloud come back, and Max crunched his knee down a little harder, until the man whimpered.

"He's not worth it. Let the police take care of it."

"She's right," a voice said.

Looking up, he saw Allie standing on the end of the porch, obviously having come out the kitchen door. "We heard the noise."

Wonderful. His grandfather was right behind her, watching wide-eyed. He was practically bouncing on his toes, looking ready to leap right into the fight. Of course, Max would be willing to bet he had also snuck a peek or two at Sabrina. Max certainly would have, eighty or not.

Man, I am gonna be him someday.

Her sister slipped out of her bathrobe and tossed it over. Catching it in midair, Sabrina put it on and tied the sash tight around her waist. "Thanks." Then she sneered at Peter. "Let the police take him and throw him in jail. It's where he belongs."

The pig on the floor glared and sputtered. "You fucking bitch. You and your stupid cunt sister can go to hell."

Max ground his knee harder, that red cloud bursting into his brain again. "I'm gonna break your jaw for that."

Sabrina grabbed his arm again. "No. Breaking and entering. Attempted burglary. If he's got any kind of weapon, that might even be considered home invasion, right?" she asked, her voice cold and steady as she stared hard at the man who'd messed with the wrong sisters.

Peter stopped wriggling. Max lowered his fist.

"Sure might," Allie said, coming closer—though not too close. A gust of wind blew through the porch like a wind tunnel, causing Allie's flowing nightgown to press hard against her big stomach. Peter, looking like a cowardly trapped animal, appeared completely unmoved by the image.

"Not something any court of law would look kindly on in a custody case, I think," Allie added.

Max immediately got it. If he beat the shit out of this man, the charges against him might be muddied by his physical condition. And for Allie and Sabrina, having him charged—giving him a record—was the best thing that could possibly happen.

He considered. Weighed the options. Knew what he would have done a few years ago. He also wondered what his brothers would do in this situation.

Morgan probably would have gotten the guy to sign an agreement that he'd never bother the sisters, then turned him over to the police.

Mike probably would have bashed his head in.

Max, however, did the only thing he could. Slowly removing his knee, he grabbed Peter Prescott and jerked him to his feet, twisting his hands behind his back. He walked the man down the stairs to the lawn, directly toward the twirling blue lights of the car coming up the driveway. And when Chief Joe Bennigan stepped out of that car, he shoved Prescott right over.

CHAPTER SIXTEEN

"YOU'RE SURE you don't mind missing the Founder's Day festival?" Max asked Saturday morning.

Sabrina tapped the tip of her finger on her cheek, pretending to think it over. "Hmm, mingling with maniacal old ladies, nudist inn-owners, gossipy waitresses and murderous hoteliers versus lying here in this bed with you, naked, having the best sex of my life?"

"Life's full of tough choices."

"But this is *not* one of them," she said with a laugh. Wrapping her arms around Max's neck, she drew him close for another deep, slow kiss, like the several they'd shared since returning to bed after seeing the others off this morning.

They were in Max's bed, in the high turret room of the house, alone and happy to have it that way. Mortimer and Allie had gone off just after breakfast to the town festival. Allie had been nearly out of her mind with excitement over the possibility of being named Miss Trouble. And Mortimer looked forward to strutting around the crowd amid the whispers of his ménage a trois with the Feeney sisters.

Don't go there.

Definitely not. She'd much rather be here. Safe in Max's strong arms—away from any prying eyes, which was why she and Allie had moved out of the tent yesterday.

She'd slept in Max's arms for the past two nights and couldn't think of anyplace that would have felt more right. Including home.

Unfortunately, however, home was where she had to go. Real life—in the form of her boss—had intruded yesterday. Nancy had called Friday afternoon, providing good news and bad.

The bad news was that Sabrina was out of vacation time and had to get back on the job. Pronto. As in Monday.

But she didn't want to think about that right now.

The good news had been a bit of a silver lining, at least. Grace Wellington was engaged. She'd reeled in a rich fish, one with a high-society family. Not wanting her in-laws to read stories about her participating in the kind of activities usually reserved for the pages of *Penthouse,* she'd demanded to buy back the rights to her book.

That was good news on a lot of fronts. Mainly on the Max front. Because now she didn't have to worry about him being publicly maligned in Grace's sordid memoir. His life would not be affected by a spoiled woman's embellishments and lies.

It amazed her that she could have believed them—had honestly *believed* he was the man Grace had made him out to be.

Now, she knew better. The man who, Thursday night, had put aside his own rage and fury to do what was best for Allie...the man who'd made such sweet love to her in the tent...who'd shared his most painful memories in order to help Sabrina deal with her own pain—well, he was not the man Grace had invented.

The whole incident had left Sabrina feeling slightly

uncomfortable—dirty almost. She'd been a part of something that could have ruined the reputation of the man she now knew she loved.

It truly made her rethink what she had done. And made her anxious to go out to the tent, get the copy of the manuscript from her briefcase and put a match to the whole thing.

With Grace's book not being published, Sabrina knew her chances of a possible promotion at Liberty Books had diminished. But since Allie had steamed full speed ahead in taking responsibility for her own life, it just didn't seem to matter as much.

Though still saddened by her sister's decision, Sabrina had to admit to feeling a certain pride in Allie. She'd already officially agreed to become an employee of Max's grandfather's corporation, complete with benefits, like health insurance.

She'd also agreed it was time to stop acting like a scared kid and try once more to reach out to their mother. Though they hadn't been able to get her on the phone yesterday, they'd left her a message, each telling her how much they loved her and how they hoped someday to see her again.

That was all they could do. It was in Mom's hands now.

"What are you thinking?" Max asked as he twirled her hair around his fingers.

Oh, what she was thinking. About her regrets…her sorrow…her fears. She regretted having to leave him. She was sorry—so very sorry—for deceiving him. And she greatly feared she would never in her lifetime love anyone the way she loved Max Taylor.

Loving, she knew, meant more than great sex and laughter and magnificent plane rides. If anything, talking Allie into reaching out to their mother had taught Sabrina

one thing: you couldn't hide from the people you loved.
You had to take chances, to count on them to understand—
forgive. Reach back. That love was worth the risk of
having your heart broken.

Max had had his heart broken. Sabrina did not want to
be the one to do it to him again.

But she had to be honest with him. Completely honest.
Then, if she made him understand—could make him see
how genuinely sorry she was about having deceived him—
perhaps she could also make him believe that she loved
him. And that they could have a future together.

She didn't know how, considering she'd told Nancy
she'd be back at work on Monday. But she had to try. "I
need to talk to you about something," she said, wondering how to find the words.

"About how many times you came last night? I'm sorry.
I know it was only twice," he said, cupping her waist pos-
sessively. "I'll do better next time."

"No," she said with a giggle. "I'm serious."

"I don't want to be serious. Thursday night was about
as serious as I want to get."

She had to agree. "Have you heard anything more
about *him?*"

"As of last night he was cooling his heels in the town
jail on breaking and entering and attempted burglary
charges." His smile was devoid of humor. "Seems there's
only one lawyer in Trouble and he declined to take Mr.
Prescott's case."

She could just imagine why.

"So it might be a while before he can get out. They have
to bring in a public defender from Weldon."

"Excellent."

"In the meantime," he added, "we've got that one

lawyer in Trouble working on getting a restraining order
to keep Peter off this property and away from you, Allie
or her baby." He pressed a kiss to her temple. "He won't
bother you again, I promise."

There was no logical way Max could keep that promise,
but somehow, she knew he would. He would not let
anything happen to harm Allie or the baby any more than
he'd let anyone get close enough to hurt Mortimer again.
Not even the Feeney sisters.

"Thank you, Max." Taking a deep breath, she added,
"But I have to talk to you about something else."

He nibbled her neck, as always the touch of his mouth
on her skin making her brain fuzzy and her muscles weak.
"Tell me how much you want me."

More than anything.

"Tell me you're dying for me."

No doubt about it.

"Tell me you'll come to California with me next week."

She froze. She couldn't have heard that, right? Max
hadn't just made some kind of suggestion that they
continue their relationship past this crazy, wild vacation
in Trouble, had he?

"What are you…?"

"Come with me, Sabrina," he whispered. "Come fly
with me."

Fly with him. Oh, God, she wanted to. And if it were
really that simple—if she'd been the normal, honest person
she'd presented herself to be, she would have leaped upon
the man, kissing every inch of his face and telling him
she'd never let him out of her sight.

She wasn't that woman.

"Max, I don't think—"

"Don't think," he ordered, pinning her tight. He kissed

her neck and her jaw, nibbled his way down her collarbone, then began to tickle her bare middle.

She giggled, unable to help it. "Stop."

"Say you'll come." He tickled some more.

"Max, I mean it," she said, her voice so weak she knew
he couldn't possibly believe her. Hell, she didn't believe
herself.

"I'll talk you into it if I have to. I'm very persuasive."

Oh, no doubt of that.

"Did I tell you I have a beautiful house on the beach?
Perfect place for a writer—you can sit on the patio looking
at the ocean and write to your heart's content."

Oh, it sounded amazing. Perfect. If she'd really been in
the position to do it, she'd have said yes in a heartbeat.

But she couldn't, not without making the biggest admission of her life. An admission that could cost her the
one thing she *wanted* most in her life: him.

Knowing she needed some physical distance, she
wriggled out from under him, rolling away. And promptly
fell to the floor. "Ow," she yelped.

He immediately shot out of bed to help her. "You okay?"

She wasn't sure. The wind had definitely been knocked
out of her when she landed on the hard wood. Not to
mention she was lying here on her stomach, bare-ass
naked, beside a man with whom she really needed the
upper hand right now. Not easy considering he was
kneeling right beside her, also naked. Deliciously—
accessibly—naked, his thick, glorious sex just about level
with her face. He must have seen her eyeing him, because
his body began to react in a way that made her mouth water
and her body dampen.

But even as she reached out to play with some of that
oh-so-accessible male yumminess, something under the

bed caught her eye. It glistened, winked. A sparkle of light flashing quickly and then disappearing. "There's something under here," she said, blinking and staring under the old-fashioned double bed.

"Why don't you crawl under and I'll watch your back for you?" he asked, his tone absolutely lascivious.

She really didn't care about the sparkle, but she did like the naughty tone in his voice. Max was so incredibly playful—in bed and out of it. And Sabrina had discovered she really liked to play.

Chuckling, she shimmied under the bed, reaching for the little sparkle. Max's hand immediately moved to her butt, caressing, stroking, driving her wild. When he moved it around so he could playfully cup her cheek, then slide his fingers between her legs to toy with her, she nearly said to heck with it and backed out from under the bed so she could take him right now. "You're distracting me," she said with a groan, seeing the sparkle again, about a foot away from her fingertips.

"Good. Don't give up. Keep looking. I'll handle things… back here."

She closed her eyes while he stroked and caressed her, moaning deep in her throat at how good his hands were. He thoroughly massaged her, gently squeezing her backside, kneading the muscles in her legs, all the way down to the soles of her feet. And she just remained there in a boneless heap, half her body stuck under a bed, loving every minute of it.

When he began working his way back up her legs, she finally opened her eyes. The shiny object—so stark on the broad, pitted expanse of the wooden floorboards—remained slightly out of reach, but she'd obviously writhed a bit closer during Max's erotic massage.

She strained a bit more, her fingers finally reaching it. But when Max's mouth replaced his hand on that delicate bit of skin where the back of her thigh met her bottom, she gasped and twisted, watching as the thing skittered an inch farther.

"You are *so* evil."

"You *so* don't want me to stop, though," he murmured, his mouth moving between her legs, covering her from this amazingly sexy, wicked angle.

She didn't. Oh, no, she didn't. Instead, she gave herself over to the incredible sensations. His hands on her hips, he tilted her up to gain access to her hot, wet core, and made thorough love to her with his tongue. Shaking and moaning, Sabrina quickly felt tremors of delight rolling through her. Reaching her climax quickly, she jerked and gasped. When she could breathe again, she realized the sparkly thing she'd been looking for was now between her fingers.

Catching it, she slid backward—Max's hands on her legs to help her, then between them to arouse her all over again. Once out from under the bed, she saw that he'd already taken care of protection. She crawled onto his lap right there on the floor, taking him into her body with one hard thrust.

"Thanks for watching my back," she muttered through choppy breaths.

"Anytime, sweetheart."

They stopped talking, able only to pound and writhe. Max took hold of her legs, wrapping them around his waist, then stood up and leaned her back against the wall. He drove into her so deep Sabrina could only scream at the pleasure of it, her fingers digging tightly into his shoulders as she hung on for the ride.

Soon crying out his own release, he turned back to the

bed and lowered them both onto it, careful to roll to his side to avoid crushing her. They panted heavily for a few moments, Sabrina wondering how on earth she was ever going to survive without him once she left here.

"I think you drew blood with those nails," he said with a shaky laugh.

"Oh, baby, I'm so sorry!" She sat up to peer over his shoulder, tugging him toward her so she could examine his back. He seemed to like the position, judging by the way he immediately covered her nipple with his mouth and lazily sucked it.

"Mmm," she moaned. Then she carefully touched the small red scratch on his back—just one, and not a bad one at all. But at the end of it, something shiny was stuck into his skin. "Not from my nails." She plucked the object free. "It's the sparkly thing from under the bed."

He sighed and tugged her back into his arms, her head tucked under his chin. "What is it, a straight pin?"

Sabrina looked at the object, at first thinking it was a piece of broken glass. But as she brought it closer and shifted it to catch the brilliant sunlight coming in through the front window, she saw dozens of flashes of light dancing around the room.

"What the hell?" he asked, immediately pulling away so he could see better. "Is that…"

"Yes," she murmured, knowing what the pea-size, faceted thing she held in her hands truly was. "It's a diamond."

For a brief second, her heart stopped and wonder coursed through her mind—*was Max proposing?*

No. It was too soon—he'd never even told her how he felt about her, at least not with words.

Besides, if the thing had been set in a ring, she could see him doing something playful and sexy like luring her under a bed so he could have his wicked way with her. But it was loose—and a little dusty. Like it had been there a long time.

"Do you have any idea how this got here?" she asked.

He shook his head, taking the stone from her hand and holding it up for them both to see. Blowing off the dust, he turned it to catch the light again. "I don't know jewels, but this thing looks absolutely flawless. More than a carat, I'd think."

"Two at least. What I don't get is how it got there. No woman would drop something like this and not tear the place apart trying to find it."

"Plus no woman has lived in this house for the past couple of decades."

"It's oddly shaped for a ring," she murmured. "Not as pointy as you'd think. It's probably from a drop pendant or something."

"It sure felt pointy."

Laughing, she explained, "It's sharp, but I mean, the surface is more flat and the point less deep than you'd expect for a solitaire setting. How weird that it was sitting there—almost winking at me like an eye when I fell."

Feeling Max stiffen in the bed beside her, she dropped her hand onto his bare chest, stroking those thick, rippled muscles. "What?"

"Like an eye…" Grabbing her hand, he kissed it, then slid out of the bed. "I need to check something."

Curious, Sabrina watched as he walked to the corner of the turret room and opened a small door, probably used to access attic space. He disappeared through it but came back a moment later holding, of all things, a cuckoo clock.

"Ugh. Take it back. It belongs there where no one can hear it."

"I know. That's why I tore it down the day I moved in. Dropped it, then tossed it among the eaves." Crossing back to the bed, his big, naked body moving so gracefully it was like watching art in motion, he sat on the edge of the bed.

"Oh, my God," he muttered as he tugged open the small doors through which the cuckoo bird emerged every hour.

"What?" Dropping her hands on his shoulders, she rose to her knees and peeked over. And immediately saw what he'd seen. "Max, there's only one eye. The other one…is that…?"

"Yeah. I think it is. Another diamond." Turning his head to meet her stare, he looked stunned. "Sabrina, I think we might have just discovered what old Wilhelm Stuttgardt meant about the stolen money being found *in time*."

TOM KING REALIZED someone was still in the house only after he'd already begun searching the clocks on the second floor. "No," he'd muttered when he'd heard a loud *thump* from overhead in the turret bedroom. Sounded as though someone had taken a hard spill to the floor.

No one was supposed to be here. They were all to have gone to the festival, leaving him with a full day to continue his search. "Why?" he whispered, the dejection weighing on his whole body. "Why does nothing go right?"

It never did. Hadn't for a long time.

He'd known Thursday night had been a gamble. The family would be on alert when they were home, so his nighttime hunts would have to be few and far between. But it had been worth it. Tipping off the police that a dark-haired stranger was trying to break into the old Stuttgardt place had done two things—eliminated his competition, and, hopefully, relieved Taylor's suspicions about who had been lurking around the house.

Being more careful and not searching much at night had been the tradeoff. Which was why today had seemed like such a godsend. The house would be empty, everyone gone for hours. Perfect.

Someone, however, had stayed behind.

He remained still, behind the door in one of the large, empty bedrooms, obviously not occupied judging by the sheets covering the unused furniture. It looked ghostly, and made him jumpy. The thud from upstairs had nearly had him running for the door.

Standing there for several minutes, he craned his ears. The house was old and sound carried. So soon he was able to make out bits of conversation. There were two voices— a man's and a woman's. Then some more pounding and wild cries that could only be the kind that came from good, solid boinking.

He could barely remember *bad* boinking, so he had to smile at whatever wild things were going on right above his head. Damn, he missed being young. Having no cares. Being able to laze around on a Saturday morning bouncing the bed springs.

His missus had liked that—before she'd up and left him three years ago. He didn't blame her. He wasn't exactly the laughing, jovial man she'd married. Once Stuttgardt had ruined him—and the town—the guilt had weighed on Tom until he found it nearly impossible even to get up every day, much less manage a smile or a laugh.

Tears welled up in his eyes. Unmanly. But he couldn't help it. Jerking the sleeve of his shirt across them and cursing his own weakness, he thought about what to do. He should leave—call it a day. Or even just give up on the whole thing and pretend he could forget the hell he'd helped create in his own hometown.

That was the part he couldn't live with.

Because he was to blame, at least partly. He'd helped old Willie with some of his financial shenanigans, his job as bookkeeper at the clock factory allowing him to play fast and loose with the numbers when his boss had asked it of him. Only, he hadn't realized Willie was playing fast and loose with other people's money—not until it was too late. He'd thought the wily old bastard was just trying to keep some of his own money out of the tax man's hands.

By the time he'd learned the truth, it'd been too late. Willie had hidden the money but good. Probably would have tried to make a getaway once he found out Tom was on to him—but, of course, a clock to the face had put paid to that idea.

The loss of his job and pension might well have been bad, the shame of what it had cost everyone else worse. But worst of all was when that old witch Ida Mae had started putting the screws to him. Stuttgardt had shared some pillow talk with her—and likely her sister, too, knowing them—and they'd realized Tom had something he wanted to keep hidden.

If Trouble had found out he'd been party to what Wilhelm had done, he'd have been ridden out of town on a rail. It would have cost him the last things he had left—his friends and neighbors. His home. So he'd paid...until his money had dried up. And still Ida Mae wouldn't pull her claws out of him.

"Gotta find that money," he muttered, wishing he could let it go but knowing he could not.

Hoping that whoever was upstairs had just decided to have a little hanky-panky before going off to the festival, he remained where he was—waiting. After a while, he began to suspect his good luck had returned, because he heard them coming down the attic stairs, talking fast and excitedly. Something about the festival—finding Mortimer. Talking to the mayor…

Why they'd want to talk to her, Tom had no idea. Nor did he care. Long's they got out of the house, they could go down to hell and talk to old Willie if they wanted to.

Smiling, he nodded and put some stiff in his spine, determined to find something in this house before he left it. He oughta have lots of time—and to make certain of that, he reached for his cell phone and had a whispered conversation.

Once it was done, he continued waiting—a long while—until there were no more voices, no sounds at all. Then he carefully opened the door, patted the gun resting comfortably against the small of his back and crept out into the hall to resume his search.

CRUISING DOWN the driveway of his grandfather's place, Max shook his head and marveled again over what he and Sabrina had discovered. The awful clocks he'd been cursing since the day he'd arrived were worth a fortune. Not because of their craftsmanship, but because of their eyes.

"Unbelievable," he muttered as he turned and headed toward town. But he had to believe it, he'd seen the proof. A cursory inspection of a few of the cuckoos in the living room had revealed the truth he'd never even noticed. Some of the birds had emerald green eyes and some ruby red ones. Some glittered like diamonds or shone a pretty sapphire blue.

He'd never suspected. Not once. After all, he'd done everything he could to avoid the damn clocks, so he sure hadn't been looking at them closely when the squawking little birdies had popped out to do their hourly song.

How incredible that murder victim Wilhelm Stuttgardt
had transformed his stolen money into jewels and hidden
them right in plain sight. *In time.* "Pretty smart," he
admitted, ruefully shaking his head. Not smart enough,
though, considering the man had paid to keep that secret
with his life.

Needing to talk to his grandfather about the discovery—and unable to call since the old man loathed cellular
phones—he was on his way down to the festival. He felt
sure Mortimer would agree to his plan to ask the mayor
and the chief to return to the house with them for a
thorough search. There was no question of keeping the ill-
gotten gains. Those stones represented not only the bank-
ruptcy of this town, but also the lost pension of a lot of its
residents.

"Hallelujah, maybe they'll buy it all back," he whispered, seeing another silver lining. Hopefully his grandfather would be out of this quagmire before too much
longer.

Sabrina had offered to come with him, but they'd both
realized it would be better if one of them stayed and started
gathering all the clocks together in one room. It would
make examining them easier. She'd just finished taking a
quick shower when he left. By the time he got back, he
expected her to be smelling sweet and fresh, her golden
hair bouncing, busily digging the eyes out of cuckoo birds.

Laughing at the mental image, he was distracted by the
ringing of his cell phone. "Max Taylor."

"Mr. Taylor, this is Chief Bennigan. There's something
I need to talk to you about."

"Sure, Chief."

"Maybe you could come by the station?"

"Actually, I'm on my way to the Founders' Day Festival. And I have something I want to talk to you about, too."

"Perfect, I'll meet you there."

Smiling, Max added, "I think you're going to like what I have to tell you."

Bennigan sighed. "Wish I could say the same."

Immediately imagining the worse, he asked, "Is it my grandfather? Is he all right?"

"Oh, he's fine, Mr. Taylor. Sorry, I didn't mean to scare you like that. It's nothing all that bad—and not unexpected. But I know you're not going to be too happy about it."

Well, his curiosity certainly wouldn't let him wait until he found Bennigan to hear the details. "Why don't you just tell me and get it over with?"

The man cleared his throat, then sneezed and blew his nose. Finally he admitted, "Well, that fella we caught trying to break in Thursday night got bailed out of jail early this morning."

Damn. He certainly hadn't expected Prescott to remain locked up for long, but he'd hoped to have a few more days. At least until the restraining order came through. "What time, Chief?"

"About eight o'clock. It was the damndest thing—those Feeney sisters came in with some attorney from the next county, demanding to see the judge. Had cash money for Prescott's bail and everything."

The Feeney sisters... He shook his head in disbelief. He never had found out what Sabrina's ex had been doing with the women the other day when Allie had seen him. But suddenly he *really* wanted to know. "Why would they help him?"

"No idea. When we told him it'd be Monday before we

could get the public defender down here from Weldon, he asked for his one phone call—and then he asked for Ida Mae's phone number." The chief grunted. "Danged if I can figure it out."

"Thanks, Chief. I appreciate the heads-up," he said. "Will you do me a favor and make sure somebody swings by the house to keep an eye out?"

"Already arranged it," Bennigan said.

"Good. Then I'll see you shortly." Smiling as he pictured the man reacting to *his* news, he disconnected the call.

Max thought for a second about turning the car around and going back to make sure Sabrina was all right. He didn't though, doubting Peter would dare go there again after what had happened Thursday night. Knowing what he did about what a cowardly prick the guy was, he imagined he was already halfway back to Philadelphia by now.

Plus, the house was locked up tight, with brand-new stick-on alarm devices on every door and window. They were a makeshift measure until a new system could be put in next week. He'd reminded Sabrina to set them when he left, sighing as he'd realized that Mortimer and Allie had *not*.

Still, to be on the safe side, he dialed her cell number. Getting no answer, he left her a message to be extra alert, told her why, and that he'd be back soon.

As he hung up, he realized he had just passed the twin falling-down ruins where the Feeney sisters lived. Though he frankly would have liked nothing better than to never see them again, especially after some of Mortimer's stories, he couldn't help doing a fast U-turn and pulling up outside Ida Mae's house.

He wanted to know why they'd helped Prescott, if they had some kind of connection to the man...and where he might be now.

Parking out front, he walked up the steps on to the porch and lifted his hand to knock on the screen door. Before he could, the inner door opened with a long, slow creak, and Ida Mae peered at him through the screen. "What do *you* want?"

Not tea, that was for sure. "I'd like to talk to you."

"Got nothing to say. And if I did, I sure wouldn't say it to you after you skulked out of here the other day without so much as a good day. That was rude, young man."

Uh, rude. Rescuing his naked, kidnapped grandfather from the clutches of two horny old women—rude. There was a new one for Miss Manners.

Ida Mae started to close the door.

"It's about Peter Prescott."

She paused. "Don't know him."

Max tsked. "You bailed him out of jail this morning."

"Oh. *That* Peter Prescott."

"Yes. Can I come in?"

She shook her head, but did open the screen door a little so he could see a few inches of her face. "No."

"Why did you bail him out?"

"None of your business. Now, shoo, young man, I've got things to do."

Before she could disappear back inside, slamming the door behind her, a ghostly figure appeared, emerging from the shadowy interior of the house. It was her sister, Ivy. She was wearing a long, feathered negligee—once white, now yellowed with age. And more appropriate for a woman fifty years her junior.

"Well, hello there, handsome. Won't you come in?"

Pursing her lips and shaking her index finger, she added, "You were naughty to sneak your granddaddy away from us—you aiming to take his place?"

He gulped, taking the tiniest step back on the porch. Pushing the door wider, the younger Feeney sister gave him a welcoming smile. He imagined it was how a she-wolf would smile at a baby deer.

"No, he will not. He's asking about Mr. Prescott."

Ivy, much less adept at hiding her feelings than her sister, frowned darkly. "That's a bad one."

"Ivy, hush."

Max forced a friendly expression onto his face and leaned in closer to the younger sister, noting the bright red lipstick and makeup-caked face. "Why did you help him, then?"

Ivy shook her head, her false eyelashes fluttering, one of them getting caught briefly in the puffy gray bangs teased down over her forehead. "Do you know that man tried to extort us? He had the most foolish idea that he knew information about us that could be damaging."

Max wouldn't be surprised if these two had a body stashed in every room of their house. But he thought it best merely to shake his head, feigning disgust, rather than to try to form any words.

"We bailed him out of jail merely so we could sit him down and straighten that boy out, proving to him just how wrong his suppositions were," Ida Mae finally said, crossing her arms and sticking out her chin. "I don't much like being accused of things I didn't do."

As opposed to the many more she probably *had* done?

"And was he convinced?"

Ivy smiled. "Oh, yes. Very. We worked everything out, then we had a nice chat along with our tea and cakes."

Tea. He tensed. And when he heard a loud *thump* coming from upstairs, his body went rigid.

"We thought about brewing up Mama's favorite kind—spiked with a lovely almond liqueur—but that's just for *special* occasions."

"Yes, indeed it is," Ida Mae said.

As if speaking to herself, Ivy mumbled, "Almond for abusers."

"I beg your pardon?"

She cleared her throat, offering him a vacant smile. "We gave him some nice orange blossom tea." Her heavily made-up eyes sparkled. "Since your grandfather liked it so well, we thought a younger man might enjoy it, too."

Another muffled thud came from the second floor.

"Radiator problem?" he asked Ivy.

She shook her head, a coy smile playing about her lips. Batting her lashes again and smoothing her negligee, she said, "Rats."

"Big rats," Ida Mae added.

Rats. Yes. Of course.

Max thought it over, then nodded. "You don't plan on doing any—*exterminating* yourself, do you?" He stared hard at Ida Mae, who stared right back, her gaze steely. "Because I don't think taking such drastic measures to get rid of rodents is a good idea and I might have to prevent you from doing that."

Ivy giggled. "Of course we're not. We'll just…wait a while. I'm sure the creature'll walk out of here on his own sooner or later."

Another *thump*. Max stared at Miss Ivy's feathered negligee and Miss Ida Mae's more modest housecoat. "A few days, then. That should suffice, I'm sure."

Ida Mae nodded once, silently agreeing to his terms.

"You're sure the problem won't return?"

She shook her head. "Oh, no. Not unless he wants the other rats to see pictures of how thoroughly he enjoyed his time here."

"Oh, they do enjoy their time here," Ivy said, her voice almost a purr. "Ida Mae and I must have the most alluring entertainment to offer any kind of creature, because they always end up loving every minute."

His eyes closing briefly, Max cleared his throat. "Very well. I guess I'll leave you, then." But before he went down the porch steps, he added, "If your Mr. Prescott does return here sometime, be sure to tell him an injunction has been filed, ordering him away from my grandfather's house, as well as the Cavanaugh sisters. He'll be arrested if he comes anywhere near them."

Ida Mae nodded. "We'll be sure to pass that along if we see the man."

Ivy pushed her sister out of the way and leaned her head all the way out to call, "Do give your grandfather our best, won't you?"

Nodding, Max turned on his heel and walked to the edge of the porch, hearing one more thunk from inside.

A very large rat, indeed. And how appropriate, really—the sexual predator targeting young girls for revenge schemes getting caught in a trap just like the one he'd constructed.

Smiling, he got into his car, then looked up at the second-story window—the room where he'd found his grandfather.

As he backed out of the driveway, he murmured. "Hope you have a great weekend, Peter."

CHAPTER SEVENTEEN

WHEN SABRINA saw the man with the gun, she somehow managed not to scream.

"This can't be happening," she whispered—quiet, so quiet as she watched, crouched close against the wall on the second-floor landing. She peeked around to see where the stranger who'd just slipped from the dining room into the living room was.

The stranger with the gun tucked into the back of his pants.

God, Max, why aren't you here?

He should be soon. He'd been gone an hour. How long could it have taken to find Mortimer and bring him back?

"Any minute now," she whispered, hearing the false bravado in her own voice. So much for all her boasting about her self-defense training at the community center back home. Every trick she'd ever learned had involved hand-to-hand defense. Not hand-to-gun.

Apparently, she hadn't gotten Max's voice message soon enough. He'd called shortly after he left—while she'd been wrestling a large clock off the dining room wall—letting her know about Peter getting out. She'd done exactly as he'd asked, making sure every one of those window alarms was set.

But apparently someone had already been inside.

Not Peter, though. She'd seen the back of the intruder's balding head as he disappeared into the living room, and it definitely hadn't been her ex. That didn't surprise her. Peter had looked like he was ready to wet his pants the other night when Max threatened to break his jaw, and she didn't imagine he'd risk coming up here.

So who is that guy?

She had no idea. She just knew she wanted more than one story separating them. Moving as quietly as she could across the creaky floor, she made her way back to the third-floor stairwell. Carefully going up it—avoiding the third from the top, which squeaked the loudest—she had a bizarre thought and giggled, only mildly hysterical. *Oh great,* she thought, *I'm turning into a scary movie heroine, going up the stairs toward the attic instead of getting the hell out of the house.*

She suddenly had some sympathy for those heroines. Because there was no way she could go anywhere on the first floor without being seen by the man in the living room. The entrance was directly at the bottom of the stairs.

Creeping into Max's attic bedroom, she stepped on one loud floorboard, which screamed like a virgin at a frat party. She froze, praying the intruder had been too far away to hear. When she heard nothing that sounded like an ax-wielding maniac racing up the stairs, she moved again.

Her cell phone was in her purse, which sat on the table beside Max's bed. Grabbing it, she looked toward the door, wishing she could close it to create one more sound barrier. Max was at a festival, and he might not hear the shaky whispers of a terrified woman.

But she couldn't risk it—that door not only squeaked, it slammed whenever it was shut.

Thinking quickly, she moved toward the tiny attic door, the one Max had disappeared behind earlier. She didn't think it had made much noise, but was still careful when opening it. Once inside, she closed it behind her, then leaned against a bare studded wall in relief.

She dialed quickly. "Max," she said as loud as she dared the moment he answered.

"Sabrina?"

In the background, she heard voices and laughter. The *ding* of a bell indicated someone had just impressed his girlfriend by swinging a sledgehammer onto a weight. God, would she rather be with them. "There's someone in the house."

"Peter?" He sounded shocked.

"No. Someone else. And he has a gun."

He muttered an obscenity. "Get out, Sabrina, now."

"Can't. He's near the bottom of the stairs."

She heard him talking to someone else, then the sound of heavy breathing—as if he was running. "Hide," he ordered, and she heard a car door opening.

"Already doing it. I'm in the attic space beside your room."

"Good. Stay there. I'm on my way, and the cops are, too."

The car engine started. The tires squealed. *On his way. Five minutes. Ten tops.*

"Keep talking to me, sweetheart."

"Uh…how's the festival?"

His bark of laughter made her hope he hadn't heard the note of terror she was trying so hard to keep out of her voice.

"Crowded with people who are going to be very happy to find out what you and I have discovered in that house."

"Yeah, I was thinking about that. Whoever's down-stairs…"

"Did you start moving the clocks? Does he know what we discovered? Maybe he'll just take the damn things and leave."

If only. Sighing, she moved deeper into the attic, balancing her way across the studs and kicking tufts of pink insulation out of her way. "Don't think so. I hadn't had a chance to do much with that yet. So unless this guy was here all morning and heard us...oh, no," she groaned, suddenly thinking of what she and Max had been doing before their discovery. "You know, I could happily go the rest of my life without suspecting someone spied on us making love."

He laughed softly. "Does that mean you think we'll be making love for the rest of your life?"

Sabrina's heart rolled over, and it had nothing to do with the fear of the stranger in the house. Sinking slowly down onto a plank-board section of the attic, she murmured, "Max..."

"Because that's what I'm picturing. You and me. For life."

Oh, please no, he couldn't be doing this now, could he? Couldn't be telling her he loved her when she still had this big, nasty secret hanging over her head to tell him. And, oh, by the way, was in fear for her life. "Max, please..."

"I know. Wrong time. Wrong place." His voice lowered. "And I'm not alone in the car. That doesn't change how I feel."

"Stop," she ordered, "not yet. Tell me later. When you get me out of this mess."

He hesitated.

"Please, Max. There's something I need to say to you, too. First. We'll talk soon."

And they would. She'd tell him everything—after he

saved her ass from the psychopath downstairs, who probably kept his gun in his pants so his hands would be free to hold the butcher knife and chainsaw.

Sighing, he gave in. "All right."

About to ask him to describe just how excited Mortimer was over this latest adventure, she heard a noise and sucked in a breath. The door to Max's room. It had creaked. And slammed. Her stomach started somersaulting. "Oh, shit, he's in your room."

"Look around. Is there anything you can use for a weapon?" he asked, staying calm. A major feat there, because she could tell by his tense voice that he was feeling anything but.

She glanced around the attic space, which was empty except for something wooden sticking out of the insulation. Crawling toward it, she brushed away the pink fluff. "There's a big clock back here. You told me you only murdered one of them."

"I did. That was back there before I moved in. Can you break something off it to defend yourself?"

She reached for an ornate, decorative cuckoo carved into the wood over the little house. Remembering what had happened to the former owner, she wondered if she could wield it carefully enough to stab someone directly in the eye. Gushy. Yucky. But she'd do it if she had to.

"Survival instinct, mister," she muttered.

Though she twisted it—hard—the thing would not come off. Careful to be as quiet as she could, she lifted the clock into her lap, the chains and weights making the tiniest *clink*.

"Quiet, Sabrina," she heard Max whisper through the phone—he'd obviously heard. *Oh, please, please, please, don't let the bad guy have heard, too*.

Trying desperately again, she twisted the bird. The

stupid thing obviously *could* come off with enough pressure, because there was a broken stump on the other branch where another bird had once been.

Still nothing. Not the slightest creak or shift.

Realizing she wasn't going to be able to do it, she decided to go for the chains. She'd seen garrotes in movies. If she could get around the guy without him blowing her head off, maybe she could choke him from behind.

Grabbing the weights, she started to tug, then saw something strange. The dark brown, pine-cone-shaped weights were sparkling in spots. Lifting one and squinting to study it under the sunlight sifting through the eaves, she realized the paint on the weight had chipped in a number of places. Rubbing at one spot, she saw what was beneath it, and it sure didn't look like iron or brass.

No. It was much shinier than iron, not as bold as brass—a bit softer. Unmistakable. "Max, I think Mr. Stuttgardt invested in more than jewels," she whispered, hearing the shock in her own voice. *Wonder what gold is selling for these days.*

She didn't have time to dwell on it, because suddenly the door from Max's bedroom began to swing inward. Thinking only of having something with which to defend herself, she lifted the clock—straining under its weight, wishing she had room to swing like the person who'd killed Wilhelm Stuttgardt.

Then she caught a glimpse of the clock face, saw a dark clump of hair tangled in the minute hand. And blood. A bunch of it.

She thought about the missing bird.

And realized this was *exactly* what the person who'd killed Wilhelm Stuttgardt had been holding when he murdered him.

"SABRINA!" Max shouted into the phone. "Answer me."

She said nothing. She'd said nothing for a good fifteen seconds. He'd heard her strange comment about the jewels, some deep breathing, then a tiny *clunk* and silence. He had the very real fear that she'd dropped the phone and it was right now lying in a mound of insulation.

"She'll be all right, boy," Mortimer said, reaching over and placing a hand on Max's arm. "We're almost there."

"Hurry," Allie said from the back seat.

Glancing in the rearview mirror at the girl's stricken face, he knew she was terrified. "She'll be fine," he muttered, trying to convince Allie. Not easy when he was half out of his mind with worry, too.

Then he spied the driveway, let the gas pedal off the floor—where it had been since they'd left the carnival grounds—and made a sharp, screeching turn. Right behind him were other cars, including Chief Bennigan's. The mayor, too, had been standing nearby when Max got the call, as had several other locals. Hell, they might as well lead a parade up to the house so everyone could see him annihilate the bastard Sabrina was hiding in terror from right now.

Not even cutting the car engine, he hopped out the second he reached the house. Heading toward the porch, he ignored a yell from Bennigan, kicked in the front door and burst inside. "Sabrina!"

She didn't reply—he heard only the wail of the stick-on door alarm, which he quickly flipped off.

"Where are you?"

Nothing. Not a whisper. Not a sound. *She has to be okay*.

He took the stairs three at a time, then went for the attic ones, pounding up them and into his bedroom. And stopped dead in his tracks, not quite believing what he saw.

Sabrina was sitting on his bed, her arm across the shoulders of an older, balding man…who was sobbing quietly into his hands.

"Found it. Can't believe you found it. Here all the time," the man was mumbling.

"Sabrina?"

She looked up, saw him there and flew into his arms. "Max, I'm so glad you're here."

He held her tight, picking her up off the floor so he could squeeze her like he'd never let her go. She coughed a little, then wiggled out of his arms.

The man lifted his head, watching them, tears pouring over his ruddy cheeks. "Thought you was both gone," he mumbled. "Didn't mean to scare anybody."

Max wasn't convinced. He pushed Sabrina behind him, shielding her with his body. "Where's your gun?"

The man pointed toward the table. "BB gun. Not even loaded. It was for show—to scare you if you ever caught me."

Behind him, Chief Bennigan and one of his officers stormed in, followed closely by his grandfather, Allie, and the mayor.

"Sabrina!" Allie yelped. She moved as fast as her pregnant body could carry her and threw herself against her sister with a loud *oomph*.

"Tom, what in holy hell's goin' on here?" Bennigan said. "You broke into this house and terrified this woman?"

"Didn't mean it," Tom mumbled again. "I'm sorry, so sorry. I just couldn't give up, you see. Couldn't stop hunting until I made up for it."

Max slowly began to understand. "You were looking for Stuttgardt's money."

The man's eyes finally shone with anger rather than

moisture. He jerked his thumb toward his chest. "*My* money. *The town's* money."

Mayor Newman pushed her way past the men and walked over to Tom, taking Sabrina's place beside him on the bed. "It's all right, Tom. You're going to be fine. Everyone here knows you well enough to know you would never have hurt the lady."

Maybe not the lady. But Max had a strong suspicion that this Tom character—who he'd finally recognized as the guy who'd knocked the chicken wings out of Scoot's hands at the tavern the other day—might have hurt somebody else. This thing he had to "make up" for... "You killed him, didn't you," he said.

Beside him, Sabrina gasped. Bennigan stepped around Max and frowned.

"Tom, did you do it?"

"Don't answer that," said the mayor.

"Ann..."

Rising to her feet, she frowned at the chief. "Ever hear of a little thing called Miranda rights?"

"I didn't do it," Tom said wearily, sounding like he just didn't want to hide the truth anymore. "Didn't kill him. Might have, though, if I'd had the chance, when I found out what he did." Sniffing again and wiping his nose with his shirtsleeve, he rose to stand beside Ann. "He used me, tricked me into helping him steal. I was his bookkeeper, you see."

Sabrina slipped her arm around Max's waist and leaned her head against his shoulder. "Mr. King didn't know I was here," she murmured. "He was shocked when he opened the attic door and found me there. We both screamed— then he apologized for scaring me."

Max just grunted, not convinced.

"Woulda run away," Tom muttered, "if I hadn't seen what was in her hands." He nodded toward the attic door. On the floor in front of it was the large, broken clock, covered in insulation and dust.

The chief and the mayor saw it, too. "Oh, no," Ann murmured.

Bennigan walked across the room and stared down at the thing. "I think this is the murder weapon. All this time…it was in the house all this time."

Made Max wonder how hard Bennigan had searched— how much he'd cared about solving Stuttgardt's murder.

"There are more secrets in this house," Sabrina said. She slid out from under Max's arm and walked over to the clock, crouched down beside it.

"Don't touch that."

"Sorry to break it to you, but my fingerprints are all over this thing. When I thought Mr. King was a psycho killer, I lifted it up and planned to hit him with it if I had to."

Ann Newman gasped and the chief sighed heavily.

"Sorry. I had no idea it was the murder weapon until after I saw the blood." She pointed at the face of the clock. Even from a few feet away, Max saw what she was talking about.

"There's something else you should know about this clock—something I was telling Mr. King when you all arrived." She reached for one of the chains, lifted the weight and held it up for all of them to see. It spun around and caught the sunlight coming in through the window. When the light caught those flecks of gold on the tips of the pine cone, the whole thing glistened.

Max got it instantly. "Gold."

"Yeah, I think it is," she murmured. "Painted over to look like a regular clock weight."

Max stepped forward. "It's not the only secret hidden in one of the clocks." Quickly explaining what else he and Sabrina had discovered, he watched as every person in the room absorbed the news. The clocks in this house had kept their secret for five long years, but all was now revealed.

Only one question remained: who had killed Wilhelm Stuttgardt to try to learn that secret?

"So he was secretly buying up loose stones and gold, probably during all those trips to Europe he made, supposedly to buy Black Forest wood for the clocks," Ann murmured. "Imagine."

"Man always was a miser," Bennigan said. "Trusted nobody. I figure he liked keeping his riches right under his own roof, tucked safely away in those clocks he was so obsessed with." He bent over the one on the floor. "I guess I'll need to bag that as evidence. Should still be able to get something off it even with whatever prints you left on it, ma'am."

"You don't need to do that."

They all looked over at the mayor, who stood quietly with Tom, her hands clenched in front of her.

"Ann, don't," Tom said, putting his hand on her arm.

"You're going to find my fingerprints on it, Joe."

The chief stood immobile, his mouth opening, closing. Then he finally choked out, "Of course I will. You were his secretary. You were here all the time—hell, you found his body."

The woman was shaking her head slowly. "I've lived with this for five years. Just like poor Tom, the weight of it seems likely to kill me sometimes, as does the fear that I'll run out of hush money to keep it quiet. Trying to help him do what he's been doing has been about the only way I can make up for things, too." She glanced at Sabrina.

"I'm sorry about today—but you're right, Tom wouldn't have hurt you. I told him nobody would be in the house."

Great. Now the mayor was in on this.

"But I can't take it anymore," she continued.

King lowered his head and stared at the floor. He was the only one appearing unsurprised by the news.

"Tom showed up that day and helped me hide the clock," she admitted. "I'd found out what Wilhelm had done, you see. Came here to confront him—he'd stolen money from *me*, the woman he kept saying he was going to marry."

Max crossed his arms and leaned against the wall, watching. Sabrina stepped over to join him.

"I didn't come over here intending to kill him," she added, her tone stark and steady as if she wanted this to be over with. "I only grabbed that clock when he laughed about it. Called us stupid small-town trash and dared me to tell anyone. Said he'd tell them all I'd been his mistress for years, even before my husband died."

Secrets. So many secrets. How the hell could a town this size hold so many of them without exploding?

Suddenly, before Ann could continue, Grandfather cleared his throat and stepped into the room. He'd been standing quietly in the doorway, watching the goings-on, wide-eyed and fascinated. "Young lady," he said to the middle-aged mayor, "I think you've said enough." Turning to the chief, he added, "You do realize nothing she just said is admissible against her. Those little things called Miranda rights she mentioned earlier?"

The chief's jaw stiffened, but he said nothing, as if torn between his duty as a police officer and his obvious liking for the mayor. Not to mention his own disdain for the murder victim.

"I suggest that I retire to my office with Mrs. Newman and telephone one of my friends, a brilliant criminal attorney in Philadelphia." He walked over to the mayor and took her arm. "We will make arrangements for Mrs. Newman to turn herself in at the appropriate time—should you find evidence on that ancient, dusty old clock that in any way links our most esteemed mayor to this horrible…accident."

And then, with the sheer confidence of a man who'd once emerged from a swordfight with the Emir of Jordan with nothing but a scratch on the cheek and the everlasting admiration of his rival, he breezed out of the room, taking the confessed murderess with him.

Leaving all the rest of them to stare at one another in wonder. And Max to say, "*Man*, do I want to be him when I grow up."

SABRINA HONESTLY had no idea what was going to become of Mayor Ann Newman, or of Tom King. She suspected— given the close-knit relationship of the residents of Trouble, all of whom had been screwed over by Wilhelm Stuttgardt—that the law might take it easy on them. And heaven knows they had the best attorney Mortimer Potts's money could buy.

They'd soon have their own money, too. Once the excitement had died down yesterday, she, Mortimer, Max and Allie had spent the rest of the day going through the clocks. More than two dozen of them, all with some little surprise. It had been like going through a mountain of Cracker Jack boxes, only instead of cheap plastic rings, they found diamonds, rubies and gold.

Not all the clock weights had been replaced with gold— only about half of them. But given the per-ounce cost of the precious metal on the open market, they accounted for a big chunk of the money Stuttgardt had stolen.

With the mayor a murder suspect, they'd turned to the town council and the chief to deal with the issue. The stones and gold weights were being stored in the vault at the Trouble Savings and Loan. It had been closed for months—the building was now owned by Mortimer—but the vault was still operational. The town would decide how to handle them, but for now, thankfully, Max and his grandfather were out from under the whole mess.

Max.

She'd held him all night last night, loving him, letting him love her, though never saying the words. It was as if he'd had the greatest scare of his life, because later he'd treated her with near reverence, like she was something precious and fragile. Something he'd die to protect.

Oh, she loved him. She really, truly loved him. Yesterday, hiding in the attic—his voice the only thing keeping her sane—she'd realized that she just couldn't give him up. She could not get in her car and drive back to Philadelphia tonight, not without taking the chance to see if they could make things work despite the stupid things she'd done.

But first, she had to tell him about those stupid things. Which was why she was walking through the house now trying to find the man. He'd been missing for the past hour. Figured. She'd finally worked up her nerve to lay it all out—to tell him about her real job, her real purpose in coming to Trouble—and he was nowhere to be found.

"Where the heck is he?" she muttered, talking to herself.

"You mean Max?" Allie asked, barely looking up from the kitchen table as she jotted in the margins of a baby name book. "He went outside a while ago."

Fisting her hand and putting it on her hip, Sabrina stared at her sister. "And you didn't think to tell me this?"

"Sorry." A tiny smile tickled her sister's lips. "He's in the tent, has been in there for about an hour. I figured he was getting things ready for you two to play 'the sheikh and the virgin' or something."

Feeling her cheeks burn, she finally let out a tiny chuckle. "You like him, don't you, Allie?"

"Max?" she said, sounding completely surprised by the question. "I adore him. And he adores you. Now go out there and thank the man properly for racing to your rescue yesterday. I swear, I think he was a little disappointed that he didn't get to pound anyone for you."

Smiling, Sabrina left the kitchen, heading toward the back door. But her smile faded as she thought of the things she'd left in the tent. Like her suitcase. Her briefcase. *The book*.

Hurrying out the door, she jogged down the steps. Her heart pounded wildly because as much as she knew Max had to know the truth, she did not want him to find out by accident. She wanted to be the one to tell him.

Steeling herself for whatever she might find, she lifted the tent flap and went inside. She half expected him to be sitting on the floor, surrounded by the rumpled pages of Grace's book, completely enraged. To her great relief, however, he wasn't. Instead, Max was lying on the bed where they'd made such beautiful love the other night. Sound asleep.

Almost laughing in relief, she walked over to him and sat on the edge of the low-to-the-floor bed, running the tips of her fingers across his cheek. He didn't open his eyes, merely grabbed her fingers and brought them to his lips for a kiss.

"Hey, sleepyhead."

"Hey. Where've you been? I came out here to seduce you."

"And decided to take a nap while you waited?"

Finally opening his eyes, he reached for her. But Sabrina slid away. It would be so easy to fall into his arms and spend the rest of this day taking whatever fabulous moments she could, before admitting the truth and driving out of his life forever.

She couldn't do it. He deserved better.

"There's something I need to tell you," she said, wishing she'd brought a drink of water from the house. Her throat was suddenly so dry.

He must have heard by her tone that whatever she had to say was serious. Sitting up, he watched her, saying nothing, just waiting.

"Max, there are some things you need to know. But before I tell you about them, I want you to know this—I love you."

His eyes flared. But he didn't move, remaining almost wary. Waiting for the other shoe to drop. Oh, God, how she wished she didn't have to drop it.

But she did. It was time.

"I've been lying to you," she whispered. "I'm not a writer."

He frowned. "You're not?"

She shook her head. "I'm actually an editor." Bending down, she grabbed her soft-sided briefcase, which she'd stashed at the foot of the bed a few days before. Not saying a word, she opened it, grabbed the thick sheaf of papers secured with a rubber band and handed it to him.

He looked down. Saw the title. The author's name. And his whole body went rigid.

She tried to touch him—reached out to put her fingers on his face—but he ducked away. His mouth barely moving, he practically spit out two words.

"What chapter?"

"Twelve."

He tore the rubber band off and threw handfuls of pages to the floor. Still silent. Focused. Shocked.

When he reached the first page of chapter twelve, he started to read slowly—the muscle in his cheek tightening.

It was as if he'd never read it before. Which seemed impossible—he'd known about the book; his lawyer had tried to stop it. "Max, haven't you ever seen this before?" she asked when he balled up one sheet of paper detailing an especially raunchy encounter he'd supposedly shared with Grace and threw it hard against the wall of the tent.

"No." That was all. Then he went back to his reading.

Sabrina's eyes filled with hot tears. This was like a double betrayal—hitting him with the truth of who she was, *and* forcing him to read the horrible lies Grace had made up about him.

Finally he reached the last page. Still silent—ominously so—he shoved the rest of the stacked manuscript to the floor, sending the pages fluttering in all directions.

Sabrina dropped to her knees in front of him, grabbing both his hands in hers. "I am so sorry. I hate myself for coming here under false pretenses." His silence unnerving her, she continued. "I swear to you, I had no idea Grace had made up all those lies. I really thought that deviant she was describing was you. But I knew better once I got to know you." Hoping to offer him a little comfort, she added, "The book's been pulled. It's not going to be published at all. So you don't have to worry about someone else's sordid imagination ruining everything you've worked for."

He finally reacted, pushing her hands away and rising

to his feet. He walked across the tent, kicking papers out of his way, thrusting his hands into his hair.

"I *love* you," she repeated, not able to stand his continued silence. "I realized almost right away that you were not the vile man in that book, but by then it was too late, I was caught in the lie. To tell you the truth would mean leaving you—" Her voice broke. "I was too much of a coward—and too selfish—to do that."

Rising she stepped closer to him, reaching out a hand, needing to know if he understood. "Please, say you'll forgive me. Let me make it up to you."

He laughed, a sharp, bitter laugh unlike any she'd ever heard come out of his sweet mouth. "Forgive you? Jesus, Sabrina, you don't know what you're talking about."

"I know I'm sorry I lied. Pretended to be something I wasn't."

"You're not the only one who did that," he muttered, shaking his head as he looked at the white papers strewn all around their feet. "I'm not some judgmental hypocrite who's going to criticize you for disguising who you really were." He grabbed her shoulders, almost hurting her. "Not when I've been doing exactly the same thing."

She didn't understand, could only stare at him, wondering why he still seemed so lost—desolate—if he truly was able to forgive her. It didn't make sense. "Max, I love you."

"No, you don't."

"I do…"

He shook her a little, then let her go and took a few quick steps back. "You love the guy I let you get to know over the past couple of weeks." He covered his face with both hands, rubbing at his eyes. "Not *me*," he said, his tone laced with disgust.

Still not understanding, she reached out, but he walked around her toward the entrance of the tent. "Max…"

"Go away, Sabrina. Go back to where you came from."

She stalked after him, grabbing his arm. "Like hell I will."

He covered her hand with his, squeezing it tightly, then slowly pushing it away. Pushing *her* away. "You just don't get it, do you."

"No." She felt like screaming, completely confused by Max's attitude, his reaction. She'd expected anger and hurt. Not this strange, fatalistic withdrawal. "I don't. I don't understand—help me understand, Max."

"You hated that vile, revolting bastard you read about. Detested him." A cold, humorless smile widened his mouth, but it came nowhere near to warming his beautiful green eyes.

He stepped closer, big, strong and powerful, but offering no warmth or security. Placing his fingers on her chin, he tilted her face up and stared into her eyes. "Don't you get it? It's *true,* Sabrina." Letting her go, he stepped toward the tent opening. "Every word you read about me in that book is true."

CHAPTER EIGHTEEN

SHE'D LEAVE. Soon. As a matter of fact, she was probably already gone, driving like hell back to where she came from, thanking her lucky stars she'd escaped.

Good. Better that way. He'd be out of here in a few days, and at least this way he knew where he stood, instead of wondering. There'd be no waiting for the ax to fall, for Sabrina to figure out who he really was and run as far away from him as she could go.

Max had known, when he'd asked Sabrina the previous morning to come with him to California, that he was taking a risk. His past was always there, waiting to catch up with him, particularly close to home. At any restaurant or social event, there was always the chance he'd bump into someone who'd known him as the rich party boy, the go-to guy for any wild, outrageous activity imaginable. And even if they hadn't known him from the old days, a whole lot of them had read about him in Grace's unpublished—but widely circulated—memoir.

What had she called him? Deviant? Vile? Yeah. He supposed some would say that. At the time, he'd preferred to think of himself as someone who enjoyed anything that made him feel good—and made him forget. Whether it was booze or sex, gambling, or taking stupid, dangerous risks, he'd been willing to give almost anything a try once, as long as it involved only consenting adults and nobody got hurt. Never thinking—had he thought at all that year?—that someday his "experiments" would be the greatest shame of his life.

His only comfort was that he'd always been careful to protect himself and hadn't come out of that crazy year in hell with any medical repercussions or diseases.

"So go," he muttered as he stalked through the woods, down the hill leading away from Mortimer's house, toward the closed amusement park. "Get away from the lowlife before you're dirtied, deemed guilty by association."

It was just as well that Sabrina had found out now who he really was. If she'd gone with him—if she'd, God forbid, ever agreed to *marry* him, as he'd so foolishly been fantasizing—she'd have ended up hating him later. Someday she'd bump into some woman he'd done, whose face he didn't even remember. Or some guy he'd shared a redhead with. Or two redheads.

Then she'd have found out about the man she proclaimed to love. So fuck, it was better that she knew now. Saved them both some heartache in the future.

He grabbed his chest, which felt tight.

Not heartache. That takes a heart, and she just pointed out you don't have one.

Or maybe it was. Maybe he *did*. But it was way too late to figure out what to do with it at this point in the game.

Reaching the carousel, he found the toolbox he'd left here the last time he'd come down. He'd stashed it underneath the floorboards of the merry-go-round, knowing the thing wasn't going to get any use up at the house since Mortimer didn't seem to want to change so much as a picture on the wall.

He pulled out a wrench, some pliers. Then, muttering,

"screw it," he reached for the hammer. Crossing over the dusty floorboards to the center of the carousel, he got to work. If nothing else, he'd get this thing to go around at least once before he boarded his plane and flew away from Trouble, forever.

He worked quietly, instinctively, not thinking too much about what he was doing. Wasn't much room in his brain for thoughts of anything except Sabrina. His past. The things she'd read about him.

Realizing the woman he loved—the only woman he had *ever* loved—had seen him in that light had been the most shameful moment of his life.

As much as he hated the thought that he'd never see Sabrina again, frankly, he wasn't sure he wanted to. He didn't think he could ever look her in the eye—wondering which nasty, fully described incident from his past she was remembering.

"Max?"

Dropping the hammer to the ground, he spun around. She stood on the other side of the carousel, half hidden behind a dusty, misshapen zebra. His heart pounded. His head roared. "What are you doing here?"

She stepped on to the platform and made her way across to him, weaving among the menagerie. "I was wondering where you'd gone. Finally figured out it would be here."

Turning his back on her, he connected some newly replaced wires. The engine rumbled a little—an unexpected sign of life.

"Did you get it working?" she asked, grabbing the nearest horse and sounding surprised.

"Hardly. More like a few death throes."

She reached down, putting her hand on his shoulder, but he shrugged it off. "Look, we've said all we need to. I'm not mad at you for what you did. Just go back home, Sabrina."

"I don't have a home."

He finally shifted his gaze toward her, seeing her lips tremble and her blue eyes widen. "What do you mean?"

"I mean, the only things that made Philadelphia home were my job and my sister. Now I won't have either one."

Dropping the screwdriver into the toolbox, he stepped closer, until his shins touched the inside edge of the platform. Sabrina stood several inches above him, and he had to tilt his head back to look up at her. "You're not quitting your job. You sure don't have to on my account—the book's history, isn't it?"

She nodded, then put her hands on his shoulder so he could help her down. He did, holding her around the waist, cursing himself for wanting her so much when he felt the slow slide of her body against his.

"I'm quitting my job because I'm moving away. Somebody invited me to fly away with him to California, and that's what I plan to do."

"You don't mean that."

"Oh, yes, I most certainly do."

His jaw tightening, he said, "The guy who invited you doesn't really exist, remember? You can't possibly want to get in a little plane with a deviant."

She sucked her lips into her mouth and shook her head. Reaching up to brush her hand through his hair, she whispered, "I am *so* sorry. I never meant to hurt you."

Her voice was low, her expression so damn heartbroken he wanted to tug her into his arms, tell her he'd forgive her anything. He resisted, knowing this thing had to end here, now. He had to get this stupid idea of giving up her job and her home out of her head.

"There's nothing for you in California."

"Bullshit." Her sadness disappeared, and she now looked merely determined. "Don't play the martyr here, buddy. You think you're the only one with things he regrets in his past?"

"Those *things* sure seemed to matter to you when you read that book."

"Maybe they did. By themselves, through Grace's eyes, I saw a man who intrigued me and repelled me at the same time."

"Oh, great, thanks."

"But now when I see that man from the past, he's shadowy, his shape blurred by the man I know now. I can't feel anything for that long-ago person because, in my heart, I know he doesn't exist." She slid her arms around his neck, somehow knowing he'd never be able to resist her. "I'm not stupid, Max. I know when all of that took place. I know what was driving you."

She thought she did.

"I didn't know those things when I first read the book."

He kept his hands at his sides, though his fingers had curled into fists as he tried to control his impulse to put his arms around her and hold her so tight she'd never leave.

"You don't know everything. I wasn't just some kind of partying swinger, Sabrina. I was a drunk. I don't remember being sober after dark once that year, and there were a whole lot of daylight hours when I wasn't, either."

She twined her fingers in his hair, not reacting with surprise or disgust as he'd expected. "You think I haven't figured that out? The man in the book always had a drink in his hand. I've never seen you glance at a bottle of beer. Besides, *choirboy,* you told me yourself you don't drink, remember?"

"*Won't* drink."

"So much the better."

She stepped even closer, so the soft curves of her breasts pressed against his chest.

"You're not fighting fair."

"I'm not fighting at all," she murmured, leaning up to press a kiss on his jaw. "Come fly with me."

He closed his eyes, breathing deeply, unable to clear his head because the sweet smell of her skin and her hair completely surrounded him. "You don't know what you're asking." Her lips moved to his throat. "*Who* you're asking."

"Of course I do," she mumbled, continuing to kiss him while she played with his hair and swayed against him. "I'm asking the man who talked me through one of the most frightening moments of my life yesterday."

He rolled his eyes. "I think that guy was more scared than you were, especially when he saw that clock."

She ignored him. "The man who controlled his temper and didn't do what he wanted to do to Peter the other night, because it was better for my sister that way."

Considering where Peter had ended up, he probably would have done the man a favor by breaking his jaw.

"The man who said I should have invisible butter on my imaginary popcorn and who likes horror movies as much as I do and who looks fabulous naked and is trying so hard to fix this carousel."

He liked the naked part.

"The man who saved his grandfather from those old ladies."

"Triumphing over old ladies, *there's* white knight stuff."

She stopped kissing him. Tilting her head back so she could stare up into his face, she looked very serious, as if to make sure he heard this, even if he'd heard nothing else.

"I don't want a white knight. I don't need a hero or a Prince Charming. I want a real flesh-and-blood man with depth and warmth and kindness. And even with scars."

Somehow, her words started to sink in.

"I love you, Max." She continued to hold him tight, not letting him look away, her blue eyes shining with honesty and emotion. "I *love* you. Knowing everything about you—the man you were, the things that made you that way. The man you are today." She leaned up on tiptoe and brushed her lips across his mouth. "I love you."

He closed his eyes for just a second, all his senses alive and in the moment. Her whispered words echoing in his mind, the smell of her filling his head, her soft body curved into every inch of his.

And he finally allowed himself to believe.

"I love you, too, Sabrina," he whispered, before lowering his mouth to hers for a kiss.

She tasted sweet—as always—but maybe even better now that there were no remaining secrets between them. No walls, no hidden objectives. Just this beautiful woman in his arms, kissing him with the mouth that had said she loved him.

Holding her tightly in his arms, he leaned back against the engine wall of the carousel, wanting nothing more than to make love to her here, outside, in broad daylight. As his back hit the controls, he bumped the power switch, heard the old engine roll and rumble as it had earlier.

But this time, it *kept* rolling and rumbling. Sabrina obviously heard, too, because her eyes flew open and she pulled out of his arms mid-kiss. "Max?"

He shrugged, watching in wonder as the old machinery struggled back to life. The chugs and clangs of the engine were suddenly drowned out by the plaintive wail of the calliope crying out over their heads. He could have lived without getting *that* annoying part of the ride to work.

"Come to the circus," she said, a huge smile creasing her face. "I love that sound. Especially because it's the very sound that brought me here to you the day I arrived."

God bless the calliope.

Unbelievably, the gears and pistons, which he'd greased and cleaned in case there ever came a day when the motor decided to run, did their job. The carousel began to move—slowly, very slowly—not so merrily, but definitely in motion.

"I can't believe you did it," she said, still looking excited, like a kid at the fair.

Unable to resist, he lifted her on to the platform, following her up. Fortunately, the thing didn't stop under their weight. Spying the nearest intact animal—an oversize elephant with upraised trunk that was obviously meant to hold two, likely a parent and child—he lifted a brow and gestured toward it. "Care for a ride, young lady?"

Nodding, she put her hand in his so he could help her up. Then, looking down, she said, "Want to join me?"

"Absolutely." He put his foot in the stirrup and slid up behind her on the dusty, peeling seat.

Tucking in close behind her so the back of her body touched the entire front of his, he wrapped one arm around her waist and buried his face in her soft blond hair. Sabrina was holding on to the bar with one hand, and he covered it with one of his, squeezing, gripping. Not letting go. Not *ever* letting go.

They continued to move slowly, the music playing its distorted tune, a soft summer breeze blowing beneath the canopy as they went round and round.

After a long while, Max kissed the side of her face and murmured, "Sabrina?"

"Mmm-hmm?"

"I think this is even better than flying."

IT WAS ALMOST EVENING by the time they left the park to return to the house. With her hand clasped in his, Sabrina couldn't keep a fulfilled, happy smile off her face.

They'd wiled away the afternoon riding the carousel…and making love. With Max holding her so tenderly from behind, Sabrina had been unable to resist taking his hand and lifting it to her breast. The lazy pleasure of their ride evolved into something else—a slow and easy hunger that neither of them could wait to assuage.

Eventually, after he'd completely explored her body and she'd sagged back against him in a boneless heap, he'd helped her wiggle around to face him. Their clothes hitting the ground, she'd climbed onto his lap and taken him inside her. The relaxed up and down of the carousel and the long, languorous kisses had gone on. And on. And on.

Max had been right. It was better than flying.

"So how long do you need to settle things in Philadelphia?" he asked as they reached the back lawn, the tent coming into view. The brilliant orange and purple streaks of sunset created a magnificent backdrop.

"I have to give two weeks' notice. Then I'll join you."

"You really think I'm going to let you out of my sight for two weeks and give you the chance to change your mind? No way. I'll pack up your place while you're at work and we'll take off together on your very last day."

He was laughing, but she knew that deep inside, Max was still a bit unsure. She'd cure him of that one of these days. "I'm *not* going to change my mind, Max. You've got me for life."

"That sounds about right." He brought her hand to his

lips to kiss it. "Speaking of which, of all those cuckoo-bird eyes, which stones did you like the best—the diamonds? Rubies? Sapphires to go with those gorgeous baby blues?"

She shivered a little, though the day was still warm. "Why do you want to know?"

Never losing that nonchalant expression, he replied, "Just want to be sure I put a ring on your finger that you're never going to want to take off."

She stopped walking, facing him. "Are you asking…?"

"Well, goodness, ma'am, you don't think I'm the type of guy who'd live in sin, do you?"

Sabrina punched him in the shoulder.

Laughing, Max dropped down to one knee, looking up at her with pure, heartfelt emotion. "I love you, Sabrina Cavanaugh. Will you make an honest man out of me and do me the great honor of becoming my wife?"

She didn't have to think, pause, hesitate or wait one second. "Oh, you bet I will."

Rising, he wrapped his arms around her waist, lifting her up so they were nose to nose. "Soon."

"Yes." She kissed him quickly, then again and again, cupping his face in her hands. She couldn't quite believe this was happening—that she'd found the love of her life, here, in this crazy little town which, if not for fate—and Grace's horrid book—she'd never have come to in the first place.

"If I hadn't seen that with my own eyes, I never would have believed it happened."

At the sound of a strange man's voice, Sabrina quickly turned her head. Max let her down, mumbling something under his breath that sounded like an obscenity.

"Me, either," another voice said. "Guess we both owe Grandfather a hundred bucks."

Oh, Lord. As Max dropped an arm over her shoulder and led her toward the porch—toward the two men watching every step they took—Sabrina realized exactly who had come for a visit.

One of the men, broad shouldered but of leaner build than Max, was sitting on the top step, his elbows on his knees. His hair was the same light brown as her fiancé's, though his face was shaped differently—broader, with deep-set eyes and a stronger nose. His expression was serious, but a smile lurked behind those tight lips, she could see it from several feet away.

The other man stood on the porch, his hands shoved in the pockets of his tight, torn jeans. Leaning one shoulder against the column, he appeared serious, more tightly coiled and alert. His whole body looked tense. His hair was darker, too—almost jet black—and, while a bit shorter, he looked to be the most powerful of the three siblings.

For she had no doubt that's who she was looking at. "Those are your brothers, right?"

He nodded.

"I wonder how long they've been here."

"Hope they didn't come looking for us down the hill."

She groaned. "I thought that was never going to happen to us again."

"You keep taking advantage of me out in broad daylight, Sabrina, and somebody's bound to see."

She kicked his ankle, but still manage to keep a smile on her face. "Come on. Introduce me to your brothers, you jerk."

"I shouldn't," he muttered, shaking his head and glaring at them as they reached the porch. "You bastards finally decide to show up now that the excitement's over?"

Sabrina looked up at him, seeing the good humor in his eyes and knowing it was in hers, too. "Are you saying the excitement's all over, Max Taylor?"

He shook his head, grinned at his brothers, then tugged her into his arms. "Hell, no, sweetheart." Not caring that they had an audience, he lowered his mouth to hers, whispering, "This is only the beginning."

EPILOGUE

"HAVE I TOLD YOU, old friend, how happy I am that you've finally decided to join me here?" Mortimer asked as he sat in his living room, in his padded leather chair, sipping his cognac.

"How could I resist, sir?" Roderick said, sarcasm dripping off his words.

Mortimer settled himself more comfortably in the chair, glad it had arrived yesterday. He'd held out with the old furniture for a while, though it pained his back. But once the main decorating theme of the house—the clocks—had been removed, there didn't seem much point in not doing the place over. Which was why he was currently living in a construction zone—with a few nice, new pieces of furniture in the rooms already finished.

With the double pay he was offering for early completion of the job, he sincerely hoped the whole place would be done by Christmas. The house would be magnificent at Christmastime. Beautiful, bright, and filled with laughing, joyful people.

Oh, it had been a long time since that had happened. The boys tried to come home for the holidays, but they seldom all managed it the same year. Maybe in the future it would be easier, now that Max had a partner in his airline business to take up some of the heavy workload.

And for this year, at least, they'd definitely all be under one roof, not just for Christmas, but to celebrate Max's nuptials, scheduled for the twenty-sixth.

"It certainly took you long enough," Mortimer said, returning his attention to Roderick. "Showing up on Halloween night like that. I figured you for an intruder—you're lucky I didn't shoot you like I shot that assassin who snuck into my hotel room in Shanghai."

Roderick finished refilling the crystal decanter on the bar, pouring himself a glass of cognac, as well. "Well, now that you've rid yourself of those wretched clocks and have decided to stay in this dreary little backwater, I assumed there was no further point in resisting."

"Damn shame you missed all the fun over the summer."

"Forgive me, but I don't think I'd describe being drugged and kidnapped by those maniacal sisters as fun."

Shrugging, Mortimer murmured, "Younger one does have nice legs, though."

Roderick merely sniffed.

"Come now, admit it, you like it here. All this fresh country air."

"Soon to be awash with the smoke of that factory you insist on reopening."

"Peace and quiet."

"Except for the squalls of your secretary's baby."

Mortimer smiled. "Cute little thing, isn't he? Like his mother." He only wished Allie and her baby boy were around more, but since she'd moved out of the house into her own place in town, he only saw her from nine to five. Of course, with the wedding, there'd be lots of time to associate with all the Cavanaughs. Including the rest of his soon-to-be granddaughter-in-law's family.

"I still can't imagine why on earth Maxwell would

decide to get married *here*," Roderick said, shaking his head as he returned to his task of addressing invitations, his penmanship fine and precise as always, which was why he'd taken over the task from a much-less-careful Allie. "Of all places to have a wedding…"

Mortimer understood. "They met here. Fell in love here. Why wouldn't they come back here to marry?" He could hardly wait.

"Besides, California was too far for Sabrina's mother to go."

Mortimer was glad the girls' mother had finally reached out to her daughters, promising to come to Trouble for the wedding and bring the younger children with her. From the sounds of it, the woman was taking some serious steps toward independence, having moved out of her father's house and gotten herself a job.

He wondered if she had any experience managing movie theaters—he'd like to have more family in Trouble.

"Well, I suppose now that the town seems to be coming back to life with the return of the funds from their treasury, it won't be such a hideous place to visit."

Roderick. Such a pessimist. "Trouble's doing fine."

"Especially since you sold back all their public buildings for less than you paid for them."

"Kept the private ones, though," he pointed out. Mortimer might have a generous heart, but he wasn't stupid. He planned to turn a profit out of this investment one of these days.

"An astute business move, as always, sir."

Frowning at the curmudgeonly tone of his friend, Mortimer lowered his glass to the table with a loud *thunk*. "Roderick, we've fought together in battle. Shared foxholes. Split a quart of water across one hundred miles of desert."

Roderick didn't even look up from his writing. "Yes, sir."

He continued. "We've explored lost pyramids and battled bandits and stolen an entire harem right off the ship of the slave-dealer who'd kidnapped them."

He paused to smile at the memory. Oh, they'd been grateful.

Clearing his throat, he eventually continued. "We've gotten each other out of more scrapes than most men ever *dream* of having."

The other man finally lowered his pen, turning in his chair. A smile creased Roderick's lips and his fine gray eyes stared somewhere over Mortimer's shoulder, as if he were looking into his own past. His youth. "Indeed we have, sir," he said softly.

Rising from his chair, Mortimer crossed the room to his friend and put his hand on the stack of invitations. "So, after all these years, what am I going to have to do to get you to stop calling me *sir?*"

Roderick rose to face him, that formal smile never fading. "You have only to ask."

Mortimer's jaw dropping, he stared in disbelief at the other man. "There must have been a thousand times over the years I've told you to call me Mortimer."

Roderick nodded. "That is correct. You've *told* me, sir."

He saw the pride in the other man's wrinkled brow, the honesty in his tired eyes, and realized what Roderick was getting at. "I've told you as a servant," he mumbled.

Seeing Roderick's face tighten, Mortimer felt like a blind fool. How was it possible he'd never realized his most trusted companion still believed he was thought of as merely a butler?

"Have I ever asked you as a friend?"

A slight shake of his head preceded Roderick's answer. "I don't believe so, sir."

Nodding and placing his hands behind his back, Mortimer righted a wrong that he'd never even realized he'd committed. "Roderick, my dearest and most loyal friend, will you please do me the honor of calling me by my given name?"

Satisfaction and pride making the other man's eyes glow, he replied, "I'd be delighted to…Mortimer."

Mortimer clapped a hand on Roderick's shoulder. "Excellent. Most excellent." Then he walked around to the other side of the writing table and pulled up a chair, reaching for a pen. "Now, come, we have invitations to address."

Roderick tugged the pen out of his hand. "Your writing's atrocious. You handle the stamps."

Laughing, Mortimer looked up and gazed out the window. Snow continued to drift down as it had throughout the day.

He smiled at the thought of a white Christmas, and a snowy white bridal gown. And perhaps, someday soon, the pale delicate skin of a newborn baby girl he could cuddle in his arms. As he'd once cuddled his only child.

Oh, yes, there was much to look forward to. So very much. All coming to him right here in this place that had called to him from the first time he'd heard of it. His own little slice of heaven, called Trouble.

"You know," he murmured as he continued to stare at the world outside his window, "after all these years—all our adventures—I think I'm finally ready to settle down."

"*You*, settle down?" One of Roderick's brows cocked up in blatant disbelief. "That, Mortimer Potts, is the most outrageous thing I have ever heard you say."

They stared at one another for a moment, Roderick

silently daring him to deny it. He couldn't, of course. So breaking into a rueful smile, Mortimer admitted, "Yes, I suppose it was."

Nodding as he acknowledged his fervent hope that his most exciting days were not yet behind him, Mortimer reached for the invitations, returning to work.

And daydreaming about what wondrous adventures still awaited him.

*****

Wait! You're not out of Trouble yet... There are so many more secrets to uncover. Come back to Trouble, Pennsylvania, this Halloween to learn the whole story of Simon Lebeaux, the mysterious, dangerous owner of Seaton House. And the woman who arrives on A Dark and Sexy Night to bring him out of the nightmare his life has become.

ASKING FOR TROUBLE
Coming from Harlequin Blaze, October 2006
Turn the page for a sneak peek!

ON NIGHTS LIKE THIS, Simon Lebeaux wondered if Seaton House truly was haunted.

The power had gone out again and the cold October wind roared through the cracks in the window moldings to extinguish any unattended candles. At least, he presumed it was the wind.

Though cracking with rage in the stormy sky above, the thunder couldn't quite drown out the creaks of the old floorboards just above his head, as if someone was walking back and forth, up and down the second-floor corridor. Slowly. Deliberately. With weary, fatalistic repetition.

Yet he was the only one in the place. And had been for months.

An hour ago, hearing loud banging coming from even farther above, he'd gone to the third floor to investigate. He'd found the previously locked doors to several of the former guest rooms mysteriously standing open. Inside them, each long unslept-in bed suddenly bore the rumpled indentation of a human form, as if several of the hotel's long-departed guests had just awakened from their deep, restless sleep.

The keys to those rooms remained undisturbed, locked away. Both before he'd gone upstairs, and after he'd come back.

"And the air," he murmured. It tasted so strange—of cloves and citrus. Of secrets and age.

He was not a superstitious man. Yet in the three months he'd lived here—since inheriting the place from his uncle and deciding it would provide the perfect location to recover from his injuries—he'd experienced things that made him wonder. Even things that made him doubt his own senses.

Objects moving from one spot to another. Scratches and whispery noises in the walls. Frigid air trickling from nowhere as he prowled the house, unable to sleep, trying to walk off the pain. And those smells...

"It's the headaches," he muttered as he sat in his office late that evening, working on his laptop for as long as its battery charge lasted. He'd become accustomed to the unreliable electrical service here on his stark, private mountain above the town of Trouble, Pennsylvania, and therefore had backups for his backups, extra battery packs...He'd even purchased a second computer. He always kept one fully charged in case he ran out of power during the small number of productive hours he managed each day. And so he would never run the risk of an unexpected power incident frying his hard drive—causing him to lose the few precious pages he'd been able to eke out since returning to work.

He could have used the generator out back, but on the two occasions he'd tried to, the thing had caused the lights in the house to surge and ebb. On the first occasion, he'd been struck by the strange rhythm of it—a steady pulse—as though the house itself had a giant beating heart hidden somewhere in its depths.

Fanciful...ridiculous. In actuality, he was quite sure, the hotel's old wiring simply disliked such modern intervention and chose to thwart it.

His own thoughts startled him. *When*, he wondered, had he begun to think of Seaton House as a living entity, capable of choice, of vengeance?

Lifting his fingers from his keys, he brought his hands to his face and rubbed wearily at his temples. Because his *own* pulse had suddenly begun to beat harder. A subtle increase in pressure had him instantly on alert. "No. Not tonight," he said with a groan as he lifted the computer from his lap and placed it on the coffee table.

Shifting around on the tired leather couch, Simon stretched out, leaning his head against the arm and closing his eyes. He needed to relax. To let go of his anger and his concern that it was starting all over again.

Hopefully the subtle throbbing meant nothing. It would pass. It *had* to pass.

The doctors had said the migraines would eventually go away, as, would hopefully, the memories of what had happened that June night in Charleston. Since the pain was severe, he sincerely hoped the experts were right.

But in his darkest nighttime hours, when the cloying weight of the hotel and the vivid images in his brain pressed down on him with unbearable pressure, he knew he'd rather live with the headaches than with the memories. If he could banish one from his life it would be the still-frame snapshots in his brain. The images—the moments—that replayed night after night in his head like a never-ending horror movie.

The fear. The pain. The screams. The blood.

The crushed and broken body.

He tried deep breathing and focused relaxation techniques. *Clench, then release,* he reminded himself. The fingers—tight, then limp. The wrists—relaxed. Every muscle in the arm going slack, then the shoulders, the neck.

Calm. Breathe. *Float* over *the waves of memory crashing in your skull rather than letting* them *wash over you.*

Amazingly it began to work. The pulse slowed. The throbbing dulled. Eventually, he felt confident of his success in battling off one of the headaches that at times left him nearly incapacitated. So confident, that he opened his eyes and slowly sat up, almost smiling at that small victory. One he hadn't even been able to imagine when last in the grip of the demonizing pain.

His triumph didn't last for long. Because when he caught sight of his computer screen, he knew he had not won the battle at all. He'd merely fallen asleep again. Fallen into that strange place where his dreams and his memories met up and tormented him.

Shaking his head, Simon silently screamed at himself to wake up and end this nightmare. Yes, *only* a nightmare. It couldn't be real—he could not be seeing what he thought he was seeing.

On the laptop screen where only letters, words and paragraphs had existed a few minutes before, there was now one large, horrifying, bloody image. An image he saw in his mind every single day, but one he'd certainly never expected to see on his computer.

He reached toward the image, covering it with his hand, spreading his fingers apart in an effort to block it out of sight—out of existence. But despite the size of his hand and the sprawl of his fingers, it could not hide everything. Especially not when each brutal detail was so very familiar. His mind filled in whatever blanks his hand managed to create.

"Wake up, man," he told his dream self, leaning back on the couch and closing his eyes as he felt that throbbing begin again. "You're dreaming about the computer, just like you're dreaming you're awake."

Remembering his therapy, he counted backward from ten, willing himself to rise toward consciousness as if ascending a long flight of stairs. Going from darkness into light. From nightmare into reality.

When he reached one, he slowly opened his eyes and looked.

"Thank God," he murmured. *Thank God*. Because in front of him he saw letters. And words. And paragraphs.

"A dream. Just a dream," he whispered.

Then he saw something else and his heart tightened. Slowly fading from sight on the screen of his laptop was a shape…the shape of a hand.

His hand.

Not a dream. A hallucination? Christ, was he doomed to have the truth now thrust at him through the most innocuous of things—like his computer, his only connection with the outside world?

He wouldn't be able to stand it. Couldn't live like this, with the pain and the solitude and the grief coming at him from every angle.

Because no matter what else, Simon knew he would go insane if everywhere he looked he saw the image of her.

The woman he'd killed.

If you enjoyed what you just read,
then we've got an offer you can't resist!

Take 2 bestselling love stories FREE!

Plus get a FREE surprise gift!